THE
SOUL
GAME

Javier Castillo grew up in Malaga and studied business followed by a Master's in Management at ESCP Europe. His first novel, *El día que se perdió la cordura* (2017), became a true publishing phenomenon, translated into 15 languages and published in more than 60 countries. Rights have been acquired to produce the television series. His second novel, *El día que se perdió el amor* (2018), received both public and critical acclaim, as did *Todo lo que sucedió con Miranda Huff* (2019). *The Snow Girl* was the most read novel during the 2020 lockdown in Spain, and in 2023 it was released as a miniseries on Netflix, achieving great success. *The Soul Game* (2021) marked his global consolidation as one of the masters of suspense. To date, his novels have reached more than 2,000,000 readers. His sixth novel, *The Crystal Cuckoo*, was published in January 2023.

Follow the author
on Twitter @JavierCordura
and on his Instagram Javiercordura

JAVIER CASTILLO

THE
SOUL
GAME

Translated by Kevin Gerry Dunn

Grupo Books is an imprint of Penguin Random House Grupo Editorial, S. A. U.

© 2021, by Javier Castillo
© 2021, by Penguin Random House Grupo Editorial, S. A. U.
Travessera de Gràcia, 47-49. 08021 Barcelona, Spain
English translation ©2023, by Kevin Gerry Dunn

Originally published in Spanish in 2021 by Penguin Random House Grupo Editorial
as *El juego del alma*

ISBN: 978-1-64473-877-1

Impreso en Colombia - *Printed in Colombia*

*This novel is dedicated
to all the embraces
we left by the wayside.
To the kisses that passed us by.
To the stories we lost.*

*This is my small contribution
to our struggle against fear
in a year when we longed
for freedom.*

And who am I to judge
the devil you believe in,
if I believe in him too.

Author's note

Any reader familiar with Queens, the Rockaways, Brooklyn, Staten Island, or Lower Manhattan will see that I have endeavored to be as faithful as possible in my depiction of these places, while keeping descriptions brief enough to maintain the pace and development of the story. I should also admit to taking certain liberties—modifying the occasional setting, access route, dirt road—for strictly dramatic or stylistic purposes. The media publications mentioned in this book are entirely fictional, except for some secondary publications that are inconsequential to the plot; any resemblance this novel may bear to actual persons living or dead, real criminal cases open or closed, or specific events within or related to this story is due to simple, omnipresent coincidence.

Chapter 1
Early morning
April 26, 2011
Miren Triggs

Don't be afraid,
everything comes to an end.

"Help!" I shriek, clutching my side, blood trickling from between my ribs.

Keep it together, Miren! I tell myself, desperate. *Hang the fuck on. You need to think. Fast. Call out to someone. Get help before it's too late.*

I feel my heart regurgitating my own blood as if my soul were dizzy and sick after all these twists and turns. I made a mistake. It's over.

I
should
have
stopped.

The street is empty except for the footsteps I hear behind my own. His shadow, distorted by the streetlamps, grows and shrinks: huge, tiny, enormous, nonexistent, gigantic, ethereal. I lose sight of it. Where is he?!

"Help!" I cry into the dark, empty street, which seems to watch from the shadows like an accomplice in my death.

C'mon, Miren, you have to get the truth out. C'mon. C'mon! You have to make it.

I don't have my phone, but even if I did, I'd be dead long before the cavalry came. All they'd find would be the corpse of a thirty-five-year-old journalist, whose soul had been frozen solid since one fateful, bitterly cold night fourteen years earlier. Light from streetlamps always takes me back to that night of pain in 1997, to my screams, howling and trembling in the park, the grinning men, the trauma I'll never be free of. Maybe it was bound to end like this, under the intermittent light of another set of streetlamps in another corner of New York.

Painfully, I lurch forward. Every step is like a knife in my side. I know this long, dark road only leads to Rockaway Beach, next to Jacob Riis Park: a long, wide shoreline battered by the wind and lashed by the insatiable ocean. Nobody will be out this early. The sun hasn't risen yet and a waning moon bathes the footprints in the sand with melancholy. When I turn my head, I see it's also illuminating the fine trail of black blood I'm leaving behind me. *At least Miller will be able to track where I was headed.* That's what you think about when you're about to be murdered: the clues that will help them identify your killer. His DNA in your fingernails, your blood in his car. Once he kills me, he'll take my body away. It'll be like I've dropped off the face of the Earth. There won't be anything left but my articles, my story, my fears.

I turn left at the end of the road and, with a speed that tears at the fibers of my already wounded muscles, I duck into a recess in one of the concrete structures of Fort Tilden, an abandoned Army installation. Left to the mercy of the elements, the old fort has been reduced to inhospitable ruins on the tongue-shaped beach that protects Queens from the voracious Atlantic. And like Fort Tilden, I, who just a few days ago was a tireless journalist for the *Manhattan Press*, have been reduced to ruins. A little girl whimpering at the sound of his footsteps. A new version of my old fears. A dirty rag mopping up the world's secrets and shame. A woman killed at the hands of a degenerate.

No one asked for my help. And I had to come alone. No one begged me to get involved in any of this, but something inside me shrieked that I had to find Gina. I don't know how I missed it. I guess I had to feel... dead again.

The Polaroid. It all started with the Polaroid. That photo of Gina... How could I have been so... naïve?

I look left and right for a way out, trying to keep quiet between the gasps exploding from my chest. The sound of his footsteps mixes with the sound of the gale off the Atlantic; I feel coarse sand striking my skin like stray bullets in a battle between wind and sea.

"Miren!" he yells, rabid. "Miren! Come out!"

If he finds me, it's all over. If I stay here, I'll bleed to death. I already feel tired and woozy. The night is beckoning me. The soul game is underway in my heart. All the things they say happen when you're losing too much blood. I put pressure on my wound, and it hurts like someone's branding my flesh with the words: NOBODY'S PROPERTY.

I close my eyes and clench my teeth, trying to withstand the stabbing pain in my side, and my mind returns to an idea I'd written off as hopeless.

Run.

From my hiding place, I consider the possibilities. There's a fence around Riis Park. If I could jump it, I'd be able to sprint toward the houses across the park and ask for help, but in most places it's topped with razor wire that looks like it could slit me open and tear my guts out.

He's close, I can feel it.

It's not his warmth I sense, it's his coldness. His icy, un-moving body a few paces away, no doubt eyeing my pathetic hideout with contempt. A son of God, licking his lips at the sacrificial lamb.

"Miren!" he cries again, even closer than I'd thought.

And I make another mistake.

At the precise moment his broken voice howls my name, I jump out and make a break for it, clinging to life even as I feel everything closing in: I'm losing blood, I'm alone, I feel weaker with every step.

Gina's image returns to my mind: her hopeful expression, her painful story. She feels so close I can practically reach out and touch her fifteen-year-old face, grinning at the camera in the photo they used after she disappeared. Why didn't I see this coming?

Then everything changes: for a few seconds, it seems like he's stopped chasing me. *I'm gonna make it, I'm gonna live. I'm gonna tell Gina's story. I have to. I can do this.*

You're safe.

In the distance, I see the night skyline. Whenever I'm close to those skyscrapers I feel like a dwarf, but from this far they look unearthly, like pillars of quartz illuminated with ancestral light.

Then his shadow reappears. My strength is failing. I can barely walk. The street is deserted. *You're dead, Miren*, the full moon seems to tell me. *You always were.*

Every step tears at my insides; every scream vanishes into absolute indifference. Only the distant roar of the ocean occasionally filters through the sound of my panting and my feeble footsteps.

"Miren, stop running!" he shouts.

I stagger across the beach, fighting the sand that swallows my feet, and I climb over a low, dilapidated bulkhead. I'm in luck: I reach a paved street that connects the beach to Neponsit, a neighborhood in the Rockaways. It's lined with dark-windowed houses.

I pound on the door of the first house, trying to shout for help, but I'm so tired I can barely manage a sigh. I knock again weakly, but no one seems to be home. I look back desperately, afraid he'll reappear, but he's nowhere to be seen. The roar of the sea rushes over me. The sound brings some relief to my shattered soul. Could I really be safe?

I move to the next house, with rounded pillars on the porch and a wrought iron railing. As soon as I slam the knocker and my knuckles against the door, someone turns on a light.

My salvation.

"Help!" I cry with renewed strength. "Call the police! I'm being chased by a—"

A hand pulls back the inside curtain covering the window of the door. An elderly woman with white hair regards me with a worried expression. Where have I seen her before?

"Help! Help me, please!"

She raises her eyebrows and gives a smile that isn't even a little comforting.

"Lord, what's happened to you?" she asks as she opens the door. She's wearing a white nightgown. "That doesn't look so good," she says with a warm voice, gesturing at the gash in my abdomen. "Let me call you an ambulance."

I look down at my side. A pool of red is soaking through my shirt and down to my hips. There's blood all over my hands, all over the door knocker. *Jim might figure out I made it this far, but better for him if he doesn't. That way he'll be safe. That way at least one of us will live.*

"I'm not… not good," I manage between increasingly feeble gasps.

I swallow spit; it tastes like blood. Before I can try to speak again, I hear footsteps behind me and everything speeds up. I don't have time to turn around.

As the old woman looks over my head, a shadow fills the doorframe, a cold hand covers my mouth and, rapidly, a powerful arm wraps around my body.

It's over.

I sense death in the old woman's dark eyes, in my empty chest, in this final breath with his hand over my mouth, and without even trying…

…I remember everything.

Chapter 2
Fort Tilden
April 23, 2011
Three days earlier
Ben Miller

Run, sister,
before the monsters
they promised us arrive.

Inspector Benjamin Miller parked his car, a gray Pontiac with New York plates, in the middle of the dirt road inside the Fort Tilden esplanade—a mess of brambles, hedgerows and other wild vegetation—beside three squad cars with their lights flashing.

It was already dark when they called him—he had, in fact, just been bringing a forkful of his wife's roast chicken to his lips. Lisa had looked worried when she saw Ben bring the cell phone to his ear, his fork clanging against the plate, and her worry turned to silent regret when she saw his serious expression. She knew what a call like that meant.

"Do you think it's Allison?" Inspector Miller said into the phone. Then, after a pause: "I understand. Where? Fort Tilden? I'm on my way."

"Do you really have to leave right now?" Lisa had asked when she saw him stand. But she already knew the answer.

She hated the ubiquity of Ben's work, how it was a permanent fixture in his life and a constant factor in his mood, but they had been immersed in the desperate world of missing children for so many years that she just sat and took a sip of water, waiting not for an answer, but the reason.

"It sounds serious, Lisa," he replied. "Remember Allison Hernández?"

"The 11-year-old from Jersey?"

"No, from Queens. 15 years old. Hispanic, long hair."

"Right, right. From last week. They found her?"

"They think so."

"Dead?" she asked with routine sadness.

Ben hadn't responded. He had simply grabbed his things, pulled his jacket from its hanger, and kissed her goodbye. A small percentage of his cases ended like this: with a pair of teenagers or a couple out for an evening stroll calling 911 after they spotted a corpse that had been steeping in the Hudson for days, or—as had happened not so long ago—chopped up and stashed in a suitcase. In the latter case, the Forensic Division had been tasked with piecing together not just the sequence of events, but also the body.

"Remember, tomorrow is—" Lisa said in a warning tone.

"I know. I'll be here early," he replied dolefully.

It would be a long drive from Grymes Hill, on Staten Island, where he lived in a white clapboard house with blue window grilles and a thriving garden but a neglected old fence. To get to Fort Tilden he crossed the Verrazano-Narrows Bridge into Brooklyn, invariably hitting every red light, thinking about Allison's parents and how he would break the news. He skirted the perimeter of Brooklyn along the water until he reached the Marine Parkway Bridge, the fastest route to the Rockaways. As he crossed the bridge, he realized the traffic had eased; he was leaving the hustle and stress of the city behind. The peninsula's open spaces and uncrowded buildings were a complete contrast to the oppressive feeling around Manhattan. From the moment he crossed the bridge, he felt that the Rockaways had a different rhythm. He turned right, following signs for Fort Tilden. Halfway down Rockaway Point Boulevard, he spotted two cops outside their squad car, at the gate to the Riis Park service road.

"I'm Inspector Miller from the Missing Persons Unit," he said, lowering his window. He could smell the sea and feel the moist, salty air. "They called me about the girl you found at Fort Tilden. She could be one of mine."

The officers exchanged a concerned look.

"Where'd you find the body?" he insisted. "I'm never over here, can you tell me where to go?"

The shorter of the two summoned the courage to speak: "Keep going straight, past the fence. We're waiting for the forensics guys. It's… horrible. I've never seen anything… like it."

Inspector Miller headed down the road, spotting three police cars around an abandoned concrete structure in the dense vegetation that had invaded the park. As he drove down the unpaved road—slowly so as not to damage the Pontiac's undercarriage—he mentally repeated the officer's words: *never seen anything like it.*

Another officer was putting up police tape, tying it to the side mirror of one of the squad cars in front of the derelict, graffitied building, illuminated in red and blue by the police lights. Another officer with her hair in a bun was talking to two 14-year-old boys whose BMX bikes lay on the ground beside the cars.

Before getting out, Miller reached over to the passenger seat and grabbed a folder on which he had written 'ALLISON HERNÁNDEZ' in red. After opening it, he took a few seconds to look at the photo on the first page: a sharp-nosed girl with brown, almost black hair smiling at the camera. He didn't need to read anything else on that first page. He knew her story by heart, including the clothes she was wearing when she disappeared: black jeans and a white shirt with the Pepsi logo on it. He left the folder in the Pontiac, got out, and showed his badge to the cop putting up the tape.

"Where…?" Miller asked.

"In there. Watch out for the rusty door."

Miller pointed to the teenagers. "They're the ones who found her?"

The cop nodded.

"And you've called their parents?"

"They're on their way. They'll have to come back to the station with us."

"Could you show me where—"

"I'd rather not see her again, sir, if you don't mind. My daughter's that same age and so I, you know…"

Miller saw the officer's hands were trembling. He was around 40, and looked like he'd spent plenty of years on the force and seen plenty of action. Even so, he was shaken. Miller was surprised: a city of nine million can get pretty creative when it comes to disposing of corpses, and it doesn't take long for officers to become immune to grotesque crime scenes.

"That's fine. Where?"

"In there. You'll see Scott and Carlos. Second room on the left."

"Can I use your flashlight?" Miller asked, already holding out his hand.

The officer took it from his belt and before he had time to hand it over, a short Latino cop with dark, impeccable hair emerged from behind the door.

"That you, Inspector Miller?" he called, his voice blending with the distant sound of waves crashing. They were easily two football fields away from the shore, but the sound sailed through the wind like a song through a dream. "We're pretty sure it's Allison. Just waiting for the Forensic Division so they can confirm the fingerprints and DNA."

"Can I see her?"

"Are you religious?"

"Since when does that matter?"

"Since today, inspector. God won't be too pleased with what they've done to that girl."

"I take it you're religious?"

"Of course. When my mother was pregnant with me, the Lord gave her the strength to cross the desert and the border, and he made me the man I am today. God has been generous with me. When I get home, I'm gonna kiss my wife, get on my knees and pray for his forgiveness."

Clearly, Carlos was also shaken. He'd begun walking toward the abandoned fort's access door and gestured to Miller to follow. From the outside, the building looked like a kind of warehouse, practically in ruins, with holes in the walls that had presumably held windows now reduced to empty metal frames, their rust reflecting a reddish light from the squad cars.

Carlos walked several steps ahead of Miller and turned on his flashlight as he stepped into the darkness, revealing an interior covered in graffiti, rubble, and the springy frames of disintegrated mattresses.

"Careful where you step," Carlos said as he moved through the corridor.

"Carlos, why'd you say you were gonna pray for God's forgiveness?" Miller asked from behind.

Carlos paused for a second, turned and replied gravely: "For not blessing myself before the cross."

* * *

That sentence echoed in Miller's head. Carlos turned left and vanished through what must once have been a door, beside which lay a rusty, overturned shopping cart. Miller quickened his pace so as not to lose sight of him. When he turned into the next room, he was surprised to find it was far more spacious than it appeared from the outside. The roof was twice as high and at the top of the walls, moonlight was filtering through the broken glass. As the beam of Carlos's flashlight pierced the darkness, Miller concluded that the place must actually be enormous. Then he noticed another light dancing around a few yards ahead, illuminating the corners.

This second flashlight turned toward Miller, briefly blinding him.

"Hey Scott, this is Miller from Missing Persons," Carlos said. Scott stood waiting for the inspector in the center of the warehouse, shining his flashlight on the ground between them so Miller wouldn't trip over the dozens of grimy chairs that were aligned in perfect rows of twelve, all facing the back wall.

"What... what is all this?" Miller asked, confused.

"It's some kind of... church..." said Carlos, clearly upset. "With her," he added hoarsely, directing his flashing at an imposing red cross on the back wall that the inspector hadn't noticed in the darkness, "in place of God."

The inspector felt his legs give beneath him and his stomach sinking, as if the earth had split open and swallowed him whole, plunging him into an abyss as dark as his childhood fears. A knot formed in his chest and rose to his throat as he took in the sight of Allison's lifeless body nailed to the painted red wood. The young, dark-haired girl's feet had been stacked one atop the other, her arms stretched across the upper beam, her torso exposed, and her waist covered with a bloody shred of white fabric. It was a horror unlike anything he'd seen before.

Miller swallowed hard, mentally projecting the photo of the smiling teenager he'd just looked at onto this body. There was a broad, black brushstroke across the top of her face covering her closed eyes, almost like a painted blindfold. It made it seem like she didn't want to look. Beneath the cross there was a pool of blood that had gathered from a wound in her side. Her head was resting to one side, as if she had fallen into an eternal sleep.

"Who would do this?!" he cried in disbelief.

Chapter 3
New York
April 23, 2011
Three days earlier
Miren Triggs

When you wager your soul,
win or lose,
you'll never be the same.

My editor couldn't believe her eyes: there I was, her star author, sprinting out of the bookstore, searching for whoever had left the envelope with the strange photo. I guess she wasn't used to her authors bolting out of book signings. To be fair, I was surprised too. By the time I realized what I was doing, I was panting and nearly breathless from fear, scanning the umbrellas on the street and looking all around me for a threatening pair of eyes. I'd become unpredictable even to myself.

It was the last of the signings stipulated by my publisher's contract. I'd agreed to publish a book about my twelve-year search for Kiera Templeton, a three-year-old girl who disappeared at the 1998 Macy's Thanksgiving Day Parade. I had first told her story in an article for the country's most important newspaper, the *Manhattan Press*, where I worked.

I hadn't planned to write a book about Kiera—not while I was searching for her, not afterwards. But I couldn't pass up the publisher's offer: a manuscript, twelve signings, a million dollars. I'd asked for time off from the *Press* to focus on the book and, as I wrote, I drifted further and further from the paper and the person I'd always been. The book's unexpected success had completely sucked me in; without realizing it, I was pulled into a vortex of interviews and book signings, and I completely lost control of my life. The plan had always been to get back to the newsroom as quickly as possible, but little by little, the book's success separated me from the things with which I most identified.

At the eleven previous signings, I'd done what I had to: I'd been courageous as I explained the details of the Templeton girl's story, affectionate with readers who wanted to see my name scribbled on their books, and polite with the booksellers who had invested a fortune in the tens of thousands of copies they'd placed in windows and on display shelves across the country. My manuscript had become the number one book in the U.S., and I was utterly incapable of enjoying its success. I don't think I was ready for any of it. It wasn't something I'd been looking for. *The Snow Girl* had set half the planet searching for Kiera; the mystery had captured the imagination of a generation, and everyone wanted to know where she was, what had happened to her and, most of all, if she had suffered. But the only pain readers found suffused in those pages, saturating every sentence, was my own. And maybe in the end that's why every signing had been bursting at the seams.

Nothing is as gripping as watching someone suffer. It's impossible to look away. We're drawn to the tears and transfixed by the drama. And the media knows it. There were so many people at that last signing that I couldn't see who'd left the padded envelope on the table with all the other gifts I'd been given.

When I first noticed it, I thought it might be a love letter: maybe some infatuated fan had let themselves get carried away by a fantasy and decided my book was proof I'd be a good life partner. Nothing could be further from the truth. I knew myself better than anyone, and I wasn't a good life partner for anybody, least of all myself. On the padded Manila envelope, in uneven handwriting, someone had written: WANNA PLAY? A bookseller was helping me put all the readers' gifts in a bag, and she was the one who planted the notion of a love letter in my mind:

"It must be some kind of sexy proposition. Open it, I could use a laugh."

I couldn't remember anyone leaving the envelope, but with the throngs of readers crowding the table, taking selfies and talking as I signed, I hadn't been paying attention to the gifts; I was just grateful for the support and trying to focus on signing books.

But I had a strange intuition about the envelope, almost like I could hear it playing a tragic melody. The uneven WANNA PLAY? transmitted a sense of chaos that made me deeply uneasy.

"Maybe it's from some crazy fan. They say all writers have at least one," the bookseller added with a laugh.

"That's what it looks like from the writing," I responded seriously.

Those two simple words seemed ready to cause havoc. Some part of me didn't want to trust my intuition, and I hoped with all my being that inside I would find a well-intentioned note. All through the signing, I had been surrounded by enthusiastic faces and kind words, and my damaged soul had clung to that moment of light, which seemed to bring some much-needed balance to a dark world.

I tore open the envelope and reached inside. The contents didn't feel dangerous: just a cold, smooth piece of paper. But when I pulled it out to take a look, I saw it was a dark, poorly framed Polaroid picture with an image that hit me like a blow to the chest. In the center of the photo was a blonde girl, gagged, looking at the camera, inside what looked like a van. On the bottom border, in the same helter-skelter handwriting, was a simple caption: GINA PEBBLES, 2002.

Even once I reached the street, I could still feel the adrenaline rushing to the tips of my fingers as I held the Polaroid with utter terror, searching up and down the sidewalk for anyone I recognized from the signing. It was raining, like it always does at the worst moments, with those tiny drops that remind me of tears, and at least twenty umbrellas blocked my view on both sides of the street. I was suddenly overwhelmed by that crushing loneliness I sometimes feel, even when I'm surrounded by people.

It's hard to feel anything but alone when everyone else is walking with their heads held high, incapable of glancing down at the horrors we drag up from our nightmares.

"What's going on, Miren?" I distantly heard the voice of my editor, Martha Wiley, behind me.

I didn't respond.

Far off I could make out the figure of a man walking hand in hand with a little girl in a red coat. I remembered the girl. A few minutes earlier she had stood across from me at the bookstore and said something that had stuck in my mind: "When I grow up, I want to be just like you and find all the lost kids."

I ran towards them, dodging bodies and wet jackets. I felt the rain soaking through my sweater, spreading from my shoulders as if the drops were tiny ice cubes melting against my skin.

"Wait!" I cried.

A few pedestrians turned to look at me, but only long enough to confirm they didn't give a shit. Do you know that feeling? Like you're swimming through the street's cold indifference? If I'd cried for help, the reaction would have been the same. Everyone walks in the flames of their own private hell, and few will take the risk of trying to put someone else's flames out.

I saw the man and girl stop at a street corner, waiting under a black umbrella for just a moment until a taxi stopped beside them.

"Did you leave a—" I shrieked between breaths when I finally reached them.

The girl turned to me, frightened. The man she was with, presumably her father, gave me a worried look.

"What's happening?" he asked, confused, protectively pulling the girl to his side.

The taxi door was open, and they had already closed the umbrella. They were getting rained on, waiting for me to answer.

The little girl's look left me speechless. I felt the fear in her eyes, the confusion in her reaction. The rosy expression I'd seen at the signing was gone, and I felt ashamed.

"Did you leave a…" the question seemed to have answered itself, and I decided to leave it unfinished. "I meant to say that…" My body and my hope floundered in the rain. I backpedaled, trying to reassure the girl, "…you left something behind, this prize for being the most special little girl at the book signing." She must have been eight or nine years old. "Here you go," I said, pulling the pen I'd been using to sign the books from my jacket pocket.

The father gave me a confused look; he seemed to have realized something was up. I hated being so easy to read, but sometimes, unavoidably, people saw me for who I really was. Wordlessly, both of them got in the taxi. I saw in the father's eyes what he really wanted to say out loud: "What the hell is wrong with you, lady?"

He closed the taxi door and gave the driver an address.

"Take it, it's fine," I insisted loudly through the window, knowing it was my desperation that had caused the terror in her eyes. "It's for you. You're going to be a great journalist one day."

She silently lowered the window and took the pen sadly with her small fingers.

"Do you mind? We have to go. This was a bad idea," the father said.

I withdrew my hand, and the taxi began driving north, its red brake lights vanishing in the distance, just like my hope of finding an explanation. I felt like my body had been smashed to pieces, even if all I actually had were a few small scars on my back.

Martha Wiley's voice drove into me from behind like a knife in the back as she covered me with her green umbrella.

"Miren, have you lost your mind? You can't come across like this in front of booksellers, and definitely not in front of readers. What's up with you? This is unacceptable, you're gonna have to—"

"I'm... I'm sorry," I said, trying to mollify her. "It's just that the photo—"

"I don't care what happened, just make sure it doesn't happen again. I can't have you acting this way, Miren. I understand that you're a little... introverted, and I appreciate you making an effort to step out of your comfort zone at these signings. I really do. But you need to sell books. And that hinges on you maintaining a positive image. You can't get all histrionic on me, okay? You can't come across like a lunatic. We've got two interviews tomorrow, including *Good Morning America*, and I need you to be a little... sunnier. I want to you see you laughing and joking."

"Interviews?" I asked, confused. "I... I have to get back to the newsroom."

"The newsroom? The book is selling better than ever, Miren. We can't lose momentum now."

"The contract said twelve book signings. This was the last one."

"The last one? You really have lost your mind. There's no other explanation. That's in the contract for the author's sake, Miren. For your sake. To make sure the publisher commits to doing a minimum amount of marketing for the book. But the more events and media exposure, the better. The contract also says the author will participate in promotional activities arranged by the publisher for a year following publication. The book just came out. It's a hit. Everybody's talking about it. Everybody wants to see you."

I looked down at the photo. I'd stopped listening to Martha as soon as she mentioned that clause in the contract.

"Miren! I'm talking to you."

"I have to get back to the paper. I haven't felt... I haven't felt like a person for a long time," I said out loud, but not to her.

"There'll be time to go back, Miren," she said, getting louder. "Right now, the important thing is to focus on tomorrow's interview. Have you thought about what you're going to wear?"

I couldn't look away from Gina in the photo: her frightened eyes, her blonde hair, the terrified expression, the rag over her mouth, the position of her arms, like they were tied behind her back. The Polaroid was dotted with tiny raindrops racing down the image to the white strip at the bottom.

"Is this about that picture? That was just somebody's shitty joke, Miren. One of your fans wanted to mess with you and they succeeded. Forget about it. Go home. Take a shower, get some rest, and tomorrow I'll pick you up. Don't let me down, Miren. We've got a lot riding on this book."

I saw her hail a taxi and, a few seconds later, it stopped beside us.

"Get in, Miren. I'll apologize to the bookstore. It's embarrassing, honestly. I'll pick you up at your place tomorrow at eight."

I opened the taxi door and looked up from the photo to see Martha Wiley, with her black suit and green umbrella, gesturing at the inside of the taxi with a serious expression.

"What are you waiting for?" she asked, irritated.

I was soaked. The cold rain was just as unpleasant as the prospect of getting into that taxi and spending the next day wearing makeup, talking about the book and Kiera Templeton in front of the whole country. I sighed with resignation and moved towards the door. I hadn't expected this whirlwind when I agreed to write about Kiera. I hadn't expected to drift so far from my true self.

"I'm glad you're seeing reason," she said finally. "We're going to sell millions of books, Miren. Millions! And I haven't even told you the best news yet: I got you an interview with the one and only Oprah Winfrey. Oprah! I don't have a date yet, but it's a major break for us. We're going to make a killing!"

I looked down at the picture of Gina again. So weak. So vulnerable. So… defenseless. Her expression was mine. Her eyes were crying out for help. My soul needed to find her.

I stopped just in front of Martha and said: "This was the last signing, Martha. Cancel everything else."

She nearly dropped her umbrella in shock, but quickly rallied in order to feel personally affronted.

"Did you not hear anything I just said?" She was raising her voice now, indignant. "Tomorrow at eight, be ready outside your house. Quit being ridiculous."

"I'm done, Martha," I declared.

"I'm sorry?"

"If you want to get in touch, send me an email."

"Your contract states very clearly—"

"I don't give a shit about the contract," I interrupted, and I think that enraged her even more.

"How… How dare you just—"

"Goodbye, Martha," I said, cutting her off again because I could tell she hated it.

Without another word, I turned around and began walking away from her through the rain.

"Miren! Come back here and get in this taxi!"

I was trembling, but not because of Martha or the cold. I was trembling for Gina. Whoever had left the envelope with her photo had given me two motives to snub my editor: to save myself and, possibly, to save Gina. I heard Martha's voice in the distance and the tone of her voice reminded me of a baby throwing a tantrum.

"You're finished, Miren! Do you hear me?"

She began yelling even louder, which I would've thought was impossible.

"Absolutely finished!" she shrieked one last time before I turned the corner and lost sight of her.

I was out of breath. I was nervous. I felt that familiar obsessiveness pulsing in my fingertips. I stopped short and let my imagination lead me. First came the tears. Then the insecurity.

"Where did they take you, Gina?" I asked the photo. "Where are you?"

I had no idea that trying to answer those two simple questions would set off the series of drastic events that followed.

Chapter 4
Manhattan
April 23, 2011
Three days earlier
Jim Schmoer

The truth always finds a way
to destroy everything.

Professor Jim Schmoer sat on the table at the front of the classroom and read the morning's headlines to his 62 surprised pupils.

"Yesterday, 81 Syrian protesters were killed by their own government's national security forces," he proclaimed as his students gradually stopped talking.

Minutes earlier, he had entered the classroom silently and leaned against the table, gripping his two daily papers, biding his time. It was blindingly bright outside even though the radio had predicted heavy rain. Spring, radiant and ever-changing, had set in on campus, permeating the foliage and the spirits of the idealistic teenagers who had traveled from all around the country for what Columbia called *Saturday Immersion*, a program in which high school seniors could spend the day living like college students. Some of them had even seen the professor come in, but had nevertheless continued chatting. Most of them thought that this program at Columbia would be no harder than high school. Perhaps that was why they continued talking and getting to know one another, even though many of them would never set foot on that campus again.

Jim Schmoer knew that first year journalism students often thought of themselves as removed from world, maybe because they thought that the real world could never really fit in academia. In a sense, they couldn't be more wrong, especially when it came to journalism, a subject in which reality not only permeated every class, but also worked its way into their notes, their assignments and, often, even took the form of a professor who wasn't being paid his salary. Every day, reality was delivered to newsstands across the country and entered people's homes through their screens; it floated in on radio waves and, of course, it taught them some lessons in the classroom, where it was sometimes better not to be so detached.

"Those killed included two children," he continued without pausing, "Jamal, age three, and his sister Amira, age seven, who were caught in the crossfire between police and demonstrators."

The students froze as he continued reading the second paragraph.

"Jamal was hit by police fire as he ran across the street towards his mother. When Amira ran after him, she was struck by a brick that protesters had ripped from the ground and launched towards the security forces. Both died instantly."

A deathly silence fell over the room. Jim's tone was so severe that the entire class seemed affected. Later, this performance would cost him two emails from concerned parents, who considered Columbia's methods traumatizing and said they would be reconsidering their children's enrollment.

"So, now that I have your attention, let me ask: who read the news today?"

Only four students raised their hands. This wasn't surprising in an open house class in which high schoolers got to experience a typical day in "Introduction to Investigative Journalism." The attitude of the college students changed with every year they spent there. By the time they were seniors, his pupils were already critical thinkers, fledgling journalists hungry for the truth. But his task during Saturday Immersion wasn't to teach these teenagers about journalism so much as to instill in them a passion for the truth, to cultivate a repulsion for lies, and to hammer home that cold hard facts are the best weapon against tyrants. His goal was to turn them into information-sniffing bloodhounds. To make them indignant at the thought of all the stories that would never come to light. When second-year students took Political Journalism, his personal objective was to instruct them to question each statement emerging from the press office of a political party. He wanted them to become sticks of dynamite capable of demolishing any statement built on a foundation of lies. But his favorite was teaching seniors, to whom he explained the ins and outs of investigative journalism: how to choose a topic and go for the jugular; how to find the shadows lurking in the brilliant artificial sunshine concocted by corporations, business owners, and politicians.

"However," he said, "nowhere in their version of the story about these protests does the *Manhattan Press* mention these two children. Why do you think that is?"

A student on the left side of the classroom—contrite after not having read the morning news, despite promising his parents that he would apply himself and make the most of this weekend experience after a long car ride from Michigan—hazarded a guess:

"To avoid seeming morbid and sensationalist?"

Jim shook his head and, still sitting on top of the table, called on a student to his right, a girl with straight hair who was clearly not ready for the question:

"Because… they didn't know?" she improvised.

The professor grinned and pointed at a boy in the back row who, a few seconds earlier, had been laughing loudly:

"I don't… I don't know, professor…"

"The explanation is simple, and I want this to be permanently etched in your minds," Jim said, putting the students out of their misery. "There's only one reason the paper doesn't mention these children's deaths: I just made it up," he finally admitted, hoping to instill a vital life lesson. "Nothing matters but the truth, and the truth is the only thing serious journalists publish. The facts—no more and no less. That's why you have to become skeptics and critical thinkers. The world needs you to question any and all information you receive. If I say two children have been killed, open your copy of the paper and check if it's true. If a politician says he's allocating city funds to build playgrounds, you go to every park and slide down the goddamn slides yourself. Don't take anything for granted. Corroborate everything they tell you. If you fail to do this, not only will you not be journalists, but you'll be accomplices in the deceit."

The class held its breath, on the edge of their seats. Jim wasn't surprised by the reaction. He gave the same speech and got the same reaction every year, though he did wish that, just once, a student would work it out from the start.

At noon, after class, the 62 students applauded. Some left with the firm idea that they would study journalism. Others left certain that they weren't ready to join the ranks of a profession whose core principle seemed so combative.

As he stepped out of the building, Jim saw that Steve Carlson, Dean of the School of Journalism, was waiting for him beside the statue of Jefferson at the entrance.

"How'd it go, Jim?" Steve asked by way of a greeting.

"Oh, good, good. The same as every year. I hope I'll see some of those faces again in the fall semester."

"Good, good…" he responded absentmindedly.

"What's going on, Steve? Did something happen?" Jim asked, confused.

"Right, yeah. You know how much I admire you, Jim. You've done really invaluable work with the students, and I want you to stick around."

"Who was it this time?"

"There are more complaints."

"From my students?"

"Oh, no. They adore you. No. Don't get me wrong."

"The administration?"

Steve hesitated, confirming Jim's suspicion.

"Steve, please. You must be joking."

"It's that radio program you record at night."

"My podcast? That's a personal project. It has absolutely nothing to do with the university. You can't just…"

"You need to… reign in the attacks. Your opinions are… raising some hackles."

"Okay, so you really are joking. We teach journalism here, for Christ's sake. My show is creating friction with the administration?"

"With our donors, Jim. You can't just go after anyone and everyone. Some of the things you say have a direct impact on the school's funding."

"I'm going to pretend I didn't hear that," Jim replied, attempting to put an end to the conversation.

"Jim… I'm not telling you to give up the program. I'm just asking you to tone it down a bit."

Jim shook his head.

"It's an amateur radio show you record in your own house, Jim. Is it really worth it? What do you stand to gain? Do you really want the board to receive complaints about things you say on a show no one even listens to?"

"Oh, for the love of God, it's one of the most popular

shows among our journalism students. It serves as an example. I use it to demonstrate the spirit that true journalists ought to have."

"Listen to me, Jim. Take my advice. Give up your internet show. I know you want to feel like you're still a journalist and having this 'podcast' or whatever you call it is how you keep a foot in that world, but… Jim, it pains me to say this, but you're a better professor than you ever were a journalist. That's why you work here and not for some media outlet. Drop it already. You're just going to end up getting yourself kicked out of here, too."

Jim remained silent. A dozen insults had already crossed his mind, but he decided to keep his mouth shut. That was a low blow.

Years back, he had been managing editor at the *Herald*, where he was considered a leading economic analyst. After the paper began its seamless and inexorable transition towards sensationalism and intensified its battle against the declining number of print readers, he was unceremoniously let go. In the age of the internet, he was falling behind: the immediacy of online news set the pace for the entire industry, and his methodical, serious approach—exhaustively verifying every word he wrote—was no longer what the market demanded.

"Bye, Steve. See you on Monday."

"Listen to what I'm saying, Jim. It's for your own good!"

Chapter 5
Queens
April 23, 2011
Three days earlier
Ben Miller

Pain doesn't care if you're expecting him,
if you just saw him, or if it's been
years since you last spoke.
He just arrives at your door, whether
you're receiving visitors or not.

It was 11pm when Ben Miller approached the house where the Hernández lived, a small, wooden two-story with screens on the doors and rusted grilles on the windows. The inside lights were on and the trash bin by the door was filled with two tied-up black bags and a third which was half-open, presumably following an assault by the wirehair cat rubbing against his calves as he waited for someone to open the door. The tiny front garden looked like a potato field and the paint on the yellow façade had peeled away in places, exposing wet chipboard.

Queens was a reasonably accurate microcosm of America, with lively, wealthy areas—home to moneyed executives who worked downtown—as well as humble neighborhoods with large immigrant populations from all over the world and neglected areas rife with crime. Elmhurst fell into the second category, but in a diffuse way, its status shifting from block to block with no clear dividing lines. The radical disparity in standards of living was a ticking time bomb that exploded in the occasional street robbery. Some accepted these conflicts as the logical consequence of the clear income inequality among residents who lived practically next door to one another.

Inspector Miller rang the bell. A few seconds later, he was greeted by a grim-looking man who he'd never seen before, with a goatee and a white t-shirt.

"Hello, are Óscar and Juana Hernández home?"

"*¡Óscar!*" he hollered, "*Aquí hay un tipo que pregunta por ti.*"

In the distance, Miller heard someone grumbling something in Spanish that he didn't understand. The man who opened the door disappeared into the dark hallway and Miller stood there waiting, weighed down by the news he was about to relay. He was nervous, but also angry, as this was his first time he'd been back to the house since Allison's disappearance had been reported.

In fact, on that first visit, the girl's parents had treated him with indifference. They had reported their daughter's disappearance at the request of a teacher at the Catholic school where she studied, because Allison hadn't been to class in three days and the lack of an explanation from her or her family had triggered their standard procedures. Juana and Óscar had brushed off the disappearance, saying Allison sometimes did this after a fight, but she always came back after a few days staying with the boyfriend of the week. Even though everything seemed to suggest she had run away of her own free will, Inspector Miller had followed the protocol for forced disappearances. He reviewed security footage, spoke to her friends and acquaintances, checked her usual hangouts and even a chapel in the suburbs where, according to one of her high school friends, she went to pray. He hadn't found any leads except a long police record documenting her fondness for weed and an equally long list of ex-boyfriends.

Miller had questioned three of these boyfriends, and all of them had confirmed her promiscuous habits and the frequent family drama. A boy named Ramiro Ortega had backed up Óscar and Juana's version of events, explaining that once, after she'd had a big blow-up with her family, she'd spent several days at his home fucking nonstop. When Inspector Miller questioned a classmate named Hannah, she confirmed the story but also said that deep down Allison was a good girl, and that she was changing. She hadn't had a boyfriend for a while and she was like a whole new person: calm, easy-going, angelic even. The inspector remembered what she'd said next: "She's a good sister in Christ now."

* * *

Óscar appeared in the shadow behind the door and, seeing Inspector Miller had returned for the fourth time in a week, clicked his tongue in annoyance.

"You again?"

"Mr. Hernández," Miller began in a serious tone.

The smell of marijuana wafted through the door. Óscar Hernández was a man without stable work. He'd gone from being a mechanic in a garage to filling tanks at a gas station, then to driving a delivery truck and remodeling homes. He was clearly a hard worker, a go-getter who didn't spend much time at home, but given his circle of friends, there was no way he wasn't also involved in something shady.

"Look, boss. She's not back yet, we'll call you when shows up. She does this. We know our daughter. She's a whirlwind, but she'll be back. Sometimes teenagers hate their parents, it's a phase."

Miller had a flashback to the image of Allison nailed to the cross and had to swallow before saying another word.

"Would it be possible for me to come in and speak with you and your wife?"

"You really got to?" Óscar asked, surprised. "We're watching TV. It's 11 at night and we got work tomorrow."

Miller responded with a silence that the father understood.

"All right. Come in," he said finally, opening the screen door.

Miller followed Óscar, who made what justifications he could as he walked through the hall to the living room:

"Hey, all the weed I've got here's for personal use. It's legal now. My brother-in-law likes to smoke and… well, it's a free country. God bless America."

"You don't have to worry about that," Miller replied. "I look for people, not drugs."

"Juana, that cop's here again. About Allison," he said scornfully the moment they entered the living room.

Miller looked around and saw the room was in worse condition than the day they'd reported the disappearance. That day, they had even let him into Allison's room for a few minutes to confirm there were no signs of violence; he hadn't found any clues about her whereabouts, but he did confirm that the family wasn't too concerned with cleaning. The mattress and bedroom walls were filthy. A thick layer of dust had accumulated on the desk and on the string of lights that hung between the curtain rod and the crucifix above the bed. There weren't many notebooks or textbooks on the desk, but he did find a few notes about love that she'd written in perfect handwriting. He'd left after that first visit with nothing but a list of her school friends' names and confirmation from her parents that she didn't keep a diary, something that might have shed some light on the case. Allison's cell phone had vanished with her, and all her clothes were still in the closet. The parents said the only thing missing was their daughter's shame at running away yet again.

There was a blue haze in the living room from the smoke and the light from the episode of *Keeping Up with the Kardashians* on the TV. In an armchair to one side, the man with the goatee who had opened the door was smoking a joint; he ignored the inspector, even though he was standing right in front of him.

"That's Alberto, my brother-in-law. He's been living with us for a few months. And you already know my wife, Juana."

Juana's eyes were glued to the screen; she only turned when the inspector began to speak.

"Mr. and Mrs. Hernández," Miller said, "I have to inform you that we've found Allison."

"See? Told you she'd show. When's she coming home? She tell you anything?" Óscar asked, visibly angry. "We're gonna teach that girl a lesson when she gets home. Wasting a cop's time. She's gonna be grounded till she's twenty-one."

"No… she isn't coming. Allison…" he had difficulty speaking. "Allison isn't coming back."

"That what she says?" the father snickered. "She'll be back for money when her new boyfriend dumps her. Always the same shit. Soon as she's out of cash, she comes home for more. That's what you have kids for. So they can pick your wallet! After all we've done for her. My father used to call me and my brother a couple of ingrates. Old man got a lot of things right."

"She was found dead in a remote area in the Rockaways," Miller said flatly, trying to avoid details.

He noticed the smiley photo of Allison he'd used for his file—and which he had uploaded to www.missingkids.org of his own initiative when it became clear that the parents wouldn't lift a finger—in a small gold frame on a side table next to an ashtray full of butts.

"So when's she get here?" asked the mother, who seemingly

hadn't heard anything. "She's needs to take out the trash. We ask her to do one thing! Her grandmother's always calling from Monterrey to ask about her and I have to tell her she's got a slut for a granddaughter."

Juana turned back to the screen and shook her head, indignant.

"I don't think you heard me, Mrs. Hernández," Miller clarified, so confused by this reaction he'd barely understood what she said. "Your daughter was found dead. We're currently trying to figure out how it happened."

"Say that again?" Óscar said, frowning. His brother-in-law took another hit of his joint and blew the smoke to the ceiling so peacefully it left the inspector speechless. Óscar continued: "Just tell me where she is, and I'll give that snot-nosed brat a piece of my mind. I'm sick of her bullshit."

"Your daughter has been murdered. She's gone," Miller declared, struggling to find words they would understand. "I'm very sorry. We're trying to figure out what happened and find the perpetrator."

"Perpetrator? Murdered?" the mother repeated in disbelief.

She finally seemed to grasp what was happening, and after what felt like a dense, endless minute, she wailed so loudly the inspector jumped. Alberto leapt to his feet at the sound, startled into a defensive instinct and then quickly turned to comfort his sister. Miller tried his best to maintain detached professionalism. The father, who'd stopped moving after processing the inspector's words, slowly shifted his expression until it was settled somewhere between disbelief and overwhelming grief. He looked Miller straight in the eye.

"Mr. Hernández, I can't tell you how sorry I am," the inspector continued, fighting the knot that had formed in his throat.

But Óscar wasn't really looking at Miller; he was lost in some distant memory that brought the tears flooding to his eyes: maybe a hug she'd given him as a girl, or a kiss he'd given her in her crib. All broken families have memories like this that they turn to from time to time, reliving moments they'll never be able to repeat.

"My… my girl… my baby girl…" he murmured, almost without knowing what he was saying.

"If there's anything I can do, please know that I'm at your disposal. My unit's work, unfortunately, ends with this tragic development, but I wanted to be the one to tell you. I'm with the FBI Missing Persons Unit. The murder case will be handled from now on by NYPD. But that doesn't mean I'm not available for whatever you might need and… well, I'll share all the details of the case with the Homicide Squad and work with them to move things forward as quickly as possible. I still don't know the name of the officer who'll be assigned to the case, but please allow me to recommend that you avoid the press and grieve for your daughter in the privacy of your own home."

Miller had given that speech so many times he could practically recite it word for word. In the United States, 460 thousand minors are reported missing every year. In other words, one minor disappears every minute and seven seconds, 52 every hour, two thousand every day. In Spain, it's twenty thousand a year; in Germany, one hundred thousand. The despair is universal. An endless flow of phone calls with heartrending cries from weeping people begging "please find my child" into the emergency line only to hear "please remain calm" from the other end. The overwhelming majority of these cases turn out okay. Only a small, insistent, painful percentage end like Allison's.

Juana screamed louder and louder, and her brother had bent over to embrace his sister after seeing her collapsed distraught on the floor. He whispered into her ear as she cried. Her husband, disorientated and uncomprehending, looked down and released his first sob. Suddenly, he turned to his wife and crouched down to hold her.

Nothing can prepare parents for a blow like that. Especially when they don't expect it. Trusting that nothing terrible has happened is a double-edged sword. The suffering saved by not worrying during the search hits harder, magnified by the shock. It's a difficult hole to get out of. Guilt pervades all their pain, memories, hopes. An active search is different: there's still the hope the child will be found, and even though the hope dwindles with time, when bad news comes, the leap into the abyss isn't from quite so high. They've already fallen to the depths, descended into anguish, and by the time they reach the very bottom, they look back up and find that at least hope left them a ladder.

Allison's parents cried as hard as children who'd let go of their white helium balloon and had to watch it float off. Given the family's distance and problematic history, it seemed like Allison had lost her parents long ago.

Allison's mother lifted up her hands in anguish, wailing: "*¡Mi niña! ¡¿Qué te han hecho?! Dios mío, ¿por qué no la has cuidado?*"

Her cries echoed in Miller's head, and he stepped out of the living room without saying goodbye to let them grieve in peace. Óscar was kneeling by his wife, both of them destroyed, and beside them, Alberto held Juana up by placing his hand on her back as if he were helping her release her tears. With their sobs in the background, Miller saw from the hallway that the door to Allison's bedroom was half-open. It looked just like it had the first time he visited, except for one subtle, yet dramatic difference to which his eyes were immediately drawn, perhaps because of the gruesome image he'd seen earlier that night or perhaps because he was in some way seeking comfort.

"Where's the crucifix that was above the bed?" he asked out loud.

Chapter 6
New York
April 23, 2011
Three days earlier
Miren Triggs

If you're clinging to something
that makes you feel alive,
in all likelihood, you're already dead.

I walked in the rain, my cell ringing nonstop. My iPhone 4 kept prompting me to accept calls from Martha Wiley, my editor and the last person on Earth I wanted to talk to. I declined seven times. She also sent several messages, which I skimmed as I continued walking aimlessly. The last of her texts said: "Miren, I don't know what's up with you. This new attitude is shocking. Tomorrow morning we have to be at the Times Square Studios for Good Morning America. Don't let me down."

That last reminder seemed somehow more serious than her previous efforts, and seeing her desperately begging made me feel powerful for the first time in a long while. When had I lost control of my own life? When had the tree I had finally managed to straighten begun growing crooked again?

And then I understood.

It was as if with the book's success, some part of me had ended up hidden between its pages. There, Miren Triggs could be whoever she wanted. She could conceal her fears, paper over her insecurities, minimize collateral damage. And maybe the best part of all was that within those pages I could protect myself from danger, avoid being vulnerable. You can't destroy a character in a book, even though the person who inspired that character is made of flesh and blood, someone who cries when she gets home at night because she feels like she's both inside and outside her own life. The Miren in the book is immortal. Even if you destroyed every copy, the character would live on forever, wandering through the limbo of literary creation, waiting to return, for someone to revive her story without needing to know that the fragile, weak, damaged human being also named Miren Triggs actually existed. And perhaps with that false shield I had convinced myself that as long as Miren the character was brave, I didn't have to be. As long as she was in control of her life, I didn't need to put my own on the line, and as long as she was seeking out the truth, I could skirt around it. But if I'd learned anything, it was that the truth always shines through at the just the right moment, and that moment had clearly come.

I had been wandering aimlessly through Queens, all the while thinking about Gina Pebbles and what I remembered about her case. I still had a folder with her name on it in my storage unit. I'd reviewed it multiple times, but I still couldn't remember the details.

In 2002, when she was 15, Gina disappeared on her way home from school. She was a blonde girl and had a slight gap between her front teeth; she looked happy in all the photos in her file, despite the complicated life she'd had.

She'd been living with her eight-year-old brother in her aunt and uncle's house in the Rockaways when she vanished.

As I remembered it, her parents had died some time earlier and her aunt and uncle, Christopher and Meghan Pebbles, took them in as they were the closest surviving relatives.

As happened in so many other kids' cases, Gina's disappearance didn't get much press thanks to poor timing: the day before, June 2nd, another girl, 14, had been kidnapped at knifepoint from her family's home in Salt Lake City. The second girl came from a wealthy family, and maybe she was a little prettier. The details usually make all the difference. The Salt Lake City case ended up dominating the news for days; the country dedicated all its resources and attention, all its prayers and vigils to her. And maybe that was why Gina's case was largely overlooked.

A week after she disappeared, her pink backpack with an embroidered unicorn was found in an isolated part of Breezy Point, in front of the beach and little more than a mile from home. That was the last definitive clue about what happened to Gina, the last trace of her existence. Everything else had vanished as she had never walked the Earth.

But what did that Polaroid mean? Who had taken the photo of her tied-up and gagged? And why had they given it to me? Had some kind of sociopath taken that photo as a final memento before killing her? Was it evidence I'd never seen from somewhere in the police file? The more I thought about it, the more uneasy I became and the more I felt I had to figure out what was going on. All those questions needed an answer; her terrified look in the photograph cried out for someone to fight for her.

I stopped to hail a taxi, but all the cabs driving down Jamaica Avenue under the overhead train's steel rails had their OFF DUTY signs lit up. I checked the time on my phone and realized it was already after midnight. I'd been wandering for over an hour, trying to remember what I knew about Gina, and I hadn't noticed that with every passing block, my surroundings had grown more threatening. I'd blithely walked from one neighborhood to another, ignoring their boundaries and, suddenly, when I looked up from the wet sidewalk, I noticed the dark shadows of the city, the burning eyes of the night beasts.

A guy in a hoodie on the corner, a homeless man lying in an alley, a couple having some kind of argument. I felt like the strangers were all looking at me, even those who had their backs turned. I could practically see them licking their lips as they undressed me with their eyes. I knew this was all in my imagination, but it was impossible for me not to think about it. It was so hard to climb out of the dark pit where three scumbags had locked me up for life all those years ago.

When I thought about that night, the first thing that came to mind was the smell, then that bright smile in the darkness, and then my mind would jump straight to the blood trickling down my inner thigh. After that, I would hear myself crying. As if I were another person. As if I had never been me. Removed from my body but still inside it. Hurt on the inside, with cuts on my skin. I could hear my own cries as I ran badly injured through the night. They say some people put up mental barriers to help them forget traumatic events. Not only did I seem incapable of creating that kind of life-saving barrier, but my mind replayed that memory time and again against my will, taking me back to that night in 1997, lingering on details and reopening wounds.

Finally, a taxi pulled up.

"Christ lady, you're soaked," the driver exclaimed as soon as I entered the vehicle. "You're gonna ruin my seat."

"Do you know how to get to the Life Storage facility in Brooklyn, by the river?"

"Now? It's after midnight. That's not a great area for a—"

"I have some things there I need to pick up. Can you wait for me in the taxi while I grab them?"

The driver hesitated.

"Look lady, I know it's none of my business, but that's not a safe place for a woman to walk around alone late at night."

"Well maybe it would be if the men in this country knew how it keep it in their goddamn pants," I replied, annoyed. "Will you wait for me, or won't you?"

He sighed, but eventually agreed:

"Yeah, but I'm keeping the meter on."

"Screw the meter. You're not finding another customer around here this time of night. I'll give you twenty bucks to wait by the entrance. And another thirty to take me from there back to the West Village. Deal?"

He grumbled, but I was watching his expression in the mirror, and I knew he'd give in. He knew I was right. I pretty much always was.

"All right, I'll take you there and wait ten minutes. Not a second longer. Lotta people get mugged over there." The taxi started moving and the driver seemed to want to keep talking. All I wanted to do was think about Gina. "They come up to you, stick their gun in your stomach and… God bless America, right? Second amendment and all that shit. You know what they don't have a right to do? Shoot a guy while he's working. Or a bunch of kids at school. What a fucking disgrace. What the hell kinda country are we trying to build here? Any freak can walk around with a gun, get in a fight and, bang! You're a dead man. Any freak can stroll into a store, buy himself a gun and mow down the first guy he sees. The other day they killed one of my taxi brothers for his pocket cash. All day driving in this traffic, smelling shit and listening to idiot passengers just to get your ass shot over a hundred bucks? Blood and brains all over the windshield. You don't have a gun on you, do you lady?" he joked, making eye contact through the rearview mirror.

"I wouldn't even know how to load it," I lied, but only partially.

I did, in fact, know how to load it, but I didn't have it on me at that particular moment. It had been under my pillow for weeks, protection from my nightmares.

When I saw the Life Storage building, I felt a tickle in my stomach. A smooth and delicate current of tension climbed from my gut to my fingertips. Why had I stopped searching?

"Wait here for ten minutes. I'll be right back."

I went to my storage unit, whose turquoise metal roller door made it stand out from the rest, and entered the combination—the year my grandmother was born—into the lock. It was a cold night, but at least it had stopped raining. When I lifted the door, the rusted metal produced a shrill, haunting shriek, but when I saw the interior of the unit, I felt like I was regaining a piece of me that I had lost somewhere along the way.

A dozen well-organized metal filing cabinets lined the walls. I read the years I had written on the little cards on each drawer, from 1960 to 2000. I've always been methodical and organized. My notes in college had been a marvel. Several of the filing cabinets had names written on the drawers, and I got goosebumps as I read the first of them: Kiera Templeton. So much emotion in two simple words. Beside her were Amanda Maslow, Kate Sparks, Susan Doe, Gina Pebbles, and a long list of others. Gina Pebbles. There was her file with everything I had managed to learn about her. I leapt onto it as if I would never see it again and began placing all the files into a cardboard box whose contents I dumped hastily on the floor without looking at them, carelessly scattering papers without realizing that simple action would change everything.

I had all the files on Gina in the box and was getting ready to go back out to the taxi when I tripped over one of the piles of paper I'd just flung to the ground. Just a few sheets on the floor of the storage unit. I was surprised to see a face I thought I'd forgotten; a photo I had managed to get a hold of after fighting tooth and nail for the undisclosed summary file on my rape.

The image had been taken from police records: a man with a serious expression and dark eyes, looking straight ahead. His name was written in the margin: Aron Wallace. I crouched to pick up the photo, regarding it with the same condescension I'm sure he'd had when everything happened. I dropped the box and combed through the rest of the papers with a determination I almost didn't recognize in myself.

I was trying to find something specific, a single line of text I knew I had but couldn't find: his address. Maybe it was finally time to find him. Too many times I'd debated whether or not to continue with the plan, but the shadows from that night and the echoes of that gunshot always came back to haunt me like gargoyles hungry for my soul. Maybe having his photo at home would ease some of the rage I still felt about that night.

In the distance, I heard the taxi driver leaning on the horn and prepared to leave with the box of files on Gina and the photo of Aron Wallace, but as I lowered the door and replaced the padlock, I saw the corner of a sheet of paper sticking out. Everything would have been so different if I'd just pushed it back under instead of pulling on it...

Twenty minutes later, I was clutching Gina's box and gazing at the city's majestic skyline as the taxi crossed the Manhattan Bridge. But that light, the beauty of thousands of illuminated windows on countless skyscrapers contrasting so sharply with the sadness of the city was nothing compared to the adrenaline I felt when I looked down at the crumpled sheet of paper beside me and, in the semi-darkness, read the second line of text: '60 123rd St., Apt. 3E.'

Chapter 7
New York
April 23, 2011
Three days earlier
Jim Schmoer

Why do people want eyes
if so many will never be able to see.

The professor left Columbia's campus through the gates at 116th and Broadway with a bad taste in his mouth. When he arrived home after a long walk north, he collapsed exhausted onto his brown leather Chesterfield, the standout piece of furniture in his living room. He stared up at the ceiling for a few minutes after loosening his plaid wool tie, squeezing the bridge of his nose. Before climbing the stairs of his apartment building at the corner of Hamilton Place and 141st, he'd stopped at the deli on the corner for a sugar-free pretzel to snack on, a package of dehydrated curry noodles for dinner, and a 16-ounce latte to ease his frustration. He'd ordered it with three pumps of vanilla syrup, which was far more than a 48-year-old man ought to have, but given his emotional state, he concluded that a glucose bomb was just what he needed.

After letting the coffee cool on the kitchen counter for an amount of time somewhere between fifteen minutes and two hours, he rose stiffly from the sofa and looked out of the living room window, watching the children at the playground across the street. There were two young girls, around six and eight, swinging back and forth like coordinated pendulums on the red swings. A boy who looked about five was sitting motionless on the seesaw, firmly grabbing the handlebar, waiting for one of the other children dashing around the park to sit on the opposite end. Jim watched the little boy as nothing happened for several minutes, and it made him think of who he himself was slowly becoming: someone waiting for something, without knowing or particularly caring what.

Jim turned away, hurt on behalf of the boy no one wanted to play with, and sat down at his computer, taking a sip of his coffee. It tasted like caramel.

"Fuck!" he spat.

He loved the taste of a cooled vanilla latte, but he hated caramel syrup with all his might. The barista had screwed it up again, and he contemplated going back down and demanding a new drink, but he needed to prepare that night's podcast.

He turned on his 27-inch iMac and opened the Pages document in which he had written an outline of the day's episode. Essentially, he planned to dedicate the hour to detailing a serious botulism outbreak that had affected four hundred babies across the country and whose origin, based on his research, seemed to be a batch of GrowKids powdered milk from the pharmaceutical company GlobalHealth. The batch had been recalled from the market weeks earlier, with no explanation or media coverage. In the preceding days, he had joined a Facebook group called ChildBotulism, where the number of new posts had grown exponentially compared to the previous year. The comments in the group seemed to follow a standard pattern: "I don't know how it happened. My child only drinks GrowKids powdered milk."

The show would practically record itself. He had a wealth of material; no one would be able to poke a hole in his findings. Irked by the Dean's comments, he even considered writing an article. If he swallowed his pride, he could send it to his old newsroom at the *Herald*, where he hadn't set foot since he was let go in 1998. But then he imagined the murmurs that would cause among his former colleagues who still worked there.

He turned on the microphone, opened Podcast Studio and, after taking a deep breath, began a new recording:

"Good evening, newshounds. Today I have definitive answers about a story I've been researching for several days now. The pharmaceutical corporation GlobalHealth seems to be covering up a botulism outbreak that may have affected over four hundred children and which, if consumers are not alerted, could result in…"

He paused the recording. He'd been struck by a troubling thought as he recorded his introduction.

Jim opened Safari and went to the university's website, looking for the donor page. Two clicks later, he saw that under the Collaborators tab—as if they did something more than give money—the very first logo was GlobalHealth Pharmaceuticals.

"Shit."

That was even worse than the caramel latte. He debated what to do. He could broadcast the show live, through a link he'd share on Twitter and not make it available for followers to download. That way, if someone from the company or the administration at Columbia looked for it among his list of episodes to justify their attack, they would find nothing. But he knew that wasn't enough. If he fought to uncover a story, it was precisely so that it could come to light and have an impact: a penalty, compensation for the families, a change in protocol to keep it from happening again. Deleting the episode after broadcasting it would cast a shadow over his work and diminish his reputation. The thousands of people who listened every

Friday and Saturday would see he'd erased the story from his list of episodes, possibly ceding to pressure from powerful interested parties, and that was the opposite of everything he'd always stood for. But if he posted it as usual and the board found out, it could mean the end of his career as a professor. Repugnant.

He rose from his chair and returned to the window. The seesaw was now occupied by the two girls who had been on the swings, and the swings were now occupied by the boy who had formerly been on the seesaw. His feet hung motionless beneath him like stalactites. Jim looked for the boy's parents among the adults on a green bench a few yards away, but they seemed to be engaged in such a heated conversation that Jim was sure no one noticed the boy's loneliness.

He was on the verge of going down to the playground and pushing the boy on the swings himself, but unexpectedly, that very instant, the skies opened and the parents leapt to their feet as their children ran frantically through the rain. In an instant, the park became deserted. The image of a swing wobbling in the distance reminded him of a happier time in his life.

He picked up his phone and made a call. After a few seconds, a woman's voice came through the speaker.

"Jim?"

"Hi, Carol," he said, hopeful.

"What do you need?" She didn't seem to be expecting his call.

"Can you put Olivia on?"

"She's on Long Island. At Amanda's house."

He sighed, too quietly for Carol to hear. He was hurt.

"She is? If I'd known she wouldn't be with you, she could've come to spend the weekend with me."

"She... She would've said no, Jim. She wanted to spend a few days at her friend's house. She's been working out the details with me and Amanda's parents all week."

"But… We could have gone to see a show or—"

"What's this about, Jim?" his ex-wife interrupted. "You never call when it's not your weekend."

"I was just thinking about the two of you. That's all. And also, we have to talk. One weekend a month seems like very little to me."

"You work all the time, Jim. You can't take care of her."

"You and I both know that arrangement is from when I was still working at the paper. I have more free time now."

"Don't you dare go there. And what's with bringing this up now? Olivia is seventeen. We got divorced when she was three. And… how many years has it been since you worked at the paper? Eight? Nine?"

"Thirteen," he admitted with a sigh.

Condensing those thirteen years into one word as if it were a trivial length of time was too much for him in this state of mind.

"Look, Jim, I'm busy. Call Olivia and talk to her if you want. I don't know what's up with you, but maybe checking in on her yourself will do you good." Jim's ex-wife realized he was distressed and didn't want to make things worse. At the end of the day, he was her daughter's father. "Are you doing okay?" she finally asked.

"Yeah, yeah, I'm fine. It's just that… well, I wanted to hear from her. I was thinking about when we used to go to the park, and you and I pushed Olivia on the swings."

"She's a little big for that now, but yeah, I get it. Sometimes I remember how crafty she was at getting the other kids to play whatever game she wanted."

"She was a sly one."

"Still is, even though, well, she's in that phase where she'd rather… You know, be with her friends and pretend I don't exist."

"I understand," Jim replied.

60

"I've got to go, okay? Me and Andrew are going out. I'll drop her off with you next weekend, that still work?"

It took Jim a moment to respond.

"Jim?"

"That's perfect, Carol," he finally said hoarsely, a knot in his throat.

He went back to his desk and closed Podcast Studio without clicking save. He decided he couldn't afford to lose anything else, so he opened Twitter and wrote: "Newshounds, what would you like to hear about on tonight's episode? I think it's best for you to choose."

A few seconds and two likes later, he received his first response, from a user with the handle @GodBlessTheTruth. It included a photo of a smiling brunette girl and said only: "The death of Allison Hernández."

Chapter 8
Queens
April 23, 2011
Three days earlier
Ben Miller

The problem with seeking the truth
is always how hard it is
to accept.

Inspector Miller bolted out of the Hernández family's house, leaving the door open, and ran to his car. He grabbed Allison's file from the passenger seat and anxiously spread its contents out over the hood. He shuffled through the sheets with information and interviews he had gathered in the preceding days and eventually extracted several photographs from the file.

The first was almost like a school photo, of Allison with her brown hair, smiling at the camera, distant. There were several photos from ATM cameras in the area where Allison was last seen alive: a few benches across from a pharmacy in the middle of Jamaica Avenue, near her high school... Apparently, someone called the AMBER alert phone number to say they thought they saw her with a group of boys and girls her age the morning she disappeared, maybe two hundred yards from the Mallow Institute. He'd tried to follow the trail of those statements, but nothing seemed to fit. That morning, Allison had been in class until lunch and, according to the principal, students weren't allowed to leave campus during class or during lunch, which lasted 30 minutes.

Finally, he found the photograph he was searching for and scrutinized it in the moonlight: it was an unremarkable shot of Allison's room. In it, you could see the position of the quilt on the mattress, the crucifix above it, the books on the shelves, the papers on the desk, the chair. A small statuette of the Virgin Mary on one of the shelves acted as a bookend on one side. Miller realized that everything in her world revolved around religion. He hurried back into the house, photo in hand.

Allison's mother was still weeping in the living room, a sound like the bells of a seaside chapel reverberating against every wall in the house. The inspector turned on the light in Allison's room and stepped in, gripping the photo, concerned by the sinister difference between what he saw in the image and what he saw in the room.

He went to where the cross ought to be and saw a shiny, cross-shaped patch of paint exactly where it had been hanging. It had been a Catholic crucifix, maybe two feet tall and one foot across, he estimated.

Silently, he checked his surroundings against the photograph. Something else caught his attention. In the photo, the books on the shelf stood evenly beside one another, all of them held up by the figurine of the Virgin Mary; now, however, the books were tipping to the side, this extra space suggesting that one was missing.

Suddenly, Óscar, Allison's father, appeared behind Miller, sobbing and with tears in his eyes, and he asked:

"What are you still doing here? Haven't you done enough damage already? Get out!"

"Where's the crucifix that used to be above the bed?" Miller asked, with a surprised expression.

"Crucifix?"

The father turned to the wall, confused, not understanding what was going on.

"Please. Has Allison been here since she disappeared?"

"Allison? How could—"

"Things are missing from this bedroom. The crucifix. One of the books on the shelf, too. I took a photograph when you reported her disappearance. See?" Miller showed him the photo.

At that instant, Juana's sobs stopped.

"Things missing?" said Óscar, a little dazed. "I don't..." he added, staring blankly.

"Who took them? It could be important."

"I don't... I don't know," Óscar finally finished. "Two days ago..."

"What happened two days ago?"

"Someone broke the window by the kitchen, behind the living room."

"What?"

"They broke the window. When we saw the shards of glass on the floor, we thought we'd been robbed. But... when we saw our things... we didn't think anything was missing," he said, almost unable to keep speaking.

"Why didn't you report it? We were looking for your daughter. It could've been impor..." he stopped himself from continuing, realizing the parents were already shouldering more than enough guilt.

"We thought it was just some local kids. This is a... humble neighborhood, the kids play in the street, they play baseball and break windows. We didn't think that..." this time he was the one who trailed off, not because he wanted to stop, but because he couldn't bring himself to continue.

Each word reminded him that they hadn't worried about their daughter in a long time. Óscar just nodded, unable to speak a word. Juana's silhouette appeared in the doorframe, her face red and swollen.

"Tell me, sir," she asked falteringly, "Did my girl suffer?"

"The two of you are religious, I take it?"

Both nodded wordlessly, short of breath.

"Did Christ suffer on the cross?" Miller asked.

"I don't… I don't know," Juana answered, disturbed.

"I… I don't know how to answer your question either."

Chapter 9
Manhattan
April 24, 2011
Two days earlier
Miren Triggs

Not every door that closes
is shut forever.

I tossed and turned all night, unable to get my mind off Gina and everything I had to do to get up to speed. I got out of bed at exactly five in the morning, showered, put on some black jeans and a blouse, also black, to match the shadows that chased me through my dreams. It was my basic writer look, which I'd worn to every book signing, and which I now hoped to pull off as a *Manhattan Press* journalist.

As I stood across from the paper's headquarters in the heart of Manhattan, I felt like I was returning home or, at least, returning to a place that felt like home. I was carrying the box with my files on Gina. All around me were businessmen rushing in suits, bustling pedestrians, and gawking tourists who had apparently woken up early to make the rounds on the New York tourist circuit, which began at the Top of the Rock, included a stop for cupcakes at Magnolia, paused at Times

Square, took a few minutes to rest in front of the *Press*, then meandered over to Grand Central just in time for lunch. In the afternoon, they would stampede their way over to the Empire State Building, hoping to get a good spot at the observatory on the 86th floor and, if they were lucky, even witness a frustrated suicide attempt. I'd followed the same itinerary when I first came to the city with my parents after a long night's drive from Charlotte, North Carolina, eager to begin studying journalism at Columbia and naïve about all that would come next: pain and truth, two words that have always been synonymous.

Kiera Templeton had been the only ray of light I'd experienced in all my years in the city. I'm not saying everything had been shrouded in darkness, just that the rest had been only occasional sparks, sporadic moments of happiness; nothing else had the intensity of her story. Not even the light from the flames that led me to the *Press*.

I pulled out my ID and, as I walked through the turnstile at the entrance to the newsroom, the sound of telephones and the clicking of keyboards on the other side of the doors seemed as if it hadn't paused for an instant since I'd left. A young receptionist with a robotic smile and a headset, whom I had never seen before, turned to look at me.

"And you are?"

"Can I see Phil?"

"Phil... who?"

Her smile grew even wider, as if my question were absurd. She made me feel uncomfortable.

"Phil Marks..."

"Hmm... Let me see..."

She brought a pen to her mouth. I prayed it was covered in germs.

"Who wants to see him?" she asked, though she didn't seem to actually care.

"How about you let me through, and we talk about this later?"

"Access to the newsroom is restricted to *Manhattan Press* staff writers only. So, I'm afraid I can't allow that. But let me know who you want to talk to, and I'll see what we can do. Who did you want to speak with?"

"I already told you. Phil Marks," I replied, annoyed, putting down the box with Gina's files.

"He's not on my list," she said coldly, almost instantly. "Is there another person you'd like to see? Tell me your name and I'll check in the newsroom."

"Phil Marks is editor-in-chief at this newspaper. Your boss, ultimately. My name is Miren Triggs, I work here, in the investigative unit."

She paused to check a list she had on her desk. A moment later, she looked up, her eyes as wide as ostrich eggs.

"Not on the list, I'm sorry," she declared, indifferent. "I'm going to have to ask you to leave."

"What are you talking about? I work here," I objected, angry.

"Not according to the list."

"Fuck the list."

"Please… Don't make me call security. This is a serious paper…"

I looked around just as two journalists in plaid shirts who worked in foreign affairs were coming in. I didn't know their names, but I remembered seeing them in the newsroom.

"Hey, sorry, can you tell her I work here? I have to see Phil."

They exchanged an incredulous look. Then, one of them looked at me with a sad expression and the other willed himself to speak.

"Miren? They didn't let you go?"

"Let me go? I was on leave. You know, for my book. Can you tell her to let me in?"

They exchanged another look that seemed to last an eternity. Finally, one of them responded:

"On… leave? You really didn't hear?"

"Hear what?" I asked, confused.

Suddenly I heard a voice behind me that I instantly recognized:

"Miren?"

It was Bob Wexter, head of the investigative unit. This whole experience was giving me the creeps. I'd been working at the *Press* for over twelve years and in just a few seconds I'd become like a stranger.

"Bob! Good timing."

"You know this woman, Mr. Wexter?" the receptionist butted in.

"Of course I do, this is Miss Triggs," Bob answered. Then, turning to me, he continued, surprised to see me: "What're you doing here?" I noted a hint of joy in his voice, but also disbelief.

"I'm ready to come back. I needed some time and… Well. Here I am."

"Want to come into my office and we can talk?"

"Office? They gave you an office? How'd they manage to trap you between four walls?"

"You didn't hear? They made me editor-in-chief."

"Really? That's incredible! Congrats. I'm really… But what happened with Phil?"

"Phil's not doing so good. Come on in and I'll tell you about it. You need a coffee? You're… Sweet Jesus, you've changed. I heard you on the radio. I see your book everywhere I look."

I walked beside him, leaving behind the receptionist who was still staring at me, dumbfounded. I couldn't help but feel butterflies when I walked past my desk. Except, it was empty. Too empty, when compared to my memories. The piles of paper had disappeared. The file trays were gone. The computer had vanished. I realized that the office, despite the constant sound of telephones and loud conversations, was far emptier than before. When we got to the office where I had often fought with Bill, Bob Wexter sat down and dropped the bomb:

"The thing is, Miren… You can't come back."

"What?" I asked, surprised. This was an unexpected blow.

"It's got nothing to do with you, I promise. It's the business."

"Business? What are you talking about?"

"The board is furling the sails. A storm is coming. Actually, we've been in the middle of the storm for a while already. Didn't you notice half the office is gone?"

"I thought it was just because it's still early."

"Last month they laid off half the staff. Subscriptions have been plummeting for months. If it keeps up, we'll have to close the paper."

"That's why Phil's gone?"

"Phil stepped down as soon as they told him. He didn't have it in him to fire half the staff and then go back to work. He felt responsible for the whole thing. I'm sure you can see that morale is low. Doesn't the newsroom strike you as kind of… dead?"

"But how did things get so bad?"

"The internet, social media, lack of interest. What do I know. Now people just read headlines on Twitter and that's enough for them. It's been bad for a while. Phil used to talk to me about how worried he was. The board hasn't stopped putting the squeeze on us. Those sons of bitches only care about money. It's the only thing that really matters to them. The print runs keep getting smaller and monetizing online content isn't easy. People aren't in the habit of paying for digital information."

"It's that bad? What about the investigative unit? Where's Samantha? Who's left besides you?"

"Samantha was the first to go. Me… Well, I took Phil's job. There is no investigative unit. We can't have two or three people covering a handful of stories a year. It isn't viable. Now we're all focused on breaking news and politics, since that's where the easy money is. Cheaper, younger journalists handle breaking news, reworking content the agencies send out, and politics, well, there's not much to that either. We have a few good analysts who summarize for the editors."

"You're kidding, right?"

"I wish I were," he muttered, downcast. "Miren, I know Phil promised you a spot when you came back, but things have changed too much. I hate to tell you this. You even brought… What is that?"

I was in shock. Listening to Bob had left me frozen. He'd been in charge of investigative journalism at the *Press* for as long as I could remember. When I joined in 1998, he was already there. His relaxed approach, without a rigid hierarchy, made me feel like I was a real member of the team from my very first day, in part because that setup allowed me to follow my own lead and grow as a journalist. The investigative unit would choose two or three central issues to work on, and the research could last for months. Then, each of us chose a parallel topic, which we'd pursue independently. It was only thanks to that freedom that I was able to dig into the Kiera Templeton case. It was so disheartening to see everything falling apart; it was like I was looking at the wreckage of an era I now yearned for more than ever. If the newspaper disappeared, I'd lose my only hope of regaining the thing that had kept me feeling alive.

"It's… the story I was planning to work on."

"What is it?"

"Gina Pebbles."

He was pensive for a few seconds and then asked gravely:

"Another girl? Miren, you have to understand…"

"Not just any girl. A teenager who disappeared in 2002. She got out of school and her backpack appeared in a park a mile from her house. That was the last anyone heard of her."

"What's special about that? Why her and not... Allison Hernández, for example?"

"Allison Hernández?"

"Last night they found the body of Allison Hernández, a fifteen-year-old Mexican girl, in the Rockaways, in one of the buildings that's part of Fort Tilden, an abandoned military complex."

"Gina's case—"

"She was crucified," he interrupted. "She disappeared last week. I have current events working on it. We've only published a tiny preview in the online version, and it'll come out in print tomorrow, when we have a little more information. Something brief. I don't want to give it too much space. Everyone's eyes are on Syria right now, things are getting worse by the day and keeping correspondents on the ground costs too much to have readers paying attention to something else. The situation in Syria is dramatic and that's where we need to concentrate our efforts. Even if the local media are writing about Allison, it'll all get buried under the avalanche of stories from the Middle East. Miren, what I'm trying to say is that everything here is fucked. Things are getting worse all the time and we have to be very careful where we channel our resources. I'm really sorry, but I can't give you your old job back, especially not for that kind of story. I have to be careful about what stories we pursue and then get them out when we can achieve the broadest possible reach."

"Shit," I sighed. A fifteen-year-old girl crucified. The whole world was crashing down around us while we watched it on TV, like the collapse was just a show that didn't concern us.

"I'm looking for the right moment to give a little more oxygen to Allison's story. Something more fully fleshed out than... what we've put out so far. It could be a good national story if we can get some details from our police sources."

I went for it:

"Bob, last night someone gave me this," I said, placing the Polaroid on his desk.

"What is it?" he asked.

A young writer I'd never seen before knocked on the door and Bob shooed him away with his hands.

"It's Gina Pebbles, gagged in the back of a truck. It looks like an old photo, taken at the time of her disappearance, but maybe it means something. With all the buzz around the book and Kiera... It seems like the sociopath who took it wants to test me or something, see if I'm able to find her. Something's telling me I should try."

Bob looked at the photo for a few seconds, concentrating.

"Have you shown this to the police?"

I shook my head. Then, because I knew he'd disapprove, I added:

"Not yet. I will as soon as I make a copy. I know Ben Miller from the FBI Missing Persons Unit; I'm going to give it to him. I'm sure he's familiar with the case."

"Inspector Miller?"

"He was on Kiera's case. He and I have been... friends for years."

He paused for a long moment. I knew what his pauses meant. He was going to give me what I wanted.

"It's a good story, Miren. I won't deny you that. But I can't take you on. There's no money. Not to mention, it's probably a dead end. It's been... eight, no, nine years since this happened. That's too long. You know it as well as I do. I can't offer you the job."

"I don't want money. I don't need it. I just want to come back. This is... home for me."

"I won't have one of the best journalists in the country working for free. No way. Even though we'll spiral into oblivion if we don't stem this loss of subscribers, I can't do something that shameful. If a country is willing to let the free press die, it has to accept that democracy dies along with it."

He might have been on to something, except maybe the country wasn't letting it die so much as calling our attention to what a crappy job we'd been doing.

"You understand, right? Believe me, no one wants you here more than I do, so we can go back to how things used to be. You know I don't like being in charge. I'm uncomfortable here. I've always preferred being... closer to the explosions. And you're like me, Miren. But I promise, you don't want to be in the building when it collapses."

I waited in silence. This closed door didn't form a part of my plans. For the past few years, the *Press* had been my home, the place where I could fight to save the world. Maybe, also, the place where the world fought to save itself. We were the lifeboat after the shipwreck. There wasn't space for everyone.

"There must be a way for me to come back, Bob."

"Miren... You don't need us if you want to investigate what happened to this girl. You can do it yourself, write another book, get your ass out of the quicksand."

"I know."

"So? Why are you here?"

"Because this is *my* quicksand."

He sighed.

"Here I'm... Here I'm myself. You said it yourself, Bob. You've always preferred being closer to the explosions. When I'm working here, I'm more myself, I'm more than... Miren Triggs. Here I'm a journalist. Here I can change things."

Maybe I was making a mistake by sharing my insecurities with him. But if that avenue was closed to me, what would I do? He gave me a serious look. Then his eyes returned to the photo of Gina.

"How about this," he finally said. "You join current events, but with a full page to yourself. One article a week. It'll be a mix of investigative journalism and current events. I think something like that could work."

"Fantastic."

"You'll get paid, well, per article. It's still less than you made before, but things have changed."

"That's fine for me. I get it."

"But I decide what you write about. And you have to contribute something unique. A new point of view. From a first-person perspective. I don't just want a sequence of events; I want you to be part of what you're telling. The public already know and love you. Let's take advantage of that. Maybe that way we can sell the board on bringing you on."

"Uh… sure."

"I like the Gina story, but you and I both know that's an open-ended story. You'll start with an article for next Sunday, May 1st."

"Bob—"

"Do you believe in God?"

I raised an eyebrow, caught off guard.

"What?"

"Whatever, forget it. Allison Hernández. Go to the Rockaways, ask around the churches, talk to people in the neighborhood, chat with her friends. Cozy up to a priest or two. Religion is important to people. Everyone will be floored when they hear how she died. It's not your Gina Pebbles, but I'm sure you understand that I can't put you on a story unless I know it'll materialize into something. Work on Gina's story in your spare time."

"You said the Rockaways? It's just that that's also where…" I stopped myself: if I mentioned Gina again, I might jeopardize my return. "I don't want to bring Allison's family into it, Bob. You know how I feel about sensationalism."

"I know. I don't care. I don't want you covering their grief. I want your own view of the story. Get close with the religious community there. Be creative. I'm sure you'll think of something. You've got a week. Er, six days. I want the article Saturday night at the very latest."

"The religious community? What does that even mean?"

"Churches, chapels, schools, academies. I don't care what type: Presbyterian, Protestant, Catholic. Get a Satanist for all I care. It's what you find that matters. Figure out what Allison believed in and start sniffing around. Try to figure out how she ended up nailed to a fucking cross. Talk to NYPD, to the Homicide Squad, or whoever you think makes sense. But I want you in the article. You're the best at that. What do you think, Miren? Are you in?" he said, extending his hand across his desk.

I was unsure what to say. I hadn't expected him to propose something like that, but what could I do? I didn't know that if I accepted, my life would end up hanging by a thread. But it wouldn't have mattered: saying no would have left me dead inside anyway.

"I'm in."

What I didn't expect was that the very same afternoon, the stories of Gina Pebbles and Allison Hernández, nine years apart, would be brought together, almost bound at the hip, by a telephone call that would unleash absolute chaos.

Chapter 10
New York
April 23, 2011
Three days earlier
Jim Schmoer

Rarely does one realize that in the future
the present will be nothing
but a bad memory.

Professor Jim Schmoer reread the reply from @GodBless-
TheTruth a few times. It surprised him: he'd read about
Allison Hernández's disappearance a week earlier, but as far he
knew, no body had been found, and there was no definitive
reason to believe she had been killed.

He always kept a close eye on news regarding missing persons; it was a recurring topic on his show, though he always made
a point of avoiding more sensationalist stories. He preferred
shedding light on forgotten cases, where a kid had disappeared at
exactly the wrong moment, while all the news channels, radio
shows, and newspapers were focused on a tax hike, a labor protest, or some senator who couldn't keep it in his pants.

He Googled Allison's name and scanned the headlines from
the past few days. A few articles had appeared with her photo

beneath the words AMBER ALERT. He refined the result so he'd only see stories from the past few hours, but he still couldn't find anything new. He jumped from paper to paper, from one news agency to another, trying to find a sentence or headline suggesting where and when her body had been found, but there was nothing.

Finally, after a few minutes, Jim responded to @GodBless-TheTruth. He had an odd feeling about all this, but he didn't pay it much attention. "Allison Hernández is still missing. Let's let the authorities do their job and try to bring her back alive."

He continued reading the other comments on the thread. Some of his followers suggested he talk about politics, which he detested. Another user asked him to do a segment on the precarious conditions of workers in Asian factories used by major tech companies. A teenager asked if he was a Knicks fan.

He felt discouraged. He thought it might be better to skip that day's episode. It wasn't easy to dive into a story when you didn't feel any kind of connection to it. He took a quick look at the trending topics on Twitter, but there wasn't anything that interested him: condolences for a celebrity who was actually still alive, the debut of a movie he didn't plan to see, the names of two music groups he didn't care about. A hashtag, #KU-WTK, had ascended to the number-one spot, but when he clicked it, he saw it was just the buildup to the next broadcast of *Keeping Up with the Kardashians*.

Someone had sent him a direct message. Jim liked keeping his Twitter DMs open so anyone could write to him privately: in his view, that was an indispensable part of being a journalist. The overwhelming majority of the big stories began that way: someone with an ax to grind sending a tip to the press through an anonymous phone call, leaking confidential documents from a throwaway email account, slipping an envelope under a door. His open mailbox was just that: a place where anyone could report something they wanted brought to light.

The message was from @GodBlessTheTruth, sent at 7.05pm according to the platform, and it contained only an image. When Jim opened it, it took him a second to process what he saw in the blurry, half-dark photo.

In the center of the image, he thought he could discern a wooden cross standing on the ground, on which the pale figure of a woman seemed to have been crucified. On either side of her, two black silhouettes were holding onto the cross and, from their posture, Jim understood that they were straining to drag it back towards the graffiti-covered wall in the background. It took him another moment to absorb what he saw on the sides of the image, but on the left he could distinguish what seemed to be the shoulder of someone dressed in white, watching the scene. On the right, he could make out several rows of empty chairs facing the cross.

"What the hell is this?" Jim said to himself out loud, perplexed.

He downloaded the image and saved it to his desktop. Then he took a screenshot of the conversation showing the username and the exact time he received the image. Before replying, he reflected on what he ought to do. He didn't understand what he was looking at, but he knew he didn't like it.

The professor clicked on @GodBlessTheTruth's profile and was alarmed to see the user had never tweeted anything except that one reply. The profile picture was a white egg on an orange background and, as he could see beside the username, the account had been created that same day.

Jim decided to reply to the message and carefully considered what to say. This could just be a troll trying to screw with him, but the possibility that the image was real and that the girl was Allison Hernández prompted him to proceed with caution:

"Is that Allison? Where did you get this image?"

For several minutes, the professor wondered what kind of macabre joke this could be. He knew the internet was a cesspool. There were sickos lurking around every corner, and it seemed like he'd found one. At one point, Jim had dipped his toes into the deep web after installing the browser Tor and acquiring a private list of the most disturbing places on the internet. This image from @GodBlessTheTruth reminded him of the photos he'd seen splashed across secret occultist forums, with the critical difference that the latter were largely inoffensive and mostly just involved burning leaves or sacrifices of dead pigeons or rats in front of a pagan cross. Although this photo had similarities, its subject was a girl on a Christian cross, with the sun slanting in from one side of the image, in what looked like an old warehouse, abandoned but full of people.

And then, @GodBlessTheTruth sent a response.

It was a link to the *Manhattan Press*'s news archives, a section he visited often to view articles from past years. It was a resource available to anyone who wanted to research the past. Jim clicked the link and felt all his built-up anxiety from that unexpected conversation explode uncontrollably when he read the headline: "HAVE YOU SEEN GINA PEBBLES?"

The article was from June 2002. He remembered the case, though it was buried deep in the recesses of his memory. Gina Pebbles went missing the day after another teenage girl had been kidnapped at knife point in Salt Lake City, and not a single outlet had covered Gina's case except for the *Manhattan Press*, which printed a short article on page twelve. It was forgotten almost immediately. At the time, he had reviewed everything that was known about the case and had even tried to get access to the girl's case file so he could talk about it on his program—and talk to his students about news opportunism—but it was all so long ago he could barely remember the details.

He checked the byline and, despite everything, couldn't help but smile: Miren Triggs. Beneath the headline, the article outlined the last time Gina was seen alive, what she was wearing, and the remote area of the Rockaways where her backpack had been found, Breezy Point Tip. It was an isolated beach at the end of the peninsula, overrun with shrubs and trash, frequented only by fishermen in the winter and surfers in the summer. The story included a photo of Gina, with her long blonde hair and bright smile. Further down, there were a few descriptions of the zone where her backpack had been discovered, a photo of a group of adults and young people in the area, including a sad-looking couple who were hugging an inconsolable, weeping eight-year-old boy. It seemed like the three of them were with a group of volunteers who had formed search parties. The caption read: 'Christopher and Meghan Pebbles, Gina's uncle and aunt, join the search for their niece. Also pictured: Ethan Pebbles, Gina's younger brother, sobbing due to his sister's disappearance.'

Jim returned to the conversation with @GodBlessThe-Truth, unable to grasp the magnitude of what was happening or the implication of those messages. Fearful of the response, he asked:

"Is Gina the girl on the cross?"

A few seconds later: "No."

"Is it Allison Hernández?" Jim insisted.

"Yes."

Jim didn't hesitate: "Where is she?"

Back to waiting for an answer. Jim's eyes were glued to the screen, and he prayed this sinister joke would end. He considered the possibility that this might be one of his students. His relationship with the third years was intense enough—he was constantly testing them and setting them on complex investigations—that he could imagine them doing something like this. A few faces came to his mind, Alice and Samuel, his best students, undoubtedly capable of concocting this sort of story to test their professor's acumen. Not to mention, they had just finished the unit on disinformation, during which they discussed how easily impulsive emotions like pain, anger, sadness, or desperation can be exploited to lend credence to stories no one would otherwise believe. He read the article about Gina over and over again. He tried Googling '@GodBlessTheTruth,' but to no avail; no one on any other platform used that handle.

Tired of waiting, he decided to insist again: "Do you know something about Allison Hernández? Is that what you're trying to tell me?"

Finally, a response: "You'll soon find out."

Jim was disconcerted. "What are you talking about?"

But the user didn't reply. Jim waited a full hour for another message, so restless he was unable to sit still. He had already abandoned the idea of recording his show that night and he had tweeted as much to his followers, which cost him a few indignant messages. He returned to the profile to read the first message he'd received and noticed something he had initially missed: he'd seen that @GodBlessTheTruth had no followers and had only tweeted once—his reply to Jim's tweet—but he hadn't noticed the account was following one other Twitter user. Jim clicked on Following and was shocked to see two usernames: Miren Triggs' and his own.

Chapter 11
FBI New York Field Office
April 24, 2011
Two days earlier
Ben Miller

*Every old puzzle
has a few missing pieces.*

It was one o'clock in the morning when Ben Miller arrived at the FBI's New York field office. He didn't bother greeting the dozens of agents still sitting at their desks, all of which were covered in folders, papers, coffee cups and hopelessness. Despite the hour, the agency didn't sleep, though its pace undeniably slowed at night: people moved more lethargically; voices spoke more softly; phones rang less frequently. The atmosphere in the early morning could be bleak: the agents' faces were always suspended in a state between strain and sadness, or sometimes both at once. If you were at the office at one in the morning, you'd either just found someone or lost someone, and in either case it wasn't good news. Cases that solved themselves without incident (a minor who showed up at a friend's house after leaving without telling his parents, or a teenager who had stormed off after an argument finally coming home) tended to be sorted out with the central office by phone after the parents were notified. These cases were closed with no more fireworks than the relief of the family and a "thanks for letting us know."

But cases whose files required a detailed closure, the ones that needed an inspector's signature, were the ones with tragic endings. Allison fell into this category. No doubt the phone ringing four tables away, beside the computer where Agent Wharton wore a look of despair, was someone waiting for news about a file with a similar fate. If a person lived in that office for one year without contact with the outside world, they would think life consisted of nothing but being born, growing up, falling in love, and disappearing, assuming you had the good luck to complete the first three phases before arriving at the fourth.

Miller spent a while typing up the report on the discovery of Allison's body. He saved all his materials to a compressed file for transfer to the NYPD Homicide Squad. Finding the body changed the case's legal status, transferring responsibilities and limiting the actions that could be undertaken by the unit of the FBI which investigated the disappearances of children. By now, a new unit would already be at Fort Tilden gathering samples, footprints, clues, and statements from the pair of teenagers who found the body. As soon as he transferred the file, another unit would visit the Hernández family and the district attorney would begin his work; if some journalist learned the way the body had been found, they'd also have to deal with reporters trying to make an even bigger deal out of things.

Before closing Allison's file, he would have to log the latest data in ViCAP, the Violent Criminal Apprehension Program, adding the general details, like the time and place where she was last seen, where her body was found, her photo, and a cold description of the main events, all of which would form the statistical database on crime in each district and the incidence of certain kinds of cases.

He clicked through ViCAP to put a pin on the map in front of the pharmacy on Jamaica Avenue, two hundred yards from the Mallow Institute, and tried four times to get the application to place the pin in just the right spot, where the satellite image displayed a rectangular, bench-shaped blur. According to the statement from a woman working in the pharmacy, that was the last place Allison was seen alive. Then he flew over the digital map to the Rockaways, at the extreme southeast edge of Queens, to place another pin on top of Fort Tilden, a gray rectangle in a field of green to show where her body had been found, on a cross still etched in Miller's memory.

He was about to open the centralized AMBER alert software to deactivate her case, but before closing ViCAP, he zoomed out on the map to see the distance between the two pins he had just placed. Between them were hundreds of color-coded pins that indicated the status of other cases: green for open cases with active searches; red for closed cases where the person was found deceased; and yellow for open cases that had reached a dead end, whose investigative teams were waiting to see if any new leads emerged.

He zoomed out so far that the screen was practically covered in red pins, like drops of blood dripped across a tapestry of streets and parks. There were far more green pins, but they only remained on the map for a few hours. Cases with more-or-less happy endings—which were the overwhelming majority—were deleted from the visual registry and preserved only as local files, so the information could be retrieved if the event repeated itself.

The yellow pins were far less numerous, but just as painful. Each one represented a forgotten case, a desolate and hopeless family. At a glance, he guessed that there were only twelve or so in Queens and, to his surprise, one of them was on top of the Mallow Institute, the same school Allison had attended.

"Who else disappeared from there?"

He clicked on the pin, opening a small bubble with bold text that took him aback: GINA PEBBLES, JUNE 03, 2002.

He remembered Gina. Hers was one of the impossible cases that he'd forgotten almost entirely; it remained in his mind only as a statistic he used to torture himself. He'd wiped the details from his mind, but when he saw her name above the Mallow Institute, he recalled asking some of her classmates if they had seen her. It could just be a coincidence that a second girl had disappeared from the school nine years later, but a new suspicion began to develop in his mind, even if he wasn't ready to trust it just yet. He considered clicking on her name and accessing her file, but before he could, he realized that the application had highlighted another pin. It was on Breezy Point, at the far southwest edge of the Rockaways, barely 300 yards from Fort Tilden, where Allison's body was found. When he clicked on the pin, another orange bubble popped up: GINA PEBBLE'S BACKPACK, JUNE 05, 2002.

He began to feel euphoric over what he thought was a connection and went back to click on the first link so he could access Gina's file. A message splashed across his screen: AR-CHIVED CONTENT. FILE 172/2002.

He jumped up and dialed a phone number. A moment later, a practically robotic female voice answered.

"Yeah?

"Jen?"

"Miller? Fuck off, I was just resting my eyes."

"I need a file."

"Nobody needs things from the archives at one in the morning, Ben. Why d'you think I took the night shift?"

"So you could be closer to Markus the security guard?"

"Is it that obvious?"

"So can you get me file 172/2002?"

"2002? That's… Oh yeah that's uh… I think… yeah, it must be downstairs. When do ya need it for?"

"Would right now be too much to ask?"

Jen sighed on the other end of the line.

"You know what? I was dreaming I won the lottery, and I went around grabbing your damn files in a velvet bathrobe."

"You won the lottery, and you were still working here?"

"Y'all could never survive without me."

Miller smiled.

"All the files from back then are a little screwy, just warning you. They came the other day to keep digitizing 'em."

Miller exhaled before continuing.

"I'll wait for it at my desk."

"What's it about? Anything you can tell me?" Jen asked, curious.

"It's… just a hunch."

"You got coffee? It'll be a minute."

"I'll get two from the machine and trade you one for the file."

"I dunno what makes me so fond of you, Miller."

"It's because we're exactly the same. Part of us hates being here. And another part wants to stay in this building forever."

"For me that part's name is Markus," Jen replied.

Ben couldn't help but laugh before hanging up.

Fifteen or twenty minutes later, after Miller had finished transferring the file to the NYPD Homicide Squad, a middle-aged woman with a ponytail and no makeup appeared at the far end of the room, struggling with a brown cardboard box. When she finally made it across the room, she dropped it on his desk like a corpse.

"Where's my fuckin' coffee?" she asked by way of salutation.

"That's all?" Ben joked, handing her a steaming disposable cup. "Two sugars?"

"If you weren't so happily married with Lisa, you'd be my Markus."

"But then who'd pine after Markus?" Ben replied, grateful for the compliment.

"I didn't say I'd be faithful."

"Touché," Ben smiled.

Then he opened the box and began piling papers and folios in front of his keyboard.

"You're getting real busy, huh?" Jen asked.

Ben sat in silence, unsettled by the first page of the disappearance report: a photo of Gina Pebbles looking at the camera, blonde, smiling, full of hope, with skin so pale she looked like she might even glow in the dark.

"You need anything else, lemme know."

Miller gave a trance-like nod and Jen said goodbye, but later, he wouldn't remember her leaving.

He quickly scanned various interview transcripts, rereading the case but taking less and less in. He was tired, but that box and the fact that both girls attended the same high school had set all the alarms inside his head blaring. He took several swigs of coffee as he read in the dark. Hours passed as he reviewed countless statements in which no one said anything of substance, until he finally reached an interview in which an agent by the name of Warwick Penrose spoke to a boy named Ethan Pebbles, eight years old, Gina's younger brother.

Chapter 12
Manhattan
April 24, 2011
Two days earlier
Miren Triggs

All mistakes
have a beginning
but not an end.

I left Bob's office with butterflies in my stomach. I was return-ing to the *Press*, on the condition that I would dive into what happened to Allison Hernández, immerse myself in an unfa-miliar world, and pray I didn't rub too much salt in my own wounds as I described it from my point of view. Like it was easy to spill my guts to the world when I couldn't even recog-nize myself. My nightmares had worked their way so deep within me that I often confused them with aspirations. One day you're dreaming about winning a Pulitzer, the next day about jumping off a bridge.

I waited while HR got my old desk ready. Paper trays, pencil holders, highlighters, a landline. They also sent a guy who looked around thirty with a black IBM laptop I didn't plan on using much. The last time I was in the newsroom, I only used the laptop they gave me when I had to write, which wasn't often, or to read messages they wouldn't let me open on my personal email account. Whenever we got a leak about a story the investigative unit was working on, it had to be stored on a secure server; it couldn't leave the *Press* offices until it was for sale at newsstands across the U.S. For everyday work, I preferred my 13-inch MacBook Pro with a snazzy new i5 processor. I'd bought it a few days after receiving the second payment for my book advance, and from the first day I had it, it was all I needed.

I glanced at my phone and saw Martha Wiley had called five times that morning. She had also sent me a text that said only: "Miren, I think you're making a mistake. I think we can find a balance you'll be comfortable with. Please, call me." To be honest, I didn't know how I should handle things with her and, deep down, I knew that sooner or later I'd have to find a solution.

"Just another minute," the IT guy sitting beside me said as he set up the computer, "and I'll have your email all synced up. I didn't delete your account when you left. I knew you'd be back," he added with a look I found confusing.

"Thanks, uh—" I answered, waiting for him to tell me his name.

"Oh, I'm Matthew, but everyone calls me Matt."

"Matt," I smiled. "You work Sundays too?"

"I'm head of IT. Can you imagine what would happen if the *Press* website went down? Or they hacked our servers and got access to all our subscribers' information? I mean, I know, obviously it's shitty being always on call, but... this is the *Press*. Here you either give it your all or you get out. The world needs us. Don't you think?"

"Tell that to everyone who got laid off." I looked down the length of the newsroom. It felt like I was in the middle of a desert.

He glanced up too, then returned to the computer. He typed a few passwords, installed some programs I'd never use, then played a drumroll with his hands on the desk.

"Just one second and… *voilà*, there you have it."

My Outlook inbox flooded with three hundred messages I had no intention of answering.

"Want me to clear your inbox?"

"Nah, leave it. Gives me something to look at when I'm bored."

"Perfect. You need anything, I'm on the second floor."

"Thanks, Matt."

"And uh… if you ever feel like grabbing a drink, here's my number."

I hadn't been expecting that. He handed me a piece of paper.

"Oh… I'm not…"

A tiny part of me felt sorry for him. Another, much louder part of me felt afraid. Despite everything, all those years later, that knee-jerk reaction still kicked in, that reminder not to let my guard down.

"Oh, sorry if that was too…" he trailed off, as if he had to really think about what he was about to say. "I just really dig the way you write."

"Thanks, Matt. It's fine. I'll call you if I need anything."

"Anytime," he said, in a tone that suggested he'd already forgotten his invitation.

It was odd. Until he offered me his phone number, I hadn't thought of Matt as a member of the opposite sex. But to be honest, when he didn't seem fazed by my rejection, he gained a lot of points in my book. I noticed he was pretty slim, in a short-sleeved linen shirt, with messy hair that fell over his forehead like he didn't even care.

"You know what? Maybe I will call you," I said, backpedaling.

"Alrighty" he answered, surprised.

Then he looked back at my computer screen, made sure I was connected to the printer, and did something to the intranet or whatever.

"I've got a new computer and I really ought to… make the most of it," I said.

Clearly, I was terrible at this.

"For sure," he responded, motionless.

Any confidence I'd gained was dashed in a matter of seconds. He went back to Outlook to set up my corporate signature.

"I'll just make sure the SMTP is working right and… yep, it's working. Chill, chill. Huh, weird," he said surprised by something on the screen. "You got two emails from the same sender."

"Sorry?"

"Two emails from the same person. Must be a server error… hang on a sec. I'll delete duplicates so…"

I leaned over his shoulder to see who had sent the messages and was left almost breathless.

"Do you know a… Jim Schmoer?" he asked at the exact moment I read the name.

"Jim?!" I said, shocked.

"I'll take that as a yes."

"Are you done? Do you mind letting me get to work now?" I spat.

"Uh…"

He got out of the chair and said something, but I wasn't listening. I sat down and he spoke again, but at that moment I could only hear the sounds inside my own head.

"Sorry, what?" I asked, distracted.

"Is he your… boyfriend?"

I snorted. Then I smiled condescendingly. It was something I'd learned as a kid, watching my mom sneer at my father whenever he invented some excuse for why he got home from work so late. As a woman, sooner or later you're bound to learn that kind of smile. Removed. Expectant. Aggressive. A smile that broadcasts to the world that you're not a fucking idiot. My mother certainly wasn't, and my father knew it.

"Matt, you're a charmer and all, but I—"

"Sorry, you have a boyfriend," he said, cutting me off. "I understand. I don't… it's fine. I shouldn't have mixed wor—"

"It's fine, Matt. He's not my boyfriend. But… It's not your business. You shouldn't read other people's emails. Anyway, I have things to do… is all. Thanks for… getting everything set up."

"Yeah yeah. Sorry if—"

"Forget it," I interrupted.

I smiled like my mom again. I was starting to like it.

He turned around and gathered his things to leave, and I felt like a piece of shit. Unintentionally—because this is something nobody wants—I'd learned to drive away anyone who represented a threat to my loneliness as carelessly as those three men who had used me like a rag. That night was always lurking. Then a shot would ring in my head, and in a flash, I was back in that alley. My chest burned. In my mouth I could taste justice, but it wasn't long before I felt like a piece of shit again. Always the same sequence of feelings in the same order, always the same… sadness.

For years, I hadn't let anyone get close to me. I drove them away, distanced myself, disappeared. My wounds kept me from loving, because deep down I felt like anyone and everyone could hurt me. The only person who had managed to break through that barrier was Jim, but with him, too, I'd lifted an invisible shield as soon as I felt he was getting too close. I was incapable of acting differently, the rage had lodged itself somewhere inside me, like a three-headed beast guarding the gates to my own personal hell.

"Matt!" I called out as he walked away. "Thanks."

He lifted a hand in a you're-welcome gesture, but he accompanied it with my same smile. Damn, he learned quick.

Then I sighed and turned to the emails from Jim. I wanted to get them out of the way before going to the *Press* website and quickly reading the short article about Allison that Bob had mentioned. The first email was a brief message, just a few lines, sent around midnight. It made me feel uneasy: "Miren, it's Jim. Congratulations on the success of your book. I tried to call you, but it looks like you've changed your number. I need to talk to you. It's urgent. Warmly, Jim."

After my unexpected car accident, Jim had visited me in the hospital several times. He and I had always maintained a certain familiarity with one another, but also a certain distance, and his visits smothered me. I remember that even my mother asked why my old Columbia professor was visiting so often. I admit, I was unable to describe my relationship with Jim and I hated being asked to. I liked him, but I also detested his constant care and concern. One day when I was in the hospital, I woke from a long nap to hear a conversation echoing in my head: it was Jim and my mother talking while I slept, each with a coffee in hand. For a few minutes I pretended I was still asleep so I could hear them talk about me. I'm a journalist; curiosity is something I can't turn off. I heard him telling my mother that he cared about me. That he considered me to be a special person. That gave me such vertigo that I feigned a cry of pain so the nurses would come and drive both of them out, and I wouldn't have to say anything.

His affection pained me. It was upsetting how well he knew me. Was it true, was he really the only person who had gotten close to me in all those years?

When I was finally discharged from the hospital, I decided not to tell him and put some space between us. I didn't tell him I was leaving my old place in the Bronx and moving into a small studio in the West Village. I got a new phone number and tried to forget about him for a while. More than a while. If it hadn't been for those emails, the chasm between us would only have grown and with time, our bond might have entirely disappeared. And part of me was trying to achieve that. Not because I really wanted it, but out of fear. I nearly deleted both emails. Why did I have to open the second message? Maybe everything would've turned out differently if I hadn't.

He'd sent it at seven in the morning, an hour before I'd set foot in the *Press* building.

"Miren. I wouldn't insist if it weren't so important. I know I might've been a little annoying at the hospital, but I think I have something. It's about Allison Hernández. I saw the preview about them finding her body on the *Press* website a few minutes ago. I don't have any other means of contacting you. This is serious. It's about Gina Pebbles, too. You might remember her. Call me at (212) 555-0134. Jim."

Gina's name popped out in the email like two words with the power to raze the city to the ground. Allison's name seemed to be gaining momentum; little did I know her story was about to fan out in front of me like a deck of cards. I picked up the phone and dialed Jim's number instantly.

I heard his voice. So warm but indifferent. So close yet distant.
"Hello?"

"Professor Schmoer?"

"Miren?"

"What do you have on Allison Hernández and Gina Pebbles?"

"It's been a while. I… I'm glad you called."

"Yes, well, I've been… a little busy."

"I know. I see your book in window displays all over town. Congratulations… You deserve it more than anyone."

He paused. I didn't know how to respond to that.

"I saw your email," I finally said.

"Can I see you? It's a professional matter. I know I might've made you feel a little uncomfortable. I was just… worried about you."

"I don't need anyone looking out for me, okay?"

"I know. That's why I didn't insist. When you left the hospital, I thought it might be a while before we saw each other again."

"Why did you email me?"

"I think it's something that could interest you."

"Why couldn't you just tell me about it in your email?"

"I'd rather show you in person."

I responded with silence. I didn't feel like putting up a fight.

After an uncomfortable, silent moment, I replied: "I'm swamped. I'm back at the paper and—"

"Yesterday, in the evening, an anonymous account sent me a photograph of Allison Hernández and she had been… crucified. I'm assuming you heard they found her body? Everyone else has."

"Yeah. I just got back and I'm writing an article about her. Something that pushes the story beyond… Well, beyond just the cold facts."

"Miren, no one has written yet that she was crucified."

"They haven't?"

"The *Press* only picked up the story that her body turned up, the same as the other papers and the TV news. I guess they don't want to risk running something so gruesome before they have official confirmation. I've talked to the Rockaway police. They won't confirm it for me, but their silence when I ask tells me everything I need to know."

"And you're saying someone sent you a photo of her?"

"Yes. Someone sent me the photograph of Allison at seven in the evening. I read the article the *Press* published, and it says two teenagers found her body at eight. This person sent me the photo an hour before her body was found."

"I haven't even had a chance to read our own article yet. Can you send me the photo?"

"No, not if you're going to publish it."

"Jim…"

"In the photo, it looks like she's still alive. It's a photo of a girl on the brink of death."

"Have you shown it to anyone? The police?"

"Not yet."

"Jim… That's not—"

"I will later. First, I need to talk to you."

"Why me?"

"The person who sent me the photo also sent me your article from 2002 about the disappearance of Gina Pebbles."

Gina's name was taking on a life of its own. It was everywhere, but nowhere at the same time. Since the night before, she was like a ghost I found around every turn: in the Polaroid, in my dreams, in my memories, in the Rockaways.

"Why do you think they sent you my article?"

"Do you remember her case?"

"I spent all night reviewing her police file. I managed to get my hands on a copy back in 2002."

"You did? But why now? Did you make a connection between the cases too?"

"Connection? No, I…" I wasn't sure if I should tell him that someone had given me the Polaroid at the book signing and that the cases involved the same part of the city.

"Can you come here? The corner of Hamilton Place and 141st."

I sighed.

"I was planning to go to the Rockaways this afternoon and ask around a few churches. Maybe I'll get a different angle for the article I have to write. You can ride with me and tell me everything. Bring the photo."

"Done," he answered.

"I'll pick you up. I'm trying to break in my new car anyway."

"When?"

"Right now," I said just before hanging up.

Chapter 13
New York
April 24, 2011
Two days earlier
Jim Schmoer

It isn't easy to hide the excitement
that comes with admitting
nothing ever ended.

As soon as he got off the phone with Miren, Jim printed the photo and the conversation with @GodBlessTheTruth. He took a quick shower to clear his head after the sleepless night he'd spent reading everything that had ever been written about Gina Pebbles. There wasn't much, but the more he read, the less doubt he had that Gina's disappearance with linked to Allison's death. He put on a pair of jeans, a white shirt, his glasses, and a sweater. As soon as he was ready, he went downstairs, popped into the deli and ordered a vanilla latte for himself and a Coke for Miren. At no point in the process did he lose sight of the intersection where Miren was supposed to pick him up, at the corner of Hamilton Place and 141st.

It was noon and everything seemed to suggest that the latte would be his lunch. He waited a few minutes for the drink to cool down before taking his first sip and, just as he was bringing it to his lips, a beige New Beetle VW pulled up and honked twice.

He quickly got in and looked at Miren in the driver's seat.

"I got you a Coke," he said, as if it had only been five minutes and not several months since they had last seen each other.

"Uh… thanks," she sputtered, confused.

"Should I open it for you?"

"Leave it in the cupholder," she said.

They drove east along 141st and soon found themselves on Harlem River Road, crossing towards Queens by way of Randalls Island. Both were silent for a few minutes, perhaps searching for the right words, perhaps feeling the weight of their mistakes, when finally Miren spat out:

"You shouldn't have come to the hospital so much. My mother thought there was something between us."

"I understand."

"She asked me how long I'd been going out with my old professor."

"She did? Every time I spoke with her, I made a point of not saying anything that would suggest that."

"The flowers?"

"You were in the hospital. It's normal to bring flowers to people in the hospital."

"And the chocolates?"

"You don't like chocolate?"

"Don't play dumb."

"Look, Miren. I'm going to be very honest with you. Maybe I felt like you were lonely. Your mom even told me none of your colleagues from the paper had come to see you. Just your editor, who, actually, I got along really well with."

"You came to see me out of pity?"

"That's not what I mean."

"It sure sounds like it."

"I thought you needed someone there besides your parents. But... I can see I was mistaken."

"I don't need anyone. Is that clear? My life is fine the way it is. Without people worrying about me because I'm by myself. Did you ever ask me what I wanted? Some people enjoy being alone. Not everyone has to spend their whole life sticking their nose in other people's business. That's not how I am. I like to read. I enjoy silence. I don't want anyone near me who might—" she stopped talking abruptly.

Jim sighed. "Go ahead, say what you have to say. It makes sense."

"No, I'm finished."

"Look, Miren. My life is a mess, and you don't know the half of it. The last thing I want is more complications. I care about you because I think your writing is... different. What journalism ought to be. Personally, to me, you're nothing more than a great former student, and I want you to keep fighting for the truth. I don't have any other intention with you beyond what's strictly professional. And this thing with Allison Hernández is serious."

Miren didn't reply, but she clutched the wheel in a gesture that Jim understood to mean that those last words had affected her.

"I don't even know why I called you. I don't need your help to write about Allison."

"I know," Jim said, "but I think there's a bigger story than Allison's under the surface here."

"I do too, I just don't know what yet," Miren responded, swallowing her pride.

Part of her wanted to continue on her own. But another part needed someone she could rely on.

"There's something you haven't told me yet, right?" Jim asked.

Miren held back for a beat, protecting her secret, but ultimately decided to tell him everything.

"Open the glove compartment," she said.

Jim did as she instructed and found the Polaroid of the gagged teenager. At the bottom of the image, Gina's name and the year she disappeared. He looked at it for a few seconds before speaking.

"Is this her? Is this Gina?"

Miren nodded silently.

"Who gave you this?"

"I don't know. Someone gave it to me at my book signing last night. It was in an envelope, and someone had written 'Wanna play?' on the front. That's all I know."

"Did you see who brought the envelope?"

"There were tons of people, I didn't see who it was. They left it on the table without saying anything."

"Are you sure this is Gina Pebbles?"

"It's a little blurry and the gag is covering part of her face, but it definitely looks like her. She's wearing the same clothes as when she went missing in 2002. Blonde hair. Skinny. Based on the length of her legs I'd guess she's around five foot three, which matches up."

"So this photo is from 2002."

"Exactly. The person who left it on the table has got to be the one who kidnapped her and took this photo, before... before he did God knows what to her. I'm sure Gina is buried somewhere we'll never find her."

"No chance she's still alive?"

"Nine years later? Impossible. Only a sadist would take a picture like this. Some fetishist who took a snapshot as a souvenir. I've read a lot about these people. They kidnap their victims, play with them a while until they get bored, and then... they get it."

Jim took a photo of the Polaroid with his phone in case it got lost or damaged. Then he asked:

"Then why do you think he gave it to you now?"

"I don't know. I'm guessing he read my story about Kiera, and he's irritated I moved on from Gina. It's like he's trying to challenge me, to get me back on the case."

Jim stayed silent. They were just approaching the Marine Parkway Bridge, which connected mainland Queens with the Rockaway Peninsula.

"They found Gina's backpack in Breezy Point in the Rockaways. It's about as remote as you can get, it's all just trash and overgrowth."

"I know. I read it in the article that Twitter user sent me. I spent all night reading every story I could find."

"And you think the cases are connected?" Miren asked, not wanting to share her own suspicions.

"I think they are. I have a bad feeling about it."

"Why?"

"Both girls studied at the Mallow Institute, in Queens."

"Really?"

"I checked. I spent all night trying to figure out why @GodBlessTheTruth sent me the photo of Allison and the article."

"@GodBlessTheTruth could be the same person who left the Polaroid at my signing."

"But why would he reach out to both of us? If he wants you to look for Gina, he has no reason to contact me."

"You're in my book. You're… the mentor. Maybe whoever it is has a fantasy about pitting us against each other. Or maybe he wants to make sure someone looks for her. To make sure at least someone plays this 'game.'"

Jim nodded in agreement, still holding the latte he hadn't tasted since leaving the deli. By the time they got to the other side of the bridge, it was like they were in another country: wide open spaces, short buildings. It was as if everything in the Rockaways had spilled through the streets after falling from the sky. They parked in a clearing by Riis Park and walked a few minutes towards the middle of a neighborhood called Roxbury. Jim was holding his briefcase in one hand and his cooled-down latte in the other. Miren was wearing a backpack with some of the papers from Gina's file, and held her Coke and a Zoom H4n recorder she'd bought a few years earlier in her hands.

"You've been holding that coffee since you got in the car, and you still haven't taken a sip. Do you plan on drinking it, or is it just an accessory?" Miren asked in a facetious tone.

"I like it cold."

"Then why don't you ask for it iced?"

"No, it's not the same. The trick is getting just the right ratio of coffee, milk, and vanilla. If you put ice in it, it throws the whole ratio off."

Miren laughed and was subsequently surprised by her own laughter. Jim brought the cup to his mouth, took a swig, and subsequently spat it out as if he'd just taken a sip of bleach.

"What's wrong?!" Miren cried.

"Caramel. They gave me a caramel latte again. The barista hates me."

The professor walked up to a trash can and tossed the drink without so much as pausing.

"Okay then. What's the plan?" Jim asked, not placing too much importance on his coffee. "Who'd you come to Roxbury to see?"

Miren gave him a perplexed look.

"A whole hour waiting for it to cool down just so you can throw it out? Who gives a shit if it's caramel or vanilla? It's sugar. It makes the coffee sweet. That's it."

Jim stopped in his tracks as Miren shook her head, her eyebrows lifted in skeptical arches.

"When I was little, my parents used to make pancakes every Sunday. It was a whole event. I liked mine with caramel syrup and sliced banana. One morning, I woke up before the rest of the family and went to the kitchen. I grabbed the bottle of caramel syrup and drank it straight, like it was milk.

"Didn't you get sick?"

"Of course! I spent a week next to the toilet without sleeping. Now do you see why I have no tolerance for caramel syrup?"

"You made that whole story up, didn't you?"

"I wish. I miss the joy of eating a big stack of pancakes and caramel syrup without vomiting."

Miren couldn't hide the smile that burst involuntarily onto her face. Then she pointed to a diner on the corner of the street in the middle of Roxbury. It was called Good Awakening.

"Let me get you a coffee, and you can show me the photo they sent you?"

"There?"

"I want to… talk to people from the neighborhood. Gina's family lived a few hundred yards from here. Good Awakening was where they organized the search parties every morning. Gina's aunt and uncle bought coffees for the volunteers and decided where to search, and at night they came back to drown their sorrows."

"How do you know all this?"

"I kept track of the case and joined the search parties. We never found anything, except the backpack that turned up in the abandoned area at Breezy Point Tip, at the very end of the peninsula. I wrote an article, the one @GodBlessTheTruth sent you, but after that… nothing else showed up. No trace of what might have happened. The Polaroid is… something, I guess."

"Did you ever talk to the family?"

"Directly? I think I talked to her brother once; he was eight. I was just another member of the search parties, though I wasn't particularly welcome. After I published the article, some people got suspicious about me being there, so I tried not to get mixed up with anyone. Then, when the search parties started getting smaller, I stopped going. Everyone in Roxbury was looking for her for a month. Some of her classmates too, in the afternoons. It was... like the Earth had just swallowed her up."

"I didn't realize you'd been so on top of it."

"I was close to the story, not on top of it. Afterwards, once the fever to find her died down, I shifted to Kiera's case and... I changed my focus. Nothing had come of the searches. It didn't seem like anyone was gonna talk. There was a lot of eagerness to find Gina, but nobody had seen anything. Should we go in?"

"You haven't had any of your Coke."

"I need something a little more... caffeinated. You're not the only one who didn't sleep last night."

Chapter 14
Roxbury
Interview between Ethan Pebbles
and Agent Warwick Penrose
June 04, 2002

[*T*]*he following interview with Ethan Pebbles, a legal minor, born March 25, 1994, is conducted in the company of his legal guardians, Christopher and Meghan Pebbles, his uncle and aunt, respectively, both of whom are residents of Roxbury, Queens, and who further have guardianship of Gina Pebbles, Ethan Pebbles' sister. Cristopher and Meghan Pebbles have consented to the following interview. Doctor Sarah Atkins, child psychologist, is also present to assist.*]

Transcript

AGENT WARWICK PENROSE: Hi, Ethan. I just want to ask you a few questions to see if we can find Gina as fast as we possibly can. Does that sound okay?

ETHAN PEBBLES: [*Nods*]

WARWICK: When was the last time you saw your sister?

ETHAN: Yesterday afternoon after school, after we crossed the bridge on the way home. She said I should go the rest of the way myself and she'd see me back home. She kept going towards Neponsit and I came here, to Roxbury.

WARWICK: She let you go back home alone?

ETHAN: [*Nods again*]

WARWICK: You were walking back from school? Isn't there a bus stop right near here?

ETHAN: We walked some of the way; the rest we went on the bus. That's how we nearly always do it. We get on or off at the stop on the other side of the bridge. In the morning we leave home at eight and go to the bus stop together, and if it's nice out we cross the bridge to the other side of the bay walking and skip a few stops. The bus turns all the way around here before going back towards… Queens and the high school.

WARWICK: When you say "here," where do you mean?

ETHAN: The Rockaways. You know. The bus goes all the way to the end of Breezy Point to pick people up and then back to Seaside. That's where it turns around and heads back towards Roxbury, then crosses the bridge towards Queens. That's what we did yesterday. It was nice out, so we walked all the way across the bridge and got on the bus at the stop that's just on the other side, like ten minutes from school. Then we did the same thing but in the opposite direction after school. We got on the bus together by school then got off to cross the bridge so we wouldn't have to go all the way around.

WARWICK: Why do you bother walking that whole stretch? Wouldn't it be better to take the bus from here?

ETHAN: I get carsick. The way we do it we're not on the bus as long. Gina does it for me. Well, I mean, she likes walking across the bridge too. The view is nice.

WARWICK: It's a pretty long walk though. How long does it take you on foot? 45 minutes from here to the bus stop on the other side?

ETHAN: Yeah, something like that. The bus takes just as long to go all the way around the Rockaways, because the stops take so long waiting for the people to get on. So we don't get there any faster or slower doing it this way, but we get to spend the half hour walking and get there before the bus is back in Roxbury. Gina likes looking at the water and the boats under the bridge. Sometimes we play a game where we count all the cars that are the same color. Yesterday we got to school the same time as always. I said bye to her in the hallway and she went with a group of kids from her class.

WARWICK: I understand. So that's what you did on the way home from school, too.

ETHAN: When we come out, we get on the bus right outside school. If I start getting carsick, we get off just before the bus crosses the bridge. And do the same thing but back-wards. The bus follows the same route, but the other way. It has to go all the way around the Rockaways before stop-ping in Roxbury. It takes the same amount of time to walk, but I don't get carsick. That's what we did yesterday.

WARWICK: Okay. What you're saying matches with what we heard from one... Hannah Paulson, your sister's classmate, who saw Gina get off the bus with you at the stop you mentioned yesterday, on the other side of the bridge. Did anything happen yesterday when you were crossing the bridge on the way home? It's a long walk. Lots of cars drive by. What did you talk about?

ETHAN: Nothing really. She hasn't really been talking to me for a long time. It's like she's mad at me or something. I told her I didn't mind being a little carsick and staying on the bus, but she... wanted us to get off and walk. She was quiet the whole time and if I asked her anything she... just answered with one word. She basically didn't play our game. I count-ed forty red cars. She counted thirty-one. I remember be-cause she always counts more than me. Except yesterday. I said she was missing some on purpose.

WARWICK: Did something happen recently that made her more distant towards you?

ETHAN: She says I don't understand her, I'm just a little kid.

WARWICK: Has she been different like that for long?

ETHAN: Yeah, she talks to me but... she's... sadder. She's been like that for like six months. Since... Christmas.

WARWICK: She never told you why?

ETHAN: [*Shakes his head silently*]

WARWICK: Mr. and Mrs. Pebbles, would you mind leaving the room for a moment?

MEGHAN PEBBLES [*Gina's aunt*]: Of course we mind. We have no intention of leaving you alone with Ethan so you can traumatize him with your questions. He's just a boy, for heaven's sake. He's eight years old. This is already distressing enough, don't you think?

WARWICK: Doctor Atkins will make sure he's well cared for.

MEGHAN PEBBLES [*Gina's aunt*]: We are not leaving Ethan alone. Ethan, darling, you don't have to answer his questions if you don't want to.

ETHAN: [*Starts to cry*]

WARWICK: Ethan... I know this is hard, but I need you to try as hard as you can, okay? Your sister needs your help. You can tell me anything you're worried about.

MEGHAN PEBBLES [*Gina's aunt*]: Is all this really necessary? While we're here doing this, our niece could be anywhere. I knew this was a mistake. We're wasting time.

WARWICK: Please... it could be important.

ETHAN: [*Gestures as if about to talk, but remains silent*]

WARWICK: Do you remember anything she said to you yesterday? Anything at all. Even if you don't think it's important.

ETHAN: Yeah. In the morning she... told me she had to talk to her boyfriend Tom.

WARWICK: Boyfriend? She has a boyfriend? Her classmates never mentioned it.

ETHAN: Yeah... Tom Rogers. He's a boy from her class. He came to our house a few times. Then he stopped coming.

WARWICK: Do you know why he stopped coming? Did they break up or something?

MEGHAN PEBBLES [*Gina's aunt*]: Is this really necessary?

WARWICK: It could be, Mrs. Pebbles.

MEGHAN PEBBLES [*Gina's aunt*]: That boy isn't welcome in my home. We want nothing to do with him.

WARWICK: Why not? Did he do something to Gina? Did he—

MEGHAN PEBBLES [*Gina's aunt*]: Did he have to? Just knowing about his impure intentions was more than enough reason to forbid him from setting foot in my home. He's a degenerate. A sexual pervert. At his age, he ought to be out helping the community, not thinking about corrupting girls still young enough to play with Barbies.

WARWICK: I'm sorry?

MEGHAN PEBBLES [*Gina's aunt*]: All he wanted was to… deflower her. The boy doesn't go to church. He doesn't pray. I caught him kissing Gina in her bedroom when he came over to work on a class project. I threw him out of the house and invited him to never return. My niece will certainly not be dating a boy who doesn't believe in the life-saving goodness of our Lord and who has no respect for the family.

WARWICK: I see. When was this?

MEGHAN PEBBLES [*Gina's aunt*]: Two months ago.

WARWICK: Two months. Okay. Ethan, do you know if they were still seeing each other?

ETHAN: [*Remains silent, with his head down*]

[Mr. Christopher Pebbles, Gina's uncle, exits the room.]

WARWICK: Did your sister say if she was having any problems at school?

ETHAN: No, nothing. Just that… just that she didn't like praying.

WARWICK: I guess you're pretty religious at home.

ETHAN: I guess.

WARWICK: What's that like?

MEGHAN PEBBLES [*Gina's aunt*]: We're a Christian family, if that's what you're getting at, officer. We certainly believe in God and try to give these children the religious upbringing they didn't get from their parents. My sister-in-law was not a good mother. Ever since the children came to our house, we have striven to compensate for all those years of spiritual anarchy. I believe that what happened to their parents was the Lord's punishment for the sinful life they led.

WARWICK: What happened to them? Could you give me some background?

MEGHAN PEBBLES [*Gina's aunt*]: Their house caught fire one night while they were sleeping. They were burned alive. Thanks be to God that the children were able to escape out the window. Obviously, that isn't something I'd wish on anyone, but when you bear in mind the lifestyle my sister-in-law and her husband had, I do believe it was the best thing that could have happened to the children.

ETHAN: [*Starts to cry*]

DOCTOR ATKINS: I think we should talk about this another time. That's enough for now. Don't you both think?

MEGHAN PEBBLES [*Gina's aunt*]: They were drinkers. They didn't pray. They didn't go to church. My sister-in-law didn't deserve children. She was never grateful for the Lord's blessings.

ETHAN: My mom was good! Not like you. Gina hates you. That's why she's gone. I hate you too!

MEGHAN PEBBLES [*Gina's aunt*]: Please, Ethan, you're just saying that because you're angry. We love you here. We take care of you. We give you the best possible upbringing.

ETHAN: But you'll never be her!

[*At the urging of Doctor Atkins, the interview is postponed until a later date.*]

Chapter 15
Roxbury
April 24, 2011
Two days earlier
Miren Triggs

Where can you jump from
without shattering upon impact?

As soon as we set foot in Good Awakening Café, I saw that everything was more or less as I remembered: the sad atmosphere, the unpainted wooden tables with benches on either side instead of chairs. The man of around sixty at the back of the café leaning on the bar was so familiar to me it felt as if he'd been there drinking that same cup of coffee for a decade. There was a dartboard on one of the side walls beside a Knicks banner that seemed to have somehow accumulated all the dust in the city. On a shelf sat a television broadcasting NBC news, filling the space with sad reality. There were two other men by the bar with hats and thick beards, drinking beer, and sitting at one of the tables by the door was a middle-aged woman, absorbed in the TV, eating a sandwich and drinking a suspiciously red Fanta Orange.

Jim went to the farthest table from the door and waited for me to sit down before he did the same.

"So, this is where they organized the search parties?" He said as soon as he'd settled into his chair.

Then he looked up at the old man at the bar as if he wanted to start a conversation with him.

"Boy!" the man cried towards a little window connecting the bar and an office. "We got customers, wake up!"

The command amused Jim. I was restless. All night with no sleep, the sound of a gunshot ringing out.

"Are you okay?" Jim asked.

"Yeah," I sighed, intuiting what was about to happen.

A boy emerged from the office door and wandered around a bit behind the bar, nervous. He bent over several times like he was looking for something, then reappeared with a pad of paper in one hand, which he dusted off with the other. He stepped away from the bar and approached us in a ketchup-stained apron.

"Hi," he said with a faltering voice "Can... can I... What would you like to drink? Or eat? If you're going to eat something... I'd rather it... that you... The cook is out so I'll make it myself. I'm still learning how to use the... grill."

The old man shook his head silently like he'd just watched something embarrassing on *America's Funniest Home Videos*.

"A couple of coffees? What do you have to eat that doesn't require the grill?" Jim asked.

"A bag of potato chips. That... that's something I can do pretty well."

Jim laughed. He didn't know why I'd brought him to this particular café, but I preferred to wait. I tried to control myself. I was about to explode.

"Sounds good. Two coffees and a few bags of Lay's. You have Lay's?"

"Only Herr's actually. Cheddar flavor."

Jim clicked his tongue.

"Cheese potato chips and coffee."

"I'm... I'm sorry," the boy stammered. "They're Mr. Marvin's favorite and he always comes."

"What about the sandwich that woman is eating? Could you make two of those?"

"It's cold. Bacon."

"Uncooked bacon?"

The boy nodded, as if admitting to a catastrophe.

"Better to stick with the chips. Don't you think, Miren?" he asked, drawing me out of my silence.

"Um... Chips are good. Black coffee for me, please."

The boy left us, and I followed him with my eyes until Jim began talking.

"Do you want to see the photo of Allison?" he asked, lowering his voice.

"Yeah. Of course."

He pulled the image and screenshot from Twitter from his briefcase, printed on regular copy paper. I leaned over to look, so close you'd think I was sniffing them.

"They're not super clear. Sorry. My printer isn't very good."

"We ought to show these to Ben Miller, don't you think? And the photo of Gina too."

He nodded and I continued looking at the photo in silence. It was more gruesome than I'd imagined.

"It's really Allison?"

I could tell that he nodded, even though I didn't look.

It was, without a doubt, the most unnerving photo I'd ever laid eyes on: a white, girl-shaped blur on a cross with an almost relaxed expression and two dark, faceless silhouettes in the background. Golden sunlight was filtering in through one of the broken windows and, to the left, the shoulder and ear of someone dressed in white. To the right, there were several chairs in a row.

"When'd you say they sent you this?"

"Around seven o'clock. Like I said, the teenagers found the body at eight. Why do you ask?"

"I'm trying to figure out if that gave them time to go from wherever the image was taken to the store where I was signing books yesterday."

"And?"

"There was more than enough time. The signing finished around ten at night. They could've been at Fort Tilden when Allison was crucified, sent you the photo from a cell phone and then come to my signing to give me the photo of Gina with time to spare."

"Do you really think it's the same person?"

"There's too much in common between the cases, don't you think? They went to the same school. Gina lived here in Roxbury and Allison lived in Queens. And the last trace of either of them is in the same area: Gina's backpack in Breezy Point and Allison's body in Fort Tilden. How far apart are they? A quarter mile?"

"It might be a coinc—"

"A coincidence? A coincidence orchestrated by @GodBless-TheTruth, maybe."

As always, he raised his eyebrows before replying:

"You think there's only one person behind all this?"

"In the photo, there are several people participating in whatever is happening to Allison. I don't know. I don't like it. And that crucifix…"

"It's a good way to kill someone. The weight of your own body asphyxiates you. You don't even have to be present when the victim dies. It's… horrible, yes. I don't want to think about what that poor girl felt, or what it must've been like for her parents when they learned how their daughter died."

"I saw Gina's aunt and uncle when she went missing. They were really devastated. I think I can guess what they went through."

"But you can't guess how they felt. That's something you can only know when they take someone you really love from you. I think it's as if they… steal your whole life from you."

I was silent. I knew that emotion well: emptiness, loneliness, a sadness that invades everything. That's how it was for me, in every pore of my skin, in every drop of sweat. An empty body, a robbed innocence; but Jim seemed to have forgotten the pain that always invaded my life. I couldn't blame him. I never talked about it.

"Do you know where Gina's trail went cold?" I asked, trying to lay the foundation of everything we knew.

"No. I know it was after she left school. She was walking with her brother, who was eight back then. She left him to go to… a friend's house, I think?" Jim replied.

"More or less. Gina and her brother Ethan left the Mallow Institute in Queens and got on the bus to the Rockaways. Both got off at the stop just before the bridge—apparently, they liked walking that part. They crossed together and once they were close to home, Gina told her brother to go the rest of the way to Roxbury by himself, because she was going to visit her boyfriend Tom Rogers in Neponsit, which is in the opposite direction."

"Neponsit?"

"It's a little over a mile from here, after you pass Fort Tilden and Jacob Riis Park. The houses there look nothing like they do in Roxbury. It's full of luxury villas that always look freshly painted. Well-tended gardens, fancy cars. A more well-to-do area. Here in Roxbury… well, there's a little bit of everything. It's all unpaved streets and sand from the beach instead of asphalt. The houses are piled one on top of the other like they were trying to make the most of a giant empty plot of sand. There isn't much in Roxbury except this café, a church and… well, a mystery."

"Understood."

"After Gina and Ethan went separate ways, she was never heard from again. The cameras on the bridge caught the two of them walking across. She was captured by the cameras on both sides. And in the middle too, for that matter. Then, in the Rockaways, there's nothing. They lost her trail. According to her brother, they said goodbye where the bridge meets Rockaway Point Boulevard. He walked the remaining quarter mile to Roxbury on the sidewalk. She went in the opposite direction, towards Neponsit. Ethan said he saw her walking towards the cycle lane going the opposite way, so that's probably the path she would've taken, along the edge of Jacob Riis Park and the Beach Boulevard parking lot until she got to Neponsit. If she was going to visit Tom Rogers, her boyfriend, it should've taken her twenty or thirty minutes on foot. But she never got there. The boyfriend was waiting for her all afternoon. Nobody saw her walking there or reported anything unusual. There were several vehicles in the parking lot she would've passed, but it was a beautiful day, and everyone was on the beach, taking in the sun. It seems like no one saw her walking past."

"How do you know all this?"

"I reviewed Gina's file last night. I couldn't sleep. She was wearing blue jeans, red Converse sneakers, a gray t-shirt that said Salt Lake on it, and a white backpack with a little embroidered unicorn. Exactly the same as in the Polaroid."

"Someone must have taken her when she was walking, forced her into a van, gagged her and… finished it."

He leaned back in his chair, defeated, as if he'd just discovered Gina's corpse somewhere on the Rockaway Peninsula.

"So what do you plan to do, Miren? How do you plan to—"

"Wait," I interrupted.

The server came back with our coffees, and Jim and I stopped talking for a minute, but we didn't have time to remove the photo of Allison from the table.

"Here are your… coffees… and now I'll bring you…"

Suddenly, he stopped cold and gave us a surprised look. It was like he'd seen something he shouldn't have. He quickly walked back to the bar and, once behind it, started nervously cleaning up.

"Did you just see what I saw?" Jim asked, confused. "That boy seems like he… knows something."

"You think?" I replied, guiding him towards my plan.

"No one would react that way based on a dark, blurry photo where you can't even tell what's happening. He must know what's going on."

"Maybe. You think he knows something?" I said.

"Either that or he's fallen in love with you."

"You know how we ended up at this café, Jim?"

"You know something I don't know, right?"

I smiled, ready to drop the bomb.

"Our server is Ethan Pebbles, Gina's brother."

Chapter 16
FBI New York Field Office
April 24, 2011
Two days earlier
Ben Miller

Any time in the past
reminds you what you no longer have.

In the morning, he woke to the sound of a telephone and two agents laughing. Inspector Miller had passed out the previous night as he was reviewing Gina Pebbles' file.

"Look at how peaceful he is!" One of the agents giggled. "Like a little boy who tired himself out in the playground… and suddenly aged 60 years."

"The dude's fucked. He's not finding anybody. Poor guy. Why doesn't he retire already? How old is he anyway? Isn't falling asleep supposed to be hard when you're old?" the other agent asked.

"Shh, he's waking up!" croaked the first between laughs.

He opened his eyes and was immediately blinded by the office's fluorescent lights while he tried to place the voices of Malcolm and Ashton, which took him a few moments. They were the two thirty-something agents from the Missing Persons

Unit who had sat on either side of the table, waiting for Ben Miller to wake up.

"Rise and shine, Ben! How'd you sleep, baby?" Agent Malcolm asked jokingly.

"Not funny," rasped Ben, clearing his throat.

"Look, I brought you your coffee and your morning paper. But I couldn't find your slippers anywhere," said Ashton, a Bostonian with his hair parted down the side and a toothpaste-ad smile.

"What time is it?"

The phone rang again as Malcolm, who had a thick mustache that seemed straight out of the eighties, kept the joke going.

"Ben, wouldn't it be better if you dedicated yourself to something... I don't know... If you left these things to those of us with more stamina? You've got the best desk in the office. It's near the back window, with the screen facing away from everyone. You could watch porn for hours and nobody'd catch you."

"Don't you have missing people to find or something?" Ben grumbled.

"Oh yeah. I've got some grandpa who wandered off from his facility. The family is losing their shit looking for him. But I'm gonna let him enjoy a few hours of freedom before bringing him back," Ashton said ironically.

"You do realize a lot of the time it's people with Alzheimer's who go missing? He could need medication," Miller answered, annoyed.

"Relax, relax." He made a gesture like he could control things that happen outside the office. "According to them, he left on his motor scooter. How far can one of those go? Not too far. He'll show up after he's smoked a few joints and had his fun."

The phone kept ringing and Ben squeezed the bridge of his nose, as if that motion were caffeine and it could help him wake up.

"I saw about Allison Hernández," Malcolm said, in an ambiguous tone that was somewhere between sadness and irony. "It's horrible, I'm sorry. I don't know why you have such bad luck with your cases. Honestly, I wouldn't want to trade places with you."

Ben still felt disoriented after waking up somewhere other than his bed. The night had been devoured between papers and statements, photographs, security camera images, and text messages sent between Gina Pebbles' friends.

"Who're you onto now? Gina… Pebbles," he read on one of the papers on the desk. "Good luck with… A girl from 2002? Holy guacamole."

"How 'bout you leave me alone already?"

The phone rang again. He finally picked it up, irate.

"Who is it?" he snapped into the receiver, as if he were receiving a door-to-door encyclopedia salesman.

"Ben, where the hell are you?"

"Lisa?"

"I know your work is important, but what about me? Is our marriage not important?"

"What are you—"

Lisa let rip on the other end of the line.

"I'm not going to wait for you anymore. I reminded you before you left last night. I'm going to the cemetery, so our son knows, wherever he is, that at least one of us is still thinking about him. Father Carlson is saying a mass for Daniel. No need for you to come."

His wife hung up.

Ben brought his hands to his head. He'd forgotten. He jumped up and ran to the door, as Malcolm and Ashton continued to laugh, confused.

He drove as fast as morning rush-hour traffic would allow. He crossed the Brooklyn Bridge, merged onto I-278 and over the Verrazano-Narrows Bridge, changing lanes every few yards to get ahead of as many other vehicles as possible. Shortly afterwards, he parked his car at St. Peter's Cemetery on Staten Island, just five minutes from where they lived. He called Lisa's phone as soon as he got out of the car, but she rejected the call.

He hurried through the cemetery, zigzagging past gray tombstones pushing out from the grass like small, rectangular, marble towers. In the distance, Lisa was standing before one of those towers, motionless, her eyes closed. As soon as he reached her, he touched her hand so she would know he was there.

"Father Carlson left about fifteen minutes ago," Lisa said, visibly hurt, but without opening her eyes.

"I'm... I'm so sorry, Lisa."

"I'm the one who's sorry, Ben. I thought he'd always keep us together, you know?"

"I was at the office until late. It's been a little... traumatic."

"You know what's traumatic? When your husband isn't there when you need him because he's out looking for God-knows-who instead of holding his wife who spent the night sobbing."

"Please, don't do this in front of him," Ben protested, almost in a whisper, trying to prevent what he knew was about to happen.

"In front of him? For the love of God, Ben. Daniel isn't there. He never has been. Thirty years today. Thirty years! Jesus Christ. A lifetime. Thirty years since he went missing. I'm never going to get over it. Do you understand? He'll never be buried here because we'll never know what happened to him."

Ben said nothing, trying to compose himself. Then, finally:

"You think I'm over it? Didn't I join the Missing Persons Unit just so I could look for him? I gave up everything. Everything, Lisa. I was in forensic accounting and liked it there. They would've promoted me in a heartbeat. I was good at it. And then I changed everything to look for him. So I'd never lose sight of what really mattered."

"That's what you've always been, Ben. A simple accountant who wanted to play detective, but you could never find the one person who really mattered: our son. When did you stop looking for him? How long has it been since you've tried to find new leads?"

"That isn't fair, Lisa. You know the day-to-day gets overwhelming. New cases are always coming in, and… I hardly have time for anything."

"How long!" Lisa shouted.

Ben looked at Daniel's tombstone. He hadn't noticed the small golden frame Lisa had placed there, containing an image of their son when he was seven, the age he was when he vanished.

"Since we got him a tombstone. Fifteen years," he finally admitted.

That number hurt him. If Daniel were alive, he'd be 37. By that age, he could have had a family, could've given Ben grandchildren. Imagined lives have a way of eating you up inside, because they're always filled with the best moments you'll never have. And that was where Ben's mind went: to the Thanksgiving dinner where he would've learned his daughter-in-law was pregnant; to the toast he would've given at Daniel's wedding, his son smiling and hugging him. He fantasized about being proud at his college graduation and wondered for an instant what career Daniel would have pursued; maybe he would have become an engineer or an astronaut, like it seemed he'd wanted when he was seven. Ben imagined Daniel smiling, drinking beer by his side, chatting in the back garden about Obama being elected president. A whole vanished life had flashed before him, at the very same instant Lisa turned around and left him alone in front of the tombstone.

She stopped in her path before turning to leave definitively. She shook her head, eyes filled with tears, and added:

"Daniel disappeared 30 years ago, Ben. Do you know how

many times I've imagined you'll come home and tell me you found his body?"

Ben didn't respond.

"Every day. Every goddamn day when you come home from work. And every night, while you sleep, I mourn his death. Because I'd rather think he's dead and doesn't need us. It's better than if he needs us and we haven't found him."

Ben crouched in front of the tombstone as his wife walked away, leaving him alone. He couldn't stop himself from bursting into tears as he remembered finding Daniel's bike lying on the street, his son nowhere in sight.

Chapter 17
Roxbury
April 24, 2011
Two days earlier
Jim Schmoer and Miren Triggs

The problem with chasing the truth
is that you never know
where it will lead you.

Ethan realized Jim and Miren were looking at him and tried to slip out of the dining room and hide in the office. Once inside, he leaned against the door. He could hear them calling him:

"Excuse me!" Miren shouted after getting up and leaning against the bar. "Could you help us with something?"

The old man looked on, a bit confused, and then shouted on her behalf:

"Boy! What kind of service is this? Get outta there and help this beautiful lady."

Miren smiled at the old man and waited for some sign of life from the office, but it never came. Jim had remained at the table, trying to process the fact that this boy was Gina's brother and wondering how the hell Miren had learned he worked there.

"Ethan, it's important," she finally said. "There are some things we think you can help us understand."

Miren waited, tense, thinking that any moment now the boy would bolt out of the office and run out of her sight.

"It's nothing bad, Ethan. Please. I'm sure you'll be able to help us… It's about Gina."

The door opened slowly and first they saw Ethan's fingers gripping the door, then his ear and, finally, his concerned face.

"Are you cops? How do you know my name?" he asked uncertainly. "I don't want to talk to anyone else. I don't know anything. I already told them everything I know."

"Police? Oh, no. Don't worry about that. We're just trying to understand what happened to Allison, and we're asking around the neighborhood. Her body was found barely three hundred yards from here. We know this is where Gina went missing too. Somewhere between her boyfriend's house and the bridge, the last time that… that you saw her, near here, in Neponsit. We're just… trying to see if there's any link between the stories is all."

"A link?"

"We know Gina and Allison both went to the Mallow Institute. Your school," Miren said.

Ethan nodded and leaned against the bar. The old man was listening closely.

"Do you mind if we talk in private?" Miren whispered, tilting her head to indicate that the old man was listening.

"Can I finish a little early, Mr. Davis? It's just fifteen minutes till my shift is over."

The old man was about to protest, but he knew no other customers would come in and that those who remained had already paid their bills.

"We'll leave a fifty-dollar tip," Miren said, making an offer he couldn't refuse.

"All right. But don't tell Louise I let you off early. She'd kill me."

"You can count on it, Mr. Davis," Ethan responded candidly. "Thank you, really," he said, looking him in the eye.

Ethan took off and carefully folded his apron before stepping out from behind the bar. He walked to the table where Jim was still sitting and waited for Miren to choose a seat before doing the same. Then he sat and scooted his chair up to the table. They were far enough from Mr. Davis to be able to speak in confidence. Jim observed Ethan, a tall teenager with thin legs but a muscular back that reminded the professor of when he himself was a strapping young man on the college rowing crew. Ethan's face was peppered with freckles, his hair was messy, and his intense blue eyes glinted in the light filtering through the window beside them.

"What do you want to know?" he asked quietly.

"I'm Miren Triggs," Miren said, trying to sow some seed of trust. "I'm a reporter at the *Manhattan Press*, and this is... Jim Schmoer, he's a..." she searched for a way to describe Jim's situation, "...he's a freelance investigative journalist. We're working on an article about what happened to Allison and we're talking with people who live in the area to get a perspective that's a little more... personal."

"But what does that have to do with Gina? Why do you have to bring that all up now? I don't want to... I don't want to deal with all that shit again."

"Like I said, we believe the two cases may be related. Honestly. We still don't understand how and that's why we need your help."

"How did you find me?"

"Facebook," Miren replied. "It wasn't hard. You should check your privacy settings. We could also see you're in a relationship with someone named... Deborah, if I remember correctly."

Ethan shook his head and looked off into the distance.

"Allison was in my class, but, please, don't... I don't have anything to do with whatever happened."

"She was in your class?"

"Yeah. She stopped coming to school a week ago. It reminded me a little of what happened with Gina, but I don't... I don't know. My sister never... never turned up. At least with Allison... they'll have a place to cry."

"It must have been hard, growing up without her."

"Hard? You don't know my aunt and uncle. Do you have any idea what it's like to thank God for every dish on the dinner table after he's taken your parents and sister from you? God's an asshole. God doesn't give a shit. And I live with two psychopaths who won't stop kissing his ass. God doesn't think about who he's punishing. He just points a finger and goes, 'you: time to suffer.' Then the worst things in the world end up happening. My parents died and then a few months later my sister disappeared. My aunt and uncle say it was the devil's work. If the devil did that, I hate God for sitting back and watching."

"So your aunt and uncle are very religious?"

He leaned forward and whispered:

"They're fanatics. It's like they're in a fucking cult. It's the same as at school. I'm just waiting for this year to end so I can go away and never come back. As soon as I graduate, I'm taking what I save working here and leaving with Deborah."

"Is the Mallow Institute that religious? I knew it was Catholic, but I never saw it as something so... sinister."

He looked around him, nervous. Then he looked down like he was afraid to speak.

"Religious? Have you ever been there? You pray before every class; you pray before lunch. If you commit a sin, Father Graham, who's like the principal, makes you do penance. If he doesn't like you, it can get really bad. I've lost track of how many times he's made me walk around the playground on my knees. He hates me."

"Penance?" Miren asked, incredulous.

"Punishment for sinning," clarified Jim. "Seeking a kind of... redemption."

"Penance is the worst part of Mallow. Ask anyone, even though I doubt anybody'll talk to you. We're not allowed to talk about what happens there. Even though the older kids are sick of it and... we break the rules sometimes. Some kids smoke weed," he paused and leaned over the table and whispered: "they even have sex. The administration knows it. They can't control everyone. The problem is if they find out. Then you're fucked."

"But it is a Christian school, right?"

"It's Christian on paper, but... something darker has always been happening in there. They don't follow any clear rules and they don't adhere to any specific... doctrine?" he hesitated, trying to find the right word. "Like, they're not really Catholic or Protestant or whatever. They pick and choose the most convenient rules and beliefs from all the different denominations and... and then they use them to destroy your life."

"How do you mean?"

"Father Graham. I hate that dude. You should go talk to him. You'll see what I mean. If there's anybody you should be investigating about Allison... it's him."

Jim wrote the name on a black notepad he'd taken from his pocket.

"What makes you say that?"

"He's in charge of the whole thing. Of the school. Whenever he wants, he calls you to his office to make a confession. When you sin... he's the one who chooses the punishment. He's..." he held back from saying whatever he was going to say.

"Do you think it'd be hard to talk to him? We're trying to take a look at both cases."

"I mean he's... the cancer of Mallow."

"Have you told this to the police?"

"Yeah, I told two cops who came asking around this morning, and an old guy from the FBI who came to the school Thursday to ask what we knew about Allison. He gave me a card. I should have it in my wallet. He said to keep it in case I heard anything. I also saw him talking to a few other kids who were on the playground. Even the ones who…" he hesitated. "He asked everyone."

"Was he from the Missing Persons Unit?"

"I guess. He talked to us all separately at lunch. He showed up like he was a… like a used car salesman or something and bombarded us with all these questions in front of Miss Harris. Asking things like, where did we see Allison for the last time, if she was acting weird, if she had a boyfriend. All the bullshit they always ask in the movies."

"What did you tell him?"

"The truth. That Allison hadn't come to class for a few days."

"Was his name Ben Miller?" Miren asked, seemingly recognizing him from the description.

Ethan pulled the card from his wallet and handed it to Miren: BENJAMIN MILLER, FBI MISSING PERSONS UNIT, with a phone number.

Jim picked up on something Miren had missed:

"What were you going to say earlier? Why did you stop mid-sentence?"

Ethan dropped his hands below the table and shifted nervously from side to side. He got up and returned with a glass of water he'd served himself from a small sink near the beer taps. He took a long sip before speaking. His heart was racing.

"A clique in the class. I don't…" he hesitated. "They're the Ra…" he seemed like he was going to say something forbidden, but he stopped himself at the last second, distressed.

"You can talk to us, Ethan," Miren said in a warm, unconcerned tone. "You're not saying anything you're not allowed to… Or anything new."

"You don't… You don't get it. If they find out…"

"If who finds out?"

"I can't say. I can't."

Miren and Professor Schmoer leaned back in their chairs. If Ethan shut down, their path forward would vanish in the blink of an eye. Suddenly, Miren sat up and in a serious tone said:

"You know what? I was part of a clique when I was in school. It was Bob, Sam, Vicky, Carla, Jimmy, and me. We called ourselves the Fallen Stars. It was like a club, a 'secret' club, but everyone knew who we were. We'd meet up in Jimmy's garage to smoke pot and listen to music. We thought we'd all be big rock musicians or movie stars and that at some point in our lives we would fall into disgrace and end up back in that garage."

"Seriously? And your parents knew about it?" Ethan asked, intrigued by the notion of a life without rules.

"Oh, definitely not. They thought we did homework and group projects. And I was crazy about Jimmy. I kept inventing new class projects so I could spend all day in his garage."

"And you lied to your parents because you liked Jimmy?"

Miren picked up her coffee and took a sip before replying. Jim put his pen on the table, picking up on the mood Miren was trying to create. If Ethan saw him taking notes, he might think there would be consequences for what he was saying and stop talking to them.

"Back then I would have done anything for Jimmy," Miren whispered decisively. "I guess as you get older, you learn that not everybody deserves so much personal investment. Then you learn that almost no one does. Later on, I found out Jimmy was just trying to see how many of us girls he could hook up with."

"And you sinned for a boy?"

Miren could see how Ethan's mind always went back to sinning, religion, a fear of straying. She could tell from his words that part of him wanted to escape from that place, break with everything, and perhaps that was the source of his insecurities. He spoke so confidently about the rules at the school the other kids broke, but he didn't seem very comfortable with the rule-breakers. He gave the impression that he understood them insofar as he also wanted to escape the clutches of their twisted methods, but he seemed overwhelmed by fear at every step.

"That too, I guess," Miren continued, "because it was fun to feel like we'd already accepted our disgrace as something inevitable, which meant that we could live carefree... in that garage, at least. If you assume life will only smile on you briefly before it smacks you in the face, it hurts a little less."

Ethan shook his head.

"No, Miss Triggs. That's not how it works. The knocks only hurt less if you get used to them. So a callus forms over the scab. It hurts less when you grow a thick skin."

"It was hard for you after Gina went missing, huh?"

He avoided looking them in the eye and clenched his jaw. A thin, reddish line encircled his eyelids until, finally, a single tear escaped just as he started speaking:

"She abandoned me. She... left me alone with my aunt and uncle. Sometimes I think I should do the same and get out of here. But... I've never been able to. But I have a plan, you know? At the end of the school year, I'm leaving, and they'll never see me again. I'll send them a postcard from Mexico and see if they manage to find me."

"You think Gina ran away?"

"No... I don't know. I just know she hasn't had to spend all these years living with my and aunt and uncle and... well, Father Graham. I still remember her saying she was going to Tom Roger's house and how she crossed the street to the road to Neponsit. Then she just... disappeared. She never made it home. And suddenly I was stuck without my... without my guardian angel, you know?"

"Was she good to you?"

"She was the best. She was everything you... everything

you could ever want from a sister. She protected me, she took care of me. She was the one... she was the one who saved me from the house fire, did you know that? She lowered me out the bedroom window after the fire blocked all the doors. She looked me in the eyes when she was holding onto my hands, with my feet dangling over the shrubs in the garden, and she said, 'Don't worry, I'm right here.' Then she let me go, and she jumped after me. She held me while we watched the fire destroy everything. At first, I wasn't even thinking about my parents, but then when I saw Gina crying uncontrollably until the firemen came, I realized what had happened. Even with all of her suffering, she always tried to take care of me and make me happy. But at my aunt and uncle's house, everything started changing. Then, after a few months... she went missing."

"Can I ask you something," Miren ventured, because she needed her intuition confirmed.

Ethan nodded as he dried his eyes with one hand.

"Did you know Allison well? Before everything... you saw the photo and you seemed to get nervous."

"Two cops told me what happened to Allison this morning. It's horrible. Seeing the cross... made me think of her instantly."

"You didn't answer me, though. Did you know her well?"

"She was in my class. She was a nice girl, even though she had a reputation for... having more fun than the rest of us. If you get what I'm saying."

"Do you think she was part of that clique you were talking about?"

"No... I don't know. Even though the past few months I did see her a few times with..." he hesitated. "I can't. Please, don't do this to me. They'll find out it was me who told you and they'll make my life at school hell."

"Ethan... Allison is dead. Do you really think this is the time for high school drama and secret clubs?"

"You... you don't know them."

"Who don't we know?"

"I can't... I really can't."

"Who?!"

"I can't tell you—"

"Who, Ethan?!" Miren raised her voice, angry.

"The Ravens of God!" Ethan shouted furiously.

As soon as he realized what he'd done, he opened his eyes to see if anyone had heard him: the two men drinking beer rose at that moment and seemed to be getting ready to leave; the woman with the raw bacon sandwich was still engrossed in the television; Mr. Davis had gone behind the bar and turned on the steam on the espresso machine to clean the pipes. For a moment, Ethan thought they had heard him and that they were only acting natural, but in reality, his outburst had coincided with the loud whistle of the espresso machine.

"The Ravens of God?" Miren said, concerned. "Who are they?"

"Please, don't..." he begged, grabbing his own hands to keep them from trembling even more than they already were.

"Ethan, please. Talk to us. It could help us figure out who did this to Allison."

Jim placed the image of Allison back on the table, in front of Ethan, who was panting, feeling ambushed.

"Who are the Ravens of God?"

"A group of people from school," he finally admitted, as if he were relieving himself of an unbearable burden. "Just like the clique you were talking about. I don't know much more than what everybody at school knows. James Cooper, one of the... popular kids at Mallow, seems like he's in it, and if you want to join, you have to talk to him. I saw the FBI guy go up to him to ask about Allison."

"James Cooper?" Jim wrote down the name.

"Does he live around here?" Miren asked, trying to get more information out of Ethan.

"Not as far as I know. He lives near school, on the other side of the bridge. I shouldn't be telling you this…" he lamented.

"You're being a big help to us, Ethan."

"Have you seen Allison with James Cooper recently?"

Ethan nodded with a clenched jaw.

"Tell us everything you know. Any little detail could help."

"The Ravens are a handful of kids from different grades. Some of them don't even go to Mallow, they just come from Manhattan for their meetings."

"What do they do when they meet?"

"They pray. They get together and… talk about God. It's like a fraternity, like in college, except… more secretive. Some kids at Mallow want to join, but not many get in. They say it began the same year Mallow was founded and it's passed from generation to generation."

"Why?"

"Because they think Mallow doesn't teach religion right. I don't know much more than that."

"Do you think Allison was in the Ravens?" Jim asked, trying to understand why the boy made a connection between the topics.

"You could tell she was a little… unhappy in class. She was always… flirting with boys. She had a reputation for being kind of, you know, loose. She'd slept with a few guys. We all knew it. I wouldn't be surprised if she was in the Ravens, looking for whatever she couldn't find on her own. They say once you're in the Ravens… you never go hungry. It opens doors to… happiness and wealth."

Jim glanced at Miren, confused, trying to understand what the boy was talking about. He couldn't help but ask:

"Go hungry?"

"It's just the kind of rumor that spreads at Mallow."

"Do you know why they call themselves that?" Miren continued.

"We study religion at Mallow. We read the Bible all the time. They say the name is from the part of the Bible about ravens and the prophet Elijah."

Miren didn't understand any of this and decided to let Ethan work this out from her silence.

"First Kings, chapter 17, verses two to six. God sends ravens to save Elijah, an Old-Testament prophet, from starving to death."

"So it's a Biblical name?"

"Everything at Mallow revolves around religion. Everything."

"Could you help us talk to someone from that... group?"

"I don't know. Ask James Cooper. Maybe he knows something. I don't know if he's part of the group, but he's the one who's always... talking about the Ravens and all that. He seems to know all the legends and rumors."

"What's your class schedule tomorrow? Do you think we could talk to him?"

"You'd have to get permission from Father Graham. Everything has to pass through his hands. But, please, don't say anything about—"

"Don't worry, Ethan," Miren said, taking his hand. "Nobody will find out you talked to us."

Ethan looked around to see if any prying eyes in the distance saw him crossing too many lines, but he didn't find them and exhaled loudly.

"Can I ask you one last thing?" Miren was attempting, one final time, to find the link between Mallow and Allison's gruesome death.

Ethan sat still for a moment, but finally shook his head.

"This is a mistake. I shouldn't—"

"Do you think Father Graham might have found out that Allison was... a little... friendly with the boys?"

"What do you mean?"

"If everyone knew Allison was a little… loose, as you say, maybe the rumor made it to his office."

"I… I don't know."

"Earlier, you said Father Graham was very strict. Do you think he might have gone a little too far with his… penance?"

"By crucifying her?" he asked, shocked. "He's a sick bastard, but… I think that's too far even for him. People respect and love him. The teachers all adore him."

"But you hate him," Miren ventured.

"Who wouldn't hate someone who makes their life impossible?"

"Ethan… we're trying to help," Jim interrupted, irritated. "Allison… is dead. Don't you see this photo? Everything you're telling us about this priest, about the oppressive culture at your school, about that group of… look, I don't know what you're trying to tell us. I think it's clear that whatever happened to Allison is related to the Mallow Institute in some way. And I have a feeling your sister's fate was the same."

"My sister has nothing to do with Allison. Everyone at Mallow loved my sister. Everyone. Father Graham always said she was a role model for how to be a good… Christian. She got good grades. She took care of me. Don't compare her with Allison, because the two of them have nothing in common."

"Except that it seems that both of their lives came to an end in the Rockaways," Jim concluded.

Chapter 18
Roxbury
April 24, 2011
Two days earlier
Miren Triggs

*Sometimes it's better not
to stir up memories,
to let them be,
perfect in the mind,
to avoid ruining them with reality.*

We said goodbye to Ethan with the feeling that we'd found the beginning of a thread to tug on, but we had no way of knowing what we'd find at the other end. He clearly regretted talking to us by the time he left. No matter how much I promised that no one would find out he was the one who'd told us about the Ravens of God, he seemed to think he'd crossed a line and there was no going back.

I paid Mr. Davis the 50-dollar tip I'd promised and ten more for the coffees and untouched snacks. Once we were outside, Jim wasted no time asking:

"Do you believe that story about the Ravens?"

"I don't know," I answered. "But it's all we've got. That and the director of Mallow, who's apparently some kind of religious despot. I don't like it at all."

"I had a teacher when I was young who was a real son of a bitch, but nothing like that."

"It seems like Mallow takes a very harsh stance when it comes to… sins and punishments."

"Yeah, but to the point of crucifying a girl?"

I sighed. That question had formed in my mind too as Ethan explained everything and talked about Allison's more promiscuous habits.

"Maybe the administration heard the rumors that Allison was running around with boys and decided to punish her, and things got out of hand."

"Miren… we're talking about nailing a girl to a cross. That's a universe away from making her say four Hail Marys or walk barefoot for a while."

"Yeah. I don't know. It's all so murky."

"What are you going to do?"

"I want to talk to Ethan's aunt and uncle. I really don't like how much Ethan… seems to hate them. If they sent Gina and Ethan to Mallow, it's because they approve of that kind of treatment. You heard how he described them. He said they were fanatics."

"Do you know where they live?"

"Here, in Roxbury. Just behind… the church."

"Seriously?"

I nodded, uneasy. In 2002, when Gina disappeared, religion had nothing to do with the investigation, even though now it seemed so relevant. I knew the Mallow Institute was a religious school and that her aunt and uncle went to church a lot, but I hadn't really thought twice about it. Now, though, with Allison's disappearance, those details seemed more relevant than ever.

"Maybe now is a good time to talk to them without Ethan around. He walked off in the opposite direction of their house."

"Do you think they can tell us anything we don't already know?"

"You know what? It's funny. When we began working on Gina's case, everything came down to just trying to retrace her steps. We looked for her on the route between the bridge and her boyfriend's house, asking her friends what they'd seen and scouring the area for some clue that would lead us to find her or... her body. Now though... with what happened to Allison, everything has taken a more sinister turn. Allison's crucifixion, and the two of them studying at the same school... it changes everything. These are the kind of puzzle pieces that might suddenly form a picture. At first, you're just fitting pieces together without knowing what you're making, until all at once, it becomes clear. But you know what the problem is?" I asked, uneasy.

Jim didn't respond, but gave me a look that suggested I should continue.

"We're still missing too many pieces."

* * *

We worked our way into Roxbury through alleyways and narrow passages between homes. It was a chaotic, unplanned neighborhood, where the houses had been built with the sole aim of making full use of every available centimeter of land along the bay to the west of the Marine Parkway Bridge. Most of the streets were unpaved, and the sand, carried on the strong Atlantic winds, formed tiny dunes beside wooden houses whose paint was being eaten away by the humid ocean air.

Gina's aunt and uncle lived on one of Roxbury's inland streets in a gray, wooden, two-story house with a white door and window frames. Finding their home wouldn't have been easy if I wasn't already familiar with that labyrinth of streets. If I remembered correctly, it was at the end of a sort of pedestrian cul-de-sac, backing onto the community church.

Jim followed me in silence, and I found his calm company oddly pleasant. I didn't really understand what he was doing, joining me for all this, when he could just immerse himself in teaching and lead a life without stress or intrigue. As we walked, I considered stopping and telling him to go away, that I didn't need him—I'd never needed anybody—but maybe I liked feeling less... alone. I smiled to myself when I heard him grumbling about getting sand in his shoes.

"Here it is," I said finally, after we walked between two houses and came out right behind the Pebbles residence.

We skirted the house and stepped onto the front porch, the wood creaking beneath our feet. With a look, Jim wished me luck. Even though he'd come with me, I felt like he was just there to support me in my search, and maybe that's why I saw that look in his eyes, framed in his dark brown glasses.

I tapped the knocker three times and waited, catching my breath. I didn't like the vibe of the place. The labyrinth of dilapidated, tightly packed houses was more oppressive than cozy. After a few seconds, a fortysomething woman with curly blonde hair opened the door, a confused look on her face.

"Hi," she began with a raspy voice, like a crackling loudspeaker. "Can I help you?"

"Meghan Pebbles?"

"Yes?" she whispered, as if she were afraid of speaking to us.

"So... I'm Miren Triggs and this is Jim Schmoer, we're investigative journalists. We've been reviewing your niece Gina's case, and we were wondering if you would mind answering a few questions."

"Don't I know you?" she said to me, grabbing the edge of the door in an uncertain gesture. "Have we talked before?"

"Yes... well, I was on some of the search parties for Gina after she... disappeared."

"You're the one who joined the search parties and then published that article in the *Manhattan Press*."

"Yes, exactly."

"Aren't you ashamed?"

"I'm sorry?"

"I remember that article. They printed it with a photo of Ethan sobbing."

"Ah, I… I don't choose the photos they run with my stories. That's the… the newspaper's call."

"Well, it was a bad call. There was our Ethan, grieving over his lost sister and then you people… well, you did what you always do. You got your pound of flesh."

"No, I… I don't think you…" I stammered.

"I have nothing to say to you. You people are a cancer on this great nation. Feeding off of other people's pain. I hope they paid you well for that story so you could at least help the less fortunate with the money."

Jim stepped in when he saw how badly I was bungling the situation. I hadn't expected such a harsh blow the minute she opened the door—I hadn't even expected her to remember the article.

"You see, Mrs. Pebbles, that's precisely why we've come: to ask your forgiveness. We deeply regret publishing that photo of Ethan, and that's why we're here. Did Christ not teach that we should forgive those who trespass against us? To err is human, but—"

"—to forgive is divine," she completed, a conviction that was clearly etched with fire in her mind.

"Gina was a good Christian. My… colleague's own Christian impulses prompted her to join the search parties. How could we not support one another in times such as these? With all the… manipulations of God's word infecting our nation, she believed she was doing what was best. All these congregations: Presbyterians, Catholics, Protestants… None of them understand the truth of God the Father, and of our Lord and Savior—"

"—Jesus Christ," Meghan whispered, apparently convinced—fervently so, even—by Jim's words.

He smiled, and Mrs. Pebbles, who looked to be around his age, seemed bewitched by his words and entranced by his two-bit Good Samaritan routine.

"Your help is… important. Miss Triggs is here to ask your forgiveness. Isn't that right, Miss Triggs?"

"Of course, yes, publishing that photo was a mistake. I'm very sorry." I really was sorry, but the paper was free to make decisions about the article's content (they get to choose the layout, which photos to use—if any—and can even decide not to run the piece at all) and they'd included the images they thought best represented the story.

My mistake was that, back then, I didn't pay much attention to how they printed my articles. I was tired. I wrote in the mornings, researched in the afternoons, and hunted the men who'd raped me by night. I had too much bullshit and pain on my mind, I didn't have the capacity for anything else.

Meghan smiled and, out of nowhere, she threw her arms around me. I didn't know how to react and stood there motionless like a teddy bear, waiting for it to be over.

"You are forgiven," she whispered in my ear.

The hair on the back of my neck stood on end when I heard her husky voice so close.

"Can we speak for a few minutes?" Jim asked, trying to free me from this improvised prison.

"Oh… of course. Come in," she released me as if her embrace had never occurred, then gave an exaggerated wave to indicate we should come inside. "I'll let my husband Christopher know you're here. He's downstairs with his… toy soldiers. He's absolutely devoted to those little things."

She left us waiting in the hallway. From where we stood, we could see a none-too-inviting living room: mahogany furniture, black-and-white photos of a young couple in gold frames, a floral pattern on the sofa. Mrs. Pebbles reappeared with her husband, who wore round glasses at the height of his hearty cheeks. He seemed a little confused, but both were smiling intensely, practically unhooking their jaws as soon as they saw us waiting for them.

"Come in, have a seat. Ah, where are my manners? I should've offered you a glass of water. Forgive me. 'For I was hungry, and you gave me food; I was thirsty, and you gave me something to drink.' That's in the Bible, isn't it?"

"Don't... don't worry, Mrs. Pebbles, we won't be here long," said Jim, who seemed to know how to handle her.

Deep down, he seemed... warmer than I did. He could look anyone in the eyes and understand who they were and what they needed to hear.

"I'm Christopher," said the man.

"Tin soldiers, eh?" Jim asked with interest, by way of salutation. "You too?"

"Don't tell me you're a collector..." Christopher said excitedly as he gripped Jim's hand. "Which battalion, if you don't mind me asking?"

"For me it's... just a little hobby. I started with a few soldiers from the Union Army."

"Really? I have at least twenty. If you have time, I can—"

"No, no thank you, really. We're just here to—"

"Of course... of course. To ask about Gina," he lamented, interrupting Jim, changing tone. "Meghan told me. If you want to sit down... make yourselves at home. We've already talked about this dozens of times, but if it'll help you find her, we might as well go over it again."

"Thank you, Christopher," answered Jim, who had seemingly gained the couple's full confidence in a matter of seconds.

We sat on the Pebbles' sofa, and I looked up at the photos on the wall. Gina and Ethan weren't in any of them, but there was no shortage of photos of a younger, newlywed Meghan and Christopher.

"Ethan isn't home, is he?" Jim asked, though he knew the answer.

"Oh no. After he finishes at work on Sundays, he and his friends go to a soup kitchen to help the less fortunate. He's a good boy... He's going to be a great person. Christopher and I have tried make sure he... wants for nothing."

"I don't know if you heard about my brother and his wife," Christopher jumped in. "It was a tragedy. A real tragedy."

"Yes... we know about it," I responded, trying not to get left out of the conversation.

"But at least the children... Even the thought of it ties my stomach in knots. Horrible. Just horrible, you know? I was the one who had to go identify my brother and sister-in-law's charred bodies. Did you know it was Gina who saved Ethan? That girl was... an angel. She was such a good girl. She didn't deserve what happened to her. She was a good Christian. She prayed, took care of her brother, stayed out of trouble."

"She was never a problem?"

"A problem? Oh, goodness no," Meghan exclaimed. "She was very good. Always willing to help. She spent her afternoons reading the Bible; she was very committed to her studies. So much so that... everyone tried to take advantage of her. Especially that pig... the Rogers boy."

"Tom Rogers?"

"That one," Mrs. Pebbles snorted. "I didn't like that boy one bit. He came to our house that day asking where Gina was. He was the one who tricked her into going to his house to do Heaven knows what. And she never arrived. He showed up here and blamed us, shouting, demanding to know what we'd done to Gina. Claiming we beat her, and he'd seen the bruises. Bruises on our girl? Where would she get bruises? We raised the two of them as if they were our own children, for the love of God. That was the last straw. I cursed at him like I've never done before and still haven't asked God's forgiveness."

"Bruises?" I asked surprised.

I'd read the report on Gina's disappearance the night before. All the statements they'd collected, places she'd been. There was no mention of that episode with Tom Rogers.

"Yes. The boy came and said we beat her and that's why she'd left home. Absolute nonsense."

"Is it possible you did? I don't mean to judge," Jim asked in a serious tone. "We're just trying to… learn what happened. It pains me to think someone kidnapped her after she said goodbye to Ethan and…" he skipped the conclusion. "If Gina is dead… it's very sad to think she hasn't received the burial she deserves."

"Of course we didn't beat her!" contested Meghan, who seemed to have taken control of the conversation.

Christopher placed his hand on Meghan's thigh, and she breathed deeply.

"Honey…" Christopher said, concerned. "It's been a long time… God has forgiven us… I think we can tell them."

"What, that? That was just one time. And she deserved it, Christopher. You agreed. That has nothing to do with this."

"I didn't—"

"Don't you start. It was that Tom Rogers… he—"

"Meghan, it might help to—"

"No, Christopher," she interrupted. "We won't stain the image of—"

"Let me speak, Meghan!" her husband exploded, using an unexpected tone.

He seemed to have been holding back while his wife talked about their happy, welcoming home, but with that reaction, Meghan's eyes grew wide as saucers, as if she didn't recognize her husband.

"Look…" he began. It was almost like he had to say something that was burning him up inside. Meghan brought her hands to her face, knowing what her husband was going to say. "We've never told anyone this, but… there was just one time… Meghan caught Gina and Tom…" he paused. His wife was giving him a look, trying to communicate that this was a mistake. I braced for anything. "…kissing in Gina's bedroom."

Jim nodded, expectant. I remained motionless, listening to the pain in his voice.

"We sent her to her room so she could pray and ask God's forgiveness. But… she snuck out. By the time we went to her room to say dinner was ready, she had climbed out the window."

"She ran away?"

"I looked for her everywhere. Everywhere. Ethan was so little; I don't think he even realized what was happening. Meghan stayed here at home with him, and I scoured the Rockaways. I was desperate. I thought the worst. I still hadn't found her when I came home at midnight. When I think about that day… the only thing I remember is… finding my wife crying in the kitchen. We were trying to be good parents to her, but… it wasn't easy. There's no guidebook, you know?"

"But what happened? In her file there are no police reports from before she disappeared on June 3rd, 2002."

"At 2.30 in the morning she knocked on the door. I cried with happiness. But… I couldn't turn a blind eye to all the damage she'd done."

"Did she say where she'd been?"

"That was the worst part," Meghan interrupted, devastated. "I remember every word as clear as if she were here saying them now. Do you really want to know what she said?"

"What?"

"She said: 'I just fucked Tom.'"

I turned to look at Jim who, in his role as a good Christian, was shaking his head. Then he added:

"What did you do?"

"What we had to!" shrieked Meghan.

"What was that?" Jim pressed.

"Thirty-nine lashes with a belt," Christopher finally said. He wrapped his arm around his wife and tried to justify himself: "I cried the whole time… But she… she didn't seem to care at all. She just lay on the bed and… waited for me to finish."

"You sick motherfuckers," I spat, unable to hold back.

"Excuse me?" said Mrs. Pebbles.

"Miren…" Jim reproached, but I ignored him.

"You heard me. The two of you are sick. Having custody over a girl didn't give you the right to… to dictate her life for her, and it sure as shit didn't give you the right to beat her like a rug."

"But she was fifteen. She was a girl! I was a virgin until I married Christopher."

"Well good for you. But it was… her body, not yours. You don't get to make that kind of decision. Do you have any idea the trauma you're causing with your fucking… virginity fetish? The complexes you must've given that girl? And worst of all, that shit stays with you for life. Maybe that's where you got the stick up your ass. No wonder Ethan wants out of here."

The way they felt entitled to make decisions for Gina upset me deeply. It was like they had bought a bag of meat and now they got to decide when and how to eat it. Me, I was living in fear after a group of animals destroyed my life, thinking they were entitled to my body. This was just like a different version of that night.

"Ethan? Wants to leave?" Mrs. Pebbles asked with a mix of surprise and rage. And then: "Get out of my house."

"Mrs. Pebbles… I think that…" Jim said, attempting to broker an apology I had no intention of making.

"Get out!" she howled. "I knew this was a mistake. You're not here to help find Gina, you're just here to dig up dirt."

"You know where you can't dig up dirt?" I countered, walking to the door, Jim stumbling behind me. "Where there is none."

Chapter 19
Mallow Institute
April 25, 2011
One day earlier
Ben Miller

*Silence is often louder
than the most honest of answers.*

Inspector Miller spent all of Sunday afternoon at home, waiting for Lisa to come back. He had called her phone several times, but she hadn't picked up. He tried to calm his nerves by tidying the house and cooking dinner for the two of them, by way of apology, but when she still hadn't shown up by 11pm, he decided it was time to call his sister-in-law Claire.

"Ben?" Claire answered on the other end of the line.

"Is she with you?"

"You're a piece of shit. You know that, I hope?"

Ben sighed, then added in a subdued voice:

"I… made a mistake, right?"

"What do you think?"

"That's exactly what she'd say."

"She's my sister. We grew up together."

"Can you tell her I made veggie lasagna? It's her favorite. Trying to apologize here."

"Ben… Lisa's gonna stay here a few days. A plate of lasagna isn't going to save you this time. You really fucked this up."

"Can I talk to her?"

"I'm sorry, Ben. She told me to say no."

"Can you tell her I called at least?"

"I know you're a good guy, Ben. But… if you don't support each other with the Daniel stuff… I think you're in for a rough ride."

"I support her. She knows I do."

"When was the last time you talked about him? Have you asked her if she's thinking about him lately? Do you know she's been writing a diary of all the memories she has of their last year together? She showed it to me. It's beautiful, Ben."

He was silent. This was all news to him.

"You forgot to be a husband. It's great for you to try and… save the world or whatever. But what about your wife? You… well, at least you get to feel like you're being useful. But she… she's been abandoned, Ben. It's like she has no place in your life. And… and like Daniel has even less. You act like he never existed, and that's even worse than what happened."

Claire was the kind of person who was close enough to know your mistakes and far enough to tell you the truth to your face without caring what nerves she was touching. That last sentence had touched them all with a salt-soaked needle.

"Tell her I'm sorry, okay?" Ben said, trying to hide the pain her words had caused.

He was crying, even though Claire couldn't see it.

"I'll tell her, Ben. But she needs more time, okay? I know my sister. You can't pretend this'll get better overnight."

"How long then?"

"Only she knows that," Claire replied before hanging up.

The conversation left Ben so devastated that he collapsed on the bed with his suit still on.

He shot awake at five in the morning: he'd been having a recurring nightmare in which he saw a bicycle wheel spinning in the air in a dark room with a floor covered in red tiles. It wasn't terrifying, just distressing, one of those dreams where not understanding what's happening generates more unease and makes your heart beat faster than an unrecognizable face chasing you down an endless hallway.

It was already Monday, and he was struggling through an emotional hangover from his conversation with Lisa. When he rolled over and saw that the other side of the bed was undisturbed, he decided it was time to start rebuilding his life, which was coming apart at the seams as he powerlessly looked on. He showered, shaved, put on a clean suit and cleaned up the plates of cold lasagna he'd left untouched on the table. He called his office to say he wouldn't be coming in that day, got in his gray Pontiac, and drove to the Mallow Institute, the place where both stories seemed to meet.

He arrived just as several buses in front of the school were releasing students of all ages. He had been at the school a week earlier to talk to Allison's classmates, but none of them had said anything particularly revelatory.

The front of the Mallow Institute was decorated with a stained-glass window in the shape of an enormous cross, above the main door through which the students were currently entering. Now that Ben knew how Allison's story had ended, he found the religious symbol disturbing. He approached the entrance and a woman jumped in front of him:

"Hi, Inspector Miller, back so soon? We heard they found Allison… it's a real tragedy. We've arranged for some special prayers for her today so that… her soul travels safely to Heaven. Allison's teachers are all deeply affected. We're going to give the kids in her class some special talks. They need spiritual guidance to help them through so much pain."

"I came to resolve a few unanswered questions. I need to talk to Father Graham and, if possible, with Allison's classmates."

"Oh, Heavens no. They'll be devastated. This isn't the time to expose them to even more trauma. Some of the parents have asked us to… to talk to their children and keep an eye on them the next few days."

"Sure, but I think it's important for us to learn what happened."

"I thought you looked for people who have gone missing. Allison is no longer missing, isn't that right? Father Graham's schedule is very tight. In just an hour he's saying a mass in the school chapel for students who wish to attend. They'll receive an excused absence from their classes during that period. After that, he has an appointment with two police officers at noon. You should have told us you wanted to talk to him. But anyway… since she's been found, doesn't that mean your job is over?"

"Another Mallow student disappeared nine years ago. My work here isn't finished. It seems like teenagers from your school keep disappearing and… it seems like no one is sufficiently concerned about the disappearance of two girls in a decade. Take me to Father Graham or I'll have to come back with a search warrant… and an arrest warrant for obstructing an open investigation."

He sidestepped the woman and entered Mallow's main hall. Once inside, he turned right, where a secretary was speaking to a teenager in a uniform of gray slacks and a white polo shirt. Ben opened a door and navigated through the hall of offices— the same place where he had discreetly spoken with the administration a week earlier. The woman from outside stumbled behind him, looking worried.

"You can't go in there. Father Graham is… preparing for the mass."

"Well, the mass will have to wait. I need to speak with him."

"Mr. Miller, please, don't make me—"

Ben reached the door to the director's office and tried to open it, but it was locked. He hurriedly beat it with his fist while the woman continued imploring him to stop, but he didn't listen.

"Father Graham! Open up. I need to talk to you." He slammed his fist against the door more forcefully, and the administrative secretary emerged from her office to see what was happening.

"Sir… Father Graham doesn't like to be disturbed when he's preparing to say a mass. I'm going to have to ask you to leave and come back another time."

"Father Graham!"

Then, there was a clicking sound and, finally, the priest opened the door and greeted Ben. He appeared confused and kept his hand on the door.

"Inspector Miller?" he said. "What's so important that it can't wait?"

Father Graham was in his fifties; he had gray hair, a thick beard, pleated gray pants, black shoes, and a V-neck sweater that exposed a white shirt underneath, buttoned so high it was practically choking him.

"I have to talk to you."

"Oh… Is it about Allison? Such a shame. That girl was… a delight. She didn't deserve to go like that. But the ways of the Lord… well, you know. That's what we believers tend to say. We don't understand life, and we certainly don't understand death when it takes away someone so young and so tragically."

"It's about Gina. Gina Pebbles. She studied here. Just like Allison. It's possible their cases ended the same way. I'm trying to figure out what we missed back then."

"Gina Pebbles?" he looked confused, but then continued. "I'm a busy man, Inspector Miller. I don't have time for this right now. If you make an appointment with Mrs. Malcolm, I'll be sure to set aside some time for you. This is a complicated week, with midterms and Community Education Council evaluations."

"I know you have a mass to officiate, but this is important. Give me ten minutes."

He hesitated, but then looked behind him, into his own office: there, on one side of the desk, sat a teenage girl with straight brown hair and a pleated skirt.

"Do you mind if we continue another time?" he said to the girl.

She silently shook her head, then stood and exited the office, slipping past Inspector Miller, who watched, puzzled.

"Come in, please. Let's get this over with," Father Graham said.

Chapter 20
Roxbury
April 24, 2011
Two days earlier
Jim Schmoer and Miren Triggs

*Fire dances even
when you aren't
watching.*

"What the hell was that, Miren?" Jim asked as soon as they left the Pebbles' house, annoyed by Miren's sudden outburst. "Have you lost your mind? We were doing alright. We were getting somewhere. They were opening up. What happened to Miren Triggs the journalist? When you're interviewing someone, you have to check your own baggage at the door. You know that better than anyone."

"Don't lecture me, Jim."

"We all have baggage, Miren. All of us. But that doesn't mean we rub it in people's faces and screw everything up. It takes self-restraint."

"They're sick motherfuckers and someone had to say it to their face. They beat a child, and for what? For God's sake… we all do stupid shit when we're young. And that doesn't give anyone to right to take us and… destroy our lives or make us into victims just because we're women."

"Your job isn't to convince others to be good people, Miren, it's to tell the world the truth about what happened to Gina and Allison. To find out what these people are hiding and bring it to light. The world will do the talking for you. The world will change if it's confronted with an ugly enough truth. Your job is to find that truth and expose it as eloquently as possible."

"This is bullshit. I didn't have to let you come, Jim. It's like you're… treating me like a child. And now you're lecturing me. Just to be clear, I'm the only one who is actually a journalist here."

"Are you serious? Do you think they would have even let you inside the house if it weren't for me? You don't inspire confidence, Miren. I saved your skin. You behave like…"

He left the sentence unfinished. He realized Miren didn't deserve all that.

"Like what, Jim? Come on, say it," she spat, raising her voice, furious.

"Hey, how about this, let's both take it down a notch."

"You're a fucking coward," she replied.

"Let's drop it, Miren. This isn't doing either of us any good."

She snorted, then continued, full of rage:

"This is why your wife left you, Jim. Because you don't have the balls to confront anybody," she hissed, thoughtlessly wounding him.

But the barb had been too sharp, and she'd thrown it at the target with her eyes closed.

"What do you know about my relationship with my wife? You don't know anything about why we separated. Anything. And getting angry doesn't give you the right to talk about others like they've got no feelings, like they're made of stone. Not everyone is like you. You don't give a shit about anyone. It's all about you, your experience, your trauma. I've always been there for you. Always. If you're at the *Manhattan Press*, it's thanks to me."

"Get the fuck away from me!" she demanded, hurt.

Jim realized that he'd done exactly what he'd accused her of—spoken to her as if she had no feelings—and tried to back-pedal, but it was useless. At a certain point in an argument, every word is like a double-edged sword.

"Miren, I—"

"Get lost!" she screamed, walking between houses toward the edge of Roxbury and leaving Jim mid-sentence.

Night was falling and she walked towards the sunset along Rockaway Boulevard, in the direction of Breezy Point. Jim watched her leave, and although at first, he considered following her and apologizing, he knew it would only complicate things.

Once she felt she was far enough away that Jim couldn't see her, Miren let the first tear escape. Then another, then more. She couldn't stand other people seeing her cry and she needed to be alone, like someone clutching their pillow at night. And in the course of those suffocating sobs that nobody saw, she realized that, without meaning to, she had walked to the far end of the Rockaway Peninsula. The sun was just about to set, and she decided to walk towards the beach, over the earth and scrubland that separated the road from the shore.

There, she watched the sun go down as she fought with her inner demons. She asked herself why she was the way she was and why her life revolved around pushing away anyone who got close to her. She felt broken and miserable, depressed and shattered. She searched the hidden chambers of her heart with the same emotional distance as she would read the newspaper, and all she found were moments in her life when she had felt alone, sad and dejected.

She took out her phone and called the only person who could pull her out of that spiral. After several rings, she heard the calm voice of a woman on the other end:

"Miren? It's so nice of you to call. I was just making dinner, and… you won't believe it, but we're making fried green tomatoes. You used to love them when you were a girl."

Miren smiled the instant she heard her mother's voice, even if some tears continued to slide down her cheeks, seemingly competing to see which could reach the corners of her mouth first.

"Miren, are you there? Oh! Before I forget: Mrs. Peters, the neighbor, she won't stop asking me to get you to sign a book for her. She's been bragging to everyone about how she used the change your diapers. It was once! She did it once during a barbecue we were having and now she thinks she ought to get royalties. I can't believe the woman. So sign one for her, but don't write anything too nice."

Miren sighed heavily before trying to speak. She thought about how she didn't want her mother to know the state she was in, but mothers always recognize their children's tears.

"Miren? Are you okay, honey?"

"Fried green tomatoes," she finally said with a knot in her throat. "I… I used to love them. I wish I could be there now with you and Dad." In front of her, the Atlantic Ocean gently bobbed, and she suddenly felt a wave touch the tips of her toes.

"Your father won't be joining me for dinner. This afternoon he wolfed down six muffins and I've banned him from the kitchen until tomorrow. The rest are for me and grandma."

Miren smiled again when she heard her grandmother was there.

"How's Grandma?"

"We bought her a motorized scooter and now she can make it halfway across Charlotte in ten minutes flat. She's drunk on life. And she asked me not to tell you, but… she has a boyfriend."

"Grandma does?" Miren laughed.

The gossip felt like a far-off lighthouse shining in her direction.

"She deserves one, don't you think? Some man from her retirement home. He's charming. They have matching scooters. It's like she's 15 again, joyriding around town, flirting, giggling like a schoolgirl."

"I'm… I'm so happy for her, Mom."

"Oh, I knew you would be."

A silence settled on the conversation, and finally, seeing her opportunity, Miren's mother insisted:

"Are you really okay, honey?"

"No, Mom. I'm not."

She felt her voice tearing like a piece of old cloth, reduced to handful of tangled threads.

"Is it a boy?"

"No," she answered with a sob.

"Work?"

"It's me, Mom. What's wrong with me? Why… why can't I ever feel like everyone else? Why does everyone think I'm cold, that I don't suffer, that I'm not… like I'm not a person? I do what I can. I swear I do. It's just that… that… I don't want anyone to hurt me again. I don't want anyone to ever think I'm vulnerable again, that they can just take me to a park and… for it all to happen again."

"Honey," her mother whispered on the other end. "It's not true, Miren. You have feelings just like everyone else."

"It is true, Mom. I've never managed to love anyone. Ever. I don't even feel things. It's like my life… like it's all happening to someone else. Like, I'm in it, but… but it's all outside of me. Nobody matters. Nothing makes me happy, Mom."

"Listen to me, Miren. I'm going to be very honest. What happened to you was hard, God knows I know it. Every day I think about how I wasn't there to protect you like I should have been."

"It wasn't your—"

"Let me finish," she said, raising her voice, angry at the world. "But… you have to try to let life move forward, honey. If you bind yourself to that night, if everything revolves around it, it'll eat you alive. Can't you see that? It'll kill you. It's been years and it still seems like it was yesterday. And that's the problem. You need to live. You need to turn the page. Relegate it to the status of a bad memory and nothing more. There was no justice. Nothing made sense. But you need to focus on yourself and your happiness. What you do—looking for people, helping others—is so worthwhile, Miren. And you should keep it up."

"But who's helping me, Mom? Who?"

"Only you can help yourself, darling. But you'll only be able to do it when you can make peace with that night."

The words echoed in Miren's head like the advice she used to receive when she still lived in Charlotte. That instant, her mind traveled to a memory of playing with her parents, running all around the house. Then she remembered how her mother would put a dollop of cream on her nose when she was making pancakes on Sunday mornings, but then those idyllic images were blotted out by the darkness of that park in Manhattan and the shadowy silhouettes all around her.

"Thanks… Mom," she finally said in a serious voice.

"I want you to be happy, Miren. If you want, your father and I can come see you for a few days."

"You don't have to, Mom. Really. I'll be alright."

"Are you sure?" she asked in a tone that only mothers possess.

"Yeah, no, it's okay Mom, I'll be fine," Miren answered before hanging up.

The sun had set while she was on the phone and, as soon as she hung up, she saw that a few groups of mopeds and bicycles had parked in remote part of Breezy Point, and their riders were all happily greeting one another. All of them seemed to be teenagers; none of them could be older than eighteen.

She spent a few moments staring off into the horizon but became uneasy as she noticed the group of teenagers growing larger and more raucous. When she looked back, she recognized Ethan Pebbles laughing with several other kids. Then she saw him approach someone in a gray hoodie—she assumed it was his girlfriend—and give her a kiss, grabbing her by the ass. Two boys poured gasoline on a pile of firewood and, the instant a girl threw her lit cigarette on it, the kindling flared. They were behaving like Miren wasn't there, and she was fascinated to see the girls acting far more liberated than she ever was at their age. They danced around the fire to a song she didn't know, then loudly sang another. One blonde girl made out with a boy and then, not long after, did the same with a girl. They were enjoying themselves, free from hang ups, not overthinking. But then, one of the youths pointed at Miren, and everyone turned to look at her.

Miren was about to turn around and walk back along the shore as if she hadn't seen them, but she was having one of those moments when she felt like she could face anything. She decided to approach the group and asked:

"Do any of you know anything about the Ravens of God?"

Ethan gave her a surprised look but kept quiet in the background as the other kids exchanged glances, confused.

"Do you know about that group? Do you know what it is?"

Ethan shook his head, disappointed, like Miren had made a serious mistake. A couple sitting on the sand continued kissing like she wasn't there.

"Come on! None of you know anything?" she insisted louder.

They all gaped at her wordlessly, as if they'd made a pact to remain silent. Miren realized she had little to gain from that conversation.

"Fine. What do I have to do? I know you won't talk to some-one who isn't part of the Ravens. So tell me, what do I have to do to join?"

A brunette girl with full lips and sharp eyes laughed.

"I don't know what you have to do, but… even if I did… aren't you a little old for the Ravens?" she said sarcastically.

A few of the boys burst out laughing. Others stayed silent, watching.

"C'mon, what do you have to do? Whatever it is. Can you reach true happiness being in the Ravens?"

"How do you know about the Ravens?" the teenage girl asked, curious.

Ethan watched but said nothing, a worried expression on his face.

"I'm interested in what happened in the place where they murdered a girl. And where another girl went missing years ago."

A boy who looked about Ethan's age, with brown hair and a square jaw, stood up and joined the conversation.

"They say… you can't ask to join the Ravens," he ex-plained. "The Ravens have to ask you to join. Even if you knew how to get in… it wouldn't do you any good if they didn't accept you."

"You're James Cooper, right? From Mallow?"

"You know me?" he laughed. "I guess even the MILFs have heard about me at this point."

"I've heard that you know how I can join the Ravens."

James gave a slight, mocking grin and eventually responded:

"They say there's a game. That's all I know… it's just a ru-mor. But… who knows. If you're looking for the Ravens, may-be they're looking for you too."

"What do I have to do for them to find me?"

"You're brave. Clearly. It'd be better if you stopped playing these games. Messing with the Ravens can get nastier than you could possibly imagine."

"I'll ask again: What do I have to do for them to find me?" she insisted, clenching her jaw.

"Hey, relax. I'm sure they've already found you," he concluded, turning around.

"What the hell does that mean?"

"Do you mind?" James replied, tired of her questions. "We're trying to have a good time here and you're... harshing our buzz."

"You do know this is where they found Gina Pebbles' backpack after she disappeared nine years ago, right?"

"Maybe she came here to have a little fun back in her day, too. Why not? We all have the right to... enjoy ourselves a little. Including you. Otherwise, what did you come out here for? To cry? Have you been crying? Your eyes are red," he snorted, giving an affected laugh.

"Leave her alone, James," said a boy in the back. "This lady doesn't even know where she is." Miren hoped it was Ethan speaking, but it didn't sound like him.

This adolescent scorn had caught her off guard and she didn't know how to react. Her mind traveled back to when she was a teenager, ignored by her entire class because she was one of the few students who took school seriously. So much time had passed since then that she'd forgotten how it felt to be ostracized, to listen to others laughing together at your expense.

"It's alright, don't worry," said the girl with brown hair who'd spoken to her initially. "Doesn't it feel good to cry? I always get a rush when I cry, from the lack of oxygen when I can't catch my breath. I love crying... I wish I could do it all day. It makes me feel more alive than... a good fuck, even."

"How old are you?" Miren asked, surprised by this kind of talk.

The girl cackled, then added:

"Get out of here, lady, I think that's enough chatting for today. I came here to... let loose." She turned around and left Miren behind.

Miren saw that the group was beginning to ignore her, laughing, going back to what they'd been doing before they saw her. That same teenage girl howled with glee when a boy turned on a portable speaker and blared the third song of the day Miren didn't recognize. She tried to make eye contact with Ethan but saw that he'd walked towards the sea with the girl he'd been kissing earlier. It must be Deborah.

Miren was out of place. She regretted walking there after fighting with Jim, and she remembered her VW was parked a few miles away in Roxbury. But just as she turned around, she heard the teenagers snickering in unison, a series of strident laughs directed at her: one voice on top of another, mixing with the gentle sound of the waves. She began walking away, towards the shore, heading for Roxbury, when suddenly she saw something fall to the ground by her feet.

Then, before she had time to figure out what had just hit the sand, something struck her head, hard, and everything faded to black.

Chapter 21
Breezy Point
April 25, 2011
One day earlier
Miren Triggs

*Not every ending
deserves a kiss.*

I woke up in a room I didn't recognize, with a crushing headache that seemed to have its own pulse. There were red curtains hanging from a small window, and I could tell there was a flashing blue light on the other side. Beneath the curtains, my backpack sat on a gray wingback chair whose arms were covered in tiny holes that looked like cigarette burns.

I heard the sound of running water to my left, but my head hurt too much for me to turn and look. I was lying on a bed, on a floral bedspread as horrible as the throbbing in my temples. I checked and was relieved to see I was still dressed. What had happened? Where was I?

At my feet, a few yards from the bed, a muted TV was on, tuned to NBC's round-the-clock news coverage. I tried to figure out what day it was based on the broadcast: Obama was giving a speech; I concluded that not too much time could have passed since the last things I remembered. Then, I heard a voice from the direction of the running water. I recognized it immediately:

"Ahh, you're awake," Jim said in a whisper, as if he were afraid the sound of his voice would hurt me.

"Jim?" I had to push myself, but after some serious effort I managed to turn my head towards him despite the pain radiating from my head to my neck and shoulders.

He stepped into my field of vision; his hair was messy and he wasn't wearing his glasses. He was also wearing the same clothes he'd had on at the Pebbles' house, so I deduced this must either be the same day or a bad dream.

"Where am I? What... what happened?"

"Someone... hit you on the head with a rock. I found you unconscious on the beach. I'm afraid I went looking for you in Roxbury when I saw you hadn't returned to the car after a few hours. I thought you needed some time by yourself, so I left you alone. But... when it was dark and you still hadn't come back to the VW, I decided to walk in the direction you'd gone. I thought I'd find you and we could have a calmer conversation, but... when I saw you lying on the ground, I got scared. Someone had hit you pretty hard. I picked you up and carried you here as best I could."

"You didn't see anyone around?" I asked.

Mentally, I navigated the last, blurry memories I had of teenagers on the beach, dancing around a bonfire.

"You were alone. There wasn't anyone. Thank goodness I found you. The tide could've come in and... well, better not to think about it."

"You didn't see any kids?"

"Kids? When I was walking towards Breezy Point, I did see a few groups of teenagers on bikes going the opposite way. Do you think they were the ones who attacked you?"

"I don't know, Jim. I'm... confused. Fuck it hurts."

I tried to sit up, but an unexpected pain caused me to let out a moan that seemed like it had a life of its own.

"Whoa, whoa, take it easy, Miren. You need to rest." He bent over to support me in the bed. "I cleaned the gash on your head as well as I could. You've still got some sand in your hair and on your neck, but I think I did a pretty good job."

"Where are we?"

"The New Life Motel in Breezy Point. I know it's not the nicest-looking place, but… it was the closest to where I found you. The receptionist insisted you should see a doctor, but I thought if I brought you to a hospital, you'd be the one bashing my head in."

"What time is it?" I asked.

I felt dizzy as I looked for a clock in the room but found nothing.

"Midnight," he said in warm voice after checking his wristwatch. "Try to rest."

"Midnight? How long have I been—?"

"I found you a few hours ago. Around nine. You had a nice long nap. And I'm… beat. I was planning to stay up to make sure you were okay, but now that you're awake… I have to be honest, I'm dead. I'll sleep in that bed over there if that's alright with you. But… if you prefer, I could get another room. The receptionist said the motel is empty. I doubt she'll charge me much for a few hours."

"No," I rushed to say, "Stay. It's… it's fine."

He gave a grin that I interpreted as a sign of approval. Then he came to the bed and offered me a glass of water, which he grabbed off the nightstand.

"Thanks, Jim," I said. "I don't know why… I…" I tried to apologize, but he cut me off gently.

"Try to rest, Miren."

"No, listen… I want you to know that… even though I can't always externalize what I… feel," it killed me to say that last word out loud, "…I promise that… I'm grateful to you for being here, helping me."

"Miren… I know. You don't have to say anything. We were angry and… I didn't understand that your past is different from my past. My experiences aren't yours and my fears—especially those fears—are nothing like the ones tormenting you. Life is subjective and I have no place questioning what motivates you and what you struggle with. We don't all start from the same place in life, and nothing ever hits two people the same way. We all just try to get through it and do our best to not lose too many pieces of ourselves along this road full of potholes and accidents."

He paused and, for the first time in many years, I felt like someone was putting into words the internal struggle that I've never fully understood. Whenever I looked at other people and thought they seemed happy or sad, or they were excited or crying, I cursed my own misfortune at being so unfeeling. But maybe Jim was right, maybe we're all doomed to drive down a difficult highway, doing our best to keep it together as we go. But ultimately, when we break down, we're the only ones who can fix ourselves.

I struggled to sit up then leaned against the headboard in silence. My head still hurt and the room was still spinning, but I knew what I needed at that moment. I grabbed Jim's hand and he looked at me, still standing. I noticed the shadows the bedside lamp was casting on his face and I remembered all the times he'd been by my side over the years, always there, as a teacher and a companion, as a mentor and something more, as a friend and a confidant.

I tugged on his hand just a little, and he obeyed my silent command, coming to sit beside me on the bed. He looked at me carefully, like he was scrutinizing my head. He knew what I was thinking, I was sure of it, but there was no way he could see the whole picture. The inner workings of my mind were inexplicable—including to me—and maybe that's why he was so observant. Maybe it was an attempt to untangle the complexities of my wounded soul.

I stroked his hair and spent a few seconds wrapping his curls around my finger. He had a serious expression. I looked at him, nervous, and then took off his glasses. The last step. I carefully placed them on the nightstand. He followed the action with his eyes, then looked back into mine and gently leaned towards me, stopping just close enough for me to feel his breath. Was it really so hard to find this? Could he really be the only person who made me feel safe? And I went for it. I felt the hair on his skin brushing against my lips.

And then it was over.

There was a loud crash as the motel room's window shattered into a thousand pieces, bathing us in a shower of glass shards. Jim stood and looked around, understanding nothing. A rock had flown to the back of the room, hit the closet door, and bounced onto the bed, landing by my left leg. Jim opened the door and ran outside. I tried to stand before realizing I was barefoot, and the floor was covered in broken glass.

"Jim?" I cried when he ran out of my sight.

He reappeared at the other side of the door a few seconds later, cursing.

"Sons of bitches. It was a couple kids on mopeds. I counted three but they rode away, laughing. I couldn't make out the license plates."

I picked up the rock beside my leg. It was about the size of a mango, with a word and some numbers written on it in red paint: 'JOHN 8:7.'

Chapter 22
Mallow Institute
April 25, 2011
One day earlier
Ben Miller

*What makes us fall into
the trap of believing
that those in positions of authority
deserve to be there?*

Father Graham hadn't even sat back down behind his desk when Inspector Miller asked his first question:

"Do you usually have closed-door chats with… your students, Father?"

"Why do you ask? Oh. Do you mean Deborah? It's… a little complicated. But yes. That's nothing unusual at Mallow."

"I have plenty of time, don't worry."

The priest sighed, and Ben noticed that he had a different air about him than he'd had the first time they spoke. The first time Miller visited the school he was confident that Allison had run away from home like she had before. Even though some of her classmates' statements seemed to suggest she had changed her ways and committed herself to her studies, her past worked its way into every conversation. That first time, Father Graham himself explained that Allison had come to speak with him a few times because she was tired of the rumors flying around the school that she was "loose", even though it was a rumor that could be corroborated. His statement matched up with Ben's conversations with Allison's classmates and seemed consistent with her history of running away, so he had treated her disappearance as no great concern. He was sure she was with one of her recent boyfriends and that sooner or later she would come home, as she always had.

"Well… let's see. Every day, first thing in the morning, I set aside two hours to help our students with their worries and give them face-to-face spiritual guidance. It's a complicated age, full of problems, insecurities, and bad decisions. I try to be available for them. Any student is welcome to come to my office to ask for advice, make a confession, or simply chat. At the end of the day, Inspector, I think it's important to break down barriers, open doors, and form close relationships with our students who are at an age when…" he paused. "When evil is lurking nearby."

"Evil? They're just… teenagers. They do the things teenagers do."

"Exactly. Evil. The devil is never closer than during adolescence, Inspector Miller. He tempts you with wicked choices, tricks you into turning from the righteous path. He promises you happiness, but you end up worshiping none other than Satan himself. It's important for the children to receive an education and clear guidance if they don't want to end up… shunning the Lord's plan."

"Did you ever have conversations like this with… Gina Pebbles?"

"Gina… I can't tell you how much I prayed for that girl. I still think of her from time to time. That was a real blow to us here at the school. She was an angel. I've never met another girl like her. She prayed more fervently than anyone else in her class. She helped whenever she could. She watched over her little brother. We all loved her. She was undoubtedly one of our finest students. I always think of her as the model Mallow student: religious, obliging, intelligent. That was... a tragedy."

"Just like Allison's case," Ben said, trying to connect the two conversations.

"Oh, yes, of course. The Lord and his plans. What happened to Gina was so long ago, we were just beginning to forget, and now... this. It has been difficult for us to convince parents that the school is a safe space, Inspector. And it is safe, truly. But things like this have a lot of impact. We're planning to send a letter to Allison's parents to express our condolences and... well, to offer them the support they need during this painful time."

"I talked to them. They're really hurting. But you know what, Father? I'm surprised a family like Allison's can afford a school like this. As I understand it, the tuition here is..." he racked his mind for the right word, "...prohibitive."

"Well, I don't know if it's prohibitive, but it is commensurate with what we provide: a high-quality religious education. Many of our graduates go on to the country's top universities—fifty percent get into the Ivy League, so we're more than satisfied with the education we offer."

"I'm sure, but... how could her family afford it?"

"Allison had a scholarship. We try to offer opportunities to students with limited resources, as part of our efforts at socially inclusive education."

"Do you give scholarships to anyone who applies for one?"

"If only we could, Inspector. We, too, have limited resources, but we try to offer four or five scholarships for high schoolers per year. It's a good opportunity financed by the Church. A high-quality education opens doors and breaks down barriers."

"Can I ask you something?"

"Of course, anything you like. I'm here to help, Inspector. This is a tragedy, and we must understand what happened as soon as possible. Every day that passes without answers is another day parents consider withdrawing their children from Mallow."

"Were Gina Pebbles and her brother scholarship students?"

"The Pebbles? I wouldn't know. I don't remember. I'd have to check. But I could look it up for you."

"Her brother is still here, right?"

"He is. Now that you mention it, I believe he is on scholarship. Yes, I suppose they both were. They deserved it. We gave them scholarships even before high school, because theirs was a special case. Their parents had passed away, and their aunt and uncle—Meghan and Christopher, if memory serves—wanted a good education for their niece and nephew. Yes. I believe that's right. In any case, I'll double-check and let you know as soon as possible."

"Well, it's certainly interesting."

"What makes you say that?"

"Doesn't it strike you as an odd coincidence that two students from your school—both teenage girls on scholarship, the same age—have disappeared in the course nine years?"

"What are you insinuating, Inspector? Are you suggesting that Mallow had something to do with this? Blaming this horror on us?"

"Of course not, I'm only saying—"

"Would you also blame the schools where a student with an assault rifle guns down his classmates? Because that's exactly what you're doing. It's as if, rather than blaming a government that makes it legal for anyone to purchase firearms, you blame us teachers for the children dying in our schools."

"No, Father, I wasn't trying to—"

"We are not responsible for what happens off campus,

Inspector. Technically, Gina disappeared after leaving class, and Allison came in that morning, as I told you, but she missed the last three hours of class. She must've left school for some reason and... well, we can't control everything that our four hundred students do, especially the ones who don't want to be controlled. The faculty had been very concerned about her attitude in recent months. The girl was a bit... libertine."

He was back on that issue again. "I don't like to say this, Inspector, but... if the Lord doesn't smile upon your behavior, the devil will".

Inspector Miller sighed. Father Graham was adept at dodging questions and Ben realized he would have to try a more aggressive approach if he wanted to learn anything.

"What happened to Allison is a travesty," the priest continued. "God knows we've kept her in our prayers, and that's why we've decided to say a mass for her, so her classmates can grieve. If you've come here to insinuate that we're... responsible for what happened, I must say that you... you may be on to something."

"Sorry?"

"We are responsible in the sense that we failed to see that Allison was crying out for our help. Her more... wanton tendencies merely indicated that she was unhappy. We all knew it. At Mallow, we keep tabs on all our students and their lives. We asked our questions. And everyone agreed that Allison had become a..."

"A what?"

"A... a harlot. And you must agree it's not something of which a girl can feel particularly... proud. She had multiple partners. And, well, as I'm sure you'll understand, this is a Christian institution, and we disapprove of any... lascivious activities. She was a sinner, like the woman in the house of the Pharisee who washed Christ's feet. Did the Lord not have a lesson to teach us? Did he not make clear that, the greater the sin, the greater must be the forgiveness?"

"Forgive my ignorance, Father, but… I'm not a particularly faithful man."

"You see, Christ entered the house of a Pharisee and let a prostitute there wash his feet. Not only did he let this sinful woman touch him, but he also washed away her sins. Are you following me?"

"I'm afraid not."

"What I'm trying to say is that at this school, we endeavored to wash away Allison's sins. And she'd begun to change. She became more applied in her studies and started earning better grades. But… sometimes our best sheep fall into a ravine, and there's little a shepherd can do but grieve the loss and move on, so he can tend to the rest of his flock and ensure no more go near the edge."

Ben nodded with concern; it took him a few moments to process what that sentence really meant. He looked around the room before speaking. He noticed the bookshelf filled with religious texts behind Father Graham. A dark wooden crucifix hung from the wall; the figure of Christ was made of silver so bright that Ben felt like he was being watched. He had left religion behind so long ago that this sudden pressure seemed oppressive.

"But what can you tell me about Gina? Did you have private conversations with her too? Did she confess to anything you found disturbing? I've read in her case file that she had a boyfriend. A kid by the name of Tom Rogers."

"It's been years since Gina disappeared, and I said everything I knew at the time in my statement to the police. She was a good student, but she couldn't get past her parents' deaths. Of course I had conversations with her, to give her advice and guidance. After that kind of tragedy, you either reach out to God or you fall into the abyss."

"What did she talk about in those conversations?"

"Her worries. She was concerned about her brother; she always wanted the best for him, and she didn't want him to feel their parents' absence. It was a very traumatic experience. But she was… charming. If she was going out with a boy, that's to be expected. We don't approve of it, of course, but it's inevitable. She was a girl with a face of an angel. And she was always smiling. In my memory of her, she's smiling."

"What do you think happened to her?"

"I don't know, Inspector. Perhaps… I don't know, some thug kidnapped her when she got out of class and… well. I'm sure God threw the gates of Heaven wide open for her."

"I understand," Miller replied.

At that moment, a woman wearing a white veil and a rosary around her neck appeared at the door and interrupted:

"Father, the archbishop is calling. It's important…"

"Will you excuse me for a moment?"

"Of course, take your time."

"I won't be long. I assure you; I will answer all of your questions on my return and assist however I can."

"I'm sure you will, Father."

The priest left his office, and Ben used these moments alone to reflect. There was something about Father Graham that didn't quite fit, but his willingness to talk and eagerness to help with the investigation had Ben baffled. He tried to remember other times when two girls from the same school had disappeared, or even disappeared from the same neighborhood. He couldn't think of any others. This had to be something more than a coincidence.

He stood up, restless under the gaze of the silver Christ on the crucifix, and glanced at the books on the shelf, which included several translations of the Bible. He picked one up and began flipping through the pages, without reading so much as a sentence. It was all so strange to him that even if he had read a sentence, it wouldn't have meant anything. He saw that many portions were highlighted in blue—outlining verses or whole passages. He thumbed through several hundred pages at once, hopping between the New and Old Testament until he reached the title page, on which he again saw the perfect, rounded handwriting, this time spelling the name *Allison Hernández*.

Chapter 23
Breezy Point
Early morning, April 25, 2011
One day earlier
Jim Schmoer and Miren Triggs

Fear is the only emotion that grows
when you can't see what's causing it.

Miren and Jim stared at the rock in disbelief. Finally, Jim walked up to her, concerned.

"Are you okay?" he puffed, out of breath.

"Yeah… no… well, it didn't hit me. What does it mean?" she asked, confused, the adrenaline still throbbing in her fingertips. "JOHN 8:7?"

"Have you read the Bible?" he asked, answering her question with another. He approached the rock for a closer look.

Miren shook her head and Jim started searching through the motel room drawers.

"What are you doing?" Miren asked.

"There must be one in here somewhere." He checked all the drawers in the TV stand, but found nothing but a discrete, empty minibar. "In this country, there's a Bible in the drawer of every hotel room and a gun under the pillow in every bedroom."

Finally, after opening the second drawer of the nightstand, he found what he was looking for: a Gideon Bible, named after Gideon International, a Christian association that, at the beginning of the twentieth century, resolved to place a Bible in every hotel room in the United States. Whenever a new hotel opened, the association would approach the management and give them enough copies for every nightstand in the building, without the owner having to spend a dime. It was undoubtedly a shrewd marketing campaign.

"Here it is," Jim said, paging through the book for the passage the rock was undoubtedly alluding to.

"Did you find it?"

"Let's see, John… chapter eight… verse seven: 'He who is without sin among you, let him throw a stone at her first.'"

Miren looked at the rock, then at Jim, who was visibly worried.

"I don't like this, Jim."

"Maybe we should get out of here," he said. "These Rockaway kids clearly don't want us investigating what happened to Allison."

"I'm the one they're trying to drive away, Jim. I remember seeing Ethan on the beach with a group of teenagers. He seemed like he wanted to tell me to leave. He kept giving me this worried look. And then… maybe it was one of the kids who knocked me out on the beach. I kept pressing them to tell me what they knew about the Ravens… I know, I know, more recklessness. Ethan warned us. Maybe… it's that group, the Ravens, who are behind this. Maybe they were the ones who killed Allison."

"What do you think they're trying to tell us with this Bible verse?"

"That they're pure and free from sin. And that we aren't… or that I'm not, really. Maybe the same things happened to Allison. Maybe… maybe it happened to Gina, too."

"Do you think the school could have something to do with it? That Father… Graham could be involved?"

"I don't know, Jim. But I want to speak with him tomorrow."

"I won't be able to join you, Miren. I have to teach, and things have been tense with the administration. I want to come, don't get me wrong, but I can't lose that job. I'm trying to… to get them to reconsider my custody arrangement with my daughter. And Carol, my ex-wife, isn't going to make it easy if I lose my job at Columbia."

"Don't worry, Jim. You've already done too much. I'll go by myself."

"Be careful though, Miren."

"Quit worrying about me, Jim. I'm fine. I'll be fine. I don't… need anyone taking care of me. Got it?"

Jim smiled and added:

"How's your head?"

"Better. At least the floor has stopped spinning."

"Can you stand on your own? Let me bring you slippers. The floor is covered in glass."

Jim grabbed a pair of complimentary slippers and placed one on the foot Miren was dangling over the side of the bed. Then, before crouching to put on the other, he looked her in the eyes, yearning to continue the kiss that was left floating in the air. Miren's heart was racing, and he could see that she was watching him, attentive. He squatted down to her level and kissed her again. The moment lasted a few seconds as he dragged the sole of his shoe through the broken glass on the ground, shards crunching under his weight like pebbles dragged by the tide to the shore. He lowered himself on top of Miren; she grabbed the back of his neck, upping the intensity. But then, suddenly, she felt a sharp pain in her chest and closed her eyes tightly, unable to heal the wound that was still there, even if it hadn't left a scar.

"I can't, Jim. Stop, please!" Miren cried brusquely, suddenly uncomfortable. This outburst was an unexpected blow for Jim.

"What's wrong?" he asked, confused.

"I can't, Jim," she said before inhaling deeply, as if she couldn't get enough oxygen.

Jim looked at her, upset, and placed the remaining slipper on her lap. Then he stood and gathered his things in silence.

"If you're okay, maybe we should go home," he said in a flat tone. "I can drive."

"Jim…"

Miren took a deep breath and tried to immobilize that internal guardian that unexpectedly leaped into action at the slightest show of affection, trying to defend her from a nonexistent enemy. She had fought this guardian many times in recent years, always in vain. He always won; he was always ready to inflict pain. He bared his fangs and claws like an abused dog that lashes out at any hand that tries to pet it.

"I'll get out at your door and take a taxi the rest of the way to my place. That way you won't have to drive home alone," Jim continued, more serious than usual.

It was still night when they left the room. Before they left, they paid the New Life Motel receptionist for the damages to the room. They walked some distance together, from Breezy Point to Roxbury where Miren's car was parked, maintaining an uncomfortable silence during which Miren wondered over and over what had happened to make Jim react so strongly. They got in the car, and it was two o'clock by the time they reached Miren's home in the West Village. They both got out of the car and Jim said goodbye with a simple:

"Let me know if you find out anything about Allison or Gina. You have my number."

"Jim, I—"

"You don't need to say anything, Miren. Maybe I don't know how to act the way you need. I don't know what you want from me. I don't know what I'm getting wrong with you. Maybe we're so different that it's impossible to… to do this. You know?"

She looked at him silently and nodded with a knot in her throat. Then she turned and climbed the stairs to her apartment, thinking that any second now she'd think of the right words. She looked back one last time, but Jim was already walking towards Hudson Street, where he could catch a taxi north.

As soon as Miren put her key in the front door of the building, a tear dropped from her eye to her hand, melting like a snowflake against her skin. She climbed the stairs to her apartment, panting, and as soon as she closed the door behind her, she released a stifled cry that no one heard except her. She broke down, sobbing, her back against the door, feeling like a little girl no one could ever love. She wondered why she was like that, asked herself if she had ever been okay in the head and felt so bad that she contemplated complete surrender, considered taking permanent refuge in the tempting, endless loneliness.

She felt like she would never understand the ever-growing hole inside her, like she would never be able to control the demon that always devoured any sign of love she received, like Saturn devouring his sons. For years now, that unexpected rage had led her to distance herself from everything she cared about, increasingly isolating herself inside an impenetrable inner fortress. Suddenly, a fire began growing inside her in the form of irreparable pain, clawing at her insides yet again, and she had no choice but to unwillingly return to the instant that beast penetrated her for the first time; to that night in the park, the pain between her legs; the dizzy sobs as she ran home, inconsolable and wounded; a scar that reopened every night she thought about what had happened. It had lodged in the deepest corner of her soul like an invisible thorn. She wailed.

Chapter 24
New York
April 25, 2011
One day earlier
Miren Triggs

No invisible thread is stronger
than the one that binds
you to a person who has done you harm.

The next morning, it was nearly noon when I woke up in my bedroom, my cell phone ringing by my ear. I'd had a horrible nightmare: I was in a dark room, aiming a gun at a sleeping man's head. I knew who he was. The calmness of his sleep disturbed me nearly as much as seeing how calmly I was holding the gun.

I looked at my phone and saw that it was Bob Wexter, from the newspaper. I answered without getting out of bed.

"Bob?"

"Miren, how's it going?" he asked. I could hear the din of the newsroom behind him.

"Good, good. Just getting started. The story is more complicated than I'd thought and… I haven't gotten much yet," I said by way of excuse. I really hadn't gotten far with Allison's story. "Yesterday I was in the Rockaways to dig a little deeper and I had... a mishap."

I touched my scalp and noticed how some of my hair was stuck to the dried blood from the gash on my head.

"What kind of mishap?"

"Someone... knocked me out on the beach with a rock. It was my fault... I shouldn't have gone out there alone."

"Sorry, what?"

"I don't know... This looks nasty, Bob. Later some kids shattered the window of our motel in the Rockaways with another rock."

"Our? And you were at a motel?"

"Yeah... I was with a friend... He found me unconscious on the beach and brought me to the motel. Then... well, the thing with the second rock happened."

"Shit... do you think it's someone who doesn't want you there? If this means putting you at risk, I want you to stop. It was hard enough getting the board to let me hire you. The last thing I need is bad news."

"I have a lead, Bob, it's just a little... tenuous. I don't know if it's something I can use to push the Allison story. But it's not looking good."

"What makes you say that?"

"So, there's a group of kids at the Mallow Institute, Allison's school, called the Ravens of God. It's a clique that seems to have its own rules. They're very secretive."

"The Ravens of God... After the way they found Allison Hernández... I think that's a thread you've got to pull on. But not if it's dangerous."

"I'll be fine, Bob."

"Do you think you could talk to any of the kids in this group?"

"I already have, but I didn't get far. They're pretty unwilling to talk. And another Mallow student—" I wanted to avoid naming Ethan Pebbles, so Bob wouldn't see that I was working on both stories at once, "—told me he'd seen Allison with some members of this group before she disappeared."

"I don't like this, Miren. Be very careful, please."

"I know, Bob. I'll try."

"And, hey, the clock is ticking."

"Isn't it always?"

I heard him give a little chuckle and, before saying goodbye, he added:

"The board asked me for a draft so they can get a sense of your new column's focus. Think you could have it for me by the end of tomorrow?"

"Bob—"

"I have no say in it, Miren. Write an article with what you've got, and we'll take it from there. You know I hate these deadlines, and that we used to spend months on every story back when we were on the investigative unit together, but… that was then, and this is now. We gotta move fast, even if we end up missing things."

I sighed.

"It's fine. I'll try to dig up something more. I'll go to the Mallow Institute today and try to talk to some of the kids, see if they'll spill on the Ravens."

"Be careful, Miren, okay? If you think you're in any kind of risky situation, drop it. We don't need it. I'll deal with the shirts upstairs. Okay?"

"That won't be necessary, Bob. I won't leave you high and dry. You fought for me and tomorrow you'll have your article."

"Thanks, Miren."

* * *

After hanging up, I jumped out of bed. I'd slept in the previous day's clothes and the bed was stained with dried blood. I stepped into the shower and let the water relax me. It was hot, and I could feel the steam rising as soon as it touched my skin. I filled my mouth with water from the showerhead and spat it out as soon I got a taste of New York's trademark quicklime flavor. Images from my nightmare filtered back into my memory: the anxious eyes of the man looking at me in the darkness; the cry of a child. Just then, someone knocked on my door.

"What time is it?" I wondered out loud as I stepped out of the shower and covered myself in a bath towel.

The person who had knocked on the door started ringing the bell. I nearly slipped on the tiled floor. I looked through the peephole to see who it was: it was just a fortysomething man in a suit and tie. He reminded me of the real estate agents I'd rented my apartment from, and maybe that's why I made the mistake of answering.

"Who is it?" I asked loudly so he could hear me through the door.

"Are you Miren Triggs?" he asked in a tone that suggested he already knew the answer.

"Who's asking?" I asked, watching him through the peephole.

He reached into his jacket pocket, and I felt a chill run down the back of my neck as he pulled out a badge.

"Agent Henry Kellet, NYPD. Do you have a minute to talk?"

"One second!" I cried. "I just got out of the shower!"

I ran to the closet and pulled on some underwear and a pair of jeans, but I couldn't find a top on any of my hangers. They must have all been in the wash. My hair was still soaking and dripped onto my shoulders. I searched for a bra, but there were none left in the drawer. While I was looking for something to cover me from the waist up, I saw the papers I'd taken from my storage unit on my desk.

The cop knocked again, and I felt like my heart was about to burst out of my chest.

"Shit," I cursed as I hurriedly threw the papers into the wastepaper basket.

"Miss Triggs? I just have a few questions," he called from the other side of the door.

I searched a few drawers—I still wasn't used to how I'd organized the apartment—and continued scouring until under my pillow I finally found a t-shirt with the Knicks logo that I sometimes wore to bed, and I quickly put it on.

"What do you want?" I asked as I opened the door nervously.

Now that I thought about it, this was the first time in the few months I'd been living in the West Village that anyone other than a delivery guy had knocked on my door.

"Miss Triggs? You are Miss Triggs, correct?"

"The one and only."

"I'm here because of a matter that I... I don't feel happy about, but I think it's important. My name is Agent Henry Kellet. This is... well, it's good news, I suppose. Last night... last night, a man living in Harlem killed himself. Shot himself in the head."

"I don't see what this has to do with me," I said, practically motionless.

"You see, Miss Triggs, it was a Mr. Aron Wallace, age 45." I remained still with a neutral expression as he continued: "He left a hand-written note in his house before blowing his brains out with a nine-millimeter Glock. In the note, he confessed to being one of several men who perpetrated a group rape in..." he hesitated and had to check something in a small folder he was carrying "...1997. I have the note, if you care to see it."

"I don't know... I don't know what you're talking about," I ventured, nervous.

"Do you mind if I come in?" Agent Kellet asked, nodding towards the apartment, as if he had to show me where to turn to find my own home. His interest had left me frozen in shock.

"Uh… I'm in a hurry," I said, hesitating. "I was about to leave."

"I can read it to you, if you like: 'I'm sorry for what I did to the girl in Morningside Park in 1997.'"

I remained immobile, waiting for the other shoe to drop.

"It's short, but clear. Aron Wallace seems to be confessing to having participated in the… assault you suffered, Miss Triggs. I'm sure you have tried to forget about it, Miss Triggs, but we… it's our job to remember. We've checked the details and his letter fits. When we put his name into the system… everything came up. You reported a case of sexual assault in 1997 and no one was ever sentenced. In your statement at the time, you alleged that three men in Morningside Park assaulted you. Only one of them was identified, Mr. Roy Jamison. The case came to a dead end because there was no evidence and the sole eyewitness withdrew his testimony. What you don't know is that we kept tabs on Jamison after he was released, to try to identify the others in the group and to see if he slipped up. We tapped his phone."

"This is all news to me," I lied. "That was so long ago and I… I've tried to turn the page. It's not exactly something you want to carry around with you."

"Well, Aron Wallace was identified as one of Roy Jamison's friends, and the two of them often went partying together, along with a third individual. We had this appended to his file along with… well, with a ton of misdemeanors, but this note… this note is confirmation."

"I can't say I'm not happy he's dead, if he confessed to it."

"Well… I guess you're right. It's a little sad, because… he took his life while his seven-year-old daughter was home. It was this morning—when the neighbors heard the girl's shrieks, they knocked on the door and found Aron's body on the living room floor and the little girl crying uncontrollably. There are suicides in this city every day, but… leaving a little girl behind… I don't know. It's a shame."

"Where's the mother?" I asked, taking an interest.

"It seems she died in childbirth. I imagine the girl will be processed by Child Protective Services and they'll place her with a foster family. Fortunately, she won't grow up near her father, but I'm sad for the girl. Some people are born to suffer, eh?"

I nodded.

"So, there's something else that may interest you, Miss Triggs. I'll tell you, since I'm here. It's the other reason I finally decided to come see you."

"What is it?"

"In 2002, Roy Jamison was murdered in an alley in Harlem, early in the morning. There were no witnesses. No one saw anything. We assumed that it was either a settling of scores or simple mugging. He was involved in all kinds of dirty business."

My heart was about to explode, and I felt a tingling in the tips of my fingers, as if I was remembering the reverberation of a gun after pulling the trigger.

"And here's the funny thing: he was also killed with a nine-millimeter Glock. It could be a coincidence—those things sell like hotcakes in this country—but still, it's a little striking, don't you think? We've ordered a bullet analysis, just in case. Protocols, protocols, protocols. That's how we do things. But, well, anyway, it's often thanks to those protocols that we end up catching the bad guys. And believe me. We always catch them. Sometimes it takes a while… but if someone has committed a crime, sooner or later we learn the truth," he said in a tone so serious that I struggled to remember his former friendliness.

"I'm sorry, Agent Kellet, but like I said, I really need to finish getting ready, I'm very short on time and I have to get to work."

"What kind of work do you do, if you don't mind me asking?"

"I'm a journalist. And you know what that world is like. The best stories are already fifteen minutes old. I don't suppose you have any anonymous tips for me?"

He returned a smile so phony I imagined he was about to pull out a pair of handcuffs.

"Nice try, but no."

I gave my own phony smile. Then I tried to get rid of him before he started snooping:

"Do you mind? Really, I'll be late."

"Of course, no problem, Miss Triggs. I just thought that… well, that you'd like to know that… two of the people we suspected back then… well, they're gone. And maybe… that'll be some comfort to you. Can I tell you something? I met my wife in a self-defense class she took after she was assaulted in a park. I know what she lives with, how she's constantly afraid when she's walking alone on the street, so I would understand if you felt the same way. People like that do irreparable damage. I thought that… well, that knowing those two men are no longer… might help you live a little more… peacefully."

"Thank you, officer."

"Can I ask you one last thing?" he said, in a tone that felt like a ticking timebomb.

"Of course, anything you like. It's nice to be the one answering questions for a change," I said with a fake laugh.

"What were you up to last night, Miss Triggs?" he inquired, very serious.

I smiled again, though I could tell he was expecting a real response. I don't know how long it took me to answer, though I'm willing to bet it was too long.

"I was here, sleeping. I came back from Queens around two in the morning. I was with a friend. You can talk to him."

"And what would your friend's name be? Like I said: protocols, protocols, protocols. I can't tell you how much paperwork I'll have to do. It's a little… chaotic."

"Um… yes, of course. His name is Jim Schmoer. He's a professor at Columbia. I can give you his number if you need it."

"No need. This is just… routine. It's also protocol for us to check to see if you have any registered weapons."

"Oh, is it?"

"I was relieved to see you don't. That saves me quite a bit of paperwork."

I smiled one last time and he said goodbye so coldly that, as soon as I shut the door, I remembered everything I'd done the previous night and it felt like the world was collapsing under my feet.

Chapter 25
Mallow Institute
April 25, 2011
One day earlier
Ben Miller

The devil is always hiding
where they can't find him.

Inspector Miller didn't know how to react when he read Allison's name in one of the Bibles in Father Graham's office. He read it over and over to confirm his eyes weren't deceiving him, that it wasn't his subconscious playing a trick on him. Questions flooded his mind, and he began eyeing every object in the office suspiciously. Could that Bible be the one he thought had been stolen from Allison's bedroom, along with the crucifix? Why did Father Graham have it? What was the meaning behind all the passages Allison had highlighted? Each question he asked himself seemed critically important and contributed to the dark shadow that seemed to loom over the priest.

He considered his options. He was alone. His discovery wouldn't amount to anything more than circumstantial evidence, and he knew it. There were a million reasons that Bible could've ended up in Father Graham's office. All of them legitimate, all of them honest. A thank-you gift she had signed for him, or even a Bible belonging to another Allison Hernández who had similar handwriting, though that was implausible since Ben knew there was no other Allison Hernández at the school.

He flipped back and forth through the passages, reading the notes and highlighted passages peppered across the pages. He was looking for something that might indicate the cause of Allison's concerns, or a pattern in the kind of verses she considered important. Ben stopped at the first such passage and, as soon as he read it, he felt that everything had taken a far darker turn than he'd initially imagined. It was a section from the Second Book of Kings, highlighted in blue. Chapter 6, verses 28 and 29:

> Then he asked her, "What's the matter?" She answered, "This woman said to me, 'Give up your son so we may eat him today, and tomorrow we'll eat my son.' So we cooked my son and ate him. The next day I said to her, 'Give up your son so we may eat him,' but she had hidden him."

Inspector Miller wasn't familiar with the Bible and had assumed it was a collection of texts praising a God he had already realized he didn't believe in. The closest he'd come to faith was the masses he'd attended when his son Daniel was declared dead, even though they had never found the body. At the time, it hurt him to see a priest saying prayers in front of an empty grave, asking God to welcome the soul of a nonexistent body. Nothing sounded falser to him than the verses Lisa had asked him to read.

He flipped through more pages until he found another highlighted section, which he read as quickly as he could—he could hear footsteps approaching in the hallway:

> Do not let her be like a stillborn infant coming from its mother's womb with its flesh half eaten away.

It was from the Book of Numbers. He didn't know if he should take the book or not. He tried to memorize the chapter and verse of every highlighted passage. The one about the half-eaten stillborn infant was easy to remember: 12:12. At the end of the Book of Revelation, chapter 12, he found another verse:

> *Its tail swept a third of the stars out of the sky and flung them to the earth. The dragon stood in front of the woman who was about to give birth, so that it might devour her child the moment he was born.*

But then, suddenly, Father Graham appeared in the doorway and, from there, raised his voice in a serious tone:

"Don't you know that rifling through someone else's belongings is a sin, Inspector? I believe that without a search warrant, it's a crime as well."

Miller looked up from the pages and waited for the priest to continue before deciding what to say. He needed more information. He had too many questions in his head, all unanswered. All waiting for him to find the link between the riddles that kept appearing before him, like an impossible puzzle of faith, loss and desperation.

"Although at this institution we abide by the laws and commandments of the Lord, we are also well aware of the laws of man and of our civil rights. But don't worry. I will turn a blind eye toward this… discourtesy. I understand that you're only trying to learn what happened to Allison, and I suppose what happened to Gina as well. I hope you succeed."

"You're right, Father. I'm not a very religious person and I've never… paid attention to what's in the Bible. I was just taking a look."

"And what do you believe our Scripture has to say?"

"I don't know. It talks about death and injustice. Half-eaten infants and mothers devouring their children. It's not a world I find very appealing, to be honest."

"But it's our world, Inspector, the one you and I share. And there are injustices, and there's pain and death. But the Lord came to deliver us from all that suffering."

"I'm at a point in my life where all I remember is suffering, Father. Seems like your God's not a great delivery man."

"Not here, Inspector. Here, we are damned. There's too much damage, too much sin. Here, we have no forgiveness. On the other side, perhaps, but there's no assurance that the gates of Heaven will open for any of us."

"Not even for you, huh?"

"For me least of all. I hear the sins of others and they devour me from inside."

Ben paused for a long second, trying to make sense of that last sentence, but the passages he'd just read had put him in such a frame of mind that all the priest's words seemed to spell was guilt.

"Why do you have Allison Hernández's Bible?" he asked suddenly, lifting the closed book so the priest could see.

"I'm sorry?" Father Graham replied in a tone that was somewhere between confusion and indifference.

"This is Allison's Bible," Ben said. "Why do you have it?"

"I don't know what you're talking about, Inspector. This is news to me. I don't scrutinize... the Bible I'm reading. All of them are equally valid. If that's hers, I suppose she must have left it here and I... mixed it up with my own things. As I said, my office door is always open to students. She came from time to time. She needed to talk. You must understand, she came from a complicated family."

"She came to have private talks with you too?"

"Yes, of course. All my students need guidance. And I'm always available to them. There is nothing worse than a lost sheep who can't find its way back to the flock."

Inspector Miller was uneasy. He couldn't understand how Allison's Bible had ended up in that office. He looked around, trying to think, then his eyes landed on a crucifix. Judging by the size, it could very well have been Allison's.

"And that crucifix? Is it yours?"

"That crucifix has been on the wall since the Mallow Institute opened its doors in 1987. And that's where it will remain for as long as I'm here."

"Do you have proof of that? It looks an awful lot like the one that disappeared from Allison's room, in her house. If you have her Bible—"

"Surely it doesn't fall to me to prove that my own crucifix has been hanging on my wall all these years?"

"I'm gonna be honest with you, Father. Something about this story doesn't sound right to me. But I can promise you one thing: if you or anyone at this school is behind what happened to Allison or Gina Pebbles, I'll find out, and I won't rest for a single second until I know what the hell made you do it."

"This is a religious school, Inspector. Here we cherish the sanctity of life above all else. And above all else we want the criminals behind all this to be found, but I would walk through fire before suggesting that anyone here laid a finger on Allison Hernández."

"Be careful, Father. You might get burned. And a burn like that leaves a scar."

"*And whosoever was not found written in the book of life was cast into the lake of fire,*" the priest said solemnly, reciting a verse from the Bible. "I don't fear fire. I fear that my name won't appear in the book of life."

"Now I understand why some of the passages Allison highlighted in her Bible are pretty… sinister."

"Sinister? There is no darkness in the Bible, Inspector. Every single verse can be understood as a beam of light for us to follow. It's only a matter of learning to read it properly."

Ben was confused, and tired of this endless back and forth. He decided to be direct.

"Were you and Allison close?" He asked, raising his voice. "What did you talk about when she came to see you? Did she talk about anything... anything that worried her?"

The priest sighed and sat back in his chair, defeated. Finally, he said:

"Okay. I'll tell you. But only so we can end this charade and you stop insinuating, time and again, that we had anything to do with what happened."

"Alright then."

"Over the last few weeks, she came to speak with me twice," he sighed. "The first time, she told me that she felt very lonely. And I think I understood. It was hard for her to make friends at Mallow. Ultimately, among new students... there's a clear difference between those who are on scholarship and those who are not, and though we do our best to ensure the students don't notice their different backgrounds, it's always a little hard for those on scholarship to... fit in. She had been studying here for a few years and... well, perhaps her classmates weren't the most welcoming to her."

"She was bullied?"

"I wouldn't say that. No. Her peers just... ignored her. Or, at least, that's what she told me. Teenagers can form very closed-off social groups, and they're reluctant to let new students into their cliques."

"I thought religion was supposed to be about helping the less fortunate and loving your neighbor and all that crap they say before they pass the collection basket."

"What we preach is one thing and what the students practice is quite another. Her situation worried me. Satan whispers in the ears of the lonely. So we decided to, how should I put it... require some students to let Allison join their group by assigning them all to work on the same class project."

"When was that?"

"That would've been… three weeks ago?"

"Who is in that group? Do you have the students' names?"

"Well, I wouldn't say there's exactly an official list. It's more… I don't know how to describe it: boys and girls who seem to have more… influence than their peers. I'm sure you understand. It happens at every school. So we try to surround the more vulnerable students with classmates with greater… social pull. This is how we create bonds that go beyond… well… something as filthy as money."

"Who are they specifically?"

"Well, let me see, there's Deborah, James, Ethan, Arthur—"

"Ethan Pebbles? Gina's brother?"

The priest nodded. Inspector Miller had found something both cases had in common, however tenuous that connection might be.

"And what did you talk about the second time? You said she came to see you twice."

"Inspector… this isn't easy for me to talk about. But I believe you must know the entire story."

"What is it?"

"The second time, Allison… came to my office and confessed that… that she was pregnant."

Chapter 26
New York
April 25, 2011
One day earlier
Jim Schmoer

*The only thing that connects you
to what's most important is love.*

Jim Schmoer tossed and turned all night, unable to stop thinking about what had happened with Miren. The harder he tried to decipher her, to understand her worries, the ins and outs of her soul, the more he doubted how he should act around her. It was strange, because he had always known how to behave naturally around women without having to try too hard, and he usually understood what they needed. He was genuinely charming and understanding, having grown up with two older twin sisters who always protected and pampered him as the miniature man of the house. Which is what he was. Jim's father, William Schmoer, had died in the Vietnam War in 1967, when Jim was just four, leaving him as the only male in the family, although in his home, gender made no difference except when it came to establishing who could use the bathroom first. His big sisters were his mentors, and he learned how to relate to women from them. The twins shared their own deepest secrets and worries with him for many years, and when he was twelve, they even taught him how to undo a bra which they'd filled with lemons.

But Miren was different. She was so secretive but at the same time so spontaneous, so mysterious... As soon as he'd arrived home that night, he'd thrown himself on the bed and tried to puzzle out whatever the hell was happening inside her head. His thoughts were interrupted at eight in the morning, when his alarm went off and he realized he was going to be late to class.

He showered, got dressed, and spent all morning telling his students about the free press and how vital it is to democracy. But as he lectured, some part of his mind was still immersed in the memory of Miren's eyes and the way she'd looked at him from that bed in the New Life Motel. He remembered the smell of her lips and her skin. He thought of the unmistakable aroma that had overwhelmed him as he'd kissed her: a subtle mix of saltwater, vanilla, and aloe. Maybe it was her shampoo, or maybe a perfume from some part of her neck.

He felt a flutter in his stomach when he thought about her and about what it meant to feel alive again. In recent years, he had immersed himself in teaching and in his podcast, in which he discussed current events, his own home-spun investigations, and news stories that flew under the radar. It kept his mind occupied so he wouldn't notice how empty and run-down his life had become.

His wife had left him in 1996, when their daughter Olivia was two years old. At first, he thought it would be temporary; a rough patch following a fling he'd had with a colleague at the *Herald*, where he worked at the time. He had regretted it, apologized, and promised to distance himself from the other woman. But the same day that Carol, his wife, came back home with Olivia in her arms, he'd accepted a promotion at the paper that would require him to work on the same team as his ex-lover. Though Jim hadn't cheated again, Carol couldn't live with the feeling that every time he left in the morning, he would share projects, articles and inside jokes with a woman he'd fucked. Two months later, after a row in which the distrust he'd sown in their relationship finally boiled over, Carol packed her bags. She had left for her mother's house, taking with her a tiny Olivia who was oblivious to the fact that her family had been torn apart by the lies of a purportedly truth-loving journalist.

Throughout the class, Jim felt empty. He spoke passionately to a set of students who only took notes out of fear the material would come up in the exam. He used several of his classic tricks for keeping the class's attention: he tore a newspaper to shreds to criticize its sensationalist writing, asked spontaneous questions about the nature of truth and its implications, and told anecdotes about the times he uncovered major pyramid schemes involving stamps or walnut trees. To his students' surprise, before dismissing the class, he posed a question:

"If a good journalist has to choose between publishing an unverified story or letting his mother starve to death, what color flowers should he buy for her grave?"

The class laughed, at least a little, and he left campus with Miren on his mind, debating whether or not he should try talking to her again.

He got home around noon and sat at his desk to review what he knew about Gina Pebbles and Allison Hernández. He had realized this was the other thing besides Miren that he couldn't get off his mind. He remembered the stone they'd thrown through the motel window and the conversation he'd had with Meghan and Christopher Pebbles. He also reflected on what Ethan had said to them. Everything seemed to revolve around God and religion. The cross on which Allison had been killed, the Pebbles' feverish devotion, the Mallow Institute and

Father Graham. Even the handle of the Twitter account that sent him the photo of Gina: @GodBlessTheTruth.

Jim thought he ought to try to build on what he knew about Gina, so he went over his notes from the previous day for a recap of what they'd learned from Ethan. Two names seemed to leap off the page, seemingly the only part of the story he could follow up: "Tom Rogers" and "James Cooper." The first was the boy Gina had been dating when she disappeared; the second was a boy from Mallow who seemed to know more about the Ravens than the rest of them. According to Ethan, James was very popular, but maybe that was precisely because he was a member of the Ravens, and everyone sensed it intuitively.

He sat at his computer and tried looking up Tom Rogers, hoping to find out if he had moved since Gina's disappearance, or if he still lived in the same old house in Neponsit that Gina had been walking to when she disappeared. Maybe if he could talk to Tom, he could learn what had been upsetting Gina and why, according to her brother, she had changed after enrolling at Mallow. He searched for Tom on Facebook, but it was useless: Tom Rogers was such a common name he'd be impossible to find. There were thousands of them online, spread across so many different parts of the planet that he seemed more like a virus than a person. They were all over Australia, New Zealand, the US, the UK, Germany, Denmark, South Africa, and even China, where it had apparently become fashionable to give children Western names so they would fit more easily into a globalized world.

He opened Google Street View and followed the path Gina would have taken in 2002, crossing the bridge with her brother until they parted ways on the other side. From there, Jim navigated towards Neponsit, continuing along Gina's most logical path down a bike route that led directly to Tom Rogers' street. The path skirted around the parking lot for Jacob Riis Park, a brick building that was part of the Fort Tilden complex, with esplanades and abandoned land and not much else. Once Jim was in Neponsit, he followed his virtual route, turning right and continuing straight to the end of the road until he reached his destination, the house where the Rogers family lived in 2002, on 149th street. It was a wood building with a green tile roof and cast-iron railings: the destination Gina never reached. She had disappeared somewhere along the way. Someone could have parked a van near the bike path, or even in the gigantic parking lot she would've walked past, and forced her inside. The strangest thing about Gina's case was the fact that her backpack had appeared on the beach in Breezy Point, which was in the opposite direction from the path Ethan had seen her walk along that fateful 2002 afternoon.

Jim thought of Miren again and entertained the idea of calling her. But it was complicated; he could wind up alienating her even more. Then, without knowing why, as he stared at Tom Roger's house on Google Street View, he remembered one of the maxims he always told himself when working on a story: *Go Return to the source.*

He stood up and walked up and down the apartment, thinking. Finally, he turned over the drawer of his desk to find his voice recorder, then groped around in his closet until he found his black backpack, the one he used to hide accounting documents leaked by administrators who wanted to report irregularities at their companies. He put the voice recorder, his black notebook, and a few pens in the backpack, along with some printed articles about Gina's disappearance. He planned to reconstruct her final movements, hoping this would help him make some progress. As soon as he pulled the straps over his shoulders, he felt the weight of an impossible undertaking.

He was nervous but, at the same time, excited. He thought maybe fate had sent Miren into his life to encourage him to return to his true path. Sometimes, you meet people along the way who help you stay true to yourself and, even though they may not stick around, you can still look back at them with gratitude. Jim loved teaching, but nothing made his heart flutter like knocking on a door, confronting someone caught off guard, and asking tough questions.

He went down to the street and entered the corner deli with a more serious expression than usual.

"The usual? Latte?" the Pakistani barista asked, reaching for a large carton.

"Yes, but no syrup."

"Diet?"

"No," Jim replied gravely. "I'm changing."

Chapter 27
Harlem
Early morning,
April 25, 2011
Miren Triggs

Nothing's more painful
than unwittingly plunging yourself
into an inescapable spiral of mistakes.

I'd forgotten how tempting it could be to feel like a threat. To know that no one can hurt you, like you're all covered in spikes. When you walk fearlessly down the streets of a city like New York, maybe you're the one people are afraid of. I'd left home with tears running down my cheeks, torn up because I was incapable of letting myself be loved. Part of me fought against any show of affection, but another part of me needed it just to stay sane.

My head still ached from getting hit by the rock. As I headed north, I didn't want to think about—or, really, I pretended not to know—where my long, decisive footsteps were taking me. I walked for over an hour, avoiding the main streets and crossing over whenever I saw an ATM whose camera might spot me. The whole way, I thought about my mother's words and my grandmother's newfound happiness, the way she had managed to rebuild her life despite years of physical abuse from the person who was supposed to love her.

My grandmother had become a kind of distant lighthouse across the bay, with a powerful light showing me the way forward. But there was one small yet obvious difference between us: my grandfather was dead, whereas my attackers—at least two of them—had taken root in my mind, sitting comfortably in an armchair made from my screams that night, eating popcorn as they watched the monster they created with their brutality destroy me from the inside. There was only one solution.

Before leaving home, gasping for breath through my own pained cries, I put on a black sweater and grabbed my pistol from my underwear drawer, the 9mm Glock I'd bought years before and never registered. The instant I picked it up, I knew this was a mistake. But it was one of those mistakes that's long overdue, the kind of mistake you put off until the crucial moment when you're forced to face it. Mistakes like that are inevitable, since just thinking about them changes you forever. I couldn't go on in this way. Either something had to give, or I was going to continue losing my battle with loneliness.

I was in tatters, but at the same time nervous and angry, filled with contradictory feelings because I also knew there was nothing left of the person I had once been: a happy, smiley, carefree young woman.

By the time I allowed myself to process what I was doing, I was at 60 and 123rd Street, staring at a red, three-story building. On the ground floor was a bodega called Best Grocery NYC. It was closed, and the door was secured with a black grate that I'm sure shrieked horribly every time they opened and closed it. There wasn't a soul in sight. A few cars cruised past at a calm, slow pace, confirming that, at that time of night, their drivers would rather be in bed. But I couldn't even think about sleeping.

I saw that on one side of the building there was a fire escape whose lowest ladder hung low enough for me to reach it easily and climb to the top floor. I stopped by the window and prayed it would be locked, thinking this might trigger the alarm that would tell me *Stop, Miren, leave it alone.* But when I pulled it up, I not only found that it was unlocked, but also that it gave me direct access to the bedroom in which a man was sleeping peacefully, not thinking about me or about what he'd done.

I slipped through the window and snuck through the shadows to the side of his bed. I watched him sleeping for a few seconds. He was well-shaven, with a snub nose that could have belonged to anyone. He was an absolute nobody, but he had transformed me into a nobody, too. He had turned me into an empty shell. He wore a tank top, and he was sleeping beneath a white sheet that looked like it'd be a pain in the ass to wash.

I drew my Glock and pointed it at his head. It could've been quick. I could have finished everything in a fraction of a second but, when I loaded the gun, the sound woke him. His eyes opened with such intensity that they looked like two eggs about to pop out of his eye sockets. He gasped and put his hands between the barrel of my gun and his own face, as if that would protect him.

"Hey, hey, hey!" he said, half-begging. "I got no money here. Please. There's nothing."

I hesitated. I waited too long and now I'd heard his voice. It was hoarse and vulnerable at the same time. I hadn't thought about how that might complicate things.

"Get up," I said, trying to mentally lower my heart rate. I kept the gun trained on him the entire time.

"Please just take whatever you want and leave... Please don't hurt me. I'm a working man, sister. I ain't got nothing fancy. Take the TV if you want. Or the microwave. It was fifty bucks. You can have it. But don't shoot."

"I didn't come here to rob you," I said. "I came because I want you to pay for what you did, because you can't keep your dick in your fucking pants."

His expression suddenly shifted from terror to sadness, and he seemed to feel some odd form of relief that I found disconcerting.

"Shit… Flaco sent you?"

"What?"

"I told him, I'll pay as soon as I got the money. I'm trying to sell. Tell him to gimme a week. Son of a bitch asks too much for pussy, last bitch wasn't even worth it."

I waited for him to continue. My whole body was gripped by an odd, unpleasant feeling of foreboding.

"And it don't cost him shit. Bitches just fall from the heavens and let him record 'em. Wish I had the same luck as that motherfucker. And everybody thinks he's a swell guy who takes care of the little skanks. Fucker has it all figured out. Tell him I'll pay up next week, all right? This week's been rough and I ain't sold no videos. My ex-wife's on my ass, makes it hard to find buyers."

"Who's Flaco? What videos are you talking about?" My own questions caught me by surprise.

"Shit… You're not working for him?" he replied, confused. He started grumbling and shaking his head as if he'd made a big mistake. But he had no idea how big.

"Who is Flaco and what are you talking about? Tell me now or I'll blow your fucking head off!" I shouted, shaking the Glock at him.

He let out a sigh and answered:

"Nobody, ain't nobody."

"Who the fuck is he and what are these videos?" I insisted in a tone that seemed calmer, even though I was about to explode.

He was silent for a long while. I took a step forward and pushed the barrel of the gun against his mouth.

"What are these videos you're talking about. This is the last time I'm gonna ask you."

He finally pointed with his eyes towards a blue zip-up DVD case in the bottom of a cupboard. On top was a hookah and several ash trays overflowing with cigarette butts. I reached for it without taking the gun off of Aron Wallace's face. I unzipped the case, nervous about what I was going to find inside. When I opened it, I saw around twenty DVDs, each in an individual envelope labeled in blue with feminine names. Three said Molly, two said Adriana, three said Jennifer, and five said Laura. They were organized by name, like some kind of pervert DJ's music collection.

"What is this?"

"Porn," he replied seriously.

"Just porn?"

He nodded, but I noticed an air of hesitation that prompted me to insist on my other question, the one he hadn't answered yet:

"Who's Flaco?"

"He's in charge of a center for..." he seemed unwilling to finish the sentence, but he didn't have to. I knew what he was going to say.

"Children?"

He nodded in silence.

"And these videos are of girls from that center?"

He nodded again and goosebumps ran all along my body, like my will for revenge was whispering to me.

"What's the place called?"

"It's called... the Happiness Shelter. But I don't have anything to do with it. I... sell what he gives me. I gotta earn a living. I could sell drugs, but this doesn't hurt anybody."

"Doesn't hurt anybody? What the fuck is wrong with your head that you would... destroy underaged girls' lives like that?"

"Destroy their lives? They're the ones who need money.

He just… offers them alternatives. These are girls who have nothing. He… provides. He gives them a future."

"They're children, you fucking degenerate! People like you really never change, huh? Once you try something you just can't stop yourself." I lifted the gun and clutched it hard. "You people are sick and there's no fucking cure. You rot everything you touch, and the problem is there's no way to get you to stop putting your hands on everything. Girls, children… or college kids who make the mistake of trusting the wrong person and end up defenseless and alone in Morningside Park, where a group of three sickos have their way with her."

"What?" he said, as if I'd unveiled one of his darkest secrets, something he thought was long forgotten.

"Don't remember me, you sick fuck?"

"You? You're…" he hesitated, confused. "That was… How did you…?"

"Get me a paper."

"What?"

"Get a piece of paper, now!"

"Why?"

"Do you know how to write? Get a piece of paper and write down what I'm about to say to you." I gestured at him with my weapon.

I followed him out of the bedroom to another, larger space. Squinting in the faint light, I could tell it served as both kitchen and living room. He rifled through a basket on the kitchen counter and tore off a piece of an electric bill. Nervously, he turned on a lamp that cast just enough light for me to see the disgusting condition the apartment was in: the arms of the couch were torn, the sink was stacked high with days-old dirty dishes, and the wood on the TV stand was warping from the humidity. He found a Bic pen in the fruit bowl and bent over the paper.

"Write: 'I'm sorry.'"

"What?"

"I said write! 'I'm sorry… for what I did… to the girl in Morningside Park in… 1997.'"

He stopped and began to sob. First, he moaned, and then he fell forward, defeated. I watched him, confused, as he collapsed over the kitchen counter. I hadn't expected this, and I didn't know what to do.

"I'm… I'm sorry," he finally whispered.

"No you aren't! You have no idea how much… how badly you broke me that night. You, Roy… and—"

"I have… I have a daughter," he sobbed.

"What?"

"Her name is Claudia. She's asleep in her bedroom. Please, don't shoot. She'll be left with no one."

"You're lying."

He exhaled hard. I couldn't tell if it was from the guilt or from fear.

"I'm… I'm sorry," he said again.

"Stop!" I shouted. "That's not how this works, got it?" I got ready to shoot.

"What are you going to do?! Please, don't… Claudia… Please… I'm changing. I promise I won't—"

"Won't what? Assault more defenseless girls? Do you really think you have the right to make that kind of promise, like it's no big deal? What kind of world would this be if everything was forgiven with a simple *I'm sorry*?" I realized I was crying too and that the tears were slipping down my cheeks as if my soul were seeping out from the depths of my fears. "I won't carry you around inside me anymore. Got it? I can't! Every time I close my eyes, it's the three of you there, smiling in the dark. No matter how many years pass, no matter how hard I try to forget. Every time. And now I don't know how to feel. I don't remember what it's like to feel protected, because I close my eyes and I see the three of you. I can't even smile without thinking I'm sharing that emotion with you. And I don't have anything in common with you, not even my pitiful and lifeless attempt at being happy. All we share is the moment you came into my life by force, and now you never, ever leave, not even when I'm sleeping."

I stopped talking. He looked at me in utter terror. I could feel his fear. And I'll be honest, I liked it.

He was crying. Both of us were, but it wasn't the same kind of crying. My tears were tears of impotence; his were tears of guilt. Those sorts of tears could lead him down a one-way road; all I'd have to do is push.

"Do you really have a daughter?" I asked in a low voice, almost unable to speak.

He nodded, looking at the floor.

"How old is she?"

"Seven." He was struggling even to speak.

"And do you think you're a good role model for her? Do you think she'll be proud of you when she finds out what you really are?"

He looked up at me, as if he feared that reality more than he feared the gun I was holding.

"Because she's going to find out. And she might not understand right now, but sooner or later she will. When she's thirteen, fourteen, twenty years old. Someone will tell her or remind her about the videos. What difference does it make if she understands now or later? At some point she'll see you for what you really were and then she'll wish she could forget you, just like I do. She'll cry at night and wish she had never been born. And she and I will share that feeling of disgust, repugnance and hate. And even though we won't know each other, together we'll curse the bad luck of ever having met you."

"She can't find out about... all this. Please..." he begged. "She doesn't deserve this..."

"You have two choices, Aron. I can shoot you and all of this will be over. I'll take those videos, I'll give them to the police, and your daughter will learn that you've always been a monster. Or I can give you this gun and leave your apartment, and you can put an end to things yourself. If you do your part, I'll burn the DVDs and your daughter will never find out about what you did to those girls from the shelter. But if you don't keep your promise, tomorrow the cops will have all the evidence they need."

"But—"

"One way or another, Aron, this is where everything ends for you. But you get to decide how your story gets told. Which version would you rather your daughter hear? The one about the monster, or the one about the father who lost his battle with depression?"

He turned towards the door he'd pointed at when he said he had a daughter and, for a second, I thought he'd tricked me. He was crying more intensely than before, but I felt no remorse. Then he looked back at me in silence and collapsed beside the door.

"Promise me you'll keep your promise," he whispered hoarsely.

I took that to mean he'd chosen the only path that would keep his daughter in the dark about who he really was. I nodded.

I grabbed the note he'd written and put it in my pocket, then wiped off the Glock, unloaded it and left it on the table. So I'd have time to leave before he loaded the gun, I threw the magazine at his feet. Then I walked into the bedroom, grabbed the videos, and before leaving through the window, I looked back and saw him gazing at the gun and stroking the grip, drowning in tears from all the horrible decisions that had led him to that point.

I climbed down the fire escape and felt the cold New York air on my face. I waited for one long, silent minute, thinking maybe I'd made a mistake by giving him the chance to pack his bags and disappear. But then there was the sudden sound of a gunshot reverberating from inside the apartment. The gun was louder than I'd remembered and, in the silence of the night, it struck me as a roar that marked the beginning of the countdown for me to get the hell out of there.

But I went back. I couldn't forget what I was there for. I peeked into the living room and saw him on the ground, a puddle of blood growing around his skull. He'd done it. I looked at his body with indifference and pulled the note from my pocket. I reread it sadly, knowing the words weren't sincere; he'd only written them because there was a gun to his head. I left it on the table and read it one more time, because it said exactly what I needed to hear. I also left the DVDs. He was dead, I had no reason to keep my word. It would help the police learn what was happening at that shelter. I heard the little girl's voice from within her bedroom, and ran off before she came out.

I thought about my grandmother. I don't know why. Maybe because I was clinging to this idea about liberating myself from my past. What I didn't know was that all these irreversible mistakes were determining my future.

Chapter 28
Mallow Institute
April 25, 2011
One day earlier
Ben Miller

Abandoning something
that is wilting isn't reasonable,
it's cowardice.

B en Miller felt a chill run down his spine when he heard Father Graham say Allison was pregnant. At that moment, the image of Allison on the cross flashed before his eyes and he fell silent; for a few seconds, he was unable to speak. This fact made her death seem that much more atrocious, and the way this priest wanted to just turn the page was sickening. Ben hadn't yet received Allison's autopsy report, from which he would have learned this information, and Father Graham's words hit him like a ton of bricks.

"What did you say?"

"I hate sharing this information with you, Inspector, knowing how all of this ended," Father Graham replied. "But I think it's important for you to know. Perhaps it will be of some help."

"She was pregnant? You're sure?"

"Let me explain. One day, a week before she disappeared, Allison came to me, sat in that chair, and… told me everything. I was even more surprised at that time than you are now, I assure you. We'd given her so many opportunities… we'd made a real effort to shape her as a good… Christian. And worst of all, she told me she was unsure who the father was."

"Why the hell didn't you tell me this when you reported her disappearance? I interviewed you and you didn't say a word about it."

"Inspector… even if you don't believe in him, only God can know a confessor's sins. She placed her trust in me by saying this. And I gave her penance: she was to leave Mallow as soon as it became impossible to conceal her condition from the other students. I made a point of not expelling her on the spot so she might still advance a bit in her studies. I assure you that I only wanted the best for Allison, and she tearfully accepted my decision. She swore that no one would find out and that, when the time came, she would relinquish her place in the school and her scholarship without making a scene. It was the best course of action for her and for the school. With this solution, no one here would have to learn of her sinful state. I offered to let her return to complete her high school degree in the afternoons as soon as she'd had the baby. I do believe I was quite understanding."

"Wouldn't it have been easier for her to just get an abortion and keep studying?"

"That does indeed seem to be the world we are creating, Inspector. A world that prioritizes pleasure, ignores consequences, and terminates life without a second thought. Heavens, no. Here at Mallow, we take it upon ourselves to uphold the only thing that makes us human: we do not destroy one another. What would come of humanity if we simply disposed of everything that was inconvenient? While we're at it, perhaps

216

we should murder the homeless? Or the elderly? If something we have created is a problem, why, let's just get rid of it. Is that your idea? Let me tell you something, the only one who can create and end life is God, and he is the one who decides when."

"She asked for your permission, then?" Ben exhaled.

"I beg your pardon?"

"She asked for your help and for permission to get an abortion. That's what she came to see you for. Her family is poor. She couldn't pay for one herself. And... she trusted you."

"I don't understand what you're talking about," the priest replied.

"That's why Allison highlighted all those passages in that Bible," Miller continued. "To show you that the Bible also talks about babies being born dead or mothers who devour their children."

"Inspector, do not come here to lecture me on the text I've read more than any other in my life. I will say this once and I hope I have no cause to repeat it: at this institution, we cherish life. And Allison—"

"That's why she told you she was pregnant. She trusted you and... and you abandoned her. You expelled her."

"She was not a good model for the other students. You must understand. We are understanding here, but... some things cannot be tolerated."

"And everything you've told me about forgiveness?"

"Oh, we forgave her. Don't misunderstand me. But... when you cross certain lines, not even God can protect you. You see..." he paused. "This isn't easy to say. But Allison had an emotional problem and perhaps that's how... she became with child. She was looking for attention, as it were."

"And you expelled her."

"Don't put words in my mouth, Inspector. She left of her own free will. It's not a crime to protect our institution's integrity and reputation. And please," he added, standing up, "if you don't mind, I have a Mass to celebrate. I've already lost too much time on this. Please, leave the way you came in. Don't come to our house to question our faith. At Mallow, we care for our students. And I have always had an open-door policy about everything that happens here. That was our approach when Gina went missing, and that is our approach now. Don't blame us for having bad luck. Because every single one of us was, is and will be disgraced, somehow or other. It's only a matter of when and how."

Indignant, Ben turned towards the door, but before leaving he stopped in the doorframe and turned back to Father Graham.

"It may not be a crime to expel a pregnant student, Father, but I have no doubt that your God and your religion are behind what happened," he said, angry. The crucifix on the wall shuddered as he slammed the door.

Chapter 29
The Rockaways
April 25, 2011
One day earlier
Jim Schmoer

*Life consists of repeating the same
mistakes until there's no time left
to make them anymore.*

Professor Schmoer felt strangely nervous as his taxi began crossing the Marine Parkway Bridge towards the Rockaways. He had asked the driver to leave him in front of the large esplanade adjacent to Fort Tilden, which had long ago been swallowed up under vegetation and vandalism, just as the Fort had swallowed up Gina Pebbles. When he got out, he exhaled loudly, thinking how, in one of the abandoned chambers of that old miliary complex, Allison Hernández had come to such a cruel end. It was a fenced-in area that consisted of around twenty concrete and rusted iron buildings. In the not-too-distant past, these buildings had been a hive of military activity and combat training. But now the fort was overrun by weeds, crushed beer cans and spray paint.

He scrutinized the area from Rockaway Boulevard and in the distance saw the bridge where Ethan had said goodbye to his sister in 2002. Then he walked to the bike lane, in the direction the boy had seen her walking. Jim looked around with concern. The place was deserted. No one was walking around, and it looked like no one had been through there in quite some time. At least not at that time of day. There were a dozen cars in the parking lot near Jacob Riis Park, and maybe twenty or so campers. Jim took a photo with his phone, then started walking towards them.

By the look of it, some of the campers had settled in that place permanently—they had even stretched out canopies and clothes lines. Near one of these vehicles was an older man, perhaps around sixty years old, with long gray hair; he was sitting in a folding chair, his shirt unbuttoned, soaking up the sun.

"Hi," Jim called out, giving a half smile. "Do you live here?"

"What's it look like to you?" the man replied with a southern accent. "With prices in the city and all, you think folks my age can afford to live across the bridge?"

"Yeah... The cost of apartments has really skyrocketed. It's crazy," Jim agreed.

"Anyways, if you came to sell me something, I think I've given you enough hints that I ain't got much to give. Try in Neponsit. Folks there got cash and they'll buy whatever you're selling. Me... I'm just a retired old man who likes the smell of the ocean. Reminds me of being a kid and... of happier times."

"Have you been living in your camper here for long?"

"Oh boy," he guffawed. "Maybe fifteen years? Since my woman died. Didn't make sense to keep living in that house. Kept seeing her in every corner, reminded me too much of the good times."

"That's a long time to be living out of a camper," Jim empathized, his face serious. "Your wife must have passed away very young."

"At fifty. Sudden stroke in the shower. Since then, this life can fuck off, as far as I'm concerned. I sold the house and bought me this camper. I was by the Grand Canyon a while. Then Yosemite a few months. Pretty spots and all, but horrible for sleeping in a camper. You get all swallowed up in the loneliness. The sound of the bears gives you chills. Later on, when I was driving along the coast, I saw some kids surfing and set up shop here without missing a beat. Bought myself a board to remind me of the old times and… here I am. I'm a little old to stand up on the board now, but I'm still a sea wolf, eh? Learned to surf in the seventies, y'know? Why back then—"

Jim decided to change the direction of the conversation. Otherwise, the man was likely to spend hours recounting one memory after another.

"My name is Jim Schmoer, it's nice to meet you," he said at the earliest opportunity.

"Marvin," said the old man, without giving his last name.

"Did you already live here in June 2002?" Jim asked, trying to guide the conversation.

"Oh yeah. Of course. Like I said, I been here… fifteen years. Yup. Not many of us left from that era. Folks tend to come, spend the weekend, then leave again. Not too many like to live in the caravan all year round. It ain't easy, you know? Filling the tank with water, pumping out the shit tank, taking care of the hot water and getting gas for the generator. Though that's only if you need light at night, of course."

"Do you remember when that girl disappeared?" Jim interrupted again, still trying to stay on topic. "Gina Pebbles. I'm sure everyone around here was talking about it."

"Ah… Of course I remember. I'd already been here a few years by that point. What a tragedy. I even helped in the search parties, ya know? Made me feel bad about seeing her that day so… sad. She was a good girl. You could tell in the way she talked."

"You saw her on the day she disappeared?" Jim asked, incredulous.

"Oh, of course, of course. Sometimes she'd come over to have a gander at my paintings. It was an intense summer and her going missing meant they had to cancel a bunch of the concerts and exhibitions scheduled for the park area. Nothing professional, don't get me wrong. But it wasn't all bad. I managed to exhibit some of my paintings as part of the program of summer cultural activities. All right with me, surfing and painting. Don't got the energy for none of it now. Like I was saying, I had 'em up beside the camper, and sometimes she'd come and have a look. One time she told me how she liked the way I painted waves in the sea."

"You two would talk?"

"I'm a sociable type. I like connecting with people. Makes me feel... alive."

"Yeah, I can see that."

"Then... I stopped. Painting, I mean. I got tired of all those brats wandering through here laughing at me. She... she was different though. Sometimes she'd come by and say hello. It's hard to find polite folks these days, you know? Everyone's suspicious of each other, like our neighbor is a murderer or something. In my day, we'd play in the street and our parents only worried about us washing our hands before supper. Nowadays... no one even says howdy. We're all afraid. The world's gone to shit, you know that? And, well... young folks don't have no respect for their elders. I'd even swear they'd rather we were dead. Save themselves a few tax dollars. That's what we are. A burden. My generation always thought about making things better for the next, but it seems like now they wouldn't lift a finger to protect us. We're going from bad to worse, I got no doubt."

"What did Gina say to you that day?"

"That day I didn't get to talk to her. I'd already left the camper to empty the tank over yonder," he said, pointing to the mouth of a storm drain a hundred yards or so away, beside the road. But I'm sure it was her. When I got back, I saw her heading toward Neponsit."

"How do you know she was sad?"

"Seemed to me she was crying. She was drying her tears. A gesture you can see from far off."

"And you told all this to the police?"

"Of course, of course. Except I don't think they paid me much mind. I admit back then I… I drank and smoked a good deal of reefer."

"Marijuana?" Jim asked.

"I haven't always been the doddering old fool I am now. I had my fun, you know? Maybe that's why the police didn't listen to me. Later they found her backpack in Breezy Point Tip, just at the other end of the Rockaways, on the beach, in the opposite direction of where I saw her walk off, but they never asked me anything about it again."

"I understand. Things are never… easy. Several agents are always in charge of these cases and each one has different priorities, and sometimes details get lost in the bureaucracy."

"You looking for her?"

Jim nodded in silence. Then he continued:

"Can I ask you a favor?"

"Course. We're here to help one another, aren't we?"

"Would you mind if I saw the inside of your camper?" he asked, after remembering the polaroid of Gina gagged in what seemed to be the inside of a truck.

"What for?"

"I liked hearing about your trips. It seems like a nice way to travel, I might want to buy one," he said in a tone that he himself didn't believe.

"Hell, great! It's a complicated life, I ain't gonna deny it. But the freedom you get… it's like no other. Best years of my life were with my wife. But the camper here has taken good care of me. Go on in, be my guest. She's getting a little up there in years, but she's got her charm. There's more modern models out there, with hidden beds that come down when you press a button, but there's something about this baby that those newer ones just don't got."

"Are the walls white on the inside?" Jim asked with interest.

"Go on in and see for yourself. Be my guest. Not too tidy though, I'm sorry."

The man waved him into the vehicle, and Jim followed his invitation.

But the instant Jim put a foot inside, he heard the sound of a gun loading behind his back and the old man's voice:

"Who're you tryina' fool, fella? Get the fuck outta there if you don't want a hole in the head."

Chapter 30
New York
April 25, 2011
One day earlier
Miren Triggs

The only rule in the soul game
is don't play if you can't afford to lose.

After Agent Henry Kellet's visit, I thought maybe leaving the suicide note had been a mistake. I'd decided to leave it on a thoughtless impulse, in an attempt to signal to the cops that I never lied or made anything up. I will never forget the look on the faces of the two agents who took my statement at the police station the morning after. I remember their hurtful questions, their incredulous gazes:

"And where did you say this was?" a very serious blonde, middle-aged cop had said back then, from behind a typewriter.

"Morningside Park. I went there with a guy I'd met... with Christopher. His name is Christopher. I was sure that... and... three men showed up. I... I don't remember real well."

His fellow officer was standing behind him, drinking coffee from a disposable cup. There was a scrutinizing look on his face, as if he were watching a street performer and deciding whether to throw a few dollars his way. I felt like a circus monkey reporting a rape.

"Had you had anything to drink, miss?" asked the cop behind the typewriter, shaking his head.

"Uh... I'd had one drink, but... I think... it didn't sit well with me."

I stopped talking as soon as I saw the cops exchange a complicit gaze, I could practically see them laughing internally. One of them even snorted as he asked:

"Do you often... go with men to the park in the middle of the night?"

"Well, I..."

"Do you remember anything that'll help us get started? A face, a name. Where does this... Christopher live? We'll need to get a statement from him. Give us something we can use to... find whoever assaulted you."

They gave each other that look again. I could feel their disdain. And I started crying. There was pain between my legs, and on my knees, and on the bottoms of my feet from running barefoot, fleeing without looking back. The strength and certainty I'd felt when I walked into the station had dissolved in the waters of their asphyxiating disbelief.

"Hey... don't worry," said the one behind the typewriter. "We'll open a file and... we'll send a unit to review the area, cameras and all that. If what you say is true, we'll get to the bottom of it. Do you have a doctor's report?"

I shook my head between tears.

"Did you take a shower before making your report?"

I nodded. They looked at each other again. As if trying to cleanse myself of all that filth, of the blood and of... what was left of their rot was a worse crime than rape.

Later, I learned the reason for that question: they wanted to collect a sample of the attackers' DNA, but I remember how miserable they made me feel for showering, as if it were my fault those men got away. Leaving the suicide note was my way of telling the cops: "You were pathetic."

* * *

I changed clothes and took two bites of a Sun-Maid cinnamon roll, the kind they sell in those sliced bread sleeves to make them look healthy. I got in the car and summoned all the courage I had to call Inspector Miller. It had been his suggestion, but the time had come to tell him about the polaroid of Gina. A few seconds later, through the car's speakers, I could hear his voice as he picked up the phone in a relatively chipper tone.

"Miren, is that you?"

"Ben, I have something. Can we meet up somewhere?" I asked, by way of hello.

"It's nice to hear from you. I saw all the success your book is having. You deserve it."

"Thanks," I said, quickly dismissing the congratulations. "But can we meet?"

"I'm, uh… not in Manhattan. I can't right now."

"When can you?"

"I'm in Queens. Reviewing an old case. I don't know if you heard, but they found the body of… Allison Hernández. It's horrible. You don't want to know how they found her. Thank God the press didn't get hold of too many details. They would've had a field day."

"They found her crucified, right? The *Press* was considering running the story, but I think they decided not to give too much detail until it was confirmed. I'm working on an article about it, though I don't know what to think."

"I can't tell you anything, Miren. It's an open investigation and any detail—"

"That's not what I called about."

"What is it, then?"

"I have something I think you'd be better off seeing in person. Where are you?"

"Just leaving the Mallow Institute. I have a bad feeling about this place. Allison studied here."

When I heard the name of the school, I intuited we were both unknowingly following the same trail. I didn't know if I should take a chance and tell him everything or if I should wait to see him in person.

"There was another girl who disappeared in 2002—" he continued, confirming my theory that we had reached the same conclusion.

"Gina Pebbles," I interrupted.

"You remember her, right? I guess you've found the same link I have: Mallow."

"That's why I called, Ben. It's important, and… I think there's new evidence. Someone gave me a photo of Gina."

"What are you talking about? A photo of her how?"

"Wait for me where you are, will you? Better for you to see it yourself."

Chapter 31
Neponsit
April 25, 2011
One day earlier
Jim Schmoer

Not all loners are crazy, but
all who wander in madness feel alone.

Professor Schmoer turned around and saw the barrel of a Colt pointing at his head.

"Get out now, or I'll shoot."

"Hey, hey. I just wanted to see the inside of your camper," Jim cried, nervous about taking a false step.

"What for? What're you looking for?"

"Gina Pebbles."

"Didn't I just tell you I was looking for her myself? What is it? You think just because I live in a camper, I'm some pervert who'd do that to a poor girl?"

"You're alone. Loneliness can be very unnerving... I just wanted to... be sure. You were here when she disappeared. I needed to see the inside of your camper to rule it out."

"Not everyone who's alone is crazy, you know that? I like being alone, surfing. I want to die near the sea. You don't got the right to come here and… insinuate I did something to that poor girl."

"Would you put down the gun? It was a mistake. I'm sorry. But please don't shoot."

The old man hesitated for a few seconds before finally lowering the weapon. But he didn't hesitate to fire off the sentence that left Jim destroyed on the inside.

"I'd rather live the whole of the rest of my life alone than lose someone else. I lost my wife. I chose this lonely life because I didn't want to suffer like that again. Call me a coward if you like. But I would never lay a hand on a teenager. Especially not someone like her."

"I understand. Please accept my apology—" Jim implored one last time, even as his heart was thundering in his chest.

"Now get the hell out of my sight."

Jim walked as quickly as he could away from the camper and out of the parking lot, with a large knot in his throat that made it hard to breathe. He continued to Neponsit on the bike lane that skirted the Jacob Riis Recreational Center. Jim had just had a gun pointed at him for the first time, and it wasn't an experience he hoped to repeat. When he reached the residential area of Neponsit, he turned to the right on 149th St., following the shortest route Gina could have followed the day she disappeared after saying goodbye to her brother. As he walked towards the Rogers' house, at the end of the street, he noticed that all the houses were elegant wooden homes, recently painted. It seemed to be a well-to-do area, based on the well-maintained gardens, the amount of space between the houses, and the high-end cars parked outside the garages. It was a far cry from Roxbury, just a few miles away. If the Pebbles' home was lost in a labyrinth of streets and alleys, the Rogers' residence shone bright at the end of the street, with a beautiful porch, Victorian columns, wrought-iron railings, a green roof and a covered garage at the end of an asphalt driveway, with an impressive wooden front door.

From there, as he climbed the stairs to ring the doorbell, the professor noticed that the ocean was so close, it felt like a wave was about to break on him. The house was a mere twenty meters from the Rockaway Beach access point, and the wind was heavy with a salty smell that brought him back to the moment he found Miren unconscious on the beach. He wondered how she was doing and if he ought to call her. He hoped she'd recovered from the head injury. There was no doubt that for Jim, Miren had become a person so complex and incompatible with how she seemed at first that the two of them couldn't even have a conversation that didn't end in a draining argument. But at the same time, she was so enigmatic he couldn't get her out of his head. She was like an impossible puzzle, full of riddles, hiding places and secrets, one which he felt that one day he might be capable of solving.

He knocked and waited. A few seconds later, a tanned, well-shaven twentysomething opened the door, looking confused. He was wearing jeans and a white polo shirt; after the initial expression of surprise at this stranger at his door, his mouth stretched into a smile.

"Hi, can I help you?" he greeted Jim, interested and expectant.

"May I... speak to Tom Rogers, please?"

Jim mentally calculated how old Tom Rogers ought to be by now and considered that it could be the young man in front of him.

"That's me. Has something happened? What do you need?"

"Hi, Tom. So, my name is Jim Schmoer, I'm a freelance investigative journalist. I'm researching the case of a girl who disappeared here in 2002. I'm sure you know who I'm talking about."

Instantly, Tom's smile faded into an expression of concern, and he tried to close the door with a sad gesture, but Jim blocked it with his foot.

"Please, Tom. It's important. I'm sure it was incredibly difficult for you and that's why I'm asking for you to help me find her. Honestly, it'll be five minutes, that's it."

"I don't want to go back to all that, you know? I tried to turn the page. It took me a long time to put my life back together. I'm finishing a master's in film now and I want to leave all that behind. As soon as I finish my degree I'm moving to LA."

"They found the body of a girl Gina's age at Fort Tilden, not far from here."

Tom released the door, looking surprised again. The news seemed to affect him emotionally.

"Gina? Is it Gina?" he asked, almost collapsing.

"No, no, it's another girl who disappeared last week. They found her body in one of the abandoned areas of the old military installation there. Her name was Allison Hernández. She studied at Mallow too, like Gina."

"Fuck… is that why there have been so many cop cars driving down Rockaway the past few days?"

"Are you able to talk? I'm trying to reconstruct everything that happened in that case so we can figure out if… the same thing could have happened to Gina."

"I don't think that—"

"Allison Hernández studied at Mallow, like Gina." Jim paused and then continued: "Tom… I know that this is the last thing in the world you want to talk about, but maybe we'll be able to figure out who kidnapped Gina and what happened to her."

Tom swallowed hard and agreed.

"Okay, come in."

"Is it just you here?" Jim asked, once they were sitting in the living room.

"My dad's in the garage building furniture. He's a good handyman, he's making a desk for my room."

"Wow. The only piece of furniture I ever built was a Billy bookshelf from Ikea."

232

Tom smiled, but it didn't last long.

"He likes working with wood. He made himself a workshop in the garage, and he spends all day there. See those shelves? He made them. The window frames too. Grandma is in her room watching TV. Nothing gets between her and that TV."

"I guess we all get a little obsessive when we get old, trying to find ways to make ourselves more comfortable. If it makes you feel better, my father is scared to leave the house during the day," Jim said.

"Maybe one day we'll all be afraid to leave the house. It doesn't seem safe outside, after what happened to Gina." Tom paused for a long moment, then added: "Sorry, do you want anything to drink?"

"That's okay, Tom. Thank you. I'll try to be quick, so I don't take up too much of your time. Do you mind if I record our conversation? That way things will go faster."

"Sure. What do you want to know?"

"I want you to tell me what your relationship with Gina was like. What happened the day she disappeared."

"I already told the police all that. This—"

"I know, Tom. I'm just trying to piece together the steps she took that day. Maybe now, after the time that has passed, your memory will bring back some pertinent detail that will help us understand what happened."

"All right," Tom said. "It's been a long time since she… vanished. And it left me… totally destroyed, you know?"

"The two of you were going out, right?"

"Yeah. Gina and I… we were really good together. She started part way through the school year, and I remember how we liked each other from day one. I still remember how she looked at me that first time, when the teacher was introducing her. Then I offered to let her sit with me and showed her around the school. I don't know if you've seen a picture of her, but she was really beautiful. She had this upturned nose and really round cheeks, pale skin, and… I couldn't even tell you. I really liked her. Now that I think about it, it's been a long time since… Maybe I liked her nose because it reminded me of my mom's. Her parents died right before she came to Mallow, and she and her brother Ethan were adopted by their aunt and uncle. Ethan was… eight back then, if I remember right. I liked him. I went over to their house a few times and we played video games. I think he liked me, too."

"He told me that he got along well with you."

"Yeah, sure. But I mean it's not like I saw him a ton of times before Gina… when we started going out, Gina and I didn't want anyone to know we were together. In class we sat next to each other, but only like classmates, and we only really saw each other at her house or mine. Sometimes we went to Breezy Point Tip, at the far end of the beach, so we could be alone and talk. At first, since she said her aunt and uncle were really religious and they'd disapprove of her seeing anyone, we'd always meet up to do school assignments at her place or here. Or if we went to a park together, we'd make sure no one we knew was there. We shared a traumatic past and I think that brought us even closer together."

"What was that?"

"My mom died when I was really little, too. Nothing brings people together like pain, right? The problem was we were making out in her house one afternoon when her aunt caught us. She turned into, like, a demon, and threw me out of the house, furious. She called me a rapist. She kept saying horrible things to me and said I'd never see Gina again."

"When did this happen?"

"A few months before… she left."

"You think she ran away?"

"I've always thought she might have. Gina couldn't stand her aunt and uncle. If she stayed with them, it was just because she was taking care of her brother and she didn't have any-where else to go. But maybe something happened with them that she never told me about and that's why she left."

"In the missing person's report, it says Gina was going to your house the last time she was seen. Ethan got off the bus on the other side of the bridge and they crossed it together. Once they were on this side, they said goodbye and he saw her walk-ing in this direction in the bike lane. She was already in the Rockaways and, after saying goodbye to her brother, it's like she was swallowed up by the world. I found a man who says he saw her a little farther along on that road, and he confirmed that she was heading towards Neponsit. Something must have hap-pened to her on that stretch, between the parking lot and here."

"We'd agreed to meet up after class. She had been acting weird for a few weeks. Like, she was just checked out all the time. When I talked to her, she'd avoid making eye contact, and she stopped sitting next to me in class. Then, finally, that day, she said we had to talk, but we couldn't do it at school. She had something important to tell me. She got off the bus on the oth-er side of the bridge with her brother and told me she'd walk to my house. I asked her to stay on the bus and get off in Nepon-sit. I said her brother could go the whole way by bus and just get off in Roxbury, near her house. But Ethan got car sick that day and she got off with him before crossing the bridge so she could skip the whole part of the bus route through the Rocka-ways. I offered to walk with them, but she said she needed to take a walk anyway, to think about what she was going to say. I was sort of worried she was gonna break up with me, so I obviously didn't want to push it, and I gave her some space. But I never found out what she was going to tell me."

"I see... Why do you think she started behaving differently around you? When did you realize she was acting strange?"

"Hmm," he hesitated. "That's hard to answer."

"Please, Tom... it might be important," Jim insisted.

"It was after her aunt caught us making out," he said with a sigh. "That day, she ran away from home and showed up at my door. It had been raining, and she was soaked. She came up to my room and I told her she should go home. Then she took off all her clothes and she... she kissed me. We made love, almost in silence, because my dad was downstairs in the living room. It was really intense. I remember it as... the best night of my life."

"What happened afterwards?" the professor asked.

"I told her she had to go back home to her family, since they'd be worried about her."

"And what did she do?"

"She got mad at me. I'd never seen her like that."

"She felt betrayed," Jim filled in, remembering Miren's anger towards him and how the two of them seemed incapable of reconciling.

"I... I wanted what was best for her. Her aunt and uncle must have been worried. It was almost midnight. It was still raining, so my dad offered to drive her home. It's a short drive, but at night and in that weather, he couldn't let her go alone. Before leaving that day, she gave me this really desolate look. The next day was when she started acting differently. She avoided me and didn't want anything to do with me. I can't tell you how much I loved her and what the two months after that night were like. So when she disappeared, it completely destroyed me. I wish... it hadn't turned out that way. I wanted to tell her I was sorry, but I couldn't figure out how. She'd shut me out and pushed me away without ever saying why. When she said she wanted to talk, I thought it would be a good chance to sort everything out. I didn't even eat when I got back home, I just tidied up my room, picked some flowers from the garden and put them on my bed, and wrote her a letter. I spent all afternoon waiting for her to knock on the door. I remember my grandma was in her room watching TV and my dad was in the garage, like today. Some people don't change, I guess. Now that I'm saying it all out loud, it feels like the world froze that day. It's sad to think that life goes on, and we all just carry on, despite a sudden tragedy like that."

"What happened afterwards?"

"I called her house to ask about her and her aunt yelled at me. She told me to tell her what I did to her niece. That was when I went out to look for her and her brother told me she'd been heading towards my house. And from then on, there was just nothing."

"Did you join the search parties?" Jim asked.

"The first few days I did, but… After a while, as everyone's hope dwindled, her aunt and uncle didn't want to see me there. They blamed everything on me. And I was sure they were punishing me for sleeping with her. When her backpack showed up in Breezy Point, everything blew up. That proved she hadn't gone to my house, but in the opposite direction, towards the end of the Rockaways. It's a pretty deserted area, I don't know if you've been. I know she liked looking at the ocean. I guess you already know the rest of the story."

"In Mallow, did you ever notice anything… strange going on?"

"Mallow was definitely strict, but nothing crazy ever happened there. Like, it was a religious school, but they didn't brainwash us or anything. Does that make sense? I'm an atheist and I went there. I think most of the students end up rejecting religion no matter how hard they try to push it on us."

"What about punishments?"

"I mean, I guess it depends on what you do. They got creative with punishments, but it's not like they were handing them out all the time. Most of the time you just had to say a prayer and apologize. When I was there, the worst thing they made us do was hold a bunch of books in each hand until we couldn't keep them up anymore, it was supposed to be like a way of humiliating you in front of the class."

Jim sighed. Not only did this account not clarify anything, but it actually made what he already thought he knew murkier.

"I think that's enough," Jim said. "You've helped me a lot, Tom. Thank you."

"Of course. To be honest... talking about it with you has reminded me how much I loved her. I haven't forgotten her face. Sometimes I think about her, you know? And I feel like she's in front of me, smiling. It's become a kind of... recurring memory. And it's painful like that. I hope one day I find out what happened to her or why she ran away."

Jim turned off the recorder and got up. Tom accompanied him to the door and, before saying goodbye, Jim hesitated on the porch and thought about telling Tom why he was really there. Maybe that would help him feel less guilty.

"The death of the other girl from Mallow is not the only reason I'm investigating Gina's case now, Tom. There's something else."

Tom raised his eyebrows, confused, and waited for Jim to continue.

"A journalist from the *Manhattan Press* has received a photo of Gina, from the time she disappeared. In the photo, she's tied up in the inside of a truck. I'm telling you this so you'll know she didn't run away on her own, it was something someone did to her. It wasn't your fault, Tom. Someone hurt her and that's why she never made it home."

Tom swallowed hard. He hadn't been expecting this. Then he asked:

"Is that really true?"

Jim nodded silently.

"Can I see the photo? Do you have a copy?"

Jim remembered taking a photo of the polaroid with his cell phone.

"I do, but I don't know if it's the best idea—"

"Please," Tom begged, nervous. "I've spent nine years thinking she left because of something I did. Don't do this to me."

Jim hesitated for a few moments, but finally agreed. He pulled out his phone and found the photo. Tom looked at it closely for a few moments, almost in tears, and then finally sighed:

"That girl isn't Gina."

Chapter 32
Mallow Institute
April 25, 2011
One day earlier
Miren Triggs

*One spark, and everything turns
into a mystery, but also, into love.*

Soon I was parking my car opposite the Mallow Institute. I looked for the café where Miller had agreed to wait for me. I noticed four yellow buses stationed outside the door, and I imagined Gina and Ethan leaving class, climbing into one of them and driving off towards the Rockaways.

Just as I got out of my car, I heard a bell ringing within the school and, a few seconds later, the doors to the building burst open, unleashing an incessant torrent of students who dispersed in all directions. Some of them got in the buses while other sat on nearby benches and talked in groups. A few rode off on bicycles or found the mopeds they had parked by the curb, riding off in pairs. The school was clearly lively, and the students seemed happy. The image contrasted sharply with the one I'd formed based on what Ethan had told me, not to mention what I knew about how Gina and Allison died.

I saw the inspector waving through the café window and began walking towards him with a serious expression. On his table sat a coffee cup and plate of breadcrumbs; he was wearing a gray suit and a black tie.

"Miren, I don't know how you do it, but you're always on top of everything. I would've thought that... with your book you would have... pulled back from this world a little. Anyway, congratulations! You didn't let me say so properly before. I see you are in all the bookstore windows. I'm so happy for you. What you did for Kiera... I think it demonstrates how much this world needs you. Do you know how she's doing?"

"No. Her parents have called me a few times, but... I don't think I have much place in their lives anymore. I've tried to distance myself from them. I think it's better if no one interferes in their life now, you know?"

"Well, you helped that family in a way that can never be repaid. I'm sure they would like to see you and thank you for what you did," he said in a comforting tone I tried to ignore.

"Have you spoken to anyone from the school?" I asked. "What'd they tell you?"

"Miren... I can't tell you anything."

"It's fine," I said, sliding the polaroid of Gina over the table.

It took him a few seconds to process what he was looking at, but the name written on the bottom margin left little room for doubt.

"What is this?"

"I received it in an anonymous envelope that had 'WANNA PLAY?' written on it."

"Do you have the envelope?"

"If you're asking if I have any evidence, I doubt it'll be much use. They put it on my table during a book signing a few days ago, and people were moving gifts and letters I'd received all over the place the whole time. It'll have been too handled to use."

"Maybe, but we could try getting fingerprints or DNA."

"I have it in the car, I'll get it for you."

"So, what's your theory? What do you think this photo might mean? Why'd they give it to you?"

"Tell me what you know about Mallow, and I'll tell you everything I know," I challenged him.

Even though he trusted me, it was a risk, considering how damaging leaked information could be.

"Oh, come on, Miren. You know I can't do that. You're a journalist."

"I won't publish anything without you signing off on it, Ben. Besides, you know we're in the same boat on this."

"I don't know, Miren. I don't think we're in the same boat. We're in the same storm, but not the same boat. You're trying to go by speedboat, and I can't work that way. I don't think I ought to—"

"I'll tell you what I know and then you do the same. I won't publish anything without the green light from you. We'll review everything together. You know I'm only interested in the truth, same as you."

"All right," he finally relented, grudgingly. Just as I'd hoped. "What do you know?" he said.

"Last week I was here, at Mallow, talking to a few students. I heard about it from Ethan, Gina's brother, who still goes to the school. I know the priest in charge here has a reputation for being a real son of a bitch, and I know that Allison and Gina both studied here. I also know how Allison was murdered: she was crucified in an abandoned part of Fort Tilden. There's a group of kids at Mallow who call themselves the Ravens of God, some kind of secretive fraternity that's hard to join. You'd think it would just be some adolescent clique, but… it seems like it's existed for years. They meet up, pray, talk about God. That's what Ethan says."

"How do you know all this?"

"Asking questions and sniffing around. Is there any other way?"

"All right then," he said. "Tell me about these Ravens."

"I don't know much. It's like a gang of schoolkids, but that's about all I know. Ethan saw Allison with a few of them before she disappeared. It seems like the same group existed at Mallow back when Gina went missing too."

"Do you know the names of the kids who are in it?"

I shook my head, then continued:

"But there's a group of kids from the Rockaways who apparently don't want me investigating. When I was walking on the beach they hit me on the back of the head with a rock, and then later they broke the window of a motel where I was staying with another one. The second rock had a Bible verse written on it, I'm sure you know it, something along the lines of 'Let he who is without sin…'"

"'…throw the first stone,'" Ben completed.

"So, clearly, I have reason to believe the school has something to do with Allison's disappearance. Okay, now it's your turn. What do you know?"

"You can't publish any of this, alright?"

"Got it. You get to decide what gets printed and what doesn't."

He thought for a few seconds before finally coming out with it:

"Allison was pregnant."

"What?!"

"Father Graham told me. He seems like he's willing to help, though I don't trust him. I called the medical examiner's office in charge of the autopsy while I was waiting for you, and they confirmed it. She was two months pregnant."

"Jesus Christ…"

"Don't even think about printing it, Miren. Please. It's confidential."

"Of course. What else do you know?"

He pulled a Bible from his briefcase and put it in front of me on the table.

"What's this?"

"Allison Hernández's Bible. It was in Father Graham's office. It had vanished from her house, along with a crucifix that was hanging over her bed. All the underlined passages are parts of the Bible that could be about abortion. My theory is she wanted to get an abortion and the priest said absolutely not. So she tried to find the parts that talked about dead babies and mothers who eat their children, stuff like that. Read this one, for example: 'Do not let her be like a stillborn infant coming from its mother's womb with its flesh half eaten away.' Or this one." He pointed at the passage which read:

Then he asked her, "What's the matter?" She answered, "This woman said to me, 'Give up your son so we may eat him today, and tomorrow we'll eat my son.' So we cooked my son and ate him. The next day I said to her, 'Give up your son so we may eat him,' but she had hidden him."

"I can't believe the Bible seriously says all that," I murmured, confused.

"Yeah, I'm as surprised as you. Damn book talks about everything, I guess. The Bible's actually a whole collection of books, some of them talk about this stuff. And worse."

"And what do you know about the priest? Is he like Ethan Pebbles described? Based on what he said, the guy's practically abusive."

"I don't know what to think of him. He has a kind of sinister air about him, definitely, but I don't know much more. It hasn't been easy to talk to anyone at Mallow. But one thing about him struck me as very strange."

"What?"

"He has private talks with his students, with the door closed. He says they're normal, but this morning, when I got there, there was a girl… around Allison's age. She was in there with him, with the door closed and locked."

"Do you think he… he does something to them?"

"I don't know. Like I was saying, he's spent his whole life being very… accessible to the students and they trust him, talk to him about their problems. I don't know what to think."

"Have you run a background check?" I asked.

"No. He wasn't on my radar… until now."

"Can you look into it? If he's some kinda perv, those things come up again and again. One report from a teenager, one case of inappropriate touching, a girlfriend who reported him for weird fetishes… there are hundreds of cases of the Church and religious schools being implicated in sexual abuse of minors. Too many for it to be a coincidence."

"Do you think this priest—?"

"Don't you think a person like that would be capable of crucifying a girl who… who he certainly considers a… a sinner? Ethan told me the punishments at Mallow are horrible. Maybe in this instance things got out of hand."

I sat thinking in silence. The owner of the bar was giving us a look that said, 'order something else or get out.'

"And what do we know about Gina?" reflected Miller. "As I understand it, she was a kind and religious girl. It doesn't seem to fit that she would meet the same end as Allison."

"Do you know Gina and Ethan's aunt and uncle?" I asked, answering his question with another question.

We seemed to be getting to the bottom of something.

"Christopher and Meghan. I talked to them a few years ago. They were involved in the search. They were a little odd, but they seemed to be good people. It was a shame they didn't have more resources to look for Gina."

"I've talked to them."

"And?"

"They're extremely religious. I guess that comes as no surprise. That's why they enrolled Gina and Ethan at Mallow. And… here's the best part," I said, preparing to establish the connection between both cases: "They told me one day Gina got angry with them and ran away. She reappeared at night, after they'd been looking for her all over the Rockaways. And do you know where she said she'd been?"

He shook his head, waiting for me to continue.

"At Tom Roger's house, her boyfriend at the time, having sex. If the priest found out—and I'm sure the Pebbles told him—in his eyes, Gina would have become a… a sinner, like Allison. It's even possible she might have been pregnant. It's a religious school, I doubt they have very comprehensive sex ed or access to birth control."

"Jesus, I like this guy less and less. I'll run a background check. How do the Ravens of God fit into all of this?"

"I'm not sure. Maybe Father Graham is part of it. If it is some kind of cult, they usually have a spiritual leader, right?"

"To the point of crucifying someone?"

"All I know for sure is that… whoever did it, they know both Gina and Allison were sexually active and… deserved punishment."

The coincidences kept adding up.

"And the polaroid? Did you show it to Ethan? Or to his aunt and uncle? I don't think you ought to—"

"The only people who've seen it are you, me and Jim Schmoer."

"Jim? He's part of this?"

"Someone contacted him online and sent him a photo from when they were crucifying Allison, from the moment just before they raised her on the cross. There are several people in the photo. Then Jim found me on the beach, unconscious after I'd been hit in the head. If it weren't for him, I might've drowned when the tide came in."

"Fuck, I don't like this at all. Do you have that image? Or

the email it was sent from? Why didn't you give it to us earlier? It might help us find the perpetrator. We're friends, Miren, but that's withholding evidence."

"We had to confirm it was the real deal, Ben. You can't… say no to a story like that."

"C'mon, Miren. Not sharing information about a crime is a crime in itself."

"Ben… I'm sorry…"

He huffed, angry. I really did understand him, but after knowing him for so many years, I knew he was going to give in.

"I'll see if I can find a way to keep your asses out of hot water," he finally conceded. Then he started asking questions again.

"How'd this person contact him?"

"Over Twitter. I have a printed copy of the photo in the car. Should I give it to you?"

"Maybe I ought to talk to Jim. The computer nerds might be able to determine where the photo was taken or even the IP address it was sent from. Can you ask him to call me?"

"Here's his number."

I showed him my phone screen with Jim's number, so I didn't have to talk to him. After our fight, I wasn't brave enough to call if I could avoid it.

"Great, I'll call him. Anything else? Theories on how all this pieces together? The more I find out, the more murky it all sounds."

"Let's see. I do have a theory that fits like a glove, but I need to move forward on a few leads to figure out the next step to take."

"Go on."

"It's possible that Father Graham is part of the Ravens. It's possible that he encourages students to join and then… well, he explains the darkest parts of the Bible to the students who are the most… curious. But I don't think there's anything so innocent about it. Ethan told us it's not easy to figure out who is and isn't in the Ravens. There are even people who are a different age and don't go to the school. Maybe Father Graham found out Gina was sleeping with Tom, no doubt from her aunt and uncle, and he punished her the same way he punished Allison. The only difference is that Allison was found by two kids who were hanging out in the area and Gina... we don't know where she's buried. It's possible they planned to hide Allison's body once she was dead, like they could've done with Gina's, but she was found before they had the chance."

"I don't think so," Ben corrected. "If that were the case, they wouldn't have given you the polaroid or sent the image of Allison to Jim Schmoer. They want you to know about them. They want you to be investigating them. But... why?"

That question was floating in the air when, suddenly, there was a loud bang in the street, and a car alarm began blaring loudly.

"What the hell?!" I cried.

Chapter 33
Mallow Institute
April 25, 2011
One day earlier
Ben Miller and Miren Triggs

There's no controlling the blaze
after lighting a fire
in an inflammable heart

Inspector Miller followed Miren outside to see what had caused the boom echoing in their eardrums. Both had identified the sound of a car alarm and, as soon as he stepped outside, the inspector realized there were still dozens of Mallow students standing in circles, older kids waiting to board the buses. Everyone was looking intently at Miren and Ben and, at first, neither understood why. It was as if the students were silently awaiting their reaction to something. The sound was coming from Miren's car. The alarm was blaring and grew louder and more unbearable the closer they got.

"What the…" Miller began to say from behind Miren, but he didn't finish the question.

He suddenly understood what had happened: Miren's rear windshield had been smashed and the tiny pieces of glass had scattered across the floor and back seat, twinkling like diamonds in the afternoon light.

Miren looked around, trying to identify the guilty party, but in every face, she saw only indifference. Ben felt a strange sense of vertigo when he thought that some of those students had been capable of smashing the rear window of the car and yet were perfectly calm, not giving themselves away.

"Who was it?!" Miren cried furiously, with a shriek that took Ben by surprise. "Who?!"

Miren turned to one of the girls she recognized from the group she'd seen on the beach and cried:

"What do you want? What? You think you're untouchable in your silence, but that same silence makes you its victim," she screamed.

Then she spotted several students on the opposite side of the street, all of them between fifteen and sixteen years old, grinning silently. They weren't happy smiles, but satisfied smirks. As if Miren's outburst were the flames of a bonfire which they had deliberately set ablaze. The bus honked its horn, the sound blending with the car alarm, and the students continued climbing aboard, staring at Miren all the while.

Inspector Miller tried to calm her down, but to no avail. On one of the doors of the car, someone had used a sharp object to scratch the word 'PLAY.'

"Motherfuckers…" Miren muttered when she saw it. "Play what!?" she cried in the students' general direction.

All the students on the bus were pressed against the windows, watching her expectantly. Miller approached to try to cool things down.

"They clearly don't want us here," he said in a serious tone.

"I'm not leaving until I find out what happened to those girls. What the fuck is happening at this school? Have they all lost their minds?"

But then Miren caught sight of a small, yellowish piece of

paper that was crammed between the driver's side window and the door.

"What is this?" she exclaimed.

Ben approached, confused, stepping on a few pieces of glass that crunched beneath his feet like gravel. It was a handwritten note, penned in black ink. When Miren read it, she felt as if her heart was loudly imploring her not to continue onward. The note read:

IF YOU WISH TO JOIN
THE RAVENS OF GOD
YOU MUST COMPLETE THE SOUL GAME

RULES:
I. CROSS THE BRIDGE ON THE OUTSIDE OF THE GUARDRAIL.
II. BURN SOMETHING OF PERSONAL VALUE.
III. ASCEND THE CROSS BLINDFOLDED.

Miren clenched her jaw and breathed deeply, trying to understand the message's implications. She didn't know what it was, but she remembered how before the incident on the beach, James Cooper had told her that to join the Ravens, you had to pass a test. She looked among the students on the bus for some kind of signal, and then, suddenly, she saw James among them, in the back of the bus, looking at her with the same expression of satisfied indifference as everyone else. They were a pack of animals watching their prey walk into a cave with no way out, salivating, their eyes glimmering with hunger. James' bus began driving off to the east; Miren realized she didn't have much time.

"Fine!" she cried at the bus. "If you wanna play, I'll play!" she screamed angrily as she opened her car door and got in.

"Miren, where are you going?" Ben asked, raising his voice. "This is exactly what they want. Snap out of it. Don't do anything stupid. This is dangerous, Miren."

"Ben," Miren said from inside the car before closing the door. "If I'm not back tonight, come looking for me."

"What are you talking about?" he yelled.

"I'll be fine. Find out what Father Graham is hiding. I'll figure out who's behind this fucking game. Maybe Allison played and that's why..." Miren chose not to finish the sentence and closed the door.

"Miren, wait!" he pleaded one last time, just as she turned the ignition and accelerated as fast as she could towards the retreating bus.

She weaved through traffic, speeding up and braking as necessary to avoid an accident. When she finally managed to pull up beside the bus, both vehicles were driving onto the Marine Parkway Bridge towards the Rockaways, with its two trademark steel towers. When she saw the bus filled with Mallow students, Miren's mind went straight to Gina and Ethan getting off at the start of the bridge so they could cross on foot, in the pedestrian lane. She put her foot to the floor, listening to the sound of the car roaring through the broken rear windshield. When she finally managed to get ahead of the bus, she jerked the steering wheel to cut it off, forcing the driver to slam on the brakes. The bus skidded for several yards, causing all the students on board to hold their breath. Miren closed her eyes as she realized that maneuver had been a mistake; she clung to the wheel, knowing the bus wouldn't have time to fully brake, and that it was about to run straight into her.

"No!" she howled.

Chapter 34
Neponsit
April 25, 2011
One day earlier
Jim Schmoer

Sometimes the truth appears before you
so late there's nothing you can do.

"What do you mean it isn't Gina?!"

"That girl isn't Gina, Mr. Schmoer. It isn't her," Tom replied, in a tone so serious there was no doubt about his confidence.

"Are you sure?"

"I mean, the girl looks similar, but it's not her," Tom confirmed. "It's some kind of prank. That girl isn't Gina."

"Look closely at the photo, Tom, please. She's wearing the same clothes Gina had on when she disappeared. The gray Salt Lake t-shirt, the red shoes…"

"I remember Gina really well. Honestly, that's not her. The shape of her face… even… look, look at her right arm."

"What about it?" Jim asked, incredulous.

"She had a burn on her arm from the fire, but there's nothing on that girl's arm. So either the burn vanished or that isn't her. That girl isn't Gina. I'm really sorry," he said in a tone that was somewhere between grief and relief.

"Fuck," the professor cursed, openly expressing his exasperation. A knot formed in his throat as he tried to piece together an understanding of what was happening. "If that girl isn't Gina... who the hell is it?"

"I don't know. But whoever gave you that photo is messing with you."

"Not with me," he said, "But with..." He paused when he remembered Miren. "I have to tell her."

He took his phone out of his pocket and searched his contacts for Miren's number. He called, nervous, with Tom watching on without understanding. After ringing a few times, he heard Miren's voice on the other end of the line, so distant and removed it seemed like it was showing him how far apart they had really drifted.

"Hello?"

"Miren?"

Suddenly he heard a metallic crunch and a strange, muffled cry from Miren that Jim didn't know how to interpret. Unexpectedly, the call cut off.

"Miren?!" he cried into the phone, confused. "Miren?!"

He tried calling back several times, but her phone seemed to have lost its signal. At first, Jim thought perhaps something had happened, but then, knowing Miren, he also knew she was capable of hanging up on him.

Tom sighed heavily the instant he heard the voice of an elderly person calling from upstairs:

"Tom? Who are you talking to?" the voice said.

He exhaled and called back:

"Coming, Grandma!" He turned back to Jim without knowing how to say goodbye. "I'm... sorry. I have things to do. My grandmother—"

"Thank you so much, Tom. You've been a big help. Don't worry."

"If you need anything else—"

"Don't worry. Go help your grandmother," Jim said. Then he continued: "Do you think I could talk to the neighbors, in case they saw anything? I've seen Gina's file and it doesn't look like any of them made a statement at the time. No one said they'd seen Gina that day, except... a man I spoke to, a guy who lives in a camper in the parking lot."

"Oh, old Marvin. He's a good guy. A little reclusive I guess, but I think he's the only decent person over there. Everyone else in the Rockaways... they all seem to have secrets. Absolutely all of them. Marvin always helps everyone else as much as he can. I don't think there's anyone around who doesn't know him. Sometimes the weirdos are the kindest people."

Jim nodded, though he wanted to tell Tom how Marvin had stuck a Colt in his back. Then Tom continued:

"As for my neighbors... yeah, I mean, talk to whoever you like. I talked to everyone at the time, and nobody had seen her. It wasn't the right time of day; everyone was either at home having lunch or at work. There was no one on the street. But you can try. They're not bad people. They're a little distant, maybe, but I guess everyone is these days."

"Thank you, Tom," Jim said by way of goodbye. "I'm sorry about everything you've been through."

"Me too, Mr. Schmoer," Tom replied.

* * *

Jim was nervous as he left the Rogers' house, not knowing how to process the fact that the girl in the polaroid was not Gina Pebbles. In his mind, more and more questions were piling up and becoming increasingly complicated. None had a clear answer. If that girl wasn't Gina, who was it? Who had staged that photograph, even down to the clothes Gina was wearing at the time? And the question that ate him up inside: Who had given

Miren that photo, and why? What kind of macabre game were they trying to play with her?

He thought the person behind the image might be the same Twitter user who had sent him the photo of Allison, and he found that even more alarming. He called Miren, again unsuccessfully. Her phone seemed to have shut off the instant she picked up, and part of him preferred to think her battery had died. That was better than thinking she was angry with him.

Jim ambled along 149th street in Neponsit analyzing houses and, when he finally had his thoughts straight, he knocked on the first in the row. No one answered. Despite how well the house was maintained, there didn't seem to be anyone home. He knocked on several more doors, all with the same result. He realized that with the exception of three houses in the neighborhood, there weren't cars parked at any of them, and he supposed they must be summer homes that remained empty most of the year. Finally, he knocked on the door of a house that had blue a Vauxhall with New York plates parked in front of the garage. A blonde, curly-haired woman opened the door for him; he seemed to be interrupting her first sip of a favorite tea, and she greeted him with an air of confusion upon seeing a strange man on her porch. She was wearing an elegant red suit and her brows were drawn on with eyeliner.

"What do you want?" she asked, arching her kohl eyebrows.

"Hi, my name is Jim Schmoer, I'm a freelance investigative journalist. I'm reviewing the case of a girl who disappeared here in 2002. Do you remember her?"

"Oh... I was just about to—" she said, trying to conclude the conversation.

"This will only take a moment, honestly," Jim implored with concerned eyes.

"I don't like... talking about other people, you know? That was a tragedy and what happened to that girl is a shame, but I'd rather not... stir up any shit, if you know what I mean. The housing prices around here plummeted for years after she disappeared. Who would want to move into a neighborhood where a girl went missing? Makes people think it's not the right kind of place to raise a family."

"But…"

"Oh, I remember how that just destroyed the Rogers. The price of their home sank so much, and they were just about to sell. No, please. Don't bring all this up again. You're going to tank my business. Do you mind?"

"Your business?"

"I'm a real estate agent. If you'd like I can give you a card. Haven't you seen the ads? Hello?" she said, as if he surely must recognize her. "That's my photo."

Jim looked around and noticed that several of the houses had signs out front placed by Mrs. Evans Properties, each of which featured a photo of Mrs. Evans wearing a suit and brandishing an impeccable smile.

"I handle all the houses in Neponsit. It's my… hunting ground. If you want a house here, I get a commission. Five percent. Ten if you want me to get you a mortgage. You're not looking for a house, are you?"

"I'm afraid not. I supposed it's going well for you, then."

"Well? Have you been living under a rock for the past four years? We just got through the worst financial crisis in a century. I haven't sold a damn house in years. And now things are finally looking up, here you are wanting to dig up all this old stuff. No. I won't."

"The Rogers were selling their house?"

"Well, yes. They wanted to move and, you know, find something a bit more affordable, but when the boy's girlfriend went missing, the value of their house fell by fifty percent. The rest of the neighborhood dropped thirty percent. That may not seem like much, but it's enough to mean you won't cover your mortgage when you sell, and you end up saddled with a massive amount of debt."

"How do you know all this? Who told you they wanted to move?"

"Mr. Rogers himself. I was selling his house. I'd shown it to several families, and it was perfect. Very well maintained. He's quite the handyman, and he gave the house the perfect touch with that green roof. That house is just beautiful, it's like something from a magazine, honestly. But, of course, with a fifty percent drop… how could they possibly sell?"

"It seems like they didn't. They're still living there," Jim replied.

"Well, it was all very sad, and I think Mr. Rogers decided to settle things as best he could. He had a workshop in the garage, and to improve the house a little, he personally started replacing the exterior wood, he put on a whole new roof, and also renovated the garage, all in a bid to bring up the price. He's always been a very hard-working man. He spent a great deal of time on those projects. But of course, he wanted to save to send his son to college and… well, sometimes things don't turn out how we'd like. Not everyone who lives here is loaded, you know. Lots of people have money, of course, but others just… have a bout of good luck and after that they have to go back to the same old grind."

"Are you saying the Rogers don't have enough money to stay here?" Jim asked.

"I mean… I'm only telling you all this because you strike me as very handsome," she smiled, catching Jim off guard. "But… you have to promise me you won't publish any of it."

"I'm just trying to find out what happened to Gina Pebbles. It's not for any article. I don't work for any paper, if that's what you're worried about."

"You see, when things started to go well, and the prices started climbing again—after the gossip from her disappearance died down—I paid the Rogers a visit. There were several interested buyers. One couple offered them some real money for it."

"And what happened?"

"He rejected the offer. He said he didn't want to move. He worked so long on that house it seemed like he was practically building a shopping center, and then, when I find him an offer over the asking price, he turns it down. Can you believe it? Then came the recession and, well, I nearly had to sell my own house at a loss because of the damn banks and their subprime mortgages. You want some free advice? If you can, never take out a mortgage. It's death by a thousand cuts with the fees, and in the long run they'll gouge you."

"Those thousand cuts include your commission, I suppose," Jim volunteered, unable to stop himself in time.

"Business is business, buddy. I got bills to pay, same as everyone. We're the same age, I'm not telling you anything you don't already know."

"And you're saying he didn't want to sell the house?"

"They were offering half a million above asking. He could've paid for his son to go to school and more."

"Why do you think he said no?" Jim asked with interest.

"He'd grown fond of the house. Like I said, it's gorgeous, and very comfortable. Right there by the beach, two floors... and plus the garage-workshop. He must have other sources of income, I don't know."

"I understand. Thanks so much, Mrs.... Evans."

"You don't want to come in for a quick... tea?"

"No, that's very kind, thank you."

"A quick fuck then?" she said abruptly, leaning against the doorframe.

"I'm sorry? I think I... I have to go. I have to—"

"Are you gay?"

"No, it's just that... I have to... you see... thank you for the interest..." he stammered, unsure how to get out of the situation. "But I'm... busy."

"Well, if you're suddenly less busy, give me call," she said, her tone dropping by two octaves. "You can find my number on all the for-sale signs."

"Thank you, Mrs. Evans," replied Jim, who hadn't expected such a sudden proposition.

Mrs. Evans made a call-me gesture with her hand then closed the door. Jim left the house with an uneasy feeling he couldn't quite place. He looked at the Rogers house again and, certainly, it was a much more beautiful house than those surrounding it. It was painted a banana yellow that looked lovely with the eucalyptus color of the roof. He looked at the Rogers' car: a gray Dodge Ram parked by the sidewalk, since the garage was being used as a carpentry workshop. The garage was at the end of the paved driveway, and Jim remembered Tom had told him his father was busy in the shop.

He approached the garage and heard the sound of a disc saw coming from inside; it was cutting a few wood boards behind a green garage door that matched the roof.

"Hello?" he called. "Mr. Rogers?"

He knocked on the garage door a few times and several seconds later the door rose, revealing a man with brown hair, a sloppy beard and fat fingers. The man looked as if he had been working in that garage for weeks. He glowered at Jim through his protective glasses.

"Who're you?" he asked, confused.

"Mr. Rogers?"

The man nodded. He took off the protective glasses, which left an outline on his skin like two wrinkles created by an invisible mask.

"Would it be possible to speak with you? It's important. It concerns your son's girlfriend."

"Girlfriend? My son doesn't have a girlfriend," he replied, genuinely annoyed.

"I'm talking about… Gina Pebbles. I'm sure you remember her."

Chapter 35
Marine Parkway Bridge
April 25, 2011
One day earlier
Miren Triggs

*Life is about playing a game
with rules that we don't know.*

It was fascinating to feel how my emotions shifted as I drove across the Marine Parkway Bridge, knowing that if I made a single mistake I would careen off into nothingness. I'd let myself act on an impulse, the kind of instant decision you make without considering the consequences and, when I opened my eyes after hearing the squealing wheels of the Mallow school bus, I felt like it was an absolute miracle that the vehicle managed to stop barely six feet from my car. I got out and heard the bus diver honking his horn and yelling furiously at me, and felt the adrenaline pulsing in my fingertips. I smelled the salty sea air rising from Jamaica Bay, drifting on the wind and into my nostrils, and I could hear the unmistakable roar of the ocean. I was frozen, staring at the bus and watching the students leaping to their feet inside, expectant. Behind the bus, other cars were beginning to come to an impatient halt; their drivers had no idea what was happening and honked their horns as if that could influence what was about to happen.

I remembered the words from the note that had been left on my car, and which had prompted me to be so impulsive:

IF YOU WISH TO JOIN
THE RAVENS OF GOD
YOU MUST COMPLETE THE SOUL GAME

RULES:
I. CROSS THE BRIDGE ON THE OUTSIDE OF THE GUARDRAIL.
II. BURN SOMETHING OF PERSONAL VALUE.
III. ASCEND THE CROSS BLINDFOLDED.

As soon as I read that note, I knew what it was referring to, even though it was more sinister and malicious than I had expected. When I was a teenager in my own little clique, the Fallen Stars, I'd had to pass tests devised by my classmate Vicky, but it was all far more innocent than this new test created by Mallow's Ravens of God. Everything in their orbit seemed to be shrouded in secrecy and danger, and it made me wonder if it was really just a group of teenagers or something far worse.

The first of the three rules of the Soul Game seemed to be a test of bravery. Jumping over the guardrail on the bridge and climbing on the other side was meant to demonstrate the player's valor. If you're capable of doing something that crazy, you are undoubtedly a person who is either brave or thoughtless, and either way, you'd be a good fit for the group. The Marine Parkway Bridge was suspended twenty meters above the bay, and falling from such a height could undoubtedly break your bones.

The second test, burning something of personal value, seemed to challenge your capacity for sacrifice. Burning an important possession required a certain emotional strength that would leave a scar on your soul. The third, ascending the cross, struck me as the most macabre, and it didn't take long to draw a link between this feat and Allison Hernández's death. Was that how I would die, trying to complete the Ravens' three challenges?

Each of the rules in the Soul Game seemed to be designed with the exclusive intention of undermining the three main attributes of a person's integrity, like three locks guarding access to the soul, and passing through each one would require opening the doors so anyone could insert their own rotten ideas inside.

I was able to deduce all of that because I remembered how, when I was a teenager, we would also impose tests—though far more innocent—along the same lines in order to join the Fallen Stars. I remembered that ours involved small, inoffensive challenges: the test of bravery, telling a boy you liked him; the test of trust, sharing a secret written on a piece of paper, which was kept in a small box to which we all had access. Though after a while, we opened the box, and that was the reason the Fallen Stars ceased to exist. The third was the strangest of all, and only Vicky and I completed it, on the first day we established the group. It was an absurd game that involve pricking yourself with a needle and letting a drop of blood fall on a piece of cardboard we had cut into the shape of a membership card. When Bob, Sam, Carla and Jimmy wanted to join the group, that challenge struck us all as so pointless and gross that none of them did it.

I looked up and saw every student on the bus staring at me. The driver was furiously gesturing for me to get out of the way, but I simply clenched my jaw and silently gripped the guardrail as I lifted one leg over. I sat there, straddling it for a moment, unable to place either foot on the ground.

I looked at the bus again and, to my surprise, saw that some of the students had opened their windows on the side closest to me and were rhythmically banging the bus's metal siding at a pace that made reminded me of a beating heart.

I recognized Ethan among the students; he was giving me a concerned look. The students increased the volume and rhythm at which they were banging on the bus, and the hair on the back of my neck stood on end as I considered the prospect that I was making exactly the mistake the Ravens wanted me to. A bell started ringing somewhere on the bridge and I thought maybe they had alerted the police that a woman was climbing over the edge.

I clutched even harder and tried to lower myself down on the other side. My hands were shaking. The wind was strong and when I tried to lower my second leg, I looked down. I saw two tiny fishing boats floating across the bay; their crews seemed to be busy with some fishing nets, unaware that sixty feet above them, I was one false step away from disaster. A sailboat with its sail retracted was slowly approaching the bridge. Just then among the students' cries, I was able to identify one voice in particular:

"Don't do it! Stop!" cried Ethan. "Don't do it!"

The students were banging on the bus faster and faster. Soon I couldn't distinguish between that sound and the throbbing sound in my own chest. Despite Ethan's cries, many other students were yelling at me to do just the opposite:

"You have to walk on the other side!" cried a male voice.

"Don't be a coward!" cried a girl.

"Jump!" shouted a third voice.

Others urged me to do the same, and suddenly the banging on the other side of the bus was accompanied by a chant: 'Jump! Jump! Jump!' rising in volume, that, along with the sound of the bell, was like a chorus waiting for me at the gates of hell.

The same instant that I placed my foot on the exterior of the bridge, as if that movement had always been part of my destiny, as if everything had been planned from the beginning, I noticed my phone was ringing and vibrating in my pocket. I felt safe, despite the height. I hooked one arm around the railing, and from there contemplated the shorelines the bridge connected: the Rockaways and Queens, so close and yet so far. Now that I can look back and see what happened through the eyes of death, I know that everything would have been very different if I hadn't tried to answer that phone call.

I let go with one hand and extracted the phone from my pocket. I don't know why I thought I had everything firmly under control. Maybe some part of me wanted what happened next to happen, maybe a small part of my subconscious was sick of fighting against my own disappearance. I saw Jim's name on the screen, and I couldn't help but feel a spark, a fire, when I remembered our kiss at the motel, as well as my fear of feeling protected. I answered the call with a gentle:

"Hello?"

But just at that moment, I heard a loud metallic crunching sound and felt a vibration running through the bowels of the bridge. I instantly clung to the railing with both hands, and I watched the phone slip through my fingers and plummet into the bay. The whole structure was vibrating powerfully, and when I looked back, I realized the bus remained unmoving as my own car and I were rising straight up with the central part of the bridge. I had forgotten the Marine Parkway Bridge was a vertical-lift bridge and from time to time the middle portion would rise like an elevator to allow taller ships through. I wanted to climb back to the interior part of the bridge as I rose nearly one hundred feet, but any movement felt too dangerous. The Mallow students pounded on the bus even harder as the driver gestured at them to stop. A few got out of the bus and ran to the edge of the bridge to watch the massive hunk of metal rising as I clung to it, now half a football field above the water. The rising section of the bridge came to a sudden halt when it reached the top and, I admit it, at that moment I thought about jumping.

It wasn't something I had planned, it was more like a flash-bulb in my brain, an idea that flew in through somewhere in the deep recesses of my soul until, little by little, that one thought began to devour all the rest.

I took a deep breath, and, at that height, walked thirty-five or forty feet along the exterior of the bridge, my whole body overwhelmed by fear and vertigo. The students seemed to have fallen silent and, interrupted only by the bell giving the signal that the bridge was about to move again, I thought that perhaps this test of courage was affecting me more than I had initially expected. Was this what the Soul Game was about?

The middle section of the bridge slowly descended with me still clutching the railing, and eventually it reached its former position, loudly clunking into place. The bell stopped ringing, and all the students looked on silently as I moved back to the safe section inside the guardrail. And I looked back at them, with all the rage in my soul, and made out the face of Ethan nodding with satisfaction while the others appeared immune to what they had just seen. I noticed James Cooper get on the bus with a serious expression and then, suddenly, I heard the bus driver screaming in my face:

"Are you fucking crazy? Why did you do that? You almost killed us! You almost killed yourself!"

I walked away from his shouts and toward my car. Several other cars stuck in a line behind the bus were honking their horns, desperate to move; and at that moment, the only thing that my heart desired was to continue to the second test:

II. BURN SOMETHING OF PERSONAL VALUE.

Chapter 36
Mallow Institute
April 25, 2011
One day earlier
Ben Miller

Sometimes you can have the
truth right in front of you,
but it's hiding in the shape of a lie.

Inspector Miller sat watching Miren's car drive off at full speed, trying to catch up with the bus. He didn't know how to react. He didn't understand anything. Miren had always been a mystery to him and, even though they got along well, he didn't know what she was capable of. That part of Miren had always been hidden in the shadows of her soul, a mysterious dark side no one could solve. Ben had forgotten the taste of adrenaline, and the blast of energy Miren gave him left him reeling. It reminded him of when, many years back, before Daniel disappeared and before he joined the Missing Persons Unit, Ben had chased a car that two bank robbers had carjacked at gunpoint, and which had a three-year-old girl in the back seat. In those days he had been young and energetic; it was before Daniel was born and Ben had nothing to lose. It was the early eighties, he had just met Lisa, and he used that story (with a few embellishments) to win her over.

He knew Miren was a calm and fairly shy woman, and that although she could be somewhat brittle, she also had indestructible willpower. Everything she had done to save Kiera Templeton had been a good example of her tenacity, even though he also thought she owed a good part of her success to luck. But he had no doubt she was a box of surprises, and he didn't know what to expect from her as he watched her speed off down the street. He noticed how all of a sudden, the students were gone, the buses had disappeared, and the crowd of people walking in all directions had vanished, just as Gina Pebbles had years earlier.

Ben went back to the café to pay for the sandwich and coffee he had ordered while waiting for Miren; he also made sure the polaroid of Gina was still on the table.

The more he looked at the photo, the less sense he could make of it, and, for a moment, he even thought of making a copy and giving it to her family. But he immediately rejected the idea, realizing it would only bring more pain to her brother Ethan, who had already lost his parents in a fire before his sister Gina disappeared.

"Who the hell took this photo?" he whispered to himself.

He sat back down, shattered, and the owner of the café approached to ask if he wanted anything more.

"Another coffee, please. I need to think," he said without looking up.

He sat there for a good while, looking at the polaroid and trying to find something in the image that would indicate where it was taken. But to no avail. The photograph was framed in such a way that he could only see Gina in the center, a little blurry, looking scared at the camera, with a gag on her mouth. Unable to find any leads in the photo, he returned to Allison's Bible and thumbed through the pages. He was looking to see if he'd missed any underlined passages. Nothing made any sense, and yet, everything seemed connected in some way he was incapable of understanding.

He noticed that the owner of the café wouldn't stop looking at him; every time he looked up, the man quickly looked away.

"Can I help you with something?" Ben asked, annoyed.

Then the man approached him nervously and said:

"You're a police officer, right?" He said it in a whisper, and then he quickly looked around to make sure no one was nearby.

"More or less. FBI."

"So… I don't like trouble, but… with the school across the street… I don't think I should keep quiet."

"What is it?" Ben asked with interest.

"So, sometimes the principal comes here…"

"The principal?"

"Father Graham, from Mallow. Sometimes he comes here. I heard you and your friend talking about him. I know it's none of my business, but… the guy comes in sometimes in the mornings and…"

"Makes sense. This is the only café nearby," Ben justified, trying to get this man to be more explicit.

"So, let me explain. I mean he doesn't come alone."

"He gets coffee with some of the other teachers? Is that what you mean?"

The man shook his head, as if he were trying to shape the knot that had formed in his throat.

"With a student. I don't know. I don't think it's normal."

"What do you mean? He takes students out to breakfast?"

"A student. He usually only comes with one. A girl. And… I don't know. I have a feeling he's too… affectionate with her. I had to tell you."

"Affectionate how?" said Ben, trying to get something more specific out of the man.

"Okay. I'll tell you. But, please, don't tell anyone you heard it from me. I have a bad feeling about that guy."

Ben nodded. If it was something important or incriminating, he'd have time to convince the man to make a formal statement.

"A few weeks ago… he came here with the girl I'm talking about, probably fifteen or sixteen years old, a Mallow student. I know from the uniform. It was probably mid-morning. The café was empty. Getting customers in here is tough, and no one ever comes that time of day."

"And what happened?"

"I thought it was strange he would sit on the same side of the table as her. A guy of his age… so close to a high school girl… I don't know. You can see how close he'd have to sit. If nothing else, it was strange. And even stranger knowing that… I mean, he's a priest. Purity, sin, all that. Right?"

"What are you trying to say? I don't follow."

"I saw the priest put his hand on her thigh in a way… I don't know how to explain it. It was too affectionate. I went to the table to ask if they wanted anything else. I wanted to interrupt whatever was going on under the table."

"And did anything happen?" asked Ben, who wasn't at all happy about the direction this was taking.

"She was crying. When I went to their table, she was silent and her food was untouched, but her face was covered in tears. The priest pulled his hand up from under the table and took a bite of his sandwich, trying to look all casual. Watching him chew made me sick."

"What did the girl look like? Would you be able to recognize her?" Ben asked, with a hunch he expected was about to be confirmed.

"She had long brown hair. I haven't forgotten her face and… I thought about going to the cops, you know? But who were they going to believe? Priests aren't supposed to lie, and I've invested so much in this café, I can't afford to alienate Mallow. Most of our business comes from there, you know? I remember when I started this place, having a religious school across the street was a plus. I thought God would bless my investment, but this… this place has been a disaster. I think it was cursed by the devil."

Jim quickly searched his briefcase for Allison's file. He extracted the photograph from the first page and showed it to the man.

"Have you ever seen this girl here with him?"

"Doesn't look familiar. Lately I've only seen him with the brown-haired girl I'm talking about. Always the same one. She doesn't seem very happy, you know? I don't know. That's just the feeling I got. Like she was begging for help with her eyes."

"I understand," Ben said with a nod, trying to figure out what to do with this information. "Can I ask you one last thing?"

"Yeah, I just… I only want to help. I'm not religious, you know? But I'm a good person. My father taught me that the only god that exists is within yourself. That how we behave is what's important."

"Have you been here long? When did you start this café?"

"In 2000. New century. End of the world. Remember? They said the planes were gonna fall from the sky and all that. Then on January first, when I saw that nothing happened, I said to myself, 'Alright, Kevin, you're going to start your own café, finally start following your dreams.' And here I am, trapped. All my savings tied up in these walls. Either I keep working here, barely scraping by, or I lose all that investment."

"Do you remember seeing anything else during all those years? Any strange behavior from Father Graham or anyone else from Mallow? Teachers, students…"

The man shook his head.

"Okay," Ben finally said. "This has been a lot of help. Would you be willing to make an official statement about all this at the police station?"

"Will they know I was the one who talked?" he said, worried.

Ben nodded.

"I'd prefer not to, then…"

"This could be far more serious than you realize. They found the body of this girl in an abandoned part of Fort Tilden on Saturday. She studied here. At Mallow."

The man brought his hands to his mouth.

"The missing girl? I've seen the posters. Do you think he did it?" the man asked, horrified.

"I can't tell you anything," Ben replied, "but any information you can provide could be important. This… I don't know. I don't feel good about it."

The man's eyes filled with tears. Then, after a long pause during which he seemed to swallow his fears with a gulp, he exclaimed:

"There!" He pointed towards the street, towards the door of the school.

"What?"

"That's her! She's there! At the door!"

Ben turned and looked out through the café window and saw a girl with long brown hair, head down, in her school uniform, hurrying out of the school, now a considerable time after the other students had left.

"That's the girl I saw with the priest!" he cried, alarmed.

Ben hurried out behind the young woman, who was walking briskly towards a moped parked in front of Mallow. He raced across the street, and a car had to slam on its brakes not to run him over. The driver honked, but Ben tried to ignore it as he approached the girl before she could get on the moped and leave.

"Hi!" he called out, almost breathless.

She had already put on her helmet and started the motor. She looked at him in silence, and Miller realized that behind the visor her eyes were bloodshot, suggesting she had been crying.

"Can we talk? I'm from the FBI."

Chapter 37
Breezy Point
April 25, 2011
One day earlier
Miren Triggs

*We fall hundreds of times in life
and even though we don't
always know it at first,
sometimes these falls are attempts at flight.*

I drove down Rockaway Point Boulevard, leaving Jacob Riis Park behind, and stopped at the first gas station, across from Fort Tilden, to buy a can of gasoline. I loved the smell of gasoline, though that wasn't something I'd admit in public. I remembered when, as a little girl, I'd go with my father to inflate the tires of our station wagon and I'd crouch down to unscrew the plastic caps so he could check the pressure. That's all life is: flashbacks that arise when they're prompted by specific smells, arguments or emotions, and then disappear, as if you'd never even lived them, unless some spark brings them to the surface again. It was sad for me to think how that moment only existed in my mind when I inhaled the smell of gasoline, and yet the night I remembered more than anything else was so vivid I could touch it and feel the pain all over again just by closing my eyes.

I reached the end of the road to Breezy Point Tip, the remote area where Gina's backpack was found, and parked my car as close as I could to the beach. I checked to see if there was anyone around, but that place was a veritable wasteland on the edge of the Atlantic, not somewhere you'd expect to find company, except from the unrelenting, frigid wind.

I sat in the car for one long hour, alone except for the salty air flowing through my broken rear window, contemplating how to handle the second test. Finally, several Mallow students on scooters arrived. They didn't seem to see me, and they ran straight for the beach, laughing, shaking their arms and yelling like they were enjoying pure, unadulterated freedom. That's how it seemed to me, anyway. A few girls were carrying plastic bags full of beer bottles, and some of the boys had taken off their t-shirts to enjoy the last rays of sun. Two of them hurried to gather pieces of dry wood to stack on the remains of the previous night's bonfire. I recognized James Cooper and Ethan in the crowd.

I considered all the possibilities, every conceivable alternative, but none seemed convincing enough for me to change my plan.

I got out of the car, opened the trunk and grabbed the can of gasoline, fearing that the fire I felt within me would suddenly ignite. I poured the gasoline all over the car, covering the hood, roof, windows, and interior. The smell was so strong that I felt like a little girl again, crouching down beside my father's car at the gas station in Charlotte. When I looked, I saw that all the teenagers had begun watching me intently, in silent expectation. I walked towards them and saw Ethan swallow hard when I bent over to pick up one of the pieces of wood from the bonfire they'd lit. The students exchanged looks with one another, and from their faces I could see they didn't believe I was capable of taking the next step. My feet sank in the sand just as I felt my soul becoming one with the fire I was carrying. It was hard not to feel like an athlete about to light the Olympic flame, about to inaugurate a series of events it was best not to think about.

"I want in," I said, just before throwing the burning strip of wood through the broken read window of my new VW.

The fire spready quickly and soon I had to back away because I couldn't stand the heat. As the flame grew stronger and stronger and I watched the fire's fearsome dance, I noticed the students had come to watch the car burn with me. Ethan came up beside me. The flames were burning through the side windows, which quickly melted, releasing even more uncontrollable, scorching heat. It was hypnotizing to watch the whirlpool of flames slowly devour the roof, warp the metal, and create bubbles in the paint that quickly burst like soap. The black smoke rising from the car was pushed inland by the wind, like a signal trying to warn the world not to make another mistake. But things were only about to get worse. Soon the fire spread to the tires and, all of a sudden, when everything seemed about to calm down, one of the girls in the group shrieked and opened her arms as if she were embracing a complete sense of freedom. Another dark-haired girl joined in the battle cry, and then James Cooper did the same, looking at me with a wide grin from ear to ear, clearly so satisfied that I could practically hear what he was thinking: 'You're unbelievable.' The other students smiled and joined in the collective howl.

One of the girls approached me with a look of admiration.

"You're a fucking psychopath and I love it," she said with a complicit smile.

Then she walked as close as she could to the burning vehicle and began dancing around it.

"You shouldn't have done that," whispered Ethan, without taking his eyes off the fire. "You don't know what you're getting yourself into."

I felt an incessant tingling in my belly, like I was finally getting closer to what I was after. I saw my burning car reflected in Ethan's eyes and I felt, based on what he had said to me, that I was making the biggest mistake of my life. I knew, but even so, I decided to carry out my plan. Now that I think about it, everything would have gone so differently if I had just stopped there... everything would have turned out another way if I'd only paid attention to that warning he communicated to me with his eyes... but how can you see the flames in someone else when you yourself are on fire?

It wasn't long before the smoke brought firefighters. I could see their lights and sirens crossing the Marine Parkway Bridge, driving towards the site of the fire as quickly as they could. The teenagers didn't waste any time, running straight to their scooters to get out of there before the firefighters arrived. Ethan was the last to leave, and I thought it was strange that his girlfriend wasn't with him. As James Cooper rode off, he yelled:

"Tonight at midnight. Wait at the motel. You'll hear from... them."

Chapter 38
Neponsit
April 25, 2011
One day earlier
Jim Schmoer

Loneliness is the only demon
that grows stronger and stronger
the more time you spend together.

Mr. Rogers' expression changed the instant he heard Jim say the name Gina Pebbles; it was as if Jim was alerting him to the presence of a ghost.

"Gina?" he muttered.

"I guess everyone around here got an AMBER alert on their phones about Allison Hernández. The girl who disappeared last week in Queens. She was a student at the Mallow Institute."

"Uh… yeah yeah, I did. What's happening? What does this have to do with us or with… Gina? It's just… we already did everything we had to do to try to find her. It fucked Tom up real good, and I'm trying to protect him from any more of that. I'd rather not have to relive this over and over. It's like a nightmare that never ends."

"So, as you know, Gina also studied at Mallow. It may only be a coincidence, but I'm reviewing both cases to see if I can learn what happened."

"You're with the police?" he asked, confused.

"I'm... a freelance journalist. I'm revisiting Gina's case and trying to help with Allison's."

"Look... I don't want Tom to have to go through all this again. You understand?"

"I've already spoken with your son, Mr. Rogers," the professor blurted out before Mr. Rogers could say any more.

At that point, he finally seemed to put his guard down.

Jim continued: "I've also spoken with your neighbor, Mrs. Evans. And... with a gentleman who lives in a camper next to Jacob Riis Park, who I recommend avoiding if possible."

"Old Marvin, right? He's been here for years. He's kinda odd, but he's not a bad guy."

"It seems everyone in this neighborhood is a little odd, wouldn't you say?"

Mr. Rogers smiled and went back into the garage, which Jim could finally see. In the workshop, he had power saws, sanders, work benches and tools everywhere. Mr. Rogers turned on a saw. The blade began to spin rapidly as he placed various pinewood boards on the table to measure and mark them. The saw's constant buzzing filled the workshop and echoed against the walls. The floor was covered in sawdust and Jim noticed the many handsaws, hammers, rulers and drills hanging on a panel at the back of the garage. A workshop like that had to be a dream come true for a handyman who loves woodwork, and Jim tried to use this to win Mr. Rogers' trust:

"So... looks like you've got everything you could ever need here. You seem to really enjoy carpentry."

"Wood doesn't lie, you know?" he replied, marking a few boards with a pencil. "I think it's the only living thing that speaks the truth. If it's dry, it cracks; if it's low quality, it warps when it's humid. You can test its resistance, strength, where it comes from, what it'll be like years from now. It doesn't hurt you."

"Well, I've never liked splinters," Jim smiled.

"Splinters are the wood's way of fighting against all the cutting, hammer blows, and other changes we try to impose on it. We'd all put up a fight if someone wanted to force us to be something else, don't you think?"

"May I ask you a personal question?"

"Is there ever an answer that isn't personal?" he responded, moving one of the boards and aligning it with the saw.

"Is the finger you're missing also the casualty of a battle with wood?"

Tom's father looked at his own hand, as if he'd only just discovered in that moment that he was missing a finger.

"A battle with the saw, actually. Don't ever put your hands anywhere near one of these things. They're merciless. This one here's a good girl, real tender, treats the wood with care, but… as soon as she's got some flesh in front of her, she slices through like butter."

"That's another reason I don't think I could ever have a workshop like this. Everything inside it strikes me as just a little threatening."

"Including me?" Mr. Rogers said in an ambiguous tone; Jim wasn't quite sure if he was joking.

Then the man smiled, and Jim smiled back with a sense of unease he couldn't quite hide.

"Guys like you have soft hands. Like sponges for splinters," he continued.

"You see, Mr. Rogers, I'm not great with a hammer, but I can hit the nail on the head when it comes to asking questions. So… could you tell me what you remember about your son's girlfriend? And then I'll leave you alone."

Mr. Rogers paused for an instant; his expression was serious, as if he were about to strike Jim with his workman's hands. Then he gave a phony smile:

"All right then. What do you want to know?"

"Would you mind turning off the saw? It's a bit loud…"

Mr. Rogers grabbed the board he'd marked with pencil and slipped it into the blade, which sliced through it like a sheet of paper.

"I'm working. I gotta fix one of the back walls. If you've gotta ask me questions, you'll have to deal with the saw."

Jim took a deep, resigned sigh.

"It's fine. Did you know Gina? Did you know she was going out with your son?"

"He didn't tell me he was going out with her for a while, but yeah. Tom is a good kid, he's not some kinda player. He introduced me to Gina here one day, at the house. I thought she was nice. Although it wasn't important if I liked her or not."

"Did you know anything about her family?"

"The Pebbles? I didn't meet them until Gina and Tom started going out. If that's what you're asking."

"Are you aware that your son had a sexual relationship with her at the time?"

"Are you seriously asking me that?" he protested. "Sure, I guess. Like all boys his age, right? Look, I don't get involved in what my son does, and he doesn't meddle in what I do. Ever since my wife hasn't been around, I've tried to make sure he doesn't feel like I'm on his ass all the time. You know what I mean? We have a rule: if either of us is with someone, we close the door and we don't ask questions."

"I'm sorry to hear about your wife."

"Don't be. She left in '95. Since then it's been the two of us and… well, and my mother. Who's already old."

"Sorry, are you saying your wife died or…?" Jim asked, perplexed by the way he referred to his wife's absence.

The man sighed and looked at the ground. He seemed to want to avoid looking Jim in the eye, and stared instead at the grille on the sawdust collector. Jim got the feeling it was a difficult topic for him. Mr. Rogers swallowed before continuing:

"Look... I don't like talking about this... but the long and the short of it is... some freaks brainwashed her into joining a cult. One day I woke up and she was staring at me with her eyes wide open and she asked me what I'd dreamed about. I said I couldn't remember, and she got fierce like a wild animal. I chalked it up to her having had a miscarriage a few months earlier, but things only got worse. She'd wake up in the middle of the night sobbing. You'd find her in the garden at sunrise digging holes in the ground with her hands. I tried to get professional help but... one day she just left. A few times she'd talked about joining a community, but I didn't understand it at all and, one day, when she was more lucid than she'd been in months, I saw her at the door, all ready to go, her bag packed. She said goodbye to me with a kiss on the forehead, and she said goodbye to Tom without even touching him. He was nine back then. I've tried to do my best to keep him from missing his mother and to make sure he doesn't want for anything here, and I think I've done a decent job. I'm not saying it's been easy, but I think I raised a strong boy with a future ahead of him. He's gonna be a big movie director."

"A cult?"

"I didn't realize that... my wife was losing it. I was working too much. Back then I had a used car dealership, and I was working as much as I could. But... you know. Running a business isn't easy. I had to close up shop and... well, we lived off my little carpentry gigs. Here in the Rockaways the humidity from the ocean is what puts food on our table. The ocean takes bites outta people's houses and they hire me to fix them."

"So how long has it been since you've seen your wife?"

"For us, Ava has been dead since the moment she decided to leave. I told Tom she died, even though I get the feeling he doesn't believe it so much anymore, he's never asked where she's buried."

"I understand," Jim said with a nod, hoping to return to the topic of Gina. "Your son told me about an episode involving Gina… how one day she ran away from home. Do you remember that day? It would've been a few months before she disappeared."

"That was a long time ago… but I haven't forgotten how crazy the girl's aunt and uncle got that day. Gina and Tom had been studying at her house and, in the middle of the afternoon, Tom comes back here in a rage. The Pebbles had kicked him out. He didn't wanna say much more than that, but a little while later, Gina knocked on the door and they went up to his room."

"They slept together," Jim said incisively, "your son told me."

Mr. Rogers looked down, as if he were ashamed to know that his son was sexually active at the time.

"Did you know she'd run away from home, and that her aunt and uncle were looking for her?" Jim asked.

"I didn't know that. Later that night, Tom asked me to drive Gina back to their house."

"Did you notice anything about her? Your son said she was different after that day. She told her aunt and uncle she'd slept with Tom."

"What do you mean?" he replied, clearly annoyed.

"Did she seem strange to you? Did you talk about anything in particular on the car ride?"

"She was silent the whole time. She was… a shy girl. I dropped her off in front of her house in Roxbury. She thanked me for the ride and got out. That was a few weeks before she disappeared. I don't see what this has to do with what happened. You ought to focus on when she disappeared. Her brother said goodbye to her by the bridge. Go sniff around there. She never made it here."

"It might help me understand what Gina was like. Can I ask… just one thing? What time did you drive her home? Was it after midnight?"

Jim's question hit like lightning, and it required an answer.

"It would've been… around two in the morning."

"Got it," Jim said distantly.

Something didn't fully fit about the answer Mr. Rogers had given, and he seemed to notice Jim was analyzing him.

"Then all the craziness started. Tom had final exams and it totally threw him off. He joined the search parties, and he lost a whole year."

"His girlfriend disappeared, I guess that's normal."

"Yeah, but… I don't know. Throwing away a whole year like that over a girl… with my wife, I learned you shouldn't put so much stake in a person, you know? Because they can leave at any moment, and it'll destroy you. If you fall in love, you're lost. They can do whatever they want with you, manipulate you, cheat on you, blackmail you. And if they lose their heads, they hurt you with all the things you never managed to do."

Jim noticed the anger behind his words.

"I think you just had bad luck. You shouldn't—"

"Don't come to my house and tell me how to live my life, buddy."

"I just mean we all have our demons, and it's hard to find someone who understands yours and knows how to deal with them," Jim said, thinking of Miren again.

He realized he hadn't been able to subdue Miren's demons or take the time to put himself in her shoes.

"You finished?" Mr. Rogers spat, trying to conclude the conversation.

"Just… one more thing I can't understand."

"What's that?"

"Your neighbor, Mrs. Evans, told me that after everything with Gina, you rejected several offers to buy your house. You'd been planning on selling it but then changed your mind. Why? Wouldn't it have been better to put some distance between Tom and… everything that happened?"

"Mrs. Evans?" he replied, as if Jim had spoken the name of an enemy. "The real estate agent? I'm sure she didn't speak too highly of me."

"Not particularly, no."

"That bitch is obsessed with getting me to sell the house," Mr. Rogers replied, "but, of course she is, that's how she earns her living. If it were up to her, all of Neponsit would be for sale. The better the house, the fewer times it's sold, and the fewer times she earns a commission. She chose the wrong neighborhood for her turf. Lots of families think this is the perfect place to live. I think she'd earn a better living selling houses elsewhere, and if she'd shut her goddamn mouth occasionally."

"You do have a beautiful house though. I wouldn't even know how to put panels on the roof. How much could you ask for it? Two million?"

"It's not for sale. So there is no price."

"But it was for sale at one point, right? Why'd you decide not to sell?"

"What's that got to do with the girl? What do you care?"

"No reason, it's just… it's not something you change your mind about overnight."

Mr. Rogers looked at Jim in silence for a few seconds, and it felt to Jim as if he were being dissected by the man's gaze.

"They weren't offering enough," Mr. Rogers declared. "They used the girl's disappearance as a pretext to offer less than the house was worth. And that pissed me off. So I refused to sell."

"Okay, I see," Jim replied with a knot in his throat.

"You finished now?"

284

Mr. Rogers grabbed some sandpaper from among his tools in the back of the workshop and continued working the wood. Jim couldn't help but notice a half-built wooden doll's house resting on one of the tables in the corner. He decided to leave on a positive note, in case he had to speak to Mr. Rogers on another occasion.

"Did you make that doll's house? It reminds me of… a person that… I was looking for at one point."

Mr. Rogers caressed the doll's house.

"Yes. Sometimes I make… wooden toys. You don't always feel like cutting planks for people's porches, you know?"

"It's… beautiful."

Jim looked closely at the details: it was probably twenty inches tall, and you could clearly identify the living room, the bedrooms, the kitchen and the bathroom, which you could tell apart because they had painted walls that differentiated them from one another. The rooms were all connected by little doors. In the bedrooms, there was miniature furniture: a bed, a desk, a cradle. In the bathroom there was a bathtub carved from pinewood. There was even a basement beneath the living room, where Mr. Rogers had made a sofa with several pieces of cloth stuffed with padding, beside which were two beds. Mr. Rogers explained how he built the doll's house.

"It's nothing. Making toys is just more fun. You get to be creative and add a little magic to things. When you're working on a house you just replace warped pieces of wood with new ones. You've gotta follow someone's instructions. And I've never liked being told what to do. I do it because we need the cash to keep living here, but there's no mystery to it."

Jim nodded, pleased with himself for wearing down Mr. Rogers' thick defensive outer layer, and then, at that moment, he asked an innocent question that would change everything:

"Does your house have a basement?"

Chapter 39
FBI New York Field Office
April 25, 2011
One day earlier
Ben Miller

Everything always begins
with one simple question:
Who are you?

Young Deborah's hands were shaking, and she was clutching them together; her thin, pale fingers were unable to contain the trembling. She was still wearing her Mallow school uniform, and Inspector Miller was waiting outside the room for her parents to arrive so he could take a statement from her. He could tell the whole situation was overwhelming for her, and she kept glancing around the room for any form of a threat. Ben had to make sure a psychologist was present for the interview, so he had called a specialist, Sarah Atkins, who had been on the force for years; she would make sure Deborah felt comfortable and relaxed enough to describe what had happened. Deborah's parents were a middle-aged couple, both very tall and blonde; they were originally from Finland, but now lived in Queens. When they finally arrived, Ben did his best to calm them befor .hey saw their daughter:

"Mr. and Mrs.... Korhonen? I assume you're Deborah's parents? I'm Inspector Benjamin Miller, from the FBI. I'm sorry we had to call you about something like this, but it's..." he searched for the right adjective, hoping to find one that wasn't too upsetting, "...serious."

Deborah's father glanced at his wife, who nodded with a concerned expression as Ben spoke.

"What are you accusing my daughter of? Why is she under arrest?" Mrs. Korhonen asked, confused.

"Oh no, no, she hasn't... she's not under arrest. Your daughter hasn't committed any crime."

"What's going on, then?" Deborah's father demanded, raising his voice.

The extent of his anger made Ben think he should have explained everything from the outset.

"We brought Deborah in to make a statement because we believe she is the object of ongoing sexual abuse from a member of... from an employee of the Mallow Institute."

"Sexual abuse?" both parents exclaimed, exchanging a shocked expression. "No... you can't be right. Our daughter... hasn't told us... no..." they refuted.

They hadn't been expecting something like that. No parent ever is. One day they notice their child is skipping lunch, the next they don't want to come out of their room, and often they think they're just acting like a teenager. Silences grow longer, conversations become monosyllabic. Parents stop knowing their kids' interests; they become strangers. For a while, they think it's just that phase all parents talk about, when their kids don't want to see them and everything they say is an insult to their maturity. They pray the phase will be brief and that their kids will come out of the tunnel of adolescence with the values they tried to instill in them intact, but then, suddenly, all the signs they confused with puberty transform into a bomb that explodes in their face: bullying, harassment or, God forbid, some irreparable trauma.

"Dr. Atkins will be present while we ask a few questions and, if there is even a minor confirmation that our suspicions are correct, we will issue an arrest warrant for the primary suspect. As your daughter is a legal minor, we will need one of you to be present in the room. It won't be easy to hear."

Deborah's mother looked through the window into the room and saw her frightened daughter looking both ways like a wounded puppy, on the lookout for the next person who might hurt her. Mrs. Korhonen covered her mouth and muttered in Finnish '*Tyttäreni...*'—My daughter...—then she opened the door and ran inside to wrap her arms around her child. Deborah's father also went inside, and Ben left them alone so they could speak for a few minutes while they waited for Dr. Atkins to arrive. Deborah broke down as soon as she saw her parents, and when Ben came in with Dr. Atkins a bit later, they were all wet with tears.

"Hi, Deborah... how are you feeling?" Dr. Atkins asked, in a warm tone and with an encouraging smile.

Deborah wiped away her tears one more time and gripped her mother's hand firmly. She responded with only a nod.

"Will both of you be staying?" Ben asked the parents, who were hugging their daughter tighter than they had ever done before.

"Yes. Whatever she has to say, we'll be here with her," her father replied in a serious tone.

"All right," Ben said. He sat at the table, and Dr. Atkins did the same.

"Deborah," the psychologist said, trying to set out the rules of the conversation, "I know this is hard to talk about, so I want you to know that if at any point you feel uncomfortable and you think you need to stop, just say so and we'll wait as long as we have to. We're not in any hurry. All we're trying to do is find out what really happened."

"I... okay," Deborah said in a hoarse voice.

Ben took a deep breath before beginning; he knew this wouldn't be easy. He felt his heart beating hard in his chest and he knew he wasn't going to like what he was about to hear.

"I'm going to try to avoid... asking you for many details. We don't need them right now, okay? I just... want to know..." he paused. "I want to know if Father Graham has ever... touched you. In a... sexual way."

Deborah initially shook her head, but Ben could tell it was because she felt vulnerable.

"The owner of the café across from Mallow saw the two of you together," Ben said. "You're not alone, Deborah. We only need you to confirm that it's true, and then we'll be finished here."

Deborah nodded in silence. She tried to swallow the lump in her throat, but it was clinging to her vocal cords in a way that only the worst of fears do. Deborah's father was pacing around the room, and her mother couldn't hold back tears.

"Was it more than once?" Ben asked as neutrally as he could.

She nodded again as a tear ran down her cheek.

"Are you able to talk to me about it, just a little? Did he make you do anything... that you didn't want to?"

She moved her head in confirmation.

Ben could barely handle it. The conversation was even more difficult than he had expected. Surely Allison must have suffered the same experience.

"When did it all start?"

Deborah finally managed to speak after swallowing.

"Three... months ago."

Her mother turned to stare at an indeterminate point on the wall and Ben realized her lips were beginning to tremble.

"Can you tell me how it started, and exactly what he did to you?"

She sighed and closed her eyes.

"Deborah, if you want, we can do this later," Dr. Atkins said, aware of the girl's internal battle. "I want you to know that this is all over now, and the person who did this to you will be behind bars before you know it. I promise."

Deborah hesitated for a few seconds, and then started speaking.

"It's okay," she said with renewed strength. "It started not long after I started going out with Ethan."

"Ethan… Ethan Pebbles?" Ben asked, caught off guard by the name.

"Yeah, he's my… boyfriend. We've been together five or six months. Everything was going great and… well, I guess at Mallow you can't really keep a secret from anyone. Soon everyone knew we were together. Dating isn't against the rules at Mallow, but… it kind of puts you under a magnifying glass."

"What do you mean?"

"They want to know everything. If you're kissing or doing more or whatever."

Ben glanced at the psychologist, looking for her approval to continue, then returned to Deborah with an expectant look.

"One day… Father Graham called me into his office. He'd heard the rumor that I had a boyfriend and… I guess he wanted to talk to me."

"Why?"

"To… talk to me about God… and love… and what it means to love someone and… virginity and chastity and how important it is to… and…" her voice fell apart as she spoke, and she had to stop.

"You're doing really well," said the psychologist, grabbing her hand so she could feel some warmth during the cold trip she was taking in her mind.

Deborah's mother stroked her back and her father sat stone-still, seething with rage, waiting for her to continue.

"Then he got out of his chair… and…"

"And what?"

"He put his crotch in front of my face. He pulled down his zipper, and—"

"All right," Ben interrupted, angry, "you can stop there, that's all we need to know."

"—then… after that… he kept calling me into his office," she continued, feeling powerless, "and he threatened to take away my scholarship and… and… I couldn't do that to my parents… and then he wanted more… and… he asked me to go to his house in the morning and—"

"That's enough, Deborah, it's okay," said Ben, who didn't want to hear any more details.

He got up and furiously left the room, leaving the psychologist with the family to manage the situation. He ran to the office of his boss, Special Agent Spencer, who looked up from some papers on his desk and gave Ben a confused look.

"What is it, Ben? Got something?" he asked. Ben hated this man, but he had to swallow his pride and work with him. He'd be retiring before too long, and he just had to put up with his unscrupulous asshole of a boss a little while longer. "If not, I need you to move on to the next case. An eight-year-old boy has gone missing on Staten Island. He was playing on the street in front of his house and then, poof, no one has seen him since."

"What?!" Ben exclaimed, confused.

That case instantly transported him back to the disappearance of Daniel, his own son, and drove what he had been about to say straight from his mind.

"You have anything on the girl or not? I can send it to Malcolm. Seems like all they found was the red jersey he was wearing, but there's no trace of the kid."

"When was this? Give it to me," he said immediately. "I think… we've found Allison Hernández's killer."

"Three days ago. Local police have asked for our help. They're not making progress and the parents… are desperate. Alright, what have you got?" Ben had noticed Spencer's confidence in him had grown after how the Kiera Templeton case turned out.

"Father Graham, the principal of the Mallow Institute," Ben answered. "Deborah Korhonen, a Mallow student, just said on the record that this guy has been abusing her. She's a scholarship student like Allison, and… they were both the same age. I need an arrest warrant immediately. And a search warrant for the school and his house. We'll detain him for sexual abuse of a minor and if he was doing the same to Allison as he was to Deborah, I'm sure we'll find incriminatory evidence from Allison's murder. He had a copy of Allison Hernández's Bible in his office. I'm sure we'll find Allison's DNA in his office or on his clothes. If we find something more connecting him to her, he'll get life. Son of a bitch deserves it."

Spencer nodded seriously. A moment later, he gave a slow smile, which Ben knew marked the greatest of victories.

"Congratulations, Ben. Let me get those warrants for you. I'll give you access to the missing boy's file, but finish this up first. I don't want any mess or hubbub. A clean arrest. Try to keep the press away and, more importantly, don't give the priest the chance to escape. This is America. Accusing a priest of sexual abuse without enough evidence would blow up in our face, in terms of public opinion."

"Thanks, Spencer. I'll bring the whole cavalry."

Chapter 40
Breezy Point
April 25, 2011
One hour earlier
Miren Triggs

And what is life,
if not a game
we're all destined to lose?

I walked as far as the New Life Motel in Breezy Point, and the receptionist greeted me as if I'd never left.

"Still haven't repaired the window in 3A. You'll have to stay in another," he said as soon as I walked in.

"I... that's fine."

He handed me the key to room 3E and, as soon as I touched it, I felt an unpleasant tickle in my stomach, as if accepting that key meant accepting everything that was about to happen.

"Can I ask you something?" he asked, bending over the counter, as if he were about to tell me a secret.

"Of course," I said.

"Will you sign my copy of your book?" he asked, pointing to a copy of *The Snow Girl* on the bookshelf behind him. "I'm a big fan. I wanted to tell you yesterday, but with the window and the condition you were in when you arrived, I thought it was... not the best timing."

I have to admit I wasn't expecting that. Since the signing at the bookstore on Saturday, when they gave me the polaroid of Gina, I'd managed to forget the whirlwind of book presentations and talks from the preceding weeks; I'd been too absorbed in the case. I remembered Martha Wiley and I figured she was probably plotting some way to seduce me into coming back. I'm sure she wanted me more places, doing more events, more interviews, an ounce of flesh here, a pound of flesh there. I had the feeling she wanted to gobble up my bones, and what she didn't understand was that if she did that, there would be nothing left of me. I felt so empty on the inside without journalism, I couldn't stay trapped in the spiral I'd lost control of my life in, filling my days with spotlights and television sets, surrounded by people who demanded more and more Kiera Templeton.

"Of... of course," I replied to the receptionist, with the feeling he was being overly kind.

"What you did... don't ever stop doing it."

That sentence was the pat on the back I needed to hear. It's odd how a stranger can have more impact on us than our loved ones. My mother had tried to tell me how proud of me she was a hundred times, and I was incapable of seeing it. But some receptionist at a hotel that smelled like ammonia says the same thing and suddenly I feel like an important person. Maybe it was imposter syndrome, and I just wanted to undermine myself and turn into the shadow-person I thought I was destined to become.

I signed his book, and he dropped a handful of complimentary pillow mints on the counter as if he were returning the gesture. I grabbed them because, truth be told, I hadn't put a single thing in my mouth in ages, and it would still be a few hours before midnight, which was the time James Cooper had told me before riding away at the beach.

I didn't know what was in store for me. I flopped onto the bed in my room, certain I shouldn't have gone there. I was exhausted and my whole body hurt. I closed my eyes to avoid the thoughts relentlessly bombarding me, but immediately opened them again when my mind showed me an image of Morningside Park. I remembered the pool of blood spreading beneath Aron Wallace's body, and I remembered Roy's corpse lying in that alley. I also remembered the pain between my legs that night, and how since that time, I had gone everywhere in life hearing my dead soul's cries.

It was impossible to feel like I would ever fill that void, because my insides were full of holes through which any emotion escaped.

I paced around the room for a while, not knowing what to expect and remembering the image of my burning car. The image of the flames was still burned on my eyes, I could still smell the burning rubber tires. The hotel bedspread had a red floral motif, and the design reminded me of a double homicide. The walls were covered in dust and grime. The place clearly didn't care about creating bedrooms that made you want to lie down and create a new life, despite the motel's name.

James Cooper had been clear that he would have news at midnight, but he hadn't told me what kind of news, and that worried me. Ethan had tried to warn me several times not to dig into the Ravens of God, and that secrecy was precisely what prompted me to try to open that locked door. I remembered that Bob was expecting the article about Allison the following day, and maybe this midnight rendezvous with a mystery person would give me the key I needed to what happened to Allison and to Gina.

My mind wouldn't stop jumping form one idea to another, from one concern to another; I kept experiencing moments of deep fear. Was I making a mistake? Absolutely. Could I have done anything differently? No way.

I regretted giving Aron Wallace my unregistered Glock, as I

wouldn't have it with me if things got ugly, but there was no predicting what was about to happen. I pulled the note with the rules of the Soul Game from my pocket and reread the last challenge:

I. ASCEND THE CROSS BLINDFOLDED.

It was the last thing I had to do, and it was impossible to read that sentence without thinking about how Allison's life had come to an end. Part of me thought that at any moment, I would understand how Father Graham fit into all this, and I would learn that crucifying Allison had been a punishment assigned by him, or perhaps a failed challenge posed by the Ravens. Anything was possible and the more I thought about it, the less sense the puzzle made, although all the pieces were scattered across the table.

I needed to talk to someone. All this time waiting was eating away at me, and the more time that passed, the more doubts I had about whether I should remain at the motel or get the hell out of there. I picked up the landline on the nightstand and dialed the only number I knew by heart. After the line rang a few times on the other end, my mother's warm voice came through the receiver:

"Hi, who's this?"

"It's me, Miren."

"Where are you calling from? I don't have this number saved."

"You don't want to know."

"Are you in prison? I told you they'd lock you up for writing all those things about the government. Those people don't know the meaning of 'freedom of the press.'"

"No, Mom, I'm in a motel. If you must know everything."

"A motel? Are you okay? What about your apartment? Why aren't you home?"

"I'm… investigating something. I had to stay here. I wanted to talk to the two of you before... some friends drop by," I hesitated, realizing I was about to say too much and worry her. "How's Dad?"

"Your father has gone out to the garden to look through his telescope. I didn't tell you. He bought himself a telescope and on clear nights he spends all his time outside. The other night he showed me Saturn. Saturn! Have you ever seen it? It's like a big white stain, but with lines on the sides. He bought himself a cheap telescope and now he's complaining that things don't look the way they do on Google."

"Dad with a telescope?"

"Retirees, honey. You stop work, and what do you do? Enjoy time with your wife a little? Plan a road trip to get some life experiences in, seeing the country and having sex in motels? No! He buys himself a goddamn telescope and just goes out to stargaze all the time. And it's all blurry. It's like having cataracts. I don't see the appeal."

"Mom! I don't want to know about those things. Ew."

"What, the sex in roadside motels? Where do you think you were conceived, the Ritz Carlton?"

"Mom, please, oh my God, stop," I laughed with a kind of giggly embarrassment. "With Dad at least you're never bored. He's always got his latest obsession."

"I don't get bored, eh? You should hear him talk. All day he's talking about distances between seals and mammoths and scales and God knows what. He's lost his mind."

I couldn't help but smile as I heard her summarize, with confusion, the magnitudes my father used to find objects in the night sky. I imagined the two of them in the back garden discussing the point of gazing out at space only to end up feeling insignificant. The truth is, you don't need a telescope to feel unimportant, all you need to do is open your eyes.

"How long ago did he buy the telescope?"

"He saw a documentary on the UFO channel, and now he's

determined to spot one. With that stubborn head of his, I have no doubt he'll find one."

"Have I told you that I love you both?"

"You don't need to say it for us to know it, honey," she said in a tone that felt like a hug.

"I know, Mom," I said, feeling the lump appear in my throat.

I realized I was about to cry and that it had been incredibly difficult for me to speak those last words. It was hard to understand how I could feel so alive under the warmth of her voice and so dead when I hung up. My mother had the ability to talk about nonsense and make you love life, but all that love ended up escaping through the holes in my soul.

"You know what?" I continued, "I miss you. I got used to having you close by at the hospital and at home."

"We could organize something for the two of us, now that your father is off looking for Martians, literally."

I laughed. I loved her sense of humor, something I hadn't managed to inherit. Or maybe I'd just forgotten it.

"Sounds good, Mom."

And then, there were three sharp knocks on the door.

"Mom, I have to go, all right?"

"Your friends are there?"

"Yes. I love you."

"I love you too, honey. If you need anything, call me. You know I'm always here for you."

"I know."

I hung up and stared at the motel room door in terror. They knocked again, the same way, and I hesitated for a few seconds, thinking about what to do. I saw that the shadows were moving in the beam of light that shone in under the door, and I knew the time had come to face the final challenge in this dark game; the time had come to discover the truth. Without waiting another second—and convinced that everything was about to come to an end—I opened the door.

Chapter 41
New York
April 25, 2011
One hour earlier
Jim Schmoer

A little lie is the first step
in the descent to a place
devoid of light.

Mr. Rogers hesitated for a few seconds before answering Jim's question, but after a moment, a smile spread across his face. It hadn't taken him long to respond, but Jim didn't like the reaction; it was offhand and yet, at the same time, charged with meaning.

"Oh, yes. There's a basement," Mr. Rogers replied in a friendlier tone than he had been using up until that moment. "Why do you ask?"

"The model house. It made me think about how much space you have here. It's a very big house for just you, your son and… your mother? Tom told me that his grandmother lives with you."

"She's been here a few years. She has… well, senile dementia. She was at a home before, but we had to pull her out. Those places are too expensive. I don't earn a bad living doing repairs around the neighborhood, but I don't earn enough to keep up the house and also keep her in a home."

"And your son takes care of her."

"What's wrong with that? You say it like keeping the family together is a bad thing."

"No... please don't get me wrong. It's just that... I thought he was focused on his studies. I know how much tuition costs. I imagine you must be making a considerable effort to—"

"We manage things all right between the two of us. There's a mortgage on the home and he's taking out a loan for college. What the hell does any of that matter to you?" he said, visibly upset. "Look, I think I've tried to be... friendly, but you push it and push it with all these questions. What are you getting at? Do you think we did something to that poor girl? She never got here that day. Tom was waiting for her all afternoon and... it destroyed him. He loved her. You weren't the one who was here, holding my son as he cried because the girl he loved had gone. I'm sorry about what happened to her, but... don't think you can show up here and question everything and act like a hero just because... why? I know this house is beyond our means, and you're not the first one to come sniffing around here asking questions about it. What's this really about? Did Mrs. Evans send you to try and convince me to sell? Are you getting a commission? Who're you working for?"

This floored Jim. Maybe it was true, maybe he was being too intrusive.

"I'm... I'm sorry, Mr. Rogers. No one sent me here. I'm doing this alone and..." Jim regretted saying that and didn't finish the sentence. "Honestly, I didn't want to... inconvenience you in any way. It's... the job, it's a professional hazard, a hard habit to kick. I'm... very sorry."

Mr. Rogers gave him a firm look for several moments, then clicked his tongue before continuing:

"Don't sweat it. It's fine. I get it. I'm just tired of this whole Gina Pebbles story. We all suffered at the time, you know? We've tried to move on."

"I understand, and I'm sorry. I was impolite and... I forgot that in this profession it's essential to... think about those who have been through a difficult experience."

"Don't worry about it," Mr. Rogers said, stepping closer to Jim and giving him a few solid slaps on the back. Mr. Rogers' fingers were thick and dry, and his hands were strong thanks to years of woodworking. Jim smiled, a little injured, and took one last look at the entire workshop before leaving. "Everyone's got baggage they can't shake. Forget about it," he smiled. "I can tell you're interested in all the machines I use. They're all... essential, they've helped me a lot. But... do you want to know what the most important thing in a workshop is?" he asked with a smile.

"The workbench?" Jim replied, saying the first thing that came to his mind.

Mr. Rogers shook his head. Then he turned and approached the giant saw behind him and give it two taps with his hand.

"The saw?"

"The saw is important, but... do you know how much sawdust these bad boys produce?" He pointed at Jim with his finger as if he were giving him a lesson, and finally he answered his own question: "The sawdust collector." He moved the finger that had been pointing at Jim towards a trap door on the floor beside the sander.

"Without a good sawdust collector, it would be impossible to run a workshop. My father taught me that, and it was the first thing I built when I started setting up this workshop. Every time you cut something, sand something, or perforate something, you produce shavings. This machine here," he said, gesturing to the saw, "collects all the sawdust from those cuts internally and deposits it in a room below the workshop."

Jim nodded, pleased that Mr. Rogers seemed to have forgiven him.

"Do you want to see?"

"Sorry?" Jim asked, confused.

"The collector. Do you want to see it? It's pretty big. It takes up the whole space beneath the workshop and... well, I figured I might as well connect it to the basement of the house."

"Wow."

Mr. Rogers crouched and pulled on the handle of the trap door, revealing a short wood ladder that vanished into the darkness."

"No... really I don't need to—"

"Don't be shy, please. I like to show off my work. If you ever start a carpentry workshop, you can't forget to set up a sawdust collector like this."

Jim bent down towards the trapdoor to look inside, and Mr. Rogers himself climbed down the ladder with a speed that demonstrated he was quite fit despite his age. He must have only been a few years older than Jim, but the physical difference between them was clear. Jim was thin and was able to pull off a fairly fit look if he wore the right clothes, but things were a different story when he was naked. It's not that he had flabby, undefined muscles, but you could tell he didn't exercise and that his diet was only so-so at best. His muscles weren't good for much besides looking adequate in the mirror. But Mr. Rogers had powerful forearms and hands that looked like they could crush walnuts.

After climbing down the ladder, Mr. Rogers turned on a light and encouraged Jim to follow.

"Come on, you have to see this," he said, waving him down with his hand.

Jim sighed and thought about the other houses on the street he still wanted to visit.

"Just for a minute. I'd better—"

"It'll only take a minute. You have to see how big it is. I'm telling you. You can even smell the ocean a little from down here. You can't imagine the seashells and fossils I found when I dug out the basement. I have a few of them around here somewhere…" Mr. Rogers disappeared into the interior of the basement.

"Shit," Jim said.

He checked the time: it was almost sunset, and he put a foot on the ladder and began to hurry down so he wouldn't lose any more time.

At the bottom, he was surprised that the space was so big the light didn't even reach the far walls. On one side of the ladder, a metal tube was carrying the buzzing sound of the saw, which was still on in the workshop; this tube led to a mountain of sawdust as tall as Jim. On the back wall, Jim could see a few shelves full of canned goods, bottles of water, and enough provisions to get the Rogers through a nuclear disaster. It struck him as funny that Mr. Rogers could also be that type of U.S. citizen who believed there would soon be a nuclear war and the only survivors would be those who had enough supplies to spend five years underground.

"Wow, I can see you have a good… deal of stuff down here."

"I haven't even shown you the best part yet," Mr. Rogers said in the distance. "Come over here."

Jim followed Mr. Rogers' voice through the semidarkness into the full darkness. He heard a noise to his side, but he could barely see anything.

"Mr. Rogers?"

Jim turned around, looked towards the area through which he had entered the basement, and saw Mr. Rogers climbing the ladder.

"You shouldn't have come," Tom's father lamented, pausing for an instant on the last step.

"Where are you going?!" Jim exclaimed, confused.

He ran towards the ladder. But Mr. Rogers moved faster and climbed out through the trapdoor. Jim looked up at him, unable to grasp what was going on. Part of his brain wanted to continue being friendly, while in another part of his mind, alarm bells were blaring; adrenaline was pulsing at the tips of his fingers. A shiver ran down his body the instant he heard a sound from deep inside the basement.

"Who else is down here?" he asked.

"Everyone's got baggage they can't shake," Mr. Rogers said from above in a serious tone.

"Hey! Hey! What are you doing!" Jim shrieked as he saw the trapdoor moving.

"And now my baggage is that much heavier," Mr. Rogers said, just before closing the latch.

"No!" Jim shouted with all his strength.

Chapter 42
Fort Tilden
April 25, 2011
One hour earlier
Miren Triggs

Fear of darkness always
emerges from those who know
what's hiding there.

I didn't know how to react when I opened the door. On the other side was Ethan Pebbles, who looked visibly upset; his face was sad, and he was wearing pants and a black pullover. I wasn't expecting to see him, but to be honest, I had no idea what to expect when I followed James Cooper's instructions.

"Ethan?" I exclaimed, confused.

"They asked me to come for you," he said with a hoarse voice. Then, after looking both ways, he whispered: "You're making a big mistake, Miss Triggs."

"Who asked you to come for me?" I asked.

The third challenge in the game was the one I feared most, and I didn't know if I should continue forward without more information.

"I can't say," he said after swallowing. I could tell he was stressed, and it hurt me to think he had been dragged into this, too. "You'll know soon."

"Ethan, it's important for you to tell me."

"We don't have time," he said nervously, coming into the room, "They're waiting for us."

"Please, Ethan, you have to tell me."

"Miss Triggs..." he whispered, "they know everything about you. Everything. They know you were here years ago looking for my sister, they know about the article you wrote, the questions you asked. You shouldn't have come. You've fallen into their trap. The game has begun."

"Do you think I'm in danger?"

"What do *you* think? Don't you get it yet? The Ravens aren't what you imagine. It's not a group of bored teenagers. This is nothing like your secret club from school. Can't you see?"

"I won't go if you tell me not to," I said.

"Now... there's no turning back. Once the game has begun, you have to finish it. There's no other choice."

"Why?"

"They've threatened me. They know you talked to me. Either you complete the final challenge, or they'll burn down my house with my aunt and uncle inside."

"They'll burn your house down?"

"I think that's how... my parents died. I hate my aunt and uncle, but... please, you have to keep going. If you pass the final challenge, no one has to die."

"The Ravens burned down your house when you were a kid?" I was becoming even more worried than I had been, and frankly I didn't completely understand everything he was telling me.

"I think Gina... wanted to join. I know she was having a hard time dealing with our parents dying and... I think she thought she'd be happier as part of the Ravens. Maybe that's why she didn't speak with me much in those final weeks. Maybe they sent you her photo to… set a trap. You're a famous journalist who's supposed to be good at finding lost people. They played you, Miss Triggs. You made a mistake by coming here and by… starting the game. They'll burn down my house… and then it'll all begin again." He was crying.

He sat on the bed and collapsed, helpless. I hadn't been expecting this. Clearly the Ravens of God had managed to terrorize Ethan, and there I was at a dead end, caught in their trap.

"No one's going to burn your aunt and uncle's house, okay? I won't let them."

"Who'll stop them?"

"I'll tell the police. They'll do surveillance."

"For how long? They'll wait… and… at some point, after one or two years when it seems like everything has blown over…"

"Fuck… what is the final challenge? Do you know?"

Ethan was really upset, and I didn't know how to make him feel better. It wasn't my forte. All I could do was sit with him as he sobbed, because pain is something I'm more used to. Sometimes all you need is someone to be with you. Someone who will wait by your side in silence as you let it all out, without trying to stop you.

"Ethan, listen to me. The last challenge. What will they make me do? You have to tell me something about what I have to do and how I can pass."

He looked up at me, his eyes full of tears, and said:

"I only know rumors."

"Tell me the rumors."

"You have to climb onto a cross. And you have to climb up it and wait. No matter what happens. You can't call for help. You can't scream. You just have to trust. That's all."

"Then what'll they do?"

"I don't know," he whispered.

"So that's how Allison Hernández died?"

He nodded silently. Then he swallowed hard and confirmed my suspicion:

"She didn't… pass the test. I couldn't… tell you. Now that you're about to do the test, you need to know."

I paced across the motel room, from one end to the other, considering all my options. I couldn't call the police, since doing that wouldn't guarantee safety for Ethan and his aunt and uncle. And I couldn't give up either, just bail out. Since I'd involved Ethan in this madness, I'd eliminated all my alternatives. I swallowed hard and finally said:

"Okay, where is this fucking cross?"

* * *

We left the motel and I climbed onto the back of Ethan's scooter. We rode from Breezy Point down Rockaway Boulevard, towards Fort Tilden and, when we were half the way there, he turned to the right down a street that opened onto the beach. I could feel the night breeze, the ocean's ever-present, sticky humidity. Finally, Ethan parked beside a rusty fence, behind which stood the vast, abandoned installations of the military complex. Ethan was well aware of what he had to do. He pulled a flashlight from the compartment beneath the seat of the scooter and illuminated a stretch of the fence, along with one of the posts holding it up. He walked up to it and lifted the wire mesh until he created an opening big enough for a person to crawl through.

"Go ahead," he said, "this is the end of the road."

I climbed through the hole, and he followed. Ethan's flashlight lit up the way ahead for several yards in front of us, and I followed him in silence to the rhythm of the waves breaking in the distance and our footsteps on the earth and undergrowth. That part of Fort Tilden had been taken over by bushes, shrubs, and trees growing wild everywhere, except along the paths created by people walking, which stretched out in front of us like a labyrinth. Ethan weaved his way through the vegetation, turning left and right. Suddenly, he stopped in front of an abandoned concrete building, in front of which four or five scooters were parked. A faint light was emerging from inside the construction, through the few windows that remained intact on the upper walls.

"We're here," Ethan whispered.

"Is this where Allison died?"

He shook his head from side to side before responding.

"I think that was in another one of the abandoned buildings. Fort Tilden is full of places like this."

I sighed. I could hear voices coming from inside.

"You have to go in alone."

"You're not coming with me?"

If nothing else, I wanted a familiar face with me as I confronted whatever was to come. But Ethan shook his head again. He looked down and touched my shoulder, a gesture I interpreted to as an apology.

"It's all right. Let's get this over with," I said, walking through the hole in the structure that I assumed served as the entrance.

I walked a few yards into the semi-darkness, treading on rubble and pieces of metal that crunched with each step. When I crushed a plastic bottle and nearly tripped over it, the voices from deeper within fell quiet as they anticipated my arrival. A yellowish light at the end of the hall was shining through a door, and I walked towards it, certain I was making the biggest mistake of my life. I thought about Bob Wexter from the paper, and about the article I would write if I managed to make it out of there alive. I tried to encourage myself by repeating that I had everything under control, but really, I knew that this was out of my hands. When I finally stepped through the door, I saw them.

There were five figures in black, all looking in my direction and waiting. They had black masks over their faces, lit up by the hundreds of candles placed throughout the chamber. The masks were all the same, and they seemed to be made of black feathers which stuck out of the top to cover their foreheads; but I could immediately tell that there were three women and two men.

"We're glad you've come," said a male voice that reverberated through the chamber.

I couldn't tell which figure had spoken. I stepped further towards them into the room, unable to control the vertigo in my stomach that made me feel as if I were falling off the Marine Parkway bridge itself. The light from the candles danced on the walls, creating the perfect atmosphere for all my worst fears to come true.

"It was brave of you to come here," one of the figures said. "Now you only need to complete the final step."

"Who are you?" I asked loudly.

My voice was full of loneliness. It would have been impossible for me to call for help in such an isolated place, regardless of how bad things got.

"We are the Ravens of God. You wanted to join, and we have shown you the door."

One of the male figures grabbed a can of paint from the floor and approached me. I could see his eyes through the mask.

"Close your eyes, please," a female voice whispered.

I sighed. There was no alternative. I closed my eyes and, a second later, I felt a wet brush sliding over them, as if my face were being covered with a crude, moist mask. A few drops trickled down my face.

"You can open your eyes."

The figure stepped to the side, and I saw that they had all moved to either side of me, forming a sort of corridor down to the back of the chamber, where they had placed a wood cross a few yards high, painted red. I was expecting them to say something more, but they remained silent, waiting; and I finally realized what was expected of me.

I took a few slow steps towards the cross as I remembered the last challenge: ASCEND THE CROSS BLINDFOLDED. When I reached the bottom, I turned around and said aloud, thinking I'd change something:

"I don't have a blindfold. I need one."

"That is our blindfold," said the same male voice that had spoken initially. "A blindfold that enables you to see. To see that you are alone, but that we are also with you."

I attempted to identify the voice, but it didn't seem familiar. Beneath the cross, there was a small, three-step ladder, and I saw there was a small footrest on the vertical beam for me to stand on. I swallowed hard and, finally, climbed up. Once on the platform, I saw two figures hurrying towards me. They grabbed my arms, spread them, then tied them to the horizontal beam with pieces of white fabric that seemed to be pieces of bedsheet. Being so vulnerable gave me vertigo. It was an overwhelming feeling of fear to face so much uncertainty. The figures pulled away the stepladder and the stools they had climbed onto to tie me to the cross. A female figure approached with a bucket of liquid and removed my shoes and socks. I felt the wooden platform beneath my feet and feared losing the support. I was paralyzed with fear, and I was about to beg them to let me down, but then I remembered Ethan's words: "No matter what happens. You can't call for help. You can't scream. You just have to trust. That's all." It was difficult for me to continue pushing myself up against the platform with both feet, and I had the feeling that if I lost my balance, I'd be in trouble. Then, unexpectedly, the person who had removed my shoes took a sponge and began washing my feet. I took a deep breath and screamed on the inside. I tried to escape to another place in my mind. And then, suddenly, a new voice cried:

"What did you feel when you walked along the edge of the bridge?"

"Fear," I replied, almost hyperventilating.

I was uncomfortable due to the posture I had to try to maintain, on tiptoes on the platform.

"And how did the fear make you feel?"

"Alive."

"And what did you feel when you burned your car?" asked a new voice, this one female.

"Freedom," I replied.

"And how did freedom make you feel?"

"Alive."

Those questions hit me like a punch in the gut. And my responses were honest, no matter how much I wanted to pretend those experiences hadn't changed me.

Everything was silent for a few moments, during which I kept expecting them to ask me another question, but, suddenly, one of them turned his back on me, and the others did the same. Then, without a single word, they walked out the door one by one, and I realized they were leaving the chamber, abandoning me on the cross with no way to escape.

"Where are you going?!" I exclaimed, thrashing my arms to try to free myself.

It seemed like no one even heard me, but just before leaving, the final figure stopped in the doorframe, looked at me in silence, and placed an index finger over their lips. Without making a sound, they motioned for me to remain silent before vanishing into the darkness.

Chapter 43
Queens
April 25, 2011
One hour earlier
Ben Miller

There are some people who, like dreams,
can quickly transform into
your worst nightmare.

When Inspector Miller arrived with four squad cars at Father Graham's home, a sprawling two-bedroom apartment a mile and a half from the school in downtown Queens, he felt like everything was finally coming to a logical conclusion. Deborah's statement had been devastating, and he couldn't help but see the priest as an unscrupulous monster, someone capable of exploiting his position and the trust of the school in order to abuse minors. Allison may have met the same fate before ending up dead on a cross, and the thought that her pregnancy may have been the consequence of that abuse made him sick to the stomach.

Before leaving FBI headquarters, he ordered a background check on Father Graham, and was surprised to see it come up clean. This monster had managed to avoid any sort of prior complaint; he didn't have as much as a parking ticket on his record. The NYPD Homicide Unit had been given Deborah's statement and they'd gotten hold of a warrant to conduct an exhaustive search of the man's home, since all the evidence clearly pointed to him: Allison's death on the cross, Deborah's statement, and the owner of the café across from the school. Not to mention Allison's Bible in the priest's office.

One of the eight agents with Ben rang Father Graham's doorbell, but there was no answer. Ben watched as two agents broke the door down at the first attempt, breaking the lock smoothly. Five of the agents entered and began their search. They called out "clear" each time they came to an empty room. Everything was far too quiet, and Ben as well as the two officers from the NYPD Homicide Unit quickly scanned the contents of each room. The place was tidy, with religious objects in all the rooms: there were paintings, crucifixes, and icons of Christ and the Virgin Mary. The whole apartment was decorated with mahogany furniture. In a small room by the entrance they saw several shelves of video cassettes, which Ben looked at with interest. He saw that all of them were in Blockbuster cases, but when he opened them, they weren't commercial movies, but tapes without any kind of label showing what they contained. The only clue as to the contents were two initials written in white on the edge of the plastic: J.F.

Suddenly, two agents deeper in the apartment yelled:

"Stay where you are! Hands up!"

All the cops ran towards the room, where they saw Father Graham behind a desk adjacent to the library, with headphones on, his hands in the air, and an amazed expression on his face. He seemed relaxed, and when he saw Ben at the back of the group of agents, he stood up calmly and smiled at him. Slowly, he removed the headphones from his ears.

"Inspector Miller... I had thought that... we were collaborating with... all you asked for. I can only assume you have a warrant to enter my house... with... with your weapons drawn? Is that really necessary? I'm a priest, for the love of God. I help the community."

"Deborah says different," Ben replied.

"Deborah?"

For a second, a look of surprise passed across his face, but then he smiled.

"That girl... she's... infatuated with me. Do you understand? I'd be curious to hear what nonsense she's told you. She has a vivid... imagination."

"You can save it for the judge, Father."

"And what evidence do you have against me? Something she said? And with that you're planning to charge me with... with what, exactly?"

"We have a witness who corroborates Deborah's story."

At that, the priest's expression changed entirely.

"How can you...? It's just words. You have nothing on me. Nothing! Do you really believe her words are more believable than... than the word of God?"

"You don't speak for God, Mr. Graham."

"I am a servant of the Lord. This is an intolerable insult. You can't arrest me. I take care of this community's children. I'm the... the shepherd of your sheep," he said with a serious expression.

As they were speaking, the two cops from the Homicide Unit had begun searching drawers and closets for evidence of further criminal activity. According to Deborah's statement, the abuse had also taken place in that house and, if that was true, there would certainly be something to corroborate her story. They entered what seemed to be Father Graham's bedroom: the bed was made, and the sheets were stretched across it so tightly it seemed the fabric was about to tear from the tension. Above the bed hung a crucifix made of redwood. The shelves and bathroom seemed to have been painstakingly cleaned, and the whole place had the faint scent of bleach, which worried the officers. On the street, the forensic unit's van was waiting for them to arrest the priest so they could enter the house to sweep for fingerprints and traces of DNA.

Just then, Miller's phone began to ring in his pocket. He hadn't been planning to answer the call, but it was Special Agent Spencer.

"We've got him," Ben said when he answered.

"Call it off, Ben."

"What?!"

"The girl's parents are withdrawing her statement."

"How?! Why?!"

"Once we started moving forward... they pulled back. They don't want their daughter going through all this."

"But—"

"They don't want their daughter dealing with this for the whole length of the trial."

Ben stepped out of Father Graham's study, leaving the priest alone with the other agents. Then he began speaking in a quieter voice.

"You have to convince them. This is—"

"We're trying, Ben. Dr. Atkins is with them right now, but... they're insisting on going home. I know it sucks. But... if you don't have anything clearly tying him to Allison Hernández, the judge will nick us for continuing with the arrest without evidence. You've got to let him go."

"Spencer... this man is—"

"There's nothing left to discuss, Ben. You've got to call it all off. It's over," he said before hanging up.

Ben put down the phone, feeling like the whole case was collapsing around him. He couldn't believe it. He was so close, then all it took was one phone call to leave him with nothing. He returned to the office with tears in his eyes, unsure what to say. He saw Father Graham behind the desk, standing beside the two agents who had put him in handcuffs and read him his rights.

"Let him go," Ben mumbled in a barely audible thread of a voice.

"What?" one of the cops replied, unable to believe what he was hearing.

Father Graham gave a smile in which Ben saw the kind of arrogance that is born only of injustice.

"They're withdrawing the charges," Ben said louder, so everyone could hear him.

The agents exchanged a confused look, and one of them approached Ben to speak in a quieter voice.

"Are you sure about this?"

He nodded silently, then looked at his feet to avoid making eye contact the priest, who seemed to grow more confident upon hearing him.

"You see? You have nothing. Nothing! Take these handcuffs off me and stop with this foolishness," he cried. "And as for you, Inspector Miller, you're finished. How dare you come into my school and my home and... accuse me of what you seem to be suggesting without evidence. Do you hear me? I will see to it that my congregation files a formal complaint about all this... bigoted persecution. You're a deeply prejudiced individual, Inspector Miller, and you certainly shouldn't be permitted to hold an important position."

"Take the handcuffs off," Ben said, defeated, trying to block out Father Graham's words.

The agents obeyed silently, and after they removed the handcuffs, Father Graham caressed his own wrists in a sign of victory. But then, suddenly, they heard one of the cops from the NYPD Homicide Unit calling from elsewhere in the apartment:

"Inspector Miller! Come here, we got something!"

Ben ran to the bedroom, where he saw the two agents crouching beside the wardrobe. One of them stood up: between his hands, he was holding a small, open shoebox filled with bloodstained clothes.

The other agent lifted the first garment, pinching it between gloved fingers. It was a t-shirt with the Pepsi logo on it.

"The clothes Allison was wearing when she disappeared…" Ben whispered.

He returned silently to the study, where the two agents were still standing beside Father Graham, who looked at Ben in confusion. His eyes flashed to the shoebox, then up at the police with a surprised expression.

"That… that isn't mine," he cried. "I've never seen that before in my life. You must have—"

"Why'd you do that to Allison, Mr. Graham?"

"I… I didn't lay a finger on the girl! You've brought that into my house to—"

"Mr. Graham, you are under arrest for the murder of Allison Hernández," Ben stated calmly.

"I didn't touch her! I swear!"

"Anything you say can and will be…"

One of the agents approached him with handcuffs—the same ones he had been wearing moments before—which swiftly returned to the priest's wrists.

"No!" he cried.

He threw himself against the table and grabbed a silver letter-opener that had been resting on a pile of blank sheets of paper. He held it to his own neck.

"Hey, okay, don't do anything stupid," Ben cried, shocked. "If you really are innocent, you have nothing to worry about."

"You people don't believe in anything. You planted that in my house. You want to destroy me and destroy Mallow! You want to destroy… God!"

The two NYPD agents lifted their guns and pointed them at the priest. Ben crouched down to put the shoebox on the ground, then lifted his hand in an attempt at de-escalation.

"Aren't you capable of facing your own sins?"

He thought that by challenging his faith, he could get through to the person behind the mask, but what he hadn't been expecting was the consequence of his simple and powerful question: Father Graham began to sob.

"I have a problem. And God knows it," he whispered between whimpers. "It's something against which I am incapable of fighting."

"You'll have psychological counseling in prison. But this is where it ends for you."

"I didn't touch Allison. I didn't place a finger on her. But… to answer your question… no. I am not capable of facing my own sins. How could I? When you live with them every hour of every day? When you're incapable of ending those thoughts?"

That was when Ben realized the significance of the VHS tapes he'd found in the closet.

"What's on those tapes?" he asked, sensing the shadow falling across Father Graham's face grow darker.

At that instant, the priest made the sign of the cross, looked at the ceiling, and took a deep breath. Then, in a voice that seemed to come from his very depths, he cried:

"Forgive me, Father, for I have sinned."

Ben was now certain of what he would find on the tapes. It wasn't the first time a sexual predator had had that sort of collection in his home. He'd discovered similar material in numerous investigations: hard drives, CDs, cassettes, even Beta tapes.

For a few seconds, Father Graham lowered the letter opener and looked straight at Ben with wild, expectant eyes, as if he were thirsty and had just discovered he would never find water.

"God is in all of us, Inspector. But so is the devil," he said, just before jamming the letter opener into his throat, severing the carotid artery.

Ben screamed and leaped towards him in an effort to prevent it, but he wasn't fast enough. Father Graham fell to the floor and Ben squatted down beside him to place pressure on the wound. Father Graham's blood pulsed furiously through Ben's fingers like a broken oil well spurting black liquid from the depths of the earth. Ben's hands were covered in blood in less than a second, and a dark red puddle spread beneath the priest's body like a bottle of wine shattered on the hard wood floor. An instant later, his eyes fixed on a spot on the wall, just where the wooden crucifix was hanging. With Ben's hands on his throat, the priest exhaled his final breath.

Chapter 44
Early morning,
April 26, 2011
Miren Triggs

There is a moment in life
that takes hold of you,
and everything changes,
because you have more to lose
than you have to gain.

They left me alone on the cross, and a few moments later, I heard their mopeds driving off. Through the upper windows of the building, I could hear the ocean. The light from the candles, arranged in haphazard groups of two, five, and seven, danced in the darkness as if the whole chamber were in flames. I could feel the paint from the mask running down my face, and I felt so alone and helpless that I nearly cried out for help.

But I remembered what Ethan had said. If I cried out, I would fail the test, and if I failed, I would meet the same fate as Allison. It occurred to me that perhaps the Ravens hadn't left—maybe they'd just turned on their mopeds and done a loop around the area; they could be hiding somewhere in the immediate vicinity to see if I cried out.

I chose to keep quiet, as if I were guarding my greatest treasure. The position on the cross was uncomfortable to maintain. I was practically standing on tiptoe, balancing on little more than a wooden peg nailed beneath my feet, with my arms outstretched and tied to the cross with shreds of cloth. I was scared I might lose my balance in that lonely place, that I would be unable to get my feet back on the small wooden platform. If that happened, I would asphyxiate. Because crucifixion is death by slow asphyxiation. Your arms pull up on your ribs and the weight of your body traps your lungs in your rib cage, just enough so that you grow more and more tired, resulting in weaker and weaker breaths. This triggers a slow and unavoidable cycle until you no longer have enough strength to breathe. That was, undoubtedly, my biggest fear: that I'd lose my balance on that small piece of wood and feel my life escaping before I found an answer to the question I hadn't had the chance to ask them: *What happened to Gina?*

I didn't know how long the test was supposed to last, but as the minutes passed, and then the first hour, I couldn't help but think they'd never come back for me.

I was exhausted, and it was becoming harder and harder to fight the fatigue building up in my ankles and wrists, both of which were holding up my entire body weight. After a while longer, I closed my eyes and couldn't help but picture my parents' faces smiling at me sadly. A second later, my mind flashed to my mother hearing about my death on that cross, and in my head, I felt I had to cry for help. What if they didn't come back? What if Allison had spent the two weeks after she disappeared hanging on the cross? And what if Ethan was wrong and they'd just sent me the photo of Gina so I'd end up in exactly this place?

Everything was beginning to fall into place. The envelope I'd received the polaroid in was labelled 'WANNA PLAY?' and in order to find Gina, I'd accepted the rules of their game without question.

The more I thought about it, the clearer it became to me that I'd never make it out of there alive. I thought about Jim, wondering where he might be and if he would find me, or if he would even look for me. I still didn't know if I'd be capable of looking him in the eyes without feeling responsible for all our false starts. Maybe dying on the cross was the best thing that could happen to me. Maybe it wasn't a trap but a path. Maybe that feeling of abandonment was exactly what the Ravens were trying to instill in me.

But then, suddenly, I heard footsteps approaching through the same hall I had used to enter. I heard the gravel and debris moving, and a wave breaking. A person dressed in black appeared in the doorway, his face uncovered, and the instant he saw me, he burst out laughing.

"Ethan?!"

A chill ran along my whole body when I saw him like that, jovial, as if seeing me in that state were something to be happy about.

"Miss Triggs..." he cried, "You are incredible. Absolutely incredible!"

"Ethan, please, get me down from here. I'm tired. I can't go on."

He approached the base of the cross gleefully, and when he reached it, crossed his arms over his chest and regarded me with contempt.

"How could it have been this easy?"

He brought his hands to his head, amazed, and started chuckling again. Then he shook his head and roared with laughter.

"Please, Ethan... get me down."

I didn't want to believe it. I couldn't believe it.

"I read your book, you know that?" he told me. "And I was fascinated how you were able to describe everything about being raped, all your loss, but you never once thought someone could use it against you. It's been so predictable. It's been... too easy, don't you think? All of this. You swallowed every single one of my lies. Please, don't..." he laughed, "please, be careful. The Ravens of God are dangerous. The Ravens..."

And then I understood.

"You're a member," I exhaled.

"No, Miss Triggs," he cried, "I created them! Give a child the proper tools and he'll grow up to be an upstanding citizen. Give him the wrong tools, and you'll create a monster. It was a long time ago. You had no idea. But that's when it all started."

"But... why?"

"I needed this. You know? I look back now, and I think this is everything I ever wanted. Remember the fire in my house? That was the night—"

"Ethan, get me down, I can't—"

"Listen to me!" His scream reverberated across the chamber. "Are you the only one who's allowed to talk? Are you the only one who has something important to say?"

"Ethan..."

He gave me a furious look, as if I had awoken a beast that had lain in wait deep in his dark interior.

"It was nighttime, and my father had been drinking, like he did every day after work. When he was drunk, you couldn't even recognize him. He was unpredictable and distant, he'd use any excuse to hit you: if you took too long to bring him a beer from the fridge, if you looked at him without saying anything, if the Knicks lost. Anything was a good enough excuse for him to push you to the floor and kick you around like a ball. That day, the same thing as always happened when he got drunk. He beat my mother over and over, over and over. OVER AND OVER!" Ethan shrieked.

I was frozen. He was like a completely different person from the boy I'd met before. Up until then he had been a tortured child devastated by his sister's disappearance, but it turns out, his traumas extended much further.

"Gina told me to hide in my room," he continued. "As usual, she was trying to protect me. That day seemed like it was going to be worse than usual. A week earlier, my mother had suggested that the three of us leave, but we never managed to make it that far. Gina went out and I heard her cries blending in with my mother's. I heard kicks, shrieks, and then, just my sister crying. You don't forget that kind of thing, you know? The silence, the uncontrollable sobbing, the darkness of my bedroom. I was there for a few minutes, hiding under the bed next to a stuffed animal of a bird I thought I'd lost. And then I heard Gina yell: 'Mom, please, wake up!' I gathered all my courage and went downstairs to the kitchen, where my sister was kneeling beside our mom's lifeless body. She was lying on the floor with bruises all over her neck and her eyes wide open."

"Your father killed your mother..." I muttered with difficulty, as I struggled against gravity and the pain in my wrists.

"Gina was devastated, and she cried like I'd never seen her cry before. I asked her where he was, and she pointed to his room upstairs. I went in and found him there, lying on the floor at the foot of the bed, sleeping or passed out. At that moment, it didn't make a difference. I saw a lighter on the nightstand beside a pack of tobacco, and I thought about burning everything. My mom was a good person, okay? But she'd ended up with the wrong guy. A sick fuck who not only beat us over and over, and who'd caused wounds that will never heal, but who had also taken away our mother. I hated him with my entire soul. I wanted to hurt him. I hit him as hard as I could, but he didn't move. Gina came into the room and said we should call the police while he was unconscious, but... I didn't think that was enough. I grabbed the lighter and lit it beside the curtains. Gina watched silently and... she whispered, 'do it,' her face covered in tears." Ethan paused to act out the movements of flicking a lighter. "I hadn't expected the fire to spread so fast. From the curtains, it spread to the closet and then to the bed and the door. Gina jumped to grab me, but before we knew it, we were trapped in the bedroom with our unconscious father, who started coughing from the smoke. Then... she opened the window, and we climbed down the ledge while the inside of the house went up in flames. We crawled a few feet until we got to a gutter drain that led to the ground, and, in a moment I've never forgotten, Gina grabbed me by both hands and let me hang from her as I lowered myself down. Remind you a little of the first challenge?"

"Cross the bridge on the outside of the guardrail," I whispered.

"When she grabbed me with both hands, while I was hanging a few meters from the ground, she said: 'Don't worry, I'm right here with you,' and then she released me. The whole time I had been hanging there, looking her in the eyes, I thought that with her, nothing bad would ever happen to me. I felt... protected. I felt alive again. The flames devoured the house, including our parents and everything we had. Something inside me was saying this would be a new beginning, that we'd be paid back for all that suffering. We held each other as we watched everything come down, and a little later, a fire truck showed up with its siren blasting."

"Burn something of personal value," I said out loud.

"Looks like you're starting to understand, Miss Triggs."

I swallowed hard when I saw how self-satisfied Ethan seemed.

"When happened then?" I asked, trying to win back his trust.

I didn't want him to turn unstable again.

"They took us to my aunt and uncle's house, and, for the first few days, I thought we would be happy. But soon, everything got sucked up by their suffocating religion, their obsessive praying, the oppression at Mallow. And then, the straw that broke the camel's back: Gina went missing."

"You didn't do anything?"

He shook his head and replied:

"Me? I was just a kid when she disappeared. You never know how to react to something like that. I'd already spent my whole life suffering, why did I deserve so much more of it? I took shelter in the search for her. I was hopeful, I thought we could find her. I joined all the search parties, even though I was a kid, and everyone thought I was just getting in the way. 'No, Ethan. You're very little. Leave it to the grown-ups.' 'No, Ethan, you've already done enough,'" he said in a sing-song voice. "And one day, when I was crying in the café while they were getting ready to go out looking for Gina again... you sat down across from me."

"I did?"

"You promised you'd find Gina. You said you'd bring her back home."

"I... remember," I said.

"I trusted you, you know?" he paused for a long, disconcerting moment, and afterwards, he took a deep breath and screamed: "I believed you! You said you'd find her, and I believed you!"

"Ethan, I..."

"'Ethan, I,'" he parroted back at me in a disturbing tone. "Ethan, Ethan, Ethan. Ethan, you have to pray. Ethan, get me a beer. Ethan, you're a piece of fucking shit," his voice grew louder with each sentence. "Ethan, it's your fault your parents died. Ethan, it's your fault your sister disappeared. Ethan, you're—"

"Please, Ethan... try to calm down."

"And then... the worst part. Father Graham and his fucking sick habits."

"Did he... touch you?"

"'Did he… touch you,'" he repeated in a mocking tone. "No! But do you really care? Deborah…" he shook his head. "He took a liking to her. You know? To my girlfriend. The only person I've loved since Gina went missing. Does everyone I'm close to have to suffer?"

"Ethan, get me down from here and we can talk about this calmly. Can you?"

"No. All this about the Ravens was… just like, a high school clique, you know? It was innocent… just a little fun. But when Deborah told me what Father Graham was doing… I knew I had to do something. We had to do something. That fucking pervert… we had to make him pay somehow. He had to… face the consequences of his sins."

"You could have told the police…" I said, trying to reason with him.

"You know what? I did."

"You reported him to the police?"

"Yeah, a few weeks ago. At the police station in the Rockaways. You know what happened? A big fat fucking nothing. I was with Deborah the whole time, encouraging her. After a while, a man from the church came. And you know what happened? The cops told us they'd take care of it. They said we shouldn't worry; they'd take care of everything. That was on a Friday. We thought that by Monday, Father Graham would be gone. They promised us justice and they gave us revenge. That same day, Father Graham called Deborah to the chapel at Mallow. She came back crying, with bruises all down her back. I didn't want to ask what had happened, because I didn't need to."

"Fuck…"

"We didn't have any evidence against him, and as far as the world was concerned, Father Graham was a good Samaritan. And then Allison tried to join the Ravens."

"And you killed her…"

"It was perfect, Miss Triggs. Can't you see? The opportunity fell from the sky. When she told us she was pregnant... that she was alone, that she didn't have any support and that she'd lose her scholarship... The first challenge of the game for her was telling Father Graham she was gonna have a baby. The second was leaving her Bible in his office. And the third, ascending the cross, just like you."

"Son of a bitch."

"She lasted a while, actually. The kids left and... when I came back the next day, she was still alive, begging for help."

"You killed her."

"I helped her die. She... had already been dead inside for a while, just like everyone else in the Ravens. You are, too. Don't think you're special. James cuts himself, Mandy's a sex addict, and you... got raped. Me... they took the most important things away from me, first by beating my mother to death, then with the uncertainty of losing the only person I had left. I read about your rape, Miss Triggs. You gave too much detail in your book. I know how it feels. You're no different than me. We've both suffered. We've both been hurt. Please, don't look at me like you're any better than I am."

"Please, Ethan, get me down."

"I said no!"

"Ethan... what did I ever do to you? I was just trying to—"

"You promised to find my sister. You promised to bring her back to me. That day in the café. You promised. You didn't make good on your promise. And not only that, but you also wrote about her disappearance in your newspaper to laugh at me."

"What are you talking about."

"'The young woman's brother, Ethan Pebbles, eight years old,'" he sang softly again, "'crying unconsolably after her disappearance.' Crying! Unconsolably! After her disappearance! You wrote that in your article and put it under a photo of me. I can't even tell you how many times I've gone back to the pain I felt in that photo. Not only do you have no shame, but you gave me false hope. Has anyone ever taken a photo of you crying? The whole country saw mine."

"Ethan… it wasn't easy. Your sister's case—"

"Shut up!"

"Wait… were you the one who sent me the photo of Gina?" I asked suddenly.

My chest throbbed and my hands were turning purple.

"Of Gina?" he laughed. "I didn't do such a bad job, right? The girl in that photo is Deborah, Miss Triggs. I got the idea when I was online one day. One time a serial killer challenged the users on 4chan to find him based on a photo of one of his victims. I thought it would be fun to do the same thing to get you to come here. I'm glad it worked. You wouldn't be hanging from that cross without… well, I mean, if you hadn't wanted to play. You know what? You don't deserve any of what you have. You sold the story of a little girl, then the story of my sister, and now your story comes to an end here."

"You sent the photo of Allison to Jim…" I whispered.

"I read in your book about how important that professor is to you. Aren't you afraid people might find out just how rotten you are? Aren't you worried someone will know how to hurt you? If you didn't come, I thought you might still fall into my trap through him."

"Ethan… please… I know how hard you had it as a kid, but you're making a serious mistake. This isn't how your sister… would want you to act. And worst of all, you've involved a group of high school kids in this spiral of… of what you're doing." I couldn't bring myself to use the word *madness*.

Ethan was unstable. Too unstable. His past had opened my eyes. He could interpret anything I said as an insult.

"We all need someone to adore, Miss Triggs. Some follow God, others the devil, and we… we just want to feel… alive. Do you understand? Father Graham has already paid the price for what he did to Deborah. Just a few hours ago he… took his own life. Deborah was at the police station when he did it and she texted me. It wasn't hard to fill the boxes in his house with Allison's clothes. If he'd only been charged with sexual abuse… it's possible he might've gotten out of it, but murder… that's a tough one. And murdering a girl. From his school. Who was pregnant. How horrible!"

He approached me with determined strides and, suddenly, he pulled a knife out from behind his back.

"Ethan… please… you don't know what you're doing."

He grabbed the wooden stepladder, placed it beneath my feet, and climbed up.

"Doesn't it strike you as strange? You're on the cross, and all you have to say is something someone else already said, when he was in your place over two thousand years ago."

"Please," I sighed, inconsolable.

"I feel sorry for you, you know?" he said. "Don't think I don't. But… I've been thinking about you for many years. Too many. It's time to get you out of my life," he said angrily.

"Help!" I cried, but I knew no one would hear me in that desolate place.

I struggled with the knots, trying one last time to break free.

"Shhh… don't shout, Miss Triggs," he whispered, "or you'll lose the game."

And at that moment, I felt the cold blade enter my abdomen. I howled with all my might, just like the wounded prey I've always been, and this time I felt the shriek emerge from my soul.

Chapter 45
Neponsit
April 25, 2011
One hour earlier
Jim Schmoer

*Sometimes, even a caress
can be a cry for help.*

Jim climbed the ladder as fast as he could with a knot in his chest. He didn't understand what was happening. Darkness had invaded every corner of the basement and in an instant, unconsciously, his heart traveled to a memory from his childhood, when he was five years old and had fallen into a well as he was playing in a field with his cousins. His family had searched for him, and after two hours that seemed endless, his cries of pain finally led them to him. During those hours, his parents had feared they'd lost him forever, and had come up with all kinds of dramatic theories about what might've happened, including the possibility that he had encountered a predator, either human or animal. When they finally found him, his tearful parents managed to pull him out of that black hole with a broken leg and a story Jim could brag about at school. But even with a happy ending, that accident had left a splinter of lifelong fear into his mind. He pushed on the trap door with all his strength, but he couldn't make it budge.

"Open up! Open the trap door!" he shouted. "Mr. Rogers! Open it!"

It was only then that he understood Mr. Rogers' insistence on keeping the saw turned on. The buzzing of the machine flew through the basement like a gust of wind, and he realized that the roar of the motor would drown out any cry for help.

He banged heavily on the trap door, calling for help over and over. With every blow against the iron, his hopes of getting out alive diminished. Once again, he was back inside that well that had lived on in his nightmares, and he relived those two hours of growing desperation.

"Help!" he shrieked. "Help me!"

It didn't take him long to realize it was pointless. The trap door seemed to be secured with something too heavy to lift, and there was no way his cries for help would be audible outside. Still, he kept trying to shake the door; his heart was sinking as he realized just how serious a mistake he had made. He felt in his pockets and pulled out his cell phone. The screen lit up with a hopeful glow and he hurriedly dialed 911. But he had no service. That place didn't seem like it had been designed as a deposit for sawdust, but to survive a holocaust.

"Fuck!" he shouted.

He was about to smash his phone against the floor, but then he realized that his iPhone had quickly become his only point of contact with the outside world. Between sighs of despair, he lifted the phone as high as he could to the top of the ladder, but the signal didn't reach underground. He ambled through the darkness, holding the phone up in his arms, hoping for coverage where there was none. Everything was so dark that the brightness of the phone hurt his eyes, but for a second, the background image of his daughter Olivia smiling was a true light in the darkness.

He had to find a way out, or something to force the trap door open. He turned on the flashlight on his phone and shone it on the rest of the space; he realized it was practically empty, except for the pillars holding up the roof and the pile of saw-dust falling through a pipe beside the ladder. The walls were bare, whitewashed plaster. He went up to a shelf to see if he could find something to use as a tool, and he saw a small wood-en horse figurine that appeared to be handmade; it was about ten centimeters high and sat on a stack of canned tuna. Mr. Rogers must have made it, just like the wooden doll's house above. Jim searched through the darkness as fast as he could, but all he found were small objects that would be of no use to him in opening the door.

"Help!" he cried again, almost losing his voice. And, to his surprise, the buzz of the saw suddenly went quiet, replaced by a silence that practically echoed in his ears.

He took a deep breath and tried to calm down, then sud-denly, he heard the same sound that had disconcerted him as soon as he came down the ladder. He remained motionless and held his breath, listening intently to something that seemed to be coming from one of the walls.

He heard it again. It was a thump, as if someone had closed a wooden box. Jim turned around quickly and shone the flash-light, which illuminated a small, white, metal door no higher than his waist.

He approached it slowly and saw it was closed with a slid-ing steel latch. His head told him that his escape route lay be-hind this door, but in his heart he feared that if he opened it, things might get worse. He crouched beside it and slipped the latch open carefully, trying to make as little noise as possible. He thought it might connect to the house and, if it did, he didn't want Mr. Rogers to hear him trying to escape. He opened the door slowly, and he felt a shudder of fear as he felt the warm, faint light illuminating his skin from the end of a long hallway with the same dimensions as the door. He scrutinized the space in an attempt to understand where the passage led and where the light was coming from.

Then he heard a voice at the end of the hallway singing a melody he recognized instantly. It was "London Bridge is Falling Down," and he remembered his mother singing him the same song. His mind also raced back to Olivia singing it over and over again as she repeatedly built and destroyed a bridge made of Legos. For a moment it seemed like this was the tunnel people describe in near-death experiences, with the light at the end consisting of the best of his life's memories. Maybe that's what death was, he thought. Returning to happy memories, spending the whole of eternity looking back on all the things that had made him feel truly alive. As he dragged himself along the passage he could make out the words to the song—very different from the lyrics he remembered—and he realized he was approaching something far more sinister than he had imagined. The voice was singing:

> *Life and hope is falling down,*
> *falling down, falling down.*
> *Life and hope is falling down,*
> *My fair lady.*

> *Build it up with wounds and tears,*
> *wounds and tears, wounds and tears.*
> *Build it up with wounds and tears,*
> *My fair lady.*

He walked down the passageway thinking about Gina and the last time Ethan had seen her alive, walking towards Tom's house, and he understood everything. For years, the search for the young woman had been based on the premise that Gina never made it to the Rogers' house in Neponsit. Everything had centered around looking for her in the vicinity, trying to figure out who might have kidnapped her on the walk from the bridge to her boyfriend's house; or else they had hypothesized that she had run away of her own free will. But aside from the formality of a few questions they'd asked Tom, no one ever considered that Gina may, after all, have made it all the way to the Rogers' house.

Jim silently approached the underground space where the light was emerging, and he saw a young woman with blonde hair, in her twenties, opening cupboards and drawers in a rudimentary kitchen as she put away a few cans of food that were piled on a wooden plank that served as a countertop. She was wearing a sky-blue dress, the bottom of the skirt black from continuous contact with the floor. Jim froze, unbelieving, like he was looking at a ghost. The woman remained with her back to him; she still hadn't heard him. She was slim, but she seemed to move as if she were tired. Then, suddenly, a child's voice called out in fright:

"Momma, a man!"

Chapter 46
Early morning,
April 26, 2011
Miren Triggs

A wild animal on the brink of death
hasn't forgotten how to bite.

I cried out so loudly I felt fire in my vocal cords. There were too many things in front of me competing for my attention, and they weren't willing to wait their turn to devastate me: death, the pain in my abdomen, the cold blade inside my body, Ethan a few centimeters away.

Guided by instinct, I launched forward with my teeth before I lost everything. There's always one final shred of hope to cling to.

I stretched forward as far as I could, stuck out my neck, turned my torso towards him, and bit hard on the soft flesh beneath his shoulder. He'd made a mistake by coming so close to me and I sank my teeth into him so hard, with all the strength I had left, that a shriek exploded from his mouth; I felt it reverberating in my ear drums.

"Aah!" he screamed.

I didn't let go. I didn't open my jaw, I couldn't. Tied to that cross, biting was all I had left, and I couldn't give it up.

Even if I bled to death, I'd make sure he stayed there with me until I didn't have the strength to clamp my mouth down any longer.

And then… in an attempt to get me off, he pulled backwards so hard he brought me with him. The cross wobbled, lurching forward, and I felt a tickling in my ribcage emanating from the very place I'd been stabbed.

We were falling.

That was when I remembered that the floor was covered in candles, and I realized I had come to the end. I thought about Jim and about our kiss; I thought about my parents; I thought about the article I had promised Bob; I thought about Inspector Miller, who may have fallen into the same trap I had. I also thought about Gina, and how I'd never find her. I thought about the desperation Allison must have felt on the cross. I tasted Ethan's blood on my lips, and I could feel his fear as I fell on top of him. The cross twisted to the left as we lurched forward, and finally, the wooden structure crashed against the floor. The first part of the cross to reach the ground was the left arm, and the whole structure split apart. I regained movement in my left hand, and with this newfound freedom, I felt like I was holding a loaded weapon. Ethan was pinned beneath me and, as I pulled my teeth off him, I realized I didn't have much time to untether myself from the cross and get the hell out of there.

He released a shriek so loud it was like it belonged to a child who had just been orphaned.

As Ethan sobbed, I fought against the knot securing my right arm to the cross. I could feel Ethan's blood in the corners of my mouth. And I managed to wriggle free. I had to escape. There was no time.

I rolled to one side, and somehow I managed to stand up. My hands were trembling. My eyes darted around for the way out. Ethan dragged himself along the floor and picked up the knife that had fallen beside him. I could have tried to fight—I could have attempted to face him—but I touched the wound in my abdomen and realized how important it was not to lose any time. I needed to get help; someone had to stop the hemorrhaging. I needed to stay... alive.

And I started to run, as best I could.

Ethan let out a cry that sounded like a hurricane magnified in the silence of that huge chamber.

"Miren!" he howled. "Miren!"

I stumbled out, and everything was lit in the moon's soft light. I didn't know where to run or how to get help. Panting, I ran through the wild scrubland of Fort Tilden, parallel to the ocean. I puffed hard with the effort, accompanied by the sound of the waves, through bushes and brambles which scratched my arms, but I barely even felt it. I was going to die. I didn't know how long I could keep going, and I needed to tell everyone about everything, I needed to find someone and get help.

I covered my wound with my hand and redoubled my efforts, besieged by shooting pain, until I finally saw an opening in the fence around Fort Tilden. But then I heard Ethan yelling, closer than I'd expected.

"Miren!"

I looked back; he was maybe half a football field away. I arrived at some kind of path between Fort Tilden and Jacob Riis Park, full of dark streetlights that intermittently lit my increasingly tired footsteps. I looked backwards again and saw a trail of my own blood behind me; I was a wounded animal on the verge of death.

"Help!" I shrieked, clutching my abdomen, blood trickling from between my ribs.

Keep it together, Miren! I told myself, desperate. *Hang the fuck on. You need to think. Fast. Call out to someone. Get help before it's too late.*

I felt my heart regurgitating my own blood as if my soul were dizzy and sick after all these twists and turns. I made a mistake. It was over.

I

should

have

stopped.

The street was empty except for the footsteps I heard behind my own. I saw his shadow, distorted by the streetlamps, grow and shrink: huge, tiny, enormous, nonexistent, gigantic, ethereal. I lost sight of it. Where was he?!

"Help!" I cried into the dark, empty street, which seemed to watch from the shadows like an accomplice in my death.

C'mon, Miren, you have to get the truth out. C'mon. C'mon! You have to make it.

I didn't have my phone, but even if I did, I'd have been dead long before the cavalry came. All they'd find would be the corpse of a 35-year-old journalist whose soul had been frozen solid since one fateful, bitterly cold night fourteen years earlier. Light from streetlamps always takes me back to that night of pain in 1997, to my screams, howling and trembling in the park, the grinning men, the trauma I'll never be free of. Maybe it was bound to end like this, under the intermittent light of another set of streetlamps in another corner of New York.

I lurched forward. Every step was like a knife in my side. I knew that long, dark road led to Rockaway Beach, next to Jacob Riis Park. Nobody would be out that early. The sun hadn't risen yet and a waning moon bathed the footprints in the sand with melancholy.

At least Miller would be able to track where I was headed. That's what you think about when you're about to be murdered: the clues that will help them identify your killer. His DNA in your fingernails, your blood in his car. But after killing me, Ethan would take my body away. It would be like I'd dropped off the face of the Earth. There wouldn't be anything left but my articles, my story, my fears.

I turned left at the end of the road and, with a speed that tore at the fibers of my already wounded muscles, I ducked into a recess in one of the structures of Fort Tilden.

No one asked for my help. No one begged me to get involved in any of this, but something inside me shrieked that I had to find Gina. I don't know how I missed it. I guess I had to feel… like my soul was on the line. I thought about the polaroid of Gina. How could I have been so naïve?

I looked left and right for a way out, trying to keep quiet between the gasps exploding from my chest. The sound of his footsteps mixed with the sound of the gale off the Atlantic; I felt coarse sand striking my skin like stray bullets in a battle between wind and sea.

"Miren!" he yelled, rabid. "Miren! Come out!"

If he found me, it'd all be over. If I stayed there, I'd bleed to death. I already felt tired and woozy. The night beckoning me. The Soul Game underway in my heart. I put pressure on my wound again and I felt the heat in my fingertips. I closed my eyes and clenched my teeth, trying to withstand the stabbing pain in my side, and my mind returned to an idea I'd written off as hopeless.

Run.

From my hiding place, I considered the possibilities. There's a fence around Riis Park. If I jumped it, I'd be able to sprint toward the houses across the park and ask for help, but in most places it's topped with razor wire that looks like it could slit me open and tear my guts out.

He was close, I could feel it. It wasn't his warmth I sensed; it was his coldness. His icy, unmoving body a few paces away, no doubt eyeing my pathetic hideout with contempt. A son of God, licking his lips at the sacrificial lamb.

"Miren!" Ethan cried again, even closer than I'd thought.

And I made another mistake. At the precise moment his broken voice howled my name, I jumped out and made a break for it, clinging to life even as I felt everything closing in.

Gina's image returned to my mind: her hopeful expression, her painful story. She felt so close I could practically reach out and touch her fifteen-year-old face, grinning at the camera in the photo they used after she disappeared.

Then everything changed: for a few seconds, it seemed like he'd stopped chasing me. I came back to life. But then his shadow reappeared. My strength was failing me. I could barely walk.

Only the distant roar of the ocean accompanied the sound of my panting.

"Miren, stop running!" he shouted.

I staggered across the beach, fighting the sand that was swallowing my feet, and I climbed over a low, dilapidated bulkhead. I was in luck: I reached a paved street that connected the beach to Neponsit. It was lined with dark-windowed houses.

I pounded on the door of the first house, crying out for help, but I was so tired I could barely manage a sigh. I knocked again weakly, but no one seemed to be home. I looked back desperately, afraid he'd reappear, but he was nowhere to be seen. The roar of the sea rushed over me. The sound brings some relief to my shattered soul. Could I really be safe? I moved to the next house, and I immediately recognized it. I was sure to find help there. I ran as fast as I could manage, passed between the round pillars of the porch, and slammed the knocker and my knuckles against the door. Inside someone turned on a light.

My salvation.

"Help!" I cried with renewed strength. "Call the police! I'm being chased by a—"

A hand pulled back the inside curtain covering the window of the door. An elderly woman with white hair regarded me with a disturbed expression. Where had I seen her before?

"Help! Help me, please!"

She raised her eyebrows and gave a smile that wasn't even a little comforting.

"Lord, what's happened to you?" she asked as she opened the door. She was wearing a white nightgown. "That doesn't look so good," she said with a warm voice, gesturing at the gash in my abdomen. "Let me call you an ambulance."

I looked down at my side. A pool of red was soaking through my shirt and down to my hips. There was blood all over my hands, all over the door knocker. *Jim might figure out I made it this far, but better for him if he doesn't. That way he'll be safe. That way at least one of us will live.*

"I'm not... not good," I managed between increasingly feeble gasps.

I swallowed spit; it tasted like blood. Before trying to speak again, I heard footsteps behind me and everything sped up. I didn't have time to turn around.

As the old woman looked above my head, a shadow engulfed the doorframe, a cold hand covered my mouth and, rapidly, a powerful arm wrapped around my body.

And I realized that it was all over.

Chapter 47
Neponsit
Early morning,
April 26, 2011
Jim Schmoer

Is there any place
darker than loneliness?

The young woman swung around and looked straight at Jim with an expression of such disbelief and surprise that both were still for a few seconds, unsure what to do.

"Who are you?" she finally said. "Cora, stay there!"

One part of her seemed to be begging Jim for help with her eyes, while the other seemed to consider him a threat.

"Gina?" Jim whispered, barely able to get the word out. "Gina Pebbles?"

She began to pant, and her lower tip trembled before she could answer the question. It had been years since anyone except Mr. Rogers had called her by her full name. She swallowed hard before nodding.

"You're... you're alive," Jim murmured falteringly.

He couldn't believe it. Then he turned to look at the little girl who had appeared and realized that the child must have been born there. After looking quickly over the space, he identified a rickety bed in one corner, a toilet, and even a shower. There was a 26-inch television sitting on top of a VHS player, next to a stack of Disney movies. In the center of the space was a table with plastic dishes and silverware covered in food stains, and in the corner, a dozen wooden toys were scattered across the floor. When Jim saw them, he recalled the doll's house that Mr. Rogers kept in the garage.

"Mr. Rogers locked you down here," he said, trying to put the puzzle together in his head. "But... why?"

"Please... don't hurt us," Gina replied, frightened. "Please..."

"Me? I'm not going to do anything to you. For the love of God... No. I was looking for you and—" he interrupted his own sentence. "I'm... Jim Schmoer... I'm a college professor. I'm... a journalist. I was investigating your case and..."

He was so shocked to have Gina in front of him that he was having trouble processing the fact that she could find his presence terrifying; he didn't realize she was defensively stepping backwards towards the little girl.

"You got here and... he locked you in this... My God," Jim said before bringing his hands to his head, calculating how many years she would've been locked in the basement and what that meant. "We have to get out of here as fast as possible."

"Get out?" she exclaimed, on the verge of tears.

She crouched down beside the little girl and hugged her. For a second, Gina's face lit up. She'd been dreaming of escape since the minute Mr. Rogers dragged her down there.

"Momma, who is this man?" the girl asked, frightened.

"Is this... your daughter?" Jim asked with a knot in his throat, trying to understand the whole story.

He spoke fearfully, as if he was standing in front of a bubble that might pop if he touched it with dry hands. Gina nodded again in silence, still holding the girl.

"But… how?" More and more questions were flooding into Jim's mind, but all the answers seemed impossible.

"How did you get here?" Gina asked suddenly in a whisper that felt like a gunshot; she was caressing Cora's brown hair. "Where is Larry?!"

"Larry?" Jim didn't know him by that name.

"Larry… Rogers. Where is he?!"

"He… locked me in the basement of the workshop," Jim said. "I came down the stairs and… he closed the trap door at the other end of the hall behind me."

Gina sighed, hopeless. She seemed to know exactly what that meant. The fact was, in all the years she'd been there, on three separate occasions she had succeeded in making it to the other side of the metal door at the end of the passage, but it had never done her any good. Mr. Rogers was far stronger than she was, and she'd never had any obvious opportunity to get out.

The first time she managed to get to the other side of the door, she'd attacked him from behind, but it was useless. She'd taken advantage of the fact that he'd forgotten to lock the white door after bringing her a month's supply of food and diapers. Gina had left the hall and lain in wait beside the trap door every day, but when he finally returned and she took her shot, Larry brushed her attack off as if it were just a scratch, and her hopes vanished. That was in 2003, when Cora was only a few months old, and Gina wished with all her might to escape and give her daughter a future. When Gina came after him, Larry didn't fight with her or even look for her in the darkness—instead, he ran towards Cora, who at that moment began to cry. She was wrapped in a blanket in the corner, waiting for her mother to finish the man off so the two of them could escape that nightmare together.

"Your brother thought you ran away…" Jim said, trying to make Gina see that he knew her story. "We have to get out of here. Lots of people are still looking for you."

"You know Ethan?!" she whispered in disbelief.

Finally, a tear rolled down her cheek. She and Ethan had grown up together, bound by pain, and separated by it, too.

"I spoke with him. You can't imagine how much he misses you…"

"Ethan…" she said, her eyes losing their focus as she allowed herself to drift into memory.

"What happened, Gina? How'd you end up here?" Jim asked. He needed to finally know what happened.

"Larry is… Tom's father… Tom was my… boyfriend."

"I know," Jim said.

Gina hesitated for a second before speaking. She held Cora in a tight hug; the girl seemed to feel protected in her mother's arms. The little girl had intense green eyes and she was staring at Jim intently, like she was looking at a ghost.

"It all started a few months before I ended up down here. I've thought about it and now everything seems to suggest that this… pit was always where I'd end up. Good things don't always happen to good people, you know? Sometimes demons feed on them. Sometimes the demons choose someone and decide to tear them apart just for the pleasure of it. It started when my father killed my mother."

"I thought… they died in a fire."

"Ethan lit the fire after my father strangled her. I saw it all. I fought with him, but… there was nothing I could do. My father was drunk and Ethan… burned everything. We swore to keep it a secret so they wouldn't separate us."

Jim held his breath as he listened.

"We ended up at my aunt and uncle's house and it seemed like things were going to get better, but… they were blinded by their faith. I don't know if you know what that's like. They enrolled us at Mallow, and every day they subjected us to punishments that were… aggressive. Our aunt beat us for messing up prayers, made us pray until we fell asleep from exhaustion.

But we held on. I wanted to be there for my brother, you know? I didn't want them to separate us."

Jim sighed, realizing her aunt and uncle's evasive attitude was really their armor against the truth. Even though they had admitted to beating their niece when she ran off with Tom, it didn't surprise Jim that their version of events differed so significantly from Gina's.

"They looked for you, Gina. I've seen how affected they were by your disappearance. I know they had a rough time of it, even though... maybe they were also driven by guilt. They told me about beating you when you left with your boyfriend, Tom."

Gina looked down for a second, as if hearing that name filled her with contradictions.

"I met Tom at school. He was nice. He had a good heart... or at least that's how I felt at the time. After everything that had happened with my father's abuse, my mother's death, and the fire, Tom filled me with hope again. I... fell in love with him. I mean, we fell in love with each other, I guess. We spent time together. We became... inseparable. And... one day my aunt and uncle caught us kissing in my room," Gina snorted, as if she'd remembered a serious mistake that now felt like little more than an anecdote. "They thought that was unforgiveable and told me I had to break up with him. They didn't want us to see each other anymore. That same afternoon, I ran away and went to see Tom." She covered Cora's ears with her hands. "We slept together," she whispered, "and... then... like none of it had mattered, he told me I needed to go home."

"You got pregnant," Jim sighed.

"Let me finish. That night, Tom asked his father to drive me back home," she huffed again, caressing the back of Cora's hand, as if that simple gesture would give her the strength to continue. "On the way, he talked to me about how lonely he felt. How his wife had left him and that... he had seen me... with his son."

348

Jim shook his head. "You don't have to continue," he said.

"We're never getting out of here. You might as well know about the devil who will be bringing you your food."

Jim nodded, even though he could predict what direction this story was heading.

"He... forced himself on me in the car. To be honest, I don't think I fought back hard enough. That has always tormented me. What if I'd... screamed? If I'd tried to escape? Or if I'd bitten him really hard? These questions have been with me my whole life. He'd stopped the car in the middle of nowhere, on a side-road near Fort Tilden, and... there wasn't a lot I could do. He's a strong man. I experienced the whole thing like I wasn't in my own body, you know? Like I was in it, but also outside of it. Then he drove me the rest of the way home, and I was crying, and when I got there, they beat me, saying they were doing it in the name of God. I was angry at them, but also at the world for feeding on me constantly. How could they be so... blind? If God was present when Larry put his hands on me, he must have been taking pleasure in my suffering."

"That was before you ended up here," Jim whispered.

"For the weeks after that I didn't have any idea how to behave around Tom. I wanted to tell him about it, but I felt like I couldn't, so I drifted away from him. It was his father. I even thought it was my fault, you know? That's how crazy I was getting. Like I just felt guilty for being a woman. And I didn't feel like anyone was going to believe me. But I think so now. Back then I was just full of fear."

"We have to get out of here," Jim interrupted, "by any means necessary."

"And then I missed my period, and a few weeks later I threw up in class. My whole world came crashing down when I took a pregnancy test, and it came up positive. I had to tell Tom. Sooner or later he was going to find out. I told him I had to talk to him, and we met after school. He said maybe we could talk at

349

his house. I… didn't want to see Larry again, but… he told me his father was working and we could talk without anyone interrupting us. They would've skinned me alive at school if they'd found out. And I… needed to tell Tom what his father had done and ask for his help deciding… I needed… someone to tell me it wasn't my fault."

She stopped for a few seconds and looked Jim straight in the eye.

"I remember that day like it was yesterday," she continued. "I got off on the other side of the bridge with my brother, because he had gotten nauseous and in any case, I appreciated the chance to think about what I was going to tell Tom. That day, the sky was full of these tiny clouds everywhere and I stopped with Ethan on the bridge for a few minutes to look at them. He was so little. He didn't know anything, even though he asked me a few times if I was okay. Then… I said goodbye to him and told him to go home, because I was going to see Tom. That was the last time I saw him. I remember how I even stopped to look at a… a painting by an old man who lived in a parking lot. It was a… painting of the sunrise over the ocean and it was full of intense colors: oranges, reds, blues, purples… but I thought it was the saddest thing I'd ever seen. It made me think of the new beginning I should have had after my father died, where after the sun came up everything was supposed to be filled with light, like I was supposed to start a new day, but in reality, it was a sunset full of nightmares. I was crying when I got to Tom's house, and I stopped on the porch to try to calm myself down. But before I had time, Larry came running from the garage and pounced on me. I froze, I couldn't believe it. When Tom told me his father was going to be working, it hadn't occurred to me that he meant at their house. It all happened so… fast. He asked me what I was doing there, if I'd told anyone, or if I was planning to. And… I hesitated. I was trembling and I… did nothing. I think he saw it in my eyes. I don't know if it was the panic I felt, but a little gesture changed eve thing. I touched my belly, because I was worried about… her," she whispered, tenderly embracing Cora.

"And he dragged you here," Jim whispered.

Gina nodded.

"He told me he couldn't let Tom find out what he'd done to me. He grabbed me by the arms like I was a garbage bag, and he threw me down that same trap door you just came through. I passed out. When I woke up, I spent the whole day alone, shouting. But no one heard me."

"They were looking for you everywhere, Gina."

"All he did was come back to throw me food from up there. I slept on the ground, used a bucket for a toilet. As my belly got bigger, he felt more and more guilty, and he started expanding the basement while I watched him, trying to figure out a way to escape. He'd come down with a few tools and a headlamp and he… I mean, he ended up building this place. Cora was born in that bed over there." She looked down and gestured towards the corner. "The… bastard has never even asked me what her name is. Better. I'd rather he doesn't know anything about her. I won't give him that power."

"My God," said Jim, who was trying to piece together the nine years Gina had spent there. But he was incapable of grasping that degree of pain. Suddenly, he remembered what Mrs. Evans had told him about the renovations Mr. Rogers had made on his house, and he remembered his abrupt refusal to sell the house. "Who is… Cora's father?"

"Does that even matter?" Gina replied. "She's all I have, and I don't want to know."

And it was true. Cora had become Gina's only reason to remain alive. Little else mattered as long as the girl was okay.

Suddenly, Cora stood and approached Jim.

"Do you want to see my toys?" she said in a cheerful tone, as if she had just then understood he wasn't here to do her harm.

Jim gave her his hand and felt a chill that traveled from the back of his neck to his heart, where it transformed into a stabbing pain. Gina saw her daughter getting excited and looked at Jim searchingly as she dried her tears.

"Can I ask you something, Gina?" Jim said as he allowed the girl to pull him towards a little wooden train.

"Save a couple questions for the next few years. I don't think we're getting out of here anytime soon."

"Has he come down again and..." he couldn't bring himself to finish the sentence.

"No. I think if nothing else, he respects that I have Cora."

Jim breathed a sigh of relief. It was a monstruous nightmare, but that at least ruled out the additional trauma of her being a... slave. Of course, it was terrible to be a prisoner, but that next level could have transformed the nightmare into a permanent night terror, her soul never able to rest.

"How often does he come down? How much time do we have?"

"It depends. Sometimes it's once every two weeks. Other times it's monthly. He brings food, vitamins, medicine. We have running water."

"What? Two weeks? No! We have to get out of here now," Jim insisted.

"And do you have a plan for doing that?" Gina replied with a worried expression. "I've tried everything. There's no moving that trap door. Don't think you can just lift it and walk out. If it's locked, there's nothing you can do. There's no other way to get out of here, no windows or other doors. He has a... kind of taser. You think I haven't already tried? Did you see he's missing a finger? That was me. I bit him and pulled it off with my mouth. That was the time I came closest to getting out, but... I didn't make it. He tased me and I fell to the ground. Cora was three then. Now... I've just lost hope, you know?"

"Listen to me, Gina. We're going to get out of here. Cora can't live in this place, and you can't be anyone's prisoner. Understood? No one deserves this. We have to find a way."

Suddenly, Cora stepped away from Jim and walked quietly down the passage, picking up an object from the floor by the entrance. It was Jim's cell phone, which he must have dropped as he'd tiptoed towards Gina and Cora.

"Who's Olivia?" the little girl said, reading the screen and looking at the phone with interest.

"Olivia? That's my... my daughter," Jim replied, confused.

"Why is Olivia vibrating?" Cora asked with curiosity.

"Vibrating? What are you...?" Jim asked, turning to look at the girl.

Cora turned the phone around and showed him the screen, on which he could read the words INCOMING CALL. Olivia was calling.

"Over here there's reception!" cried Jim with surprise.

Chapter 48
Early morning,
April 26, 2011
Miren Triggs

All your life searching for the truth
and the whole time, you had it within.

The arm around me isn't Ethan's. What's happening? Who's grabbing me?

I sense death in the old woman's eyes, in the emptiness in my chest, in my final breath held in by the hand covering my mouth.

"But Larry, what are you doing? This woman needs help," she says.

And then I realize the major mistake I made in coming here.

Mrs. Adele Rogers gives me a look of both surprise and disbelief. I remember seeing her at the search parties that had been organized to find Gina. She's the grandmother of Gina's boyfriend, Tom. The adrenaline pumping through my veins makes everything feel like it's in slow motion. In a flashback, I see her sitting at one of the tables at Good Awakening, sharing her opinion about where the search parties should try next. Seeing her now makes me feel comforted, even though I know everything is about to come to an end. Ultimately, in her eyes, I can see that she's a good person and that she's worried about me.

"Larry! Can't you see she's hurt?" she says, confused.

"Shut up, Mom!" he yells angrily as he drags me backwards, pulling me off my feet entirely so my legs are dangling a full foot off the ground, covering my mouth with his thick, rough fingers that smell like sawdust.

"Larry! What are... have you lost your mind? This girl needs help! What are you doing!"

I feel my own weakness, and I'm no match for Larry's strong arms. What's happening? Why is he grabbing me like this? I can hardly think. Carrying me under his arm, he opens the garage door and throws me to the ground like a stack of firewood. My knees hit the legs of a workbench, and the impact against the polished cement floor adds to the pain from the wound in my abdomen which is radiating down to my hip.

"Aah!" I shriek. "Why... are you doing this?" I ask him, terrified.

I look up at him, and he seems three times my size. Right now I'm little more than a wounded, defenseless animal. One of Larry's veins is bulging from his temple and his face is red with rage. He's moving around furiously from one side to the other of the garage he's converted into a carpentry workshop. He is so all over the place that he slams his head into the bare bulb hanging from the ceiling, and the light begins to dance frenetically around the room with him, as if that intermittent light was tapping out the beating of my heart.

Larry moves to a table covered with tools, grabs something off it, and an instant later, I see it's a flat-head screwdriver, which he immediately holds against my throat. I feel the tip pushing hard against my skin, ready to strike the fatal blow.

"You came with him, didn't you?" he shouts from the depths of his fury.

"I... what?" I say through the pain. "Please... help me."

"Why did you come to my house! You're a journalist, right? Like that dumbass with the glasses? Fuck!"

He moves his face closer to mine, which is half hidden by the layer of paint that's running down to my lips.

"You're… bleeding," he says all of a sudden, seeing that my belly is drenched in blood.

"Get help, please. Call… an ambulance," I whisper. I don't know if I'll be able to hold on much longer. I'm starting to get dizzy. I desperately need medical attention.

He stands back up straight and takes a deep breath. He sees that his hands are covered in my blood, and his agitation transforms into panic.

I don't understand why Larry Rogers is grabbing me, but I don't have much energy to think about it. The walls are trembling and the ground beneath me is moving. I cough up blood onto the floor. Things aren't looking good. I think I'm going to die. I feel it in my heart, which is beating harder and harder, like it's on a wild gallop to the precipice where all the lights go out. Maybe I'll find something in that darkness, even though now that I feel the end approaching, I see just how wrong I've been. I wasn't dead in life after all, because now, deep down, I'm terrified of losing all those emotions I always thought I'd felt as distant and sad. In reality, I'd only felt them within my own soul, as if it were a picture frame drawing the boundaries of who I was, drawing where my shadows lay, where my light shone, and the colors in which I presented myself to the world. Mine are dark and somber after spending so long navigating sadness, but in the end, I understand that even from my perspective, I enjoy things or suffer in the hues of my own painting. I push men away because I feel like a broken toy; I become obsessed with searches because I feel I need to find myself; I like being alone because I need to spend time exploring the nooks and crannies of my own heart…

"Please…" I say with the last strength I'm able to summon, "help me," I whisper.

"Tell me! What do you know? Did you come together? Who did this to you?"

"To...gether?" It's hard to breathe. I don't understand the question.

"Fuck, fuck!" he shrieks.

He brings his hands to his head and then slams a fist down hard on the workbench.

"I have to take you down," he says. "I can't take you anywhere else. I can't risk them... looking into this. They'll see the blood and... they'll want to see if I did something to you. And... they'll find them."

"What...?" I murmur, half-closing my eyes.

He moves a few feet away and crouches beside a trapdoor in the floor, which he opens with a struggle after removing the padlock. He seems to be in a hurry, like he doesn't want something to escape from down below.

"What... are you going to... please... I need..."

And then suddenly, he lets it all out, and I understand everything:

"I can't let them find Gina," he mutters through his teeth, as if he's thinking out loud.

Hearing Larry Rogers say the name Gina gives meaning to every move that's led me to this point. The answer was always in the same house that the earliest investigators had ruled out. I gathered enough strength to look him in the face, and I understood that he had always been the missing piece of the puzzle.

What Ethan had said was true, he hadn't hurt his sister, and neither Mallow nor the Ravens of God seemed to have anything to do with her tragic end.

"Gina made it here after all, didn't she?" I say with my last ounce of strength.

He stops and looks at me with sad eyes.

"I knew you came with him to look for her," he whispers,

357

as if I'd finally spoken the sentence he had been waiting to hear all along.

"You… him?"

He hunches over me and lifts me up like I weigh nothing; he brings me to the trap door, but just as he's about to drop me in, there's a voice at our backs.

"Dad?! What are you doing, Jesus Christ!" Tom cries from behind us.

"Quiet, Tom! I'll explain everything later! Help me get her down, quick! The trapdoor is open, and he might—" Larry says aggressively.

I think about Adele Rogers, and I hope that, in her fright, she is calling the cops. Maybe she's the one who alerted her grandson.

"Get her down? There?" Tom interrupts, confused. "Dad… this woman needs help. We have to call an ambulance." Then after looking me in the eyes, he exclaims: "She's… the journalist. The one who came to help look for Gina years ago."

"Help me get her down, Christ! Do you want to lose everything? Because that's what's going to happen if someone shows up and starts looking into things here."

"Lose everything? Dad, what are you talking about? What the hell is all this? You're scaring Grandma. And now you're starting to scare me, too."

"Tom!" he shouts. "Don't disappoint me. I've sacrificed everything for you, you know that? Everything!"

"But Dad…" his voice trembles.

I don't have the strength to move.

"C'mon. Grab her by the legs and we'll drop her in there. The entrance isn't deep."

"Dad, if we don't help her, she's going to die. Look at how she's bleeding."

He's right. I'm about to close my eyes, I'm losing all my strength, and the truth is I hate how the arms holding me are not Jim's. I even feel like I can see him in the shadows, like a memory that's being projected into the darkness where Larry Rogers wants to bury me.

But then, the projection of Jim in the shadows begins to move and shout, pouncing on Mr. Rogers. He's real. It's him. Like an angel emerging from the depths of my fears to give me some hope to cling to, or at least one last memory before I'm gone forever. Then I understand who Larry was referring to when he asked if we came together.

"Jim," I whisper, filled with hope for the first and final time.

Jim smashes something shiny and metal into Mr. Rogers' face, in a motion filled with rage and desperation. The impact makes him stagger backwards, and he drops me. As I fall, I think about what I had; I travel in my memory and think about the life I lost. And an instant later, after hitting my head against the floor, everything fades to black.

Chapter 49
Early morning,
April 26, 2011
Jim Schmoer

Stories never end the way you want,
but that doesn't make the
ending any less inevitable.

Jim Schmoer accepted his daughter's phone call desperately, taking the phone from small Cora's hands and scaring her when he leapt towards her.

"Olivia!"

"Dad! How are you? Mom told me that… you had asked about me."

"Honey! I need you to call for help. Please. I've been kidnapped."

"What?!"

"Please. Write down this address. Call the police. Do you have a pen and paper? Quick!"

"What are you talking about, Dad? You're scaring me."

"Honey, do it, please. Call the police and ask for help. I'm locked in the basement of a garage at number 16, 149th Street in Neponsit."

Olivia's voice broke on the other end of the line, like a plate cracking under the pressure of all those words.

"Dad?"

"Sixteen, 149th Street in Neponsit," Jim repeated, desperate.

Suddenly, from the hall, he heard the sound of the trapdoor unlocking.

"He's coming!" Gina cried with fright, recognizing the sound like an animal that's learned to identify the rustle of its plastic bag of food.

Little Cora ran to a corner and hid under a blanket. Jim turned to look at the small hole he'd entered through.

"I love you, Olivia," he whispered before putting the phone down on the improvised countertop, leaving his daughter without the chance to reply.

Jim rushed down the tunnel, crouching, until he reached the other end. He could hear Tom and Mr. Rogers yelling at the other end and grabbed the first thing he could from one of the shelves—a can of food. At first, he thought of hiding in the darkness and attacking Mr. Rogers the moment he came down, but then he looked through the open trapdoor and saw Miren, wounded and unconscious in Mr. Rogers' arms.

He climbed the ladder and stopped for a moment halfway up, still in the shadows, waiting for the right moment. He didn't know what he was going to achieve, but he had no doubt that the best path forward was to fight until the very last moment rather than give up. And he saw Miren look straight at him before getting lost in the space between life and death. He saw blood in her mouth. Her eyes painted black.

He didn't hesitate, leaping on Larry and slamming the can into his face, causing Miren to fall to the ground. Mr. Rogers tottered for a moment before collapsing backwards, crashing against the sheet metal of one of the machines behind him. Jim shouted with rage.

Tom cried out to his father in confusion. He didn't have

time to ask again what was happening before Jim grabbed Larry by the throat.

"Tom," Larry croaked, "Help…"

Jim's attack had caught Larry off guard, and he was sufficiently shocked for Jim to gain the advantage.

Tom stared at him, astounded, like he was looking at a ghost. He didn't understand why his father was trying to hide this badly injured woman, and even less why the journalist he had spoken to hours earlier had emerged through the trapdoor and attacked his father. He had always thought the hole in the floor was just a storage space for sawdust and tools.

Then Jim said something that revealed the truth, like a whirlwind that decimated an entire life of lies. A puzzle has the same conclusion no matter how many people complete it, but the piece that brings it all together is always different for each person who attempts it.

"Why are you doing this to Gina?" Jim asked harshly.

"Gina?" Tom muttered.

Hearing this accusation against his father was the final piece of the puzzle for Tom. Suddenly, he understood the meaning of all those times his father had locked himself in the workshop, his refusal to move to another house. He finally made sense of his father urging him to focus on his studies and forget about the trauma of Gina's disappearance.

"Why!?" Jim insisted.

"Dad…? But… what did you do?" he whispered, incredulous.

In his mind, everything was so confusing that he was frozen, racking his brain for moments that demonstrated his father had behaved strangely. And there, at that moment, all those moments seemed to explode at once into the air, forced out of his memory in a rush.

Suddenly Mr. Rogers rolled over and managed to break free from Jim; he pushed him back and then threw him onto the table. Quickly, Larry got as far as he could from Jim and began to speak rapidly and nervously to his son.

"Tom! I can explain," he said in a tone that seemed to shift between desperation and a cry for help.

And then it happened.

A sheet-white hand with skinny fingers reached up through the trapdoor. It was followed by a thin arm and, finally, Gina's head. Her eyes were flickering and bright, and they met Tom's astonished gaze. He recognized her instantly. In truth, often in his memories he reminisced about what he had felt with her during their time together and, at night, sometimes in the form of vivid dreams, he had relived her caresses and that adolescent love whose equal he still had yet to find.

"Gina..." he said in a wisp of a voice.

"Gina..." repeated another male voice from the door.

Jim turned towards the new voice and saw Ethan, clutching a knife in his right hand, his unbelieving eyes fixed on his sister. He had followed Miren, and when he saw Mr. Rogers grabbing her and carrying her to the garage, he had been unsure what to do next. He had hidden behind a corner for a few moments, but when he saw Tom run over from the house, he made the connection between that place and his sister's destination the day of her disappearance. Frightened, he had walked towards the workshop, nervous about what he would find and eager to know why Tom's father had behaved in that way. He saw the fight and the struggle through the crack in the door, and finally, Gina's fearful face emerging.

"Ethan..." she whispered.

Gina climbed the final portion of the ladder and carefully emerged. She raised both arms towards Larry so he wouldn't attack her.

"Larry... let us go. Please," Jim pleaded nervously. "The police are on the way."

"You're lying," Larry replied furiously.

He couldn't understand how, after years without making a single mistake, suddenly everything had come apart just because of a few questions from a journalist who was looking for Gina. Larry felt cornered, and Jim was sure he would attack at any moment, like a wild boar willing to destroy everything in its path to escape the barrel of a hunter's gun.

"Gina…" Ethan repeated. His mind traveled to the night they escaped the flames together when he was just a small child—he remembered the fire, the rage, the revenge…

Despite the changes in her brother since they'd said their last goodbye at the bridge, Gina recognized him instantly.

The shape of his eyebrows, the color of his eyes, and the way his nose looked like an olive, as she had always teased him affectionately. Gina felt a lightning bolt in her chest, as if seeing him again made her travel back to that moment so far-off it felt like a dream, when she'd said to him "See you back home." For years she had reflected on that final innocent sentence and thought how, if she had known what was going to happen, she would have hugged him with all her might and promised that she would never, ever stop thinking about him. But Ethan was no longer the same.

The sound of the wind coming from the ocean slid through the cracks in the wooden walls of the garage, creating a whistling sound which seemed like a fitting accompaniment for a dramatic conclusion. Suddenly, Ethan understood that the guilty parties in his sister's disappearance had been Mr. Rogers and his son, and he couldn't contain his fury.

"It was you!" he shouted. "You took her! You took the only thing I had! The only thing!"

Full of rage, he dove into the workshop and pounced on Tom, who grabbed Ethan's hand a moment too late, after the blade of the knife had already sliced into his stomach and pancreas.

"Ethan, no!" Gina shouted.

"Tom!" his father cried, jumping on Ethan and grabbing the hand that held the blade.

Tom raised his eyebrows in an expression of surprise and, when he looked at his hands, saw the blood quickly covering his fingers. His legs slowly gave way, no longer able to support the weight of his body, and he fell to the ground, holding his torso up by grabbing the leg of his father's workbench.

Apoplectic with primal fury, Mr. Rogers dragged Ethan around the workshop like a rag until Ethan's body came to a sudden halt as it slammed against the tool wall. His face instantly transformed, passing from disbelief through fear to surprise. Larry saw the confusion on his face, the expression of panic as he tried to look behind him. One of the hooks the tools had been hanging on had perforated his back and penetrated his heart. A second later, Ethan slumped, motionless, his eyes open, and Larry stepped away, terrified by what he had just done. He had spent years concealing the greatest mistake of his life, and even though he had sometimes considered putting an end to it all, he was never brave enough, nor did he imagine he would one day cross that red line that, for him, was indefensible. But, when someone takes the first step towards darkness, it's only a matter of time before they continue descending, little by little, until they look up and see just how far they have traveled from the light.

And then, to everyone's surprise, someone yelled: "Police! Hands up!" Six officers burst into the workshop, with their guns trained on Larry. Gina threw herself to the floor, terrified, and crawled to the trapdoor to hold Cora, who had been waiting on the ladder the entire time without climbing out, just as her mother had instructed. For nine years she had been dreaming of the moment that someone might rescue her; hundreds of times she had dreamed of hearing the police cries that would signal the end of her nightmare.

Jim dived towards Miren on the floor to protect her. He embraced her like he never had before, shocked to see her closed eyes, her bruised lips, her white skin growing colder by the second. And he sobbed on top of her. He wailed like nothing mattered as the cops kept their weapons trained on Larry's head. Deep down, Larry had also been wishing in a way for that day to arrive. The end of the story is never the one you hope for, but the one towards which you are inexorably dragged. Jim brought his trembling hand to Miren's face and stroked it, knowing it would be the last time. He remembered the night they spent together, and all the incisive questions she had asked when she had been his student. The kiss they'd shared, all their fights. The world they had tried to change, the truth they'd always sought.

He hugged her cooling body. He screamed and howled inside, then kissed her forehead and brought his face up to hers as he cried inconsolably. He told her he loved her and then, at the last moment, Miren exhaled a feeble: "Me too."

Epilogue

"What happened to Miren Triggs?" asked a woman in the front row as soon as they opened the floor for questions.

The woman from the audience had been ready with that question since the beginning of the presentation, and it took Jim a few seconds to respond. He was nervous and overwhelmed in front of an audience like that, so different from the classroom full of undergraduates he was used to. That day, his audience was a miscellaneous group of women of various ages with a shared love of mystery. Sitting in folding chairs, they looked at him like they knew him, but at the same time they were eager to learn more about him as a person. Jim was surprised by the smile he saw on the faces looking back at him, but he was good at managing his nerves and succeeded in seeming cool and confident.

On the table lay a photo of Miren Triggs beside a stack of copies of *The Soul Game*, and readers were squashed into every corner of the bookstore, clutching their copies tightly in a hug that, in the not-too-distant future, the entire planet would yearn to experience again after embraces were robbed by an invisible enemy.

In the front row, a blonde middle-aged woman sat making eyes at Jim and he wasn't sure how to react. Martha Wiley hurried to answer the question about Miren before Jim had the chance to screw it up:

"No comment," she said with a smile, using the cap of a pen to point at a man standing at the back.

Stillman Publishing, one of the biggest publishers in the U.S., was always looking for juicy stories to publish, and every book from their imprint became an automatic bestseller. Readers interpreted the Stillman logo on the spine as an indisputable guarantee of a book's seal of approval and their books were always be recommended by word of mouth from the moment they were published. Every booklover read their books to keep up with the conversation, and occasional readers read them because they didn't want to miss out on the big story everyone was talking about. After word spread about *The Soul Game* and its journalistic story of captivity, struggle, courage, and revenge, the book instantly topped the charts across the country. On the streets, the shop windows of bookstores advertised it as the most groundbreaking work of the year, and on the subway, it wasn't hard to find someone reading it, unable to tear their eyes from the page.

* * *

After the police arrived that fateful night, Larry Rogers was arrested and charged with the kidnap and rape of Gina, and also with kidnap of a minor for keeping Gina's daughter, Cora, in captivity. As emergency services arrived on the scene, Jim whispered continually to Miren, stroking her face. He couldn't be torn from her side, and even though she didn't open her eyes once, Jim knew she could hear him. He covered her wound as best he could and, when the paramedics arrived, he cried desperately for them to save her from what seemed like an inevitable death. Dawn was just breaking when he accompanied Miren into the ambulance. He clung to her hand, and only let go when they wheeled her into the ER. Five hours later, a doctor emerged with a serious face to inform Jim that she had too many internal wounds to stitch. He said they'd done everything they possibly could to save her, but from that moment on it would depend on her to come out of her coma. Miren's parents arrived midafternoon after taking a flight from North Carolina, and her mother embraced Jim as soon as they met. They were together for so long they each understood just how much Miren meant to the other.

* * *

In the second row, Jim spotted a short-haired woman who was leafing through the book she'd just purchased, and he remembered when Miren had been his student. He couldn't help but get emotional, and he realized that this process was going to be harder on him than he had initially expected.

"How will Gina rebuild her life after this? Will her daughter be able to integrate into society? And what about Tom Rogers?" asked another young woman who looked like a journalism student.

"Gina, as well as her daughter," Jim said, "are entering a life in which they can decide their own future. I'm certain they will succeed. They will adapt very well to the outside world. Tom spent some time at the hospital, but he has recovered, and now he has dedicated himself to helping Gina and to taking care of the little girl."

"Will they live in New York?" asked a woman in the back who was clutching her book with the enthusiasm of someone who was also yearning to start a new life.

"I would be letting myself down if I answered that. I'm sure you understand. The important thing now for the two of them is that they are safe and will receive all the support they need to move on," Jim replied.

Then he pointed to the girl in the second row, who had reminded him of Miren, who seemed to want to ask something urgently:

"Are you going out with Miren Triggs?" she asked directly.

Jim was about to speak, but Martha Wiley dismissed the question before he had the chance to open his mouth.

"We haven't got time for any more questions if we want to leave time for all of you to get your copies of the book signed. We have an interview at two and there are a lot of you here. You can speak with the author as he signs."

Jim stood, a little nervous, and apologized with his hands. For the next hour, he scribbled affectionate messages into books. He took selfies, smiled, and replied enthusiastically to all the concerns of those who had come to see him. It was strange because, despite feeling fortunate to be there, he couldn't help but think that he didn't, in fact, deserve all that success.

* * *

Two days after the operation, Miren Triggs opened her eyes, still unsure where she was. She saw her mother sitting with her head down, and her father in the adjacent chair; the two were holding hands. Jim was sitting on the floor in front of the bed with his eyes closed. He was still in the clothes he'd been wearing when she'd seen him at the Rogers' house.

Miren remained silent and observed Jim in the dim light. All the people in the world who really mattered to her were in that room, where there were no sounds except for the whistles of the monitor, like a metronome tapping out the rhythm of her hopes. Then she cleared her throat and Jim opened his eyes. They looked at each other.

There are few moments like that in life; there are few emotions that equal the significance of that gaze. Jim jumped up and approached her, delicately, afraid of touching and losing her. For a moment, he even thought he might be dreaming, but soon he confirmed that Miren was breathing, with her breath leaving vapor on the mask she was wearing. You never see that kind of detail in dreams.

"Hey… you're awake," he whispered.

Miren exhaled.

"I… owe you so much, Jim. You… saved my life."

"Miren… please, rest. Don't be silly. You would've done the same for me."

"You're right about that," she said immediately.

She pulled off her oxygen mask and smiled. Jim looked at her up close, and she understood, with a thrill, the meaning behind the shine in those eyes that, for the first time, didn't make her feel uncomfortable. Now, she felt the opposite.

Mrs. Triggs opened her eyes and let out a shout when she saw Miren awake. She shook her husband's arm so he'd see her too. When she approached her daughter, there were tears on her face.

"Miren… thank God," she whispered between sobs.

"You came…" Miren whispered.

Her mother stroked her hand and Miren reciprocated, but more softly, because she was still quite weak.

"Rest, darling… you have to save your strength…. Even though I know you're not going to listen to me. Since when have you listened to me? Who can ever control you?"

"Mom…"

Miren's father also got up, approached his daughter and, to her surprise, kissed her on the forehead without saying a word. She felt as if that simple kiss were the most important of her life. For many years, her father had been somewhat distant, and he wasn't in the habit of showing affection. He was fun—he was a cheerful and relaxed man—but he didn't often express the love within him. She couldn't help but cry when he pulled back from her forehead and she saw the two tears sliding down his cheeks. It was the first time Miren had seen her father cry; she swallowed hard and felt so loved she could barely contain her happiness.

* * *

A few days later, Bob Wexter visited Miren in the hospital, and while he was there, he showed her his scars from a bullet wound he'd sustained during crossfire while reporting on the Gulf War. Before he left, Miren surprised him with a suggestion that left both him and Jim flabbergasted.

"I want Jim to be the one to write this story."

"But…" Jim said.

"Are you serious?" Bob wanted to know.

"Yes, Jim is the best journalist I know, and… I'm a little too tired to write from the hospital. I still have to recover, and… every extra day it takes us to write the story, the less interest it will generate. You know what they say, the best scoop is the one from fifteen minutes ago."

"But Miren… you deserve this. You deserve to be the one who writes the article. It's your story…" Jim replied, confused.

"Nothing would make me happier than having you write it, Jim," she said. "You were the one who found Gina. And you were the one who saved me."

"Miren—"

"As far as I'm concerned, if that's how you want it, great," Bob stated.

"Don't get me wrong—that job at the paper is still mine," she laughed gingerly.

Two days later, the press ran an article titled "The Soul Game," by Jim Schmoer, and it began trending on Twitter the instant it was published online. The story spread like wildfire. Everywhere you went, someone was talking about the teenage girl who had been kidnapped for nine years and held prisoner in a basement in the Rockaways; how her brother had lost his mind in the years after her disappearance and how, under the crushing weight of a world of extreme religion, he had even ended up crucifying a classmate as revenge. Shortly after publishing the article, Jim got a phone call from an unknown number. It was Martha Wiley, offering to publish a book based on the story. Jim had two conditions:

"I'll only write it together with Miren. It's not just my story," he said as soon as he received the offer.

Martha agreed, despite the extent to which their relationship had deteriorated in the weeks after Miren stood her up. But she decided to treat the situation as an opportunity and to leverage the Gina Pebbles story. When Jim insisted on that condition, Martha began mentally developing a marketing plan that would only increase the buzz by the time it was published: Jim would go to book signings alone, even though both of their names would appear on the cover, and the book would end at a moment when it was impossible to know if Miren had survived. Her fate would be a mystery both in the book and in real life... and the rumors about her possible death might add an extra zero to the number of copies sold. According to Martha, that ambiguity would attract future readers, since it would leave the ending open and give them the chance to develop their own version of the story. Granted, the more informed readers would soon learn the truth when they read the column Miren had resumed writing at the *Press* every Wednesday. Although Martha Wiley might be a tough cookie to work with, in the publishing world, she was unparalleled.

* * *

On the kitchen table at his house in Grymes Hill, Ben Miller had emptied the contents of a cardboard box labeled 'Daniel' in blue marker. On one side of the table was a pile of documents: statements from neighbors, most of whom reported seeing nothing on that fateful afternoon in 1981. On the other side of the table were photos of a bicycle, clothes, toys, and license plate numbers that had been in the neighborhood on the day Ben's son had disappeared.

After Father Graham's suicide, Ben decided to leave the Missing Persons Unit and retire. He had spent so many years caught up in his day-to-day work that he had lost sight of his primary reason for joining in the first place. The sadness that imbued every case had affected him so much that everywhere he went, he was plagued by a painful feeling of loss. When he got home, he couldn't get rid of his expression of a desolate FBI agent. After resigning, Ben gathered his things and, without fanfare, left an office where he had always felt like a stranger. The only person who hugged him goodbye was Jen from the archives, who, before he left, prepared a box full of files of missing children like Daniel who had disappeared in Staten Island, Queens, Manhattan, and New Jersey. Ben had resolved to spend his retirement trying to solve the riddle that had turned him into a living martyr and destroyed his family. He was so focused on reading the statement from one of Daniel's best friends that he didn't hear the front door open or the footsteps of someone approaching him from behind.

Suddenly, he felt a hand on his shoulder and, when he looked up, he felt a knot form in his throat as Lisa warmly caressed his neck. He cried the way you can only cry when you know you've made a mistake, and Lisa did the same, because her heartache had never disappeared.

Ben got up and embraced his wife. In that embrace, she felt all the hugs she had missed on those nights she had sobbed alone in the darkness.

✳ ✳ ✳

When Jim finished signing copies, he said goodbye with a smile, leaving with a handful of love notes he intended to read when he got home. He left the bookstore with Martha, followed by a group of female readers who wanted one last selfie. Martha left in a taxi and Jim walked a short distance towards Broadway, down 36th until the intersection with 8th. As soon as he could, he called Miren, who picked up instantly:

"Where are you?"

"Behind you," she replied.

Before he even turned around, he felt two arms wrapping around him from the back. When Jim felt Miren's hands, he slowly turned around. She was wearing a sweater, leggings, and a Knicks cap the partially covered her face.

"You followed me?"

"I was at the book presentation. I like how you brush off the compliments people pay you. It's so... humble," she laughed.

"You were there? I didn't see you."

"That was the idea," she said with a smile. As soon as you started signing and I saw how many people were there, I went for a run—I ran a few miles, actually."

Then Jim kissed her, and she allowed herself to be loved.

Unexpectedly, they heard a male voice from behind Miren's back.

"Miss Triggs?"

She spun around, surprised. Jim looked up to see what was happening. It was Agent Kellet, wearing a blue shirt and a gray tie.

"Do you have a moment? I'd like to... speak with you."

Miren gave him an expectant look, and Jim sensed her tension in the way she suddenly held her breath.

"Could you give me a second, Jim?" she said quietly.

"I... of course."

He walked a few yards away, perplexed. In a serious tone, Miren said:

"Are you following me? What do you want?"

"Do you remember what I told you about Aron Wallace?" Agent Kellet asked.

Miren nodded.

"At his house we found a whole host of DVDs with videos of... child abuse."

"Then I'm glad he's dead," Miren said coldly. "Why are you

here? To tell me the man who raped me was even more of a degenerate than I already knew?"

"Well, there's something else, Miss Triggs." He extracted a photograph from his jacket pocket and showed it to her. "This image is from a security camera in Harlem, right by Aron Wallace's home. It was taken at four in the morning. Do you recognize this silhouette?"

Miren swallowed hard and looked. It was her. There was no room for doubt.

"Are you planning to arrest me? Is that what you're here for?" she asked, her heart pounding in her chest.

"You lied to me. You did leave home that night, Miss Triggs."

Miren breathed deep and stood still. She waited for him to continue.

"But do you know what? I've seen some of the confiscated videos. The world has turned into a hostile place."

Miren looked at Jim, who was out of earshot. He was watching her with incredulity.

"Do you remember what I told you about my wife?" Kellet asked.

"You said that she had also been assaulted," Miren replied, tense.

"And what kind of person do you think I'd be if I arrested you? At the end of the day… you don't own any registered weapons and… the person in this photo… could be anyone, don't you think?"

Miren took a deep breath, and then she nodded.

"Could be anyone," she repeated.

"So… have a good day, Miss Triggs. I won't bother you anymore. I just wanted you to know that today, the world is a much fairer place."

"Thank you, Agent," she said by way of goodbye.

She walked up to Jim as if nothing had happened.

"Should we eat? I ran four miles and I'm famished," she said, putting her arm around him.

"Who was that guy?" Jim asked, confused.

"One of Ben's colleagues. He was just giving me some news."

"Anything I should worry about?"

Miren smiled and said:

"All you have to worry about is finding a good restaurant. I'm starving."

"That was the plan, wasn't it?"

Miren nodded, smiling even more. Then Jim continued:

"Oh, by the way. Olivia is coming. I called her. I'd like you to… get to know each other a little better," Jim said after pausing to analyze Miren's reaction, and to make sure he hadn't made a mistake.

Miren gave him a serious look and then asked:

"But does she know about us?"

"She was the one who suggested coming."

"Seriously?"

"She read the book. She even brags about you to her friends."

Miren smiled and kissed Jim again.

"I'd love to meet Olivia," Miren said, smiling yet again. She could see how happy Jim was by the gleam in his eyes, and she realized she had wagered her soul in the most important game in life, and that she had won.

Acknowledgements

I always save a little space in my books to thank all the people who have inspired and helped me along the way, so that my stories can end up in your hands. This part of the book is critical, because it's full of sentences with double and triple meanings, and it's full of affection.

I wrote *The Soul Game* in 2020 and I think that, undoubtedly, it has been the hardest novel for me to write, especially given the uncertainty with which all of us were living. Twenty-twenty has been a year we will remember forever, and I think this time, more than ever before, these pages are filled with honest words. I thought and dreamed only of giving all of you a new window into my world, together with the key to the padlock Miren keeps deep within.

As always, I have to thank Verónica, because she was my first reader, always with the perfect critical eye, and her reactions, as she read that first draft, not only improved the story, but also helped me realize how important it was to give the novel soul. There's something of her between the lines on these pages, and there are a few specific moments in the plot that emerged from me interpreting her face and surprised expressions as she read.

I'm also grateful to my kids, Gala and Bruno, for their infinite patience, for the coffees they helped me make in the middle of the afternoon as an excuse to spend some time with them, and for all the hugs and kisses they gave me in the evenings after I'd finished writing. This novel has robbed you of some time with your father, and when you're older and read this, I hope you'll forgive me and won't hold it against me.

Thanks to the whole team at Suma de Letras, as always. You are my home and shelter, the people with whom I feel safe, and you have helped me not only to become a better author, but also taught me the true meaning of teamwork. I want to give special thanks to Gonzalo, even though he has already heard it from me, for every audio message and phone call, and for trusting in my judgement and taking a chance on this story that touches many sensitive wounds and sets so much on fire.

Thanks, also, to Ana Lozano, who this year had to endure my doubts and insecurities with a degree of patience only a great editor can possess. She has worked tirelessly against the clock to polish a story that had been bouncing around my head for years, but which always seemed to find a place to hide when I tried to extract it, just like a good villain.

Thanks to Nùria Tey, whose endless cheerfulness and shrewd eye have kept me calm during those moments when you're unable to see the end approaching. Thanks to Mar, who this year got away from me for a wonderful reason, and to Leticia, who has managed to bring me halfway around the world without ever leaving home.

Thanks also to Rita, Ana, and Pablo. I don't know how they do it, but they always find a way to get my novels into the right hands at the right time.

So much gratitude to Michelle G. and David G. Escamilla, for opening the doors to the other side of the world and fighting tooth and claw for my books. I've lost count of how many celebratory mezcals I owe you.

Thanks to Conxita for finding the perfect places for my stories to be adapted, always with a laugh and a smile. To María Reina for fighting every day to get those stories into more languages and getting my words translated just as carefully as they were written in Spanish.

I'd also like to thank Iñaki, who is eternal, and Patxi Beascoa, who I always seem to run into in every country in the world except for Spain. And thanks to Yolanda, who always gives my covers the perfect touch. Also Marta, Carmen, Nùria, and everyone who joined in the virtual celebration for the millionth copy of my novels being sold, a moment when I cried more than any other in 2020. I want to use this space to give you the hug that I couldn't give you in real life, and to thank you, with my whole heart, for this journey. And thanks to Nacho from the Guardia Civil's Homicide Unit, for opening the door to this real and tragic world of missing children.

The most important part of the acknowledgements, undoubtedly, is the part dedicated to you, my readers. In 2020, we had to forget about the book tours, signings, and presentations, and we saw all of our plans canceled. And I admit that for months, I dreamed of the moment when I could see you all in person again. The book was published two days before the state of alarm was declared and, with it, you gave me the greatest gift you can give a writer: staying in my memory as a window to the outside world at a time when all doors were closed. Thank you so much for making *The Snow Girl* the best-selling novel in Spain during lockdown, and for embracing my novel the way you did during those months we will never forget. THANK YOU, with my whole heart. Thank you for every letter, for every message, for the support, for recommending my stories. Thank you for getting this far, for staying by my side, for traveling with me and making my dreams and your dreams coincide.

Like I always say, I could thank many other people, in different chapters narrated by different characters, in other voices or in other periods of time, with twists, surprises, and cliffhangers on the final page, but I think it's better for us to keep our yearly promise: I won't stop writing, if all of you, every time you're asked to recommend a book—if you liked it—recommend *The Soul Game*, without giving away what it's about (please!) beyond a basic synopsis. This is our game, and for me to keep writing, my stories need to keep breaking barriers every time they end up on bookshelves. So let's keep this pact and, in exchange, next year, I promise I'll be back in bookstores with another story I've been sitting on for a while, and which without doubt will knock this puzzle flying into the air, leaving pieces all over the place. What do you say?

Wanna play?

Yours in madness,
Javier Castillo